CREEPER

Stuart James

ASIN : B09NGNJTW5

Cover by The Cover Collection.

Edited by Emily Yau.

*For my beautiful family, Tara, Oli and Ava, who will forever be
the light that shines the way.
Also, my parents, Jimmy and Kathleen.
I love you both so very much.*

PROLOGUE

Sometimes I leave a gap, a little time between striking. Too many bodies and it becomes conspicuous. And also, it gets a tad monotonous. I relish the feel of the hunt; my prey are like mice, scavenging across the kitchen floor and making their escape, finding a small hole in the wall, or under the floorboards, or down the back of the sofa. The thing is, they always surface again and make their way out, appearing when you least expect it. So I, the hunter, will wait, biding my time. Patient, diligent. That's what I've learned over the years: too many strikes and boom, you're out.

I wait at the front of the farmhouse and watch. I'm like a cat, purring, my tail gracefully sweeping, cutting through the air, blissfully awaiting the approach.

I wait and watch.

How I love to watch.

1

Present Day.

I think it's on. The red light was flashing before; now it's still. That means it's recording, right? OK, I'm sure it's recording – oh God, where to start. You know, it's weird, looking into the lens of a camcorder, talking to myself, alone in the house. At least I think I am. I have a few minutes – that's it, no more. That's all I have. So, bear with me. Watch this recording and make up your own mind, but promise me you'll do something.

'I look dirty. Bloody hell, I've aged ten years overnight. My long brown hair is dishevelled and has grey wisps starting to show – large swathes of them are pushing their way through. I can see laughter lines cut deep into the skin of my face, only there's nothing to smile about. Not now, not anymore.

'You may wonder why I'm whispering, why I'm keeping my voice low, faint. The truth is, I'm fucking terrified. I'm guessing if you're watching this, you've found the recording. Perhaps you've just moved in and you're settling down, making a new life for yourself, a better life that's peaceful, quiet. You have a family, a partner, children. Well, get out. Get the fuck out before it's too late.

'Listen to me. Please.

'You'll hear the stories, the rumours, that's for sure. If you've found this, whoever you are, I beg you, don't just watch this. Promise me you'll do something. Take this recording to the police, put it on YouTube, Facebook, Instagram... All of your social media platforms. Make people aware. Tell them our story. You will, won't you?

'It can't all have been for nothing. I won't let that happen.

'Fucking Creeper. God, what were we thinking? Why didn't we listen? We were so keen to make the documentary. Now look where it's ended up.

'I don't have long, but you need to understand my story, how I came to be here, hiding in the upstairs bedroom, sitting in front of a camcorder, waiting.

'Wait...

'Hello? Who's there? Hello?

'Sorry, I know my voice is low. It may be hard to hear me. I get it. But I thought I heard the front door open.

'Hello?

'Shit. I think someone's in the house. I knew this would happen. I knew it.

'But what was I saying? All I ask is that you tell people about us. About Creeper.

'This is weird, right? You're watching this, maybe months after I made the recording, perhaps even years. I might look strange. My clothes may look peculiar, out of fashion, like an odd picture from a century ago. You may snigger, mock my appearance, laugh. Go on then. It doesn't matter. I don't care.

'I need to stand. I have cramp; my legs have gone to sleep. My body is aching and sore.

'Wait, stay with me. There's the bedroom door. I'm going to be quiet so I can listen. If you can't hear me, it doesn't mean I've gone or the battery has run out. I'm going to keep quiet because I want to draw it out, being found. I want to last as long as possible. That's all.

'Is the camera steady? Can you still see me? I can see my reflection, my worried expression, in the glass of the lens, but only just. I have visions of the video coming out blurry, the lens filthy, so you won't be able to make anything out.

'Wow, that would be a waste of time. Can you imagine? How stupid would that make me look? I guess I'll never know. I'll never find out.

'If that was the case, I could be saying anything, couldn't I? I'll exaggerate my lip movements. I'll speak louder. You need to hear what I'm saying.

'Here goes.

'CALL. THE. POLICE. PUT. THIS. ON. YOUTUBE.

'There. I've made it clear. If the sound's gone, you'll still have no excuse.

'You may think I'm delusional, drugged, pissed up. Well, I'm none of those. I wish I was.

'What I'd do for a drink though – an ice-cold beer. Just the one, mind, to take the pain away, place it far enough away for a short while.

'If you can't see where I am, I'm stood by the bedroom door, listening. I'm sure I heard the front door open a few minutes ago.

'Yes, there's someone at the top of the stairs, getting closer. I'm backing away to the middle of the bedroom. I'm going to place the camcorder in a bolt hole; there's a cupboard behind me with a section cut out. Can you see it? I'll place it in there. One of you will find it, I'm certain.

'The handle of the bedroom door is moving downwards slowly. This is it. I think my time is up. Please do something. When you find this, do som—'

2

Six Months Earlier.

Monday.

'Action.'

'Hello. I'm Jenny Freeman. We're here at Greyshott Hall Psychiatric Hospital in Oxford, an abandoned asylum for the mentally insane. This is Sean, my husband and partner in crime.'

'Hello.'

'Sean, point the camera on yourself when you talk. What are you like?'

'Sorry. Blame the nerves. OK, go again.'

'Hello. I'm Jenny—'

'Shit.'

'What's up now?'

'The red light didn't come on. Hang on a second. Bloody camera.'

'Don't shake it, you lemon.'

'Right. It's on. Maybe start with a little background info, Jenny. A little about the place, you know. Set the mood before we go inside.'

'You mean light some candles? Look scared? Sound breathless?'

'Love it. You got it. Right, go again.'

'I was being sarcastic. OK, where was I? We're here at an abandoned asylum for the mentally insane, where the story goes: thirty years ago, Mark Wheelan was held in a room after having electric shock treatment that caused permanent brain damage. His family filed a lawsuit against the authorities, claiming that after he was sectioned for depression, the treatment he underwent caused him to lose his mind, so to speak.'

'Brilliant, Jenny. I've paused it for a second. I'm going to move to the side for a better angle. OK, ready. Keep going.'

'On January twenty-fifth, Sheila Eastwood, a young nurse who worked the nightshift, found Mark slumped on his bed. Thinking he was unconscious, she panicked. When she attempted to resuscitate him, he sprung up from the bed and bit her face, punching her repeatedly until she was practically unrecognisable. He removed the keys from the pocket of her uniform, and proceeded to go on a murderous rampage. Seven inmates were found that night, in a horrific state, disfigured and mutilated. Nurse Eastwood's dead body was found lying in Mark's cell. Mark Wheelan was never found. It is said he returns to the grounds late at night.'

'Fantastic, Jenny. That was bloody awesome. You nailed it.'

'You think?'

'Totally. Oh shit, it wasn't recording.'

'You're joking.'

'Got ya. You should see your face.'

'You're such a shit.'

'OK. Let's go inside. I'm recording now, so don't swear. Move forward and push the door. That will be a great shot.'

'I'm trying. It's jammed. Come on, move. Yes. OK, we're inside. Where's the torch?'

'Here. Stay beside me. This is a little nerve-wracking. We should have come earlier. I can't see a bloody thing. I'm shitting it.'

'Are you?'

'Yeah. Aren't you?'

'Sean, you're such a wuss. Just keep the camera rolling. This is going to be great. Give me the torch.'

'OK. Slowly move forward, and I'll follow behind. Try and shine the torch directly in front so the camera can pick up everything you're seeing.'

'Click the light on the top of the lens. That will give us a bit more sight. Yeah, this is great. OK. As you can all see, this place has been abandoned for some time. The walls are crumbling, the paint is flaked and patchy, there are holes in the ceilings and there's a musty, putrid smell, which you obviously won't get, but believe me, it's vile. It smells of rotten cabbage; that's the best way to describe it. I'd hate to think what it could be. It's hard to comprehend what happened here all those years ago, the mess that Mark left behind. The trail of destruction. Above us, you should be able to hear birds nesting in the beams, which have taken roost over the years. The place is covered in bird and rat droppings. As most of you will know, although we frequently explore dark and creepy places, I still have a major phobia of rats. Over here, we have the cells. Now, as you can see, the furniture and beds have been removed; they're pretty much empty shells. All that remains are the old plumbing pipes for what I'd say were a simple toilet and wash unit. I imagine it was very basic back then. My guess is these inmates were kept locked up, holed in practically twenty-four seven. Whoa. Shit.'

'Jenny, are you OK?'

'No, I'm not. Turn the camera off.'

'What happened?'

'The floor. It's rotten. I've hurt my ankle. Jesus Christ.'

'Here, let me help. Can you walk?'

'I think so. Bloody hell. The things we do.'

'Hold on. I'll lift you up. Easy. Go easy.'

'I'm fine.'

'Can you put weight on it?'

'Yeah. It'll be OK. Roll again.'

'You sure?'

'Yeah, I'll shake it off. I'm good. There's just one more thing I need to add before we get in closer. OK? Roll... We believe the last cell on the left was Mark Wheelan's.'

'OK, I've paused it. Now, let's make our way over to the cell. Slow and atmospheric.'

'Got it... It's here where Mark Wheelan was held all those years ago. The nurse was probably standing right about where Sean is now, watching him, unaware of his plan, how he purposely was lying still, playing dead. She would have removed her key, opened the cell door and moved towards his limp body. He probably waited for the right time, listening to the sound of her light footsteps on the wooden floor as she edged closer, until she was standing over him. Then *bang*. It makes me shiver just thinking about it, the horror that she and the other inmates suffered. There's an overwhelming feeling of sadness and despair in this place. I can't explain the feeling. The sense of doom, if you like. The cell is smaller than I'd imagined, that's for sure. Six feet in length, I'd guess, and the same width. How anyone could hold on to their sanity here is beyond me. See the window at the back of the cell, no bigger than eight inches in length and width? It's roughly head height, with solid-looking iron bars – I guess to stop you from reaching the glass, which is now cracked and stained. A small hole to the outside world. I wonder what went through Mark's head as he stood here, day after day, looking out at the world, knowing he'd only ever see the outside from this cage-like container that confined him. As I look out, I imagine what Mark saw all those years ago. There's a forest, lined with trees, rows of them stretching high into the air. It's dark right now, and aided by the glint of the moon, shadows appear to cast a menacing, imminent spell over this old building. There's a light wind coming from the woodland, and branches flicker in the distance, seemingly waving, stretching, beckoning for us to join them.'

'That was spectacular, Jenny. It captured the atmosphere brilliantly.'

'Thanks, I guess?'

'I think we have all we need. Shall we call it a wrap?'

'Sounds good to me. It should look great, Sean. Shit. Look down there. Blood marks. There's blood marks, Sean.'

'Let me see. Keep the torch still. Let's have a look. Oh yeah, that's disgusting. Maybe they closed this place down immediately after the slaying.'

'It makes it so much creepier, thinking what happened here,' Jenny stated.

'Eugh, I've had enough of this place. Let's go. Are you ready?'

'Yeah, next time we'll stay overnight. We'd get great

footage. Can you imagine doing a live through the night? Make it a big event.'

Sean was apprehensive about her comment. Jenny watched as he placed the small camcorder into a satchel and struggled with the zip.

'Yeah, I'll come back to you on that one.'

'So that's a no then?'

'Let me think about it. But don't hold your breath.'

They moved slowly from the cell.

Jenny peered towards the cracked windows, feeling the cold work its way into the old building. 'Do you believe it happened as they say it did? That he escaped? That he's still alive?'

Sean lifted the satchel and carefully placed the strap over his shoulder. 'You mean Mark? That he could still be out there? I don't know, Jenny. I'd hate to think he's still alive. It doesn't bear thinking about. What would he be now? Mid-forties?'

Jenny calculated the years in her mind and came to the same answer. 'Yeah, something around that. They don't get any more innocuous as they age. There are plenty of stories of documented serial killers still active later in life. Look at Michael Myers.'

Sean turned, realising her sarcasm. 'Yeah. Look at Michael Myers, indeed.'

He moved towards the front door, peering at the large holes in the walls, the rotten beams hanging from above. He held the torch, pointing the light across the floor as he tried to dodge the cracked boards. He turned, shining the torch in the direction of his wife. He eyed her long blonde hair, her blue eyes. Her pale skin was flushed and she looked aggitated.

'How's your leg?'

'I'm fine. I'll manage. I'll have a bruise in the morn—'

Suddenly, they both stopped.

'What was that?'

Sean held the torch, pointing it in front of them. 'I'm not sure. It came from outside. Was it someone banging on the door?'

'Hello? Is someone there?' Jenny placed her finger over her lip to sign for him to keep quiet. 'Sean, someone's out there.'

'How could there be? I didn't hear a car come into the grounds, and we're in the middle of nowhere. There are no other houses for miles.'

They stood for a moment, peering towards the large wooden door in front of them, Sean waving the torch erratically.

'What now?' Jenny watched as the light shone in front of her.

Sean paused for a moment. 'I say we get to the car, get out of here. We're technically trespassing; maybe someone got wind of us being here, saw the car as we drove in. We left the lights on, remember.'

Another loud thump on the door caused him to drop the torch.

Jenny screamed out, reaching forward to cling on to his jumper. 'What the heck, Sean?'

He reached down, pawing for the torch, which had now gone out. 'I need to get some light. It's pitch black. Who the hell is that outside?' He spread out his hands on the cold wooden floor.

'We need to get out. Please, Sean, just get the torch.'

'I'm trying.' He crouched down and stretched out. 'I got it. Let me find the switch. Damn. It's broken.'

'Are you kidding me? What about the camera? Set it up again.'

'There's no time, Jenny. We need to go. I'll move forward. Just keep a hold of my jumper. Don't let go, all right?'

'All right.'

Holding tightly to him as he made his way towards the door, Jenny struggled to see in front of her. They stepped on the wooden floorboards gently, fearing they'd collapse at any second.

Sean reached forward, swiping his arms through the air, feeling into the darkness. He suddenly felt the large wooden door frame. OK'OK, we're at the front door. We need to squeeze through quietly. You OK?'

'Yeah, I'm good. I'm just concerned someone will jump out from behind me, you know?' She looked over her shoulder into the darkness behind.

After moving through the gap, they emerged in the fore-court, the full lights from their car providing a welcome relief from the bleakness. They hugged, and as he held her, Sean felt his wife's body shivering, her sharp breaths caused by adrenaline.

'Do you think someone's still here, Sean?'

'I'm not planning on finding out.' He gripped her hand, holding it tight, and adjusted the strap of the camera case with his other hand. They looked around, glancing towards the dark forest to their right. Over to the left, in the distance, lights from the village gleamed.

As they made their way around the side of the building toward their car, a light came on behind them.

They swung around together, stones crunching under their feet. They both noticed a vehicle parked on the path by the edge of the forest. It looked like a small pick-up truck. Sean let go of Jenny's hand, holding his arm up across his eyes. The glare had temporarily blinded him, and he struggled to see what was happening.

The vehicle was parked at an angle, and the lights pointed to where they stood. They could make out the shape of a man sitting in the driver's seat.

Jenny squinted as her eyes adjusted to the sudden brightness. 'Who the hell is that? Was that truck here all the time?'

'I don't know. I never noticed it earlier, but it was dark. Surely we'd have heard it coming up the drive?'

The truck started to rev, smoke billowing from the exhaust, causing a thick mist-like cloud.

'Let's move to the car. Keep going, Jenny. Don't stop.'

'I've no intention of stopping. Why is the driver revving?'

'Come on, they're trying to antagonise us. Stay close to me.'

Their car was parked twenty yards from where they were, and as they walked, they moved away from the truck.

As they reached the car, Sean looked back. The truck was still stationary, the lights still on full beam.

'Can you see the driver? Is he still in the front seat?'

Sean stood for a moment, watching the truck, then he unlocked the car with his fob and felt for the door handle. 'I'm not sure. I can't see anyone anymore.' He placed the torch and the camera satchel in the back, then manoeuvred himself into the driver's seat.

Jenny climbed into the passenger side, then leant forward to see more clearly. 'Let's just leave. I don't want to be here. Can we go?'

Sean turned to her. 'Why should we let this person dictate what we do? I'm going over to see what the problem is. He could have taken our number plate. There's the possibility he may report us. I need to go over and talk to him.'

'Are you fucking with me? You are, aren't you? Please say you are.' She watched as he undid his seatbelt and got out.

'Wait there a second. If anything happens, call 999.'

Jenny held up her phone to him, showing the empty signal bar on the top right of the screen.

'OK, OK, well, drive to the nearest house then.'

'Sean, get back in the car.'

Sean grabbed the torch and tapped the end until the light came on, then he shut the driver's door and edged slowly towards the truck. The full beams from their car showered the asylum in light.

Greyshott Hall gave a sinister portrayal of what must have been a beautiful construction once. Sean looked at the large building, the grey stones forming the solid outside walls, the arched windows to the left and right of the main entrance. There were three floors in total. Most of the windows at the front had been smashed. Ivy weaved its way along the outside of the building, smothering it. There were metal steps to the side, which led to the water tanks on the roof. It was cold and desolate.

The torch momentarily lit up a sign that stood on a thin wooden pole, planted in black soil. It declared, 'Trespassers will be prosecuted.'

He turned around to look at where Jenny had pushed her head out of the window and had been calling out for him to return. But now she remained still. He suddenly felt vulnerable, worried that she would try to join him, then panic and draw attention.

He was ten yards from the truck when its passenger door opened, as if the driver was beckoning him to get in, relax, unwind.

What the hell is wrong with this idiot?

Sean stopped, weighing the situation; if he went back to

the car, he'd look weak; if he kept going, he was possibly putting their lives in danger.

'What's your problem, mate?' He waited for an answer, not expecting one. 'Are you doing this for kicks? Is that it? Come out.'

He waited, edging forward, listening to the stones crunch under his boots. His breath was sharp, silent.

'Get out of the truck, and we'll talk,' he called out, cupping his hands around his mouth. 'You're a dickhead, mate.'

He decided to go back to the car, and when he turned, the driver revved, longer this time. The noise rasped in his ears.

Spinning back around, he saw the truck's wheels spinning; stones were spraying over the forecourt, and the air was quickly filling with the smell of petrol.

Suddenly, the truck pulled away, heading straight for Sean. He held his hands out in front of his face, the glare from the full lights now blinding him, and watched the truck move towards him at great speed. He stood still, his eyes wild with fear and his legs fixed to the ground, unable to move. The truck was almost on top of him.

Sean debated whether to dive out of the way or jump onto the bonnet, but the truck came to an abrupt halt a few feet from where he stood, its tyres skidding along the ground. Dust rose, seeping into his lungs. He coughed, then stumbled back, holding his arm above his eyes to protect his vision.

He wiped the grit-like texture from his face. His skin was irritable, as if he'd been in a sudden storm in a desert. His face felt dirty, contaminated. 'What the hell is wrong with you?'

He listened to the engine, a heavy, cumbersome roar in the surrounding stillness.

Then, it cut out.

He heard a voice – loud, brash. 'You... you don't understand. Where's the lady you were with?'

'What are you talking about?' Sean was unable to see into the truck's cabin. The full lights pushed into his face, an unwelcome assault, causing major discomfort. His eyes began to water, then tears streamed down his face. He blinked, feeling a little relief.

'The woman? The woman you were with a minute ago? Did you not see the guy run towards your car?'

'What guy? You're off your head, mate.'

'No. Listen. I'm a groundsman here. I fell asleep. I watched you both coming out of the building. I tried to warn you by revving the truck. A guy was stood there, watching you both. He had a baseball bat. He was wearing a mask, like a white bag over his face. You need to get to your car.'

Sean listened as the guy pleaded with him, not believing his lies.

'I'm not messing around, mate. There's a guy out there. He's probably making his way to her as we speak.'

Sean turned and ran towards the car, thankful for the heads up. 'Jenny, Jenny, for God's sake, where are you?'

He reached the car, seeing his wife lying on the back seat.

'Are you OK?' He pounded his knuckles against the glass. 'Open the door.'

Jenny sat up, looking bewildered, then reached forward into the front and opened the driver's door. 'What's going on?'

'The guy. Did you see the guy making his way to the car?'

'No, Sean. No one has come to the car. I lay down in the back to keep hidden. Can we just get out of here?' She got out of the car and sat in the passenger seat.

Sean turned and saw the pick-up truck pull beside where he stood. Now, he could see the driver leaning forward. He could see the mask, a white cloth tied around his face. His arms were slightly extended, one hand holding a long, wooden object in front of him. As the man got out of the truck, Sean recognised it as a baseball bat.

'Shit. Where are the keys?' He sat into the driver's seat and felt for the ignition, watching as the guy moved towards them. 'Jenny. The keys. Where are they?' Sean closed the car door.

'I haven't got them. We need to go. Start the bloody car, Sean. We need to go!'

Still holding the torch in one hand, Sean frantically reached into the pockets of his jeans, then fumbled towards the glove compartment, fishing through the paperwork. 'This isn't happening. Lock the doors. Quick, Jenny. Lock the fucking doors. I need to find the keys.'

He lifted himself off the seat and peered into the back, patting the seats behind with his hand. 'Yes.'

He gripped the keys and manoeuvred back into the front, dropping the torch into the passenger well. At the same time, the driver's window smashed, shards of glass spilling onto his lap.

The bat then came down onto the bonnet.

Jenny screamed, holding her hands over her face.

As the guy moved to the front of the vehicle, Sean jiggled the keys into the ignition. He pressed the right pedal, and the car suddenly moved backwards, just as the man started to hammer on the windscreen.

They watched in horror as the man leapt onto the

bonnet, where he continued to smash the bat against windscreen.

'What the hell is his problem? Get us out of here, Sean.'

Sean hit the brakes, then rammed the car into first, jolting the car forward, the gears crunching as the car moved. He slammed the brake with his foot, throwing the truck driver over the side of the car. He paused for a second, watching the guy get to his feet, then stamped on the accelerator. He hit the driver with the front right edge of their car, knocking him backwards.

'Put your seatbelt on.'

As they pulled away, through the rear-view mirror, Sean could see the guy in the moonlight, lying on the ground.

3
———

Monday.

At the back of the living room at Sheldon's Residential Retirement Home, Billy Huxton watched the man standing at the front as he reached into the tray and pulled out a piece of paper. He held it high above him.

'Oh, it would help if I opened it now, wouldn't it? You OK, Gladys? Anywhere near a full house yet?'

She shook her head eagerly, full of anticipation for the new number.

'OK, it's better on wine, sixty-nine. Any takers?' Groans came from the room. 'Let's get another one. Remember to shout Bingo when you can't mark any more numbers on your cards, loves.'

'On its own – like most of you... I'm joking! I'm joking! – number four.'

A nurse walked into the room, making her way towards

where Billy sat.

'You have a call. Says it's urgent.' The nurse crouched beside him, waiting to see his reaction.

He stood and followed her out.

'Here, the phone's on the wall at the end of the corridor.' She pointed it out.

'I know where the bloody phone is. I've been here long enough.'

She walked into the office, still listening as Billy picked up the receiver.

He wiped the earpiece with a handkerchief he'd pulled from the breast pocket of his brown tweed suit jacket. 'Who is it? Speak up... Nurse, it's not working. Hello?'

'Billy Huxton?'

'Who wants to know?'

'I have a small personal matter that I need investigating. I think my wife may have taken a lover, and I need it looked into please. Dara O'Keefe gave me your number. I hope you don't mind that I've called?'

'Dara O'Keefe still owes me a fortune.'

'Mr Huxton, money is no object. I've heard you're good.'

'I've retired. You're ten years too late.'

'Look, Mr Huxton. As I said, I can pay whatever you need. Business is going well – we've secured deals all over Europe; we've three offices opening this year alone – so please don't worry about payment issues. I've suspected something's been wrong for a while. My wife is out most evenings, I've found a second phone and she's cold towards me. I miss her.'

'Well, get a bloody dog then.' Billy slammed the phone hard on the receiver and returned to the living room.

* * *

Gladys and Betty made their way to the front, while Declan impersonated a horse commentator.

'Ladies, ladies. Stay calm. There's plenty of me to go around. Let's check those cards. You can't have both won. OK, Betty. You've marked fifty-three. That number didn't come out, my love. It wasn't called, Betty. You can't mark willy nilly. Go back to your seat now, cheater, cheater.' He leant forward and kissed her cheek. 'OK, Gladys. Let's take a look. Yes. Yes. Yeah. We have a winner! Well done, my love. You've won a week-long stay at – drumroll please – Sheldon's Residential Home! How does that sound?'

'Oh, you are funny, Declan.'

Billy sat back down, glancing around the room. He never bothered taking part in the games and didn't care much for conversation.

His wife had died almost ten years ago, and it had hit him much harder than he could have imagined. After her death, he'd moved in with his only son, but they constantly bickered, which eventually forced him to move into a residential home.

Henry called once a week, and every time he did, Billy would reluctantly move down the hall to talk for all of two minutes.

Billy and Cheryl were married for over forty years. They'd squabbled like cat and dog, and for the latter part of their marriage, slept in separate rooms, but as Billy always declared, they were dedicated to each other. They were solid. Their relationship was complex, to say the least. He loved her, and she him, but Billy pissed her off more than she'd care to admit. Her eventual ultimatum: move out of the bedroom, keep busy and keep out of her business or find a bench to call home.

She often referred to him as the grumpiest bastard she'd

ever met.

They'd worked together in private investigations – everything from keeping tabs on unruly teenagers to marital affairs, cons let out from prison and gangs suspected of dealing shit on street corners. They took it all on, and everything was a challenge. Cheryl took phone calls, booked in work and kept the customers informed, while Billy worked all the hours his body could muster to do the investigatory work.

Cheryl had died of cancer, a six-month battle that they went through together. Every step of the way, he held her hand, and as she took her last breath, he'd vowed to retire, never to continue a day of business without her.

Cheryl would never have wanted him to mope, to give up, but she was his life, and he couldn't get over the fact that she'd been taken in such a cruel way. He had no motivation to keep working.

He watched as Declan handed out new cards, waltzing around the tables, which were tightly bunched together, his tall, skinny frame, effortlessly moving as he theatrically danced around the room as if he were on stage, soaking up the applause and willing to do as many encores as his audience would allow.

'OK, darlings. One more game, then it's bedtime. Gladys, Betty, you listening, treacles?' He brushed a hand through his curly blond hair and pinched the corners of his eyes with his thumb and forefinger. 'A new game. Don't go marking the old card now, will you? Right. The first number. Four and five, are you all still alive?'

Billy stood and walked out of the living room, nodding to Declan as he left.

'See ya, Billy. Night night. Thanks for joining us... He's the life and soul, isn't he? Three and one.'

4

'Do you hear that?' Sean asked. He and Jenny were driving along a narrow country lane, away from Greyshott Hall towards Oxford.

Jenny hadn't spoken for a couple of minutes. She was fighting to get a phone signal but the display bar remained empty. Her hands were shaking, and she shivered in the passenger seat. 'Hear what?'

'There's a hissing noise. Oh no.' Sean wound the window down. 'I don't believe it.'

He pushed his fingers through his hair, letting a couple of strands flop over his forehead, then brought his hands to his face, feeling the heavy stubble around his mouth.

'Do we have a flat tyre?' Jenny's voice was weak. Her stomach was aching and her head began to pound with stress.

'I think so. I have a spare in the boot.' He hit the steering wheel with his fist. 'This is typical. One of the coldest nights of the year, we've been attacked by a lunatic, we're in the middle of nowhere late at night and now we get a puncture. Yes, of course this is going to happen.'

He slowed the car, looking into the darkness around them. It was late and the full lights of their Volkswagen Tiguan cut into the bleakness.

They were parked in a lay-by a couple of miles from Greyshott Hall. Sean left the engine on with the heaters at full blast.

'Shit. We're almost out of petrol too.' He eyed the gauge, where the needle was resting on the bottom. 'Can our luck get any worse?'

'Turn the engine off. The lights as well. They'll drain the battery.'

They sat in total darkness. Jenny was leaning forward, her head in her hands, fighting to get to grips with what had happened at Greyshott Hall. She checked her phone. The signal was still empty.

'When we get home, we'll check the footage. Hopefully, it picked him up when we arrived. Something we can show the police.'

They sat for a few moments, listening to the radio. Though they risked the battery dying, they needed the comfort of voices.

'Christ. Why do we do this?'

'Because it makes us decent money.' With that, Sean undid his seatbelt, grabbed the torch and glanced into the rear-view mirror, making sure the road behind was clear and hoping to see a glimpse of another vehicle.

When he opened the driver's door, bright lights suddenly came on in front of them, blinding their vision. 'What the hell? Where did they come from?' The road in front of them had been a mass of blackness. 'Surely we'd have seen a vehicle coming towards us.'

He began to wave his arms.

'Go back, mate. There's no way to pass. The road's too narrow.'

He stood out on the path and flagged for the driver to back up. The lights went off.

'That's strange.' He leant into the car. 'Why would someone just turn their lights off? It doesn't make sense.'

'Sean, just back up.'

'I'm not moving.'

'Just do it. That vehicle didn't approach us by accident. It was like it was waiting.'

'Oh, Jenny. That's ridiculous. How could—'

The lights came back on, now a little further back, around twenty yards from where they were parked.

'It's fine. They're backing up. See? Nothing to panic about.' Sean waited by the car door.

In the passenger seat, Jenny listened to a local channel, where a caller was discussing the Brexit situation. As the person spoke, she watched the vehicle's lights in front go off, darkening the road completely.

As Sean climbed back into the car, he assumed two possibilities: the driver was either backing up to find a gap to let them pass, or was reversing to leave the road altogether. In any case, it was a good sign. They had little choice but to wait and see how it played out. They sat nervously, watching in front of them, the engine off and the lights out. The road seemed deserted now, only the two of them out there. Alone.

In the background, a radio commercial played. It had a lively jingle and a voice-over saying why you should buy a particular washing powder.

'They must have taken another route. Maybe they were lost. See, they've gone, Jenny.' But as he finished speaking, the bright lights came back on, this time right in front of them. The vehicle was a couple of yards from where they sat.

Jenny screamed. 'I thought they'd gone. What the fuck is going on?'

Sean started the car. 'I don't know, but we need to move. I'll back up, let them pass. This is getting ridiculous.' He shifted around to eye the road behind. The backlights of his car provided enough sight for him to see and steer the car along the dark road. The tyre was almost deflated; he could hear the rasping sound as the car struggled to move.

'Sean, the lights have gone out again. Do you think they've left the road?'

'I doubt it. I don't know what the hell they're playing at, but I'm not waiting around to see. I'll reverse until I find a safe place to turn, then I'll replace the tyre and get us the hell out of here.'

He guided the vehicle backwards gently, steering around the sharp bends, listening to the grating sound coming from underneath.

When he'd eased back and up the steep hill, Jenny spoke. 'I think they've gone. I haven't seen anything for a few minutes.'

A bead of sweat had begun to trickle down Sean's cheek, his face flushed. 'Come on. There must be somewhere to turn. Do you see anything?'

'Nothing.' She jabbed the button on the dashboard to silence the radio, then opened her window, leaning out to listen. There was only the sound of their car reversing, the high-pitched noise of the engine grinding in her ears. 'Stop a second.'

Sean hit the brakes. 'What?'

'I want to listen. See if we can hear anything.'

They sat in silence, completely still. Sean looked at the

smashed windscreen and then down at his seat where there were still glass crumbs between his legs that he hadn't brushed away yet.

Jenny turned towards him. 'Now is a good time to change the tyre. I haven't seen the lights for a few minutes. Maybe someone was stuck – a farmer with a tractor, or a lost elderly person. We probably frightened them more than they did us.'

Sean turned towards her, now able to smile. 'A farmer, working at this time of night, ploughing fields in the dark? What the hell, Jenny.'

She began to laugh and hit the side of his forearm in a don't-mock-me gesture. 'It could have been someone on a bike, pissed drunk.'

'And how would you explain both lights?'

'Maybe they had two torches. Oh, hang on – that would make it a tad difficult to steer the bike...'

They eyed each other, their fear momentarily replaced by laughter, a relief from the strain of the evening, but Sean was still concerned how the lights had suddenly appeared in front of them. They'd had the radio on loud and hadn't heard the vehicle approach, but it was more than that. It was as if someone had been waiting for them in the darkness. Whoever was out there, they'd backed up into the distance, then rolled forward silently, purposely turning the lights back on. It felt as if the person was hunting them down, tormenting them.

'Sean, what just happened? Who the fuck was that at Greyshott Hall? He was going to kill us.'

'I don't know. He didn't want us there, that's for sure.'

They sat still, listening. It had been almost ten minutes since they'd seen the lights.

'This time next week, we'll be in the Cotswolds. Our new start,' Sean said, trying to divert their thoughts.

'I know. I can't wait. We have so much to do.'

'Well, everything's packed, more or less.'

'Oh Sean, that's only the tip. There's house insurance, telephone lines, gas, electric, WiFi. Can you imagine Beth and Ethan's face if they have to spend a night without social media?'

'Oh, the thought of it. How could we be so cruel?' Sean laughed. 'Back in my day, we actually spoke to one another. Imagine that.'

'Imagine is right.' Jenny turned the radio back on, an action made subconsciously to ease the stress. She opened the car door, needing to rid the cramp that had formed along the side of her leg. As she stepped out onto the path, she looked out at the bleakness beyond. 'They've gone. I can't hear anything.'

Sean grabbed the torch. Again, he turned off the engine to preserve the battery, but left the lights on this time. Only the radio played to relieve their fear. He stepped out of the car and made his way to the boot, where he lifted the hatch. He stood back, seeing the deflated back right tyre. The car had dropped slightly, and the smell of burning rubber was overwhelming.

'It seems torn. Those stones at Greyshott Hall must have done a right job on it.' He crouched down and began to jack up the car. Then he used an angled bar to remove the nuts. 'Sorry, my friend. Your time is up. Off you come.'

He turned around to look behind. The road was pitch black, desolate.

'Any signal yet?'

Jenny looked at her phone. 'Nothing. You?'

He dipped his oil-stained hand into the back of his jeans

and retrieved his mobile. He lifted it in the air, moving it around. 'Nothing.'

'Sean, do you think he's dead?'

'The man? I doubt it. I only clipped him.' He smiled nervously. 'What the hell was his problem? I know we weren't supposed to be there, but he overreacted, don't you think?'

Jenny remained silent for a few seconds, then spoke. 'Sean. You don't think—'

'Jenny. No. Come on. Listen to yourself.' He knew who she was thinking about. Mark Wheelan. The psychopath who'd murdered the nurse and seven inmates, then escaped, never to be seen again. The idea was ludicrous.

Jenny moved to the back of the car, listening intently.

It was late. Vehicles rarely used this route at night. The road was dangerous with potholes, sharp bends and all manner of hazards. People even avoided the area during the day.

The tyre was off now, and Sean had placed it on the road beside him.

Jenny watched as her breath formed in front of her like a dense cloud. The harsh breeze sweeping down from the hills was uncomfortable and seemed to numb her bones. She wrapped her arms around herself.

As Sean lifted the new tyre, he knocked the torch, which caused the light to go off.

'Are you for real?' He banged the end of it. 'This isn't happening. For Christ's sake. Come on!'

He turned around, glancing behind the car. He listened as far into the distance as possible. The road was so quiet, serene. It suddenly dawned on him how alone they were, and only a few miles from where the attack had taken place. He was unsure how hard their car had hit the guy. He remembered how he'd stumbled backwards, landing on the ground, and how, as they'd pulled away, he'd seen the guy lying there, motionless.

He remained crouched by the side of the car, balancing the new tyre in place as he knocked the end of the torch onto the road in a bid to resuscitate it.

That's when they heard the sound of glass smashing.

'What the fuck?' Who's there?' As he stood, he heard another crash.

They both crouched at the back of the car and listened. Stones crunched not too far away. Someone was moving towards them, heavy breathes to the side of where they were hiding.

Jenny screamed, and Sean reached his arms out, moving in front of his wife to protect her. Without the torch, the path ahead was now a mass of blackness.

Sean listened to the sound of heavy shoes moving around the car. 'What the hell do you want? Leave us alone.'

They stood still, petrified. Out on the country road, they were alone, vulnerable.

'They've smashed the lights,' Sean whispered. 'I can't see in front of the car. They've smashed the bloody lights.'

'What are we going to do?' Jenny had to fight to stop her body from shaking. Her voice was broken and she struggled to speak through her whimpers. 'Sean. I'm so scared.'

The footsteps were getting closer. They heard the crunching sound of stones right beside them.

'I have a knife. I swear I'll stab you in the throat if you come any closer.'

The crunching sound stopped. Sean and Jenny held their breath.

Moments passed. They remained still, listening for a signal that the person was still there.

Jenny kept her voice low. 'Are they gone?'

'I can't hear anything. I think they're hiding by the car.' Again, Sean checked his phone for a reception. Still nothing.

Suddenly, they heard the footsteps again, only this time, they were moving away. Sean and Jenny remained still, crouched behind the car, gripping each other tightly as they waited until the sound disappeared.

There they remained, cemented in the same spots, in the cold, hidden and too frightened to move.

Five minutes passed with them hearing nothing.

'I need to change the tyre.' Sean broke the silence. 'Then we'll get away from here.'

He knocked the end of the torch on the road and thankfully, the light came on. He pointed it forwards, steering the light towards the road in front of the car. The road seemed empty. He slowly stood, then managed to fit the new tyre in place, his hands trembling as he tightened the nuts and released the clamp.

When he placed the old tyre in the boot, he could hear Jenny weeping. 'Are you OK? I'm so sorry this happened.'

She moved around to the side of the car, clutching the jumper he wore. 'Sean, it's the same guy, isn't it? He's still out there.'

'I think he's gone. I can't hear anything.'

Once he'd put the tools away, he guided her back to the car. He shone the torch at the windscreen, wanting to assess the damage. A crack had formed like a huge spider's web, creating holes large enough to push your wrists through. The bonnet was also dented, the door badly damaged, and the glass that covered the lights on either side were both smashed.

Back inside the car, they locked the doors and sat still for a moment. Sean needed to compose himself. He turned the control knob to bring on the lights, forgetting for a second that they were out.

'How am I supposed to drive? The bastard has smashed the bulbs. It's pitch black.' He raised his voice. 'What is wrong with this idiot?'

The voices from the radio helped to calm him down. He appreciated the sound of them discussing recent current affairs. It was like a welcome comfort to ease the darkness.

'Have you got any reception?'

Jenny lifted her phone from her lap. 'Nothing. Dead.' She placed her hand on the passenger door, making sure it was locked, then gazed out of the window, wondering whether the person had really gone or if he was still out there, watching from the bleakness.

Sean turned the engine on and prepared to leave. Behind him, he could see just past the car, but in front, he could see nothing. 'You'll have to shine the torch on the road ahead. It's the only way we'll see anything.'

As he pulled forward slowly, Jenny noticed something in her visor mirror, a brief flash behind the car, a few hundred yards away. 'Sean. Someone's behind us.'

Sean tapped the brakes, looking in the rear-view mirror. 'I can't see anything. What was it?'

'I don't know exactly. Lights, I think.'

Sean waited in anticipation, wondering whether the darkness was playing tricks with his wife's mind. 'Are you sure?'

'Sean, a light flashed – only for a split second, but I saw it.'

Sean sighed. He needed Jenny's full cooperation to see the road in front, but at that moment, she was still spooked.

He stopped the car, unlocked the doors and stood out on the road. Jenny joined him a moment later.

'Where? Show me?'

She lifted her arm and pointed to the side of the road. 'I think it came from over there.'

'How far away?'

'Oh, I don't know. A half a mile, maybe. It could have been more. It's hard to judge.'

'Maybe it was the farmer looking for his tractor.' He tried to control the smirk that threatened to spread across his face. He had to ease the tension somehow.

Two lights flickered in the distance, possibly the same lights that had been in front of them a few minutes ago.

Sean stared, anticipating what might happen.

Suddenly, the lights started flashing on and off, moving closer. Sean was unable to judge how close, but they were moving towards them.

Then they suddenly went off.

Standing at the back of the car, Sean peered into the distance, his heart racing. He could feel the hairs rise on the back of his neck. He glanced upwards. The sky was clear with millions of glistening specks, the moon providing enough light for them to see each other. The fields on either side of them were pitch black, with an array of trees serving as a blanket for any light that might have seeped through. Was it possible that whoever had been driving had backed away? Turned off the path, moved around full circle and was now behind them? He panicked, suddenly feeling nauseous. Out here in the open, they were so vulnerable. He moved towards Jenny, who was still staring into the distance.

'Let's go.'

'Go? How can you drive? It's too dark, Sean.'

'Jenny. Let's get in the car.'

They moved into the seats, locked the doors and were suddenly startled by the brightness that glowed no more than a hundred yards away. Once again, they heard the revving of an engine, and the sound was pelting towards them.

Jenny screamed.

Sean started the car, pressing his foot hard on the accelerator. The vehicle was right behind them, moving fast.

'Come on, you piece of shit. Go,' he demanded. 'Jenny, shine the torch.'

'I'm trying. It's broken.' She hammered the torch against her lap until the light came on, then she pushed her body over the door, hanging out of the window to shine the light on the road.

As he struggled to gain speed, Sean had to flick the bottom of the rear-view mirror to move it out of his sight, dimming the lights behind. 'I can't see enough ahead. This is crazy.'

Suddenly, they jerked forward. The small truck had hammered into the back of them.

Jenny's body jolted with great force, causing her to drop the torch on the floor of the car. She screamed out, reaching down.

'What the hell? He hit us.'

Sean pushed the gearstick hard, willing the car to pick up speed. Jenny had a hold on the torch again and was leaning out the window, shining the light on the road.

The truck was fifty yards behind them. They turned a sharp corner.

'We're losing him, Jenny. Keep the light towards the road. It's our only chance. We better not meet anyone head-on.'

'Oh Christ, Sean. Don't say that. Can you see him?' Her

voice was partly lost in the wind and she had to repeat herself.

Sean turned to look behind him. 'No. He must be a good way back. What the fuck is this guy's problem? Should we keep driving or try to hide? Maybe we could turn into a ditch and kill the engine. I can't see anything in front. It's so dangerous.'

Jenny was too confused to answer. Besides, there was nowhere to pull over.

'If we meet a car, we've had it.'

The road ahead was suddenly illuminated, his vision aided by the lights of the truck.

'Shit. He's still behind.' He hammered his fist on the steering wheel. 'No. Oh shit.'

'What?'

He peered to the right. 'We've missed a turning. That's how the truck managed to get behind us. There may not be another one for miles. Shit, shit, shit.'

Jenny sat back inside the car for a moment, then turned, seeing the lights moving around the corner. 'He's still with us.'

'OK. Just keep the light shining to the front. I can make out the road, only just, but I can't drive fast; it's too risky.'

'It'll be frigging risky if this prick catches us!'

Sean glanced in the mirror. The truck was around a hundred yards from them, clipping bushes as it moved along the country lane.

He drove, struggling to remember the route and praying that the road would narrow ahead. As they turned around another bend, he slowed up, worried they'd run out of petrol or meet another car or come to a dead end. His eyes darted towards the gauge, which was in the lowest position. He had a few seconds before the pick-up truck would come around the corner behind them.

Sean had an idea. He estimated the truck was going around twenty miles an hour; the driver would struggle along the narrow lane. This was their only chance. The road could go on for miles.

He pushed the car as much as he could. It was suicidal to speed for too long. The fear of not being able to see ahead was horrifying.

'Jenny, hold the torch as best you can. I know it's not safe to drive, but I need to get a reasonable distance between us and the truck. If my memory serves correct, there's another turning to the right a little further up. I think there's a large gap opposite, between the bushes, that leads into a field. I drove here recently with Beth, and I recall her commenting on it; she pointed to the field, saying it was the perfect spot for a picnic. There's an entrance. I may be able to steer the car in there.'

'What are you thinking? He'll see us.'

'Just trust me.' He looked at the speedometer; the needle was dancing at twenty miles an hour. The petrol gauge indicated the tank was empty.

Beside him, Jenny was kneeling on the passenger seat, her right hand supporting her left, which was aching from holding the torch. The adrenaline was pushing her body to keep going as the cold air whipped her face.

They reached another bend, and Sean slowed the car, narrowly missing a ditch. The wheels screeched as he forced the steering wheel to the right.

Come on. Where's the break in the bushes? He struggled to remember the layout. He pushed the accelerator, forcing the car to twenty-five miles an hour. 'Can you see him?'

Jenny leant back inside and turned to him. 'No. Nothing. Do you think he's given up?'

'You can be sure he's pushing the truck as hard as he can, but he'll be struggling on this road.' Sean slowed the car. 'Give me the torch a second. We haven't got long.'

He eyed his wife; her nose was dripping and her cheeks were a bright red colour.

She passed the torch across, her hand trembling and cold with fear.

Sean guided the torch to the road on his right side. 'I'm sure there's a turning here somewhere.' He jabbed the brakes and drove slowly, worried the truck would catch them and ram them from behind again. They drove for another minute. 'Is he behind, Jenny? Can you see anything?'

'Still nothing. I think we've lost him.'

Up ahead, the turning came into view.

'Yes.'

'Are we going to make it?'

'He's not going to win. Just trust me. I'll get us out of this. OK? I'm going to drive into the field on the left.' He shone the light across the road, eyeing the large gap, then slowed the car to a crawl. He turned to Jenny. 'You have to trust me.'

'Sean, he'll find us. I know he will.'

'Jenny, trust me, we have no choice. He'll kill us if we keep driving. 'He leant over and kissed her. He held her tight, handed her the torch and then spun the steering wheel hard to the left, hitting the accelerator.

* * *

The field was relatively dry due to the cold weather. The wheels spun, flicking lumps of mud onto the bonnet. Sean manoeuvred along the grass until he was sure they couldn't be seen from the road. Quickly, he killed the engine.

'Wait in the car. I'm going out on the road. OK, Whatever happens, sit tight.'

'Sean, I'm scared.'

He leant forward and kissed the top of her head, not wanting to let her know that he was just as terrified. 'Please. Just wait in the car. If he turns in here or you don't hear from me, run like the clappers through the field. Just run.'

Jenny reached for him as he grabbed the torch, gripping his hand, then let go and watched as he grabbed the angle bar from the boot and disappeared back onto the road.

Sean walked through the gap in the bushes then stood in silence. He listened to the quietness. The truck was nowhere to be seen. No lights. No sounds of the engine. He wondered whether there was another route. Maybe the man had reversed and was waiting for them further down the road. He stood, feeling the icy chill against his skin, his breath pluming in front of him like a vape cloud.

Suddenly, he saw the lights in the distance a couple hundred yards away, moving towards him. It seemed like the driver had stopped, and for some reason, turned off the lights and the engine; now, he was continuing the chase.

Sean raced across the road, looking back to make sure the car was hidden, then waited.

* * *

Still sitting in the passenger seat, Jenny locked the car doors, struggling to control her emotions. Her body shook with fear, her breathing was erratic and her limbs were aching. She had been certain the truck had given up, backed off and left them, but now, she could see the field light up, including the ground around her.

The lights were getting brighter. She prayed Sean's plan would work. Whatever he had in mind, she'd give it a few minutes, then run to him. There was no way she'd race along the field on her own. Out there in the darkness. Alone.

* * *

Sean crouched by the ditch on the side of the narrow road, facing the direction where the sound of the truck was coming from. The engine was loud, revving and getting closer. As he kept low, waiting, endless outcomes dominated his thoughts.

Suddenly, the lights were upon him, the sound of the heavy, throbbing engine grating in his ears.

This is it: fight or flight.

Sean kept low, hidden in the ditch and made himself as small as possible. Then, judging the right moment, he got to his feet quickly, ran towards the truck and turned the torch on, shining the bright light directly into the driver's face. He watched as the truck swayed, the driver now wrestling with the steering wheel. Sean smashed the side window with the angled bar. A few seconds later, the driver drove straight into the ditch.

Sean watched the front end drop and the wheels become trapped. 'Yes, you prick. Yes. Fuck you.'

The driver was slumped against the dashboard. The white sack was still tied tightly around his face, with large holes cut for his eyes.

He watched for a moment as the driver lay still, then he stepped into the field and made his way back to the car.

He tapped on the window. 'He's crashed. He took the bait. We don't have long. We need to move.'

As they drove away, Sean and Jenny looked back at the empty vehicle.

The driver was gone.

* * *

Fifteen minutes later, they were on the main road, a few miles from home. Cars were flashing as they headed towards them, drivers letting them know their lights were off. To Sean and Jenny, it was a welcome relief. Civilisation.

Sean lifted his hand, thanking people, while both of them laughed nervously, giddy from the adrenaline pumping through their veins. They'd managed to get away, escaping the clutches of a psycho, hell-bent on killing them both.

They pulled into a petrol station, thankful they made it before the last drop had left the tank.

Jenny placed her hand in Sean's lap. 'You OK?'

He paused, rubbing his face with his hand. 'I just need to get home.'

Jenny sighed. 'You and me both.'

5

He'd stood by the ditch, watching as the taillights disappeared into the distance. As they pulled away, he saw the woman leaning out of the passenger window, desperately using the torch to guide them. He'd watched as her arm dropped, the strain too much. Then, the light trailed down the road as they made their escape.

The man drove slowly, bouncing excitedly in the driver's seat, punching the roof of the car with his fist, the excitement evident as they made their way towards the main road.

Relief. That would be a strong emotion for them right now. He could almost feel the tensity ebb from each wave, seeping from the car as they celebrated their achievement. A victory, if you like. But it wouldn't last. Be assured. This was just a warning – it was only the beginning.

The driver glanced towards his small pick-up truck, the front of it hanging at a twenty-degree angle, and walked to the back where he unlocked the cover. The contents resembled a builder's yard: shovels, spades, an assortment of tools, cement. It looked like a collection of home improvement materials, but this selection was for a different reason completely.

He picked up a couple of bricks. To others, these were to build something; to him, it was a weapon, a tool that aided his sick depravity. He placed the bricks on either side of the front tyres and pushed on the accelerator.

A few seconds later, the small pick-up was back on the road.

He eyed the baseball bat, which had rolled off the seat and onto the floor. How he'd ached to watch them take their last breath, their eyes wild, strained. He envisioned them clawing the end of the wood as he reined it down on their skulls, blow after blow. He doubted he'd be able to stop once he started.

His jeans had become stained with ejaculation due to the excitement he'd felt, but the anticipation was now dissolving from his icy veins – a feeling he hated, like a singer who'd been getting ready to play to a large stadium but a power-cut stopping them at the last second – such a high and then, *boom*, all gone.

'Jack and Jill went up the hill to fetch a pale of water; they both came out and made away to elude their fucking slaughter.'

Next time.

Next time they wouldn't be so fortunate.

He moved to the hedge on his left, shining a torch into the fields. He pushed through the bushes, standing in the mud. He saw the tracks, fresh tyre marks, deep in the grass.

'Oh, you are clever. So very conniving.'

He dropped to his knees, holding his head with both hands, and screamed at the top of his lungs. A sinister wail poured from his mouth. In a tree close to where he knelt, a rustling sound could be heard as birds were woken, disturbed from their sleep. He listened as their wings flapped above him.

He removed a penknife from his jacket pocket and proceeded to make a cut in his forearm.

This is what you get. Come on now, take the pain. It's your fault they fooled you. You only have yourself to blame.

As he pressed the point of the knife deep into his skin, guiding the blade slowly up his inner arm, starting from the hand towards his elbow, a trail of blood appeared.

Stop, I'm sorry. I didn't mean for them to escape. Please stop. It hurts.

Take the pain; there's a good lad. You know what happens when you do wrong, don't you? Deeper – cut deeper, you imbecile. That's it. Keep going. Take the arm off. Do it. Do it, I said.

He fought with the voices in his head, knowing he couldn't stop them. But cutting himself gave a modest release.

He removed the white bag from his head and placed it in his jacket pocket, then tossed the penknife deep into the field. He wiped his hand over the blood, scooping it up, and smeared it across his lips.

Good boy, that's a good boy. Taste it. That's it. You have done so well.

He felt the skin on his face, tracing his fingers over the rough skin, feeling the deep burn marks. He caressed the tissue, the thick, tough, fibrous texture, and ran his fingers along the indents.

Ever since that night, he'd avoided mirrors, shop windows – anything that displayed his reflection.

The night it happened, the fire, he'd never felt such pain. He hadn't intended for his plan to backfire so cruelly. He recalled standing there, watching as the flames engulfed everything in its path as he tried to make his escape. Only he didn't. His skin burned as it melted, disintegrating. Lumps of his flesh dissolved.

As he'd ran from the house, he could hear the screams, the voices begging for help.

He still heard those screams.

6

Tuesday.

B illy Huxton woke, and eyed the alarm clock. It was just gone 10am, and he'd slept in. He could hear someone in the hall outside his room, someone pushing a frame along the wooden floor, their slippers dragging like sandpaper on a rough wall.

'Lift your bloody feet, Betty. Stupid woman.'

Billy knew the residents' habits, all their odd little quirks. Mildred Harper chewed constantly, and if she wasn't frequently chomping her mouth, she was sucking on a strong mint. Eddie Barns was as deaf as a post, and you'd have to repeat a sentence several times before he'd grasp what you said. Katherine Reilly hummed to herself all day, and Barry Soleman's false teeth often dropped from his mouth mid-conversation.

Billy lay still, debating whether he should get up at all. The boredom in this place was arduous and the days dragged, just like Betty Gilroy's slippers. He looked to the end of his single bed, where his stockinged feet stuck out over the end, and through the small stained window that gave him a view of the grounds of Sheldon's Residential Retirement Home.

This room was like a prison cell to him, but what choice did he have? He had somewhere to sleep, three meals a day, and the entertainment was bearable. Just.

He pulled himself off the bed, swinging his legs to the right. He lifted the picture of his wife that stood on the bedside cabinet, kissed it and placed it back. Then he placed his legs through a pair of pyjamas and pushed his feet into his slippers.

As he walked into the living room, he noticed Declan was up by the front, talking into a microphone. He was wearing bright green trousers and a loud yellow shirt that matched his hair. He looked as if he was ready to take centre stage at a circus.

'Testing – one, two. Testing. Billy! What a surprise. I didn't expect to see you here. When did you get here? You should have called. I'd have picked you up from the airport.'

Billy looked across the room. 'Declan, do you ever give up? It's Tuesday morning, the rain is lashing outside, and I need bloody coffee.'

'You sit there, Captain. I'll get it for you.'

Billy watched Declan move to the back of the room, and pour a coffee from a large urn into a mug. He was squeezing the lid as if he were clutching a lemon over a pancake, trying to get every last drop.

'Are you joining us for the disco this morning? We're starting with the conga. Over-eighties only, baby. I'll even let you be at the front.' He passed the coffee to Billy who proceeded to stir the contents with a spoon.

'I'll have you know I'm nowhere near eighty. Cheeky bastard. The conga indeed. I can barely lift my leg to climb into the bath.'

'Don't be a defeatist, Billy lad. How many miles are on the clock anyway?'

'Sixty-one.' He sipped the coffee, grimacing at its weak taste. 'Why do you do it, Declan?This can't be the most exciting job you're qualified for?' He placed the mug on the table and leant back in the chair with a sigh.

'It beats selling my body. I'd never be able to keep up with some of the ladies in here. They'd ruin me.'

'I'm serious. A young fella like you, stuck in here, day in, day out. What are you? Forty?'

'Almost, Billy. Almost. But hey, at least I'm first in the queue for when I'll need this place. What about you? Why don't you go back to what you love? You have a reputation. The phone rings constantly. I see you moving down the hall to answer it, the frustration in your voice as you decline, the way you hammer the receiver back in its holder. What's stopping you?'

Billy hesitated, succumbing to the memories for a second. 'I made a promise to my wife. That's a personal question anyway. Mind your own bloody business.'

Declan sat on the chair next to him. 'Oh right, and that's what she would have wanted? You, giving up? Wasting away in here? From what I heard, you were a great investigator. People talk.'

'People talk shit. As I said, I made her a promise.' Billy looked to the ground. For a brief moment, his mind drifted to the past. 'What about you, Declan? Is this where you'll be for the rest of your life? An entertainer in a retirement home?'

'Butlins weren't taking anyone on. I can think of worse

jobs. Besides, the women adore me here.' He laughed. 'I could never go back to the police force. I hated it. Bullying was rife. It nearly killed me. And anyway, I'm happy here. I enjoy it. I wouldn't want it any other way.' Declan turned towards the door as the residents started making their way inside, a smile coming over his face as he greeted them. 'Morning, lovelies! A game of paintball, anyone? Or shall we start with tag rugby?'

7

Tuesday.

Jenny sat in the kitchen with her laptop open, still shaken from the attack the previous night. She Googled Greyshott Hall Psychiatric Hospital and found loads of articles reporting on everything from patients, staff, plans for the future and early pictures of when the asylum had first been built.

She clicked on various social media platforms and found an article entitled, 'Mark Wheelan still at large: Police baffled on his whereabouts.' The report was published a few days after the massacre had happened.

The story had been featured on Twitter; an influencer in the news industry had posted it with a trigger warning, declaring that the details of the story may upset some readers. Discretion was advised for those who were easily upset.

. . .

Not much is known about the psychopath who mutilated eight people and ran into the night. There is no previous history of Wheelan and no pictures, due to him being a minor when sectioned. Sheila Eastwood, a nurse, had attempted to resuscitate Mr Wheelan, leaving the metal door to his cell open when she raced towards him. Wheelan bit off part of Sheila's nose and then proceeded to take chunks from her face until she passed out. He then punched her repeatedly until she died. It's thought that Wheelan grabbed the keys to the other cells and murdered all seven inmates in the same way as he killed Sheila.

Patients were found with missing ears, fingers and other limbs. He'd urinated on one victim and broke most of their teeth.

The police described the scene as a 'terrifying massacre – a bloodbath beyond comprehension.'

PC Richard Thornton was one of the first to arrive on the scene.

'We were called around 10.30pm on the night of January 25th by one of the nurses. She had been hiding in a store cupboard on the first floor. Others were holed up in their rooms in the staff quarters. Even down the phone, I could hear the screaming.

'I can only describe the scene as carnage. Bodies lay strewn across the floor. Each of the cell doors were open, and I could smell the flesh. It was like a butcher's shop. Officers were getting sick; I recall one or two fainting. In all the years I've served as an officer, I've never seen anything like it. The nurse and inmates that were mutilated were left in an appalling state.

'Many officers had counselling. Others retired, too distressed to carry on with the job.

What we witnessed that night was pure, unadulterated wickedness.

'I've no doubt that the person who did this, Mark Wheelan, is the devil himself.'

.   .   .

Jenny closed the page, feeling a shiver work its way up to her neck. She shut the laptop for a moment, composed herself and then opened it again so she could edit the latest documentary footage, ready to load it onto their social media platforms. She and Sean had searched each frame, but no footage had been captured of the guy who attacked them. They'd called the police when they arrived home, explaining what had happened. After they'd given a full report and a description of the attacker, as well as the vehicle he was driving, the call handler told them they'd send an officer to the area to take a look.

Sean came into the kitchen and stood by the counter, making a pot of coffee and peering into the garden. Jenny explained the search and reports she'd read on Greyshott Hall.

Sean tried to put the image from his head, what those people had gone through that night and what the police officers had found. At the window, his gaze passed over the old metal slide to the right-hand side to the trampoline, which had its safety net ripped along the front thanks to years of abuse. The kids were older now, but he couldn't face getting rid of the childhood memorabilia.

They were moving at the weekend, and he'd miss this place. They'd lived in Oxford for the last nine years, but it was time to go, time to move on, to make a better life. He could feel tears forming in his eyes at the thought.

They'd been gifted a rundown farmhouse in Painswick, a village known as The Queen of the Cotswolds, around fifty miles from where they currently lived. The property had been owned by his late uncle, Ed Berry, and had land that they couldn't pass up. The place was derelict and in need of major refurbishment – Ed Berry had abandoned the place and died in a retirement home – but Sean and Jenny wanted to make it their project. A large house with loads of space; it was the opportunity they'd been waiting for.

Their son, Ethan, was eighteen and in his second year of college, studying business and finance. His grades were excellent and he dreamed of setting up a clothing company. He had managed to transfer to a college in the Cotswolds, wanting to stay with his parents, though his decision was further aided by the fact he didn't get on with one of his lecturers.

Beth was sixteen and had just finished secondary school. She was still uncertain where her life was going, but after a conversation the previous week, she had convinced her parents that she'd follow in her brother's footsteps and go to college. That was the latest update, but she often changed her mind.

Beth had worked the summer in a small eatery – nothing fancy, but it gave her experience with customer service. The hours were long, and the pay was bearable. She'd finished her last shift a couple of days ago and now wanted to delay registering at college in Painswick.

Ethan and Beth were good kids. Respectful and honest, the two qualities Sean and Jenny had taught from an early age. Ethan was tall, well-groomed and always dressed impeccably. He had short, cropped blond hair and deep green eyes.

Beth was slightly shorter, with long brown hair, brown eyes and a darker complexion than her brother. She was shy and reserved. Beth struggled with her confidence and was often awkward around people.

Sean and Jenny worried about the move; they'd spoken in-depth about the decision to move to the old farmhouse and the fresh start in Painswick. Their documentaries' popularity had grown considerably. They'd been featured in national newspapers and participated in interviews on the radio and television. Local companies were queuing to advertise their products. Now, they had the money to move and refurbish the farmhouse.

The process was slow, building their reputation as film-makers and it would be a couple of years before they were comfortable.

Sean placed a cup in front of Jenny, and leaned over her shoulder to watch as she edited the latest docufilm. They liked to make the footage as raw as possible, with only light cuts here and there. It made for a more edgy, realistic recording.

'I'm going to do a short trailer for the Greyshott Hall documentary and explain what happened last night, before the kids wake up. I don't want them knowing. Not yet, anyway.'

'You do know that they can watch it on YouTube, right?'

Jenny leant back, stretching her neck and running the tips of her fingers through her hair. 'When was the last time they asked about a documentary we've made? They've no interest unless Stormzy or Skepta make an appearance.'

'Who?' Sean laughed. 'The latest grim stars, I presume?'

'It's *grime*, Sean.'

'Grime? What kind of name is that?' He left the kitchen, and a few seconds later, returned with the camera case. 'Where do you want to film the trailer?'

'Here is fine. I'm looking at doing a minute, no longer.'

Sean set up the camera while Jenny took a makeup set from her handbag and applied a light coat of mascara and some lipstick. She eyed herself in a small hand mirror, then adjusted the seat.

Sean reached up, twisting the fluorescent light above

and towards where she sat. 'That looks good. OK, ready when you are.'

She gave him a thumbs up, and Sean hit the record button.

'I'm Jenny Freeman, and last night we were viciously attacked after visiting Greyshott Hall Psychiatric Hospital to make a documentary. We're filming a trailer, a taster of what's to come. We'll edit the docufilm which should be available shortly, but I'd like to explain what happened to both Sean and I. Unfortunately, we don't have any footage as we were running for our lives. We've reported the incident to the police and that's all we'll say on the matter. I'm stating the circumstances as it may get out. We're film-makers and I don't want to tarnish the work we do. Often, Sean and I put ourselves in dangerous situations. It goes with our work. It's part of the territory. Anyway, I hope you enjoy our latest film which will be ready soon. Thanks for all the support.'

Later that morning, after Jenny had finished the edits and added the brief introduction, they watched the film back before uploading it to their website and social media channels.

'How are you, hun? After last night, I mean.'

'I don't want to think about it. It was horrible. We could have been killed. Do you believe it? The stories, I mean. What happened there all those years ago? What if it was him? Mark Wheelan?'

'No, Jenny. Don't go there. It's something too terrifying to think about.'

'But—'

'Jenny, come on. Let's put this behind us.'

Sean thought part of what his wife was saying made sense. Mark Wheelan. The murderous rampage at the mental institution all those years ago. The stories. The evil of that night. There was doubt playing in his mind.

What if?

Jenny turned back towards the laptop. 'You're right. We need to forget about it. Focus. Don't mention anything to the kids. I won't have them worrying.'

Sean nodded. 'I'm going to get the car fixed. I also thought I'd take a trip down to the farmhouse, have a look. Friday's approaching fast. I'll find a garage in Painswick, get the windscreen repaired and see if they can get the dents out. Do you fancy taking a spin with me?'

'Not today, Sean. I can't bear getting in the car, after... well, you know.'

'I get it. Rest up; take it easy. The first of the kids to come down the stairs, I'll nab. The promise of lunch will be too good to pass up.'

* * *

Forty minutes later, Sean and Ethan were halfway to Painswick.

The rain pelted against the windscreen and the wipers screeched as they struggled to cope with the water, which was getting in anyway thanks to the cracked windscreen. Ethan was getting soaked.

'You hit a tree? You and Mum? Jesus, Dad, you could have been killed.'

Sean looked across at his son, whose face still bared the marks from his pillow, his blond hair hidden under a cap. He also noticed that his hoodie was inside out.

'Yeah, I know. Anyway, I thought we'd get the car sorted and check out our new home. Thanks for coming, mate. You know how I hate to go anywhere on my own.'

Ethan looked across at him and smiled. 'Yeah, I know, Dad. I can't believe the state of the car. You do know they'll throw the book at you if you're pulled over?' He reached forward and touched the cracked windscreen.

'How? I can still see out.'

Ethan laughed, wiping the wet droplets from his face.

* * *

They were a couple of miles from Painswick. They'd called ahead at a garage that Ethan had found online, and the friendly voice on the phone had said they'd take a look at the car. It was quiet due to the rain, so they were instructed to drive straight over, with the promise of a replacement car for the interim.

Sean pulled into the forecourt, eyeing the shabby sign above the garage, which hung too far to the left and looked as if it might drop at any second.

He parked the car and climbed out into the car park.

A small, tubby guy moved towards them, wearing blue overalls and a cap that boasted 'Bernie's Autos' across the front. He looked to be in his mid-sixties and his hands were grubby with oil stains. When he saw the car, he gave a loud well-blow-me-down whistle through his grey beard.

'What in the name of God? Looks like you were jumped. Those dents on the bonnet – must have been a big guy!'

Sean glared at the man with a frown, trying to hint at him to shut up. He glanced at Ethan, who was running his hands over the dents.

'I'm Sean. This is my son Ethan.' He extended his arm and shook the guy's hand. 'Do you think you can do anything today?'

'Yeah. Scrap the bugger. That's what I'd suggest. What a mess.'

Sean felt irritated, but tried to hide it.

'I'm sorry, I didn't catch your name.'

'It's Bernie.'

Sean looked up at his cap, then the sign on the garage door. 'I'm guessing you're the Bernie who owns this place?'

'Nope. That was my grandfather. He started this garage many moons back.'

'Well, good to meet you.'

'Good to be met, but I'm not the Bernie you were looking for.'

Sean feared it was going to be one of those mornings.

Bernie looked over the car, grimacing like a cat nibbling on a lemon as he did so, then beckoned for Sean to pull it into the garage. Sean followed him into the office, while Ethan waited on the forecourt, tapping on his mobile phone and laughing at something on Instagram.

'OK, come in. We don't bite.' Bernie opened the door, which led into a small office. Posters of car engines were hung all over the white walls, and the smell of oil was overbearing.

Bernie moved around the desk and pulled out a folder containing pages of registration plate numbers with figures written next to them. Sean guessed they were prices for works that had been recently carried out.

'Now, I'll do what I can. We can replace the glass on the windscreen and side door, smooth over the dents, but be warned – you can't polish a shit. And I can give you the blue Volkswagen out the back. She needs a drop of petrol, but I'll take that off the bill. If I can get a signature, here and here? Oh, and fill out your address and occupation.'

Sean took the form, filled in his details and signed at the bottom of the page.

'Where is it you're moving to anyway?'

'Oh, a farmhouse a couple of miles from here, just off the A46. We're moving in this Friday. There are neighbours close by so we won't be completely alone.'

Sean watched Bernie's face suddenly drop. 'You mean the old place on Psycho Path? A little rundown, yeah? Ed Berry's old place. It's been closed down for years now. I heard someone was moving in.'

Sean laughed. 'Psycho Path. I like that. It's actually Gallows Lane. Ed died a few months back, and we got first dibs on the place. He was an uncle of mine.'

'Terrible thing – him dying, I mean. A good old stick, as they say. Kept himself to himself – a quiet chap. The place has been shut for so long now. You've got your work cut out.'

Bernie lifted the piece of paper, squinting his left eye. 'Documentary filmmaker. Is that what you do?'

'Yes. My wife and I. We make films for the internet. Investigations mostly. Urban legends, unsolved mysteries, the paranormal... People can't get enough of it.'

'Well, you'll certainly be busy here then.'

Sean straightened his back. 'Oh, why's that?'

'Ed never said anything to you?'

'I never met the man. I know he moved out of the farmhouse a while back, taken into a home, I think. My mother has taken charge and she gifted it to us. Builders have been doing it up for a few weeks now, so it's just about liveable. We'll renovate it when we move in. It'll be a long process.'

Bernie placed the form into a filing cabinet behind him. Then he handed him the car keys. 'OK, be back later this week. We close at 5pm. After that, I don't answer the phone to anyone, so you'll be wasting your time calling.'

Sean went to walk out, but something Bernie had said niggled at him. He turned around at the last second. 'What did you mean we'll be busy?'

'Son, it's one of the Cotswold's biggest secrets. But it isn't my business to go talking.'

'You asked me if Ed had ever said anything. Anything about what?'

'That old farmhouse has a history. People talk. Rumours, things that happened there and to the people of Painswick.'

Sean held the door open, looking out at his son in the car park talking on the phone. 'I'm not with you. What rumours?'

'You'll not find anything on no internet, no news reports either. The truth, I mean. About who did those awful things. Yeah, people want to forget. But it happened. He's as real as you or me.'

'Who is? Who are you talking about?'

Bernie adjusted the peak of his cap. 'Creeper.'

* * *

Sean sat in the small, blue Volkswagen. The engine revved as he struggled to push the gearstick into reverse. Any minute now, he feared Bernie would race out and order him from the driver's seat thinking he wasn't capable of being behind the wheel.

'You OK there, Dad? Having a little trouble?'

The car jolted back and conked out.

'No, I'm good, thanks.' He started the car again, and the engine clattered as if the floor was collapsing. 'Piece of cake.'

Sean followed signs for the A46, and a few minutes later, they pulled into Gallows Lane. The road was narrow with potholes ingrained in the tarmac and was surrounded by overgrown fields, wild and primitive. Tree branches that reached over onto the road clipped the car as they drove.

'It's certainly quiet,' Ethan said.

'Yeah, it does seem that way.'

They passed a couple of large detached houses on the left and Ethan commented on the front gardens. 'They're huge. I came here once when it was late so I never saw them properly. I can't believe how amazing they look. How long did you say it's been abandoned?'

'A few years now. Don't use the word "abandoned". It makes it sound haunted. Temporarily closed or waiting for repair is the way I like to view it.'

Sean was distracted. The place was much quieter than he'd expected. He'd been over a couple of times earlier in the year with Jenny, but he'd forgotten how deserted the place was, especially now that winter was drawing close. He needed to find out more of the story that Bernie had hinted at – the rumours, the farmhouse and its history.

He steered the car onto the drive. 'That's weird.'

'What?'

'I thought there'd be a van here. The decorators can't have finished already, surely? I spoke to Mario yesterday; he said they'd be here until Friday, possibly Saturday morning.'

Having exited the car, Sean stood on the drive, looking up at the farmhouse. It was bigger than the others they'd passed along the road and it would take a lot of looking after. It was a huge, two-storey building and looked old, tired and worn out. There was a large wooden door at the front, and a small garage was attached on the right with a metal shutter. Trees surrounding the front garden added some privacy, and across the road, fields spread out as far as you could see, wild and chaotic. They could hear the birds in the trees nearby, singing their morning song, and in the distance, the sound of a tractor.

Sean fished the keys from his jacket pocket and slowly opened the door. Ethan followed him inside.

'Hello? Mario? Is anyone here?'

There was no response. The walls were unfinished and only painted in parts. The wooden floor in the hallway was fully sanded but again, only varnished in certain areas. The new doors that he had asked to be fitted inside lay stacked in the front hall, and he noticed that the stairs that led to the first floor still had holes in the rotten wood. Mario had promised this would be finished a couple of days ago.

He grabbed his phone and dialled the contractor's number. He waited, but nothing rang out. He cursed, realising there was no reception. 'Damn it, what's wrong with those clowns? Your mum's going to hit the bloody roof. I'll have to finish the work. We need it done before we move in. Shit.'

Sean and Ethan inspected the other rooms, finding that the living room to the left was finished, albeit needing furnishings, and the rest of the house was liveable.

'Dad, here.'

Sean joined Ethan in the kitchen. 'What's up?'

He lifted three mugs filled with tea. 'Looks like the builders left in a hurry?'

8

Tuesday Evening.

Marie Nelson left the pub at just gone 7.30pm. It was Tuesday evening, and she had an early start the following day. The rain was heavy, and she struggled to see in front of her. Her face stung from the cold droplets that pounded against her skin. She removed her coat so she could hold it over her head to keep dry.

She walked briskly along the dark country lane – something she'd done many times before, rarely heeding the words of advice to steer clear of the area and take a taxi.

It was a typical October evening, and the lanes were pitch black, but Marie felt brave due to the three large glasses of Merlot she'd sunk with her friends earlier in the evening. She could feel the warmth from the alcohol radiating in her cheeks. She adored the buzz – it made her mood light and upbeat.

Lights appeared behind her, signalling a vehicle approaching. She could hear the spray from the wheels as it moved through a puddle; it sounded as if someone was bombing into a swimming pool. She stood to the side, watching the car pass, realising she still had a way to go to get home. At the last second, overcome by a feeling of Merlot-fuelled courage, she stuck out her thumb, then moved to the middle of the road where she waved her arms frantically. She even hurled her jacket at the window. But the car disappeared around a bend and continued up the steep hill.

'Damn it. You keep driving, arsehole. I'm getting pneumonia out here. Jesus, what's wrong with some people?'

Marie turned and looked behind. A shiver darted through her body.

She picked her jacket off the ground and flapped it dry, like she were a matador coaxing a bull, then placed it over her shoulders.

She walked in silence, thinking about the great evening she'd had, wishing she was still inside the pub, listening to the crackling of the open fire as it warmed her body and the laughter that filled the room, seeing the faces glowing, induced by the alcohol consumption.

She glanced to a house on her left, the curtains at the front drawn tight. She waved her phone in the air to search for reception. It was no use; this part of the village was secluded. Besides, it would take ages for a taxi to arrive.

I wonder if it'd be cheeky to ask them for a lift, knock the door and force them to take pity on me. Nice motor you've got there, mate. Fancy putting it to use?

She reached the corner where a few minutes ago the car had disappeared. She needed shelter. The rain was much heavier than she'd expected, and the torch on her phone was struggling to cut through the darkness.

Marie lived on her own; her parents had died six months apart, her mother taken by cancer and her father suffering a massive stroke. She'd kept the family home, unable to tear herself away from the memories.

After the death of her parents, she had tried to end her life. She'd took an overdose of sertraline, swallowing them with a half-bottle of whisky. A friend who'd called over had seen her lying on the hallway floor and called the emergency services. Marie was vulnerable, and her friends had looked after her, making sure she got the help and therapy she needed.

She had lived in Painswick all her life and had no ambition to leave anytime soon. She loved it here.

Now, she sat on the side of the ditch, wrapping the coat tighter around her shoulders and ran her fingers through her hair to push the damp water away.

Suddenly, she heard a vehicle in the distance making its way towards her. Quickly, she jumped up, watching as the car approached. She stood in the middle of the country road, determined not to let it pass. She'd lie on the ground if needs must.

She watched the large, blazing beams move towards her. The lights were irritating her eyes, but it didn't matter.

Yes, you beauty. You have to stop. Please stop.

As the vehicle approached, she reached up, arms extended, and waved her coat.

The vehicle slowed to a halt. Marie could feel the heat coming from the front. The passenger window cranked down.

'Oh, thank you. Lifesaver. I'm perished out here.'

The person in the driver's seat leant over. 'You'll catch your death. Get in. Where do you live?'

Marie pointed ahead. 'About two miles along this road. Oh my, I can't thank you enough.' She climbed in, and once seated, grabbed the seatbelt, wrapping it around her cold, shivering body.

'Have you been out tonight?'

'Yeah, a couple of drinks with friends. I didn't know the weather would be so bad. Otherwise, I'd have stayed indoors.'

'It's not a night to be out on your own, that's for sure.'

Someone jumped up from the backseat. Marie screamed, reaching for the handle of the car.

'Jesus Christ, Ethan. You scared the shit out of us. I thought you were asleep.'

Sean turned to Marie and apologised, introducing his son who'd been lying on the backseat.

Marie threw her body forward, laughing uncontrollably. 'Jesus, you hear stories about women getting into strange cars. Sorry, but you gave me the fright of my life. Wow.'

Sean looked across at her. 'I thought it was the driver who was the vulnerable one.'

He explained how he and his family were moving to Painswick, doing up an old farmhouse. He'd treated his son to dinner, and they were now driving back to Oxford.

'Wow. Well there are worse places, that's for sure. What will you do for work? You'll have to travel, you know? You're in the sticks now.'

'We make films.'

'Oh yeah?' Marie laughed.

Sean picked up on her sarcasm. 'Not the rude type, I assure you.'

'I'm playing with you.' She laughed, and in the back, Ethan tutted.

'We make documentaries. Exploring urban legends, haunted places, true-crime investigations – that kind of thing.'

'Wow. That's so intriguing. How exciting.'

'Yeah, we enjoy it. It beats working in an office, that's for sure.'

'You'll be aware of our urban legend, I'm guessing?' Marie wiggled her fingers in an exaggerated fashion as she spoke.

'I heard something earlier, but I didn't get the full story. I'll Google it later.'

Marie's body was starting to thaw out. She placed her damp coat across her legs. 'You won't see anything online – not the whole story anyway.'

'So, what's it about?' Sean was eager to hear what Marie had to say.

'Well, for years, there have been reports of residents seeing someone outside their homes – in Painswick mostly. He watches them, stalks them, if you like. Some believe he gets inside by hiding in their basements, under floors or in their bedrooms, often while the residents are home. Others will tell you he's responsible for all the missing women. Painswick has an inordinately high number of disappear-ances. Supposedly, he kidnaps people, holds them in an underground chamber and tortures and kills them. Then he dumps their bodies close by.'

'Have any of these bodies been found?' Sean asked.

'No. But people here believe there's something sinister behind it.'

Sean felt a shiver dart through his body, causing him to

jerk back. The hairs stood on his arm. In the back of the car, Ethan was leaning forward, listening intently.

'And you? What do you believe?'

'I believe there's no smoke without fire. They call him Creeper. Around these parts, he's as notorious as the banshee, someone you don't want to see standing at the end of your drive. I know of at least eight women who have vanished in the area over the last twenty years. No sightings, no leads – it's like they've disappeared off the face of the earth.'

Sean looked across at her. 'Wow. That's bloody scary stuff.'

She nodded. 'It sure is. But hey, people love an urban legend, don't they? Anyway, the last woman I know of to vanish was over ten years ago.'

'Where is this chamber supposed to be then? Where he supposedly takes the bodies? Here in Painswick?'

'Yeah.' Marie glanced across at him. 'Ed Berry's old farm-house on Gallows Lane.'

9

A figure stood at the end of the drive, peering into the dim, unlit farmhouse. The country lane was empty, the lights from the cottages in the distance having faded, like a Chinese lantern high above, rising and dissolving into the night sky. It was late, and the din from the village had quietened. It was so remote. Peaceful.

Earlier, not far from here, he'd watched as the young woman stepped out of the man's car, thanking him for the lift and saving her from the treacherous rain. He'd watched her as she waved and lifted the metal gate, then hoisted it back with great effort before jogging along the path to her front door.

As she approached, the bulb on the wall had jumped to life, draping her in light. She turned, watching as the car pulled away, the wheels spinning slightly on the wet road.

She held her red coat at her side, the material skimming the ground, making the woollen hem muddy. She turned her key in the lock and when she opened the door, she stood still for a moment, breathing in the heat from the hallway. She placed the coat on a stand to her left and then rubbed her hands along her dress to rid the water droplets that sat on top of the material. Then, without looking, she reached behind her, pushing the front door shut. But it bounced back. She turned, and everything went black.

Now, outside the farmhouse, the garage shutter was closed and the front door shut and locked. The van had gone from the drive. Work had now ceased, for them anyway.

He'd watched the workers earlier that morning racing through the door, the small tubby guy pleading with the others.

'It was nothing,' he'd shouted. 'Please, guys. We need to finish.'

He'd begged them, but the others wanted out. He'd watched their faces as they, grown men, fled like a cat that had been placed in the middle of a chicken pen.

Now, as he stood watching, he could hear voices. Unsure if they were in his head or a recent memory, he looked down towards the marks on his forearm.

'Let me go, please. I beg you. I have a boyfriend; he'll be worried sick. You can't keep me here. I beg you. I have money. He can transfer anything you need, make a drop-off. He'll look after you. You don't have to do this. For fuck's sake, let me go, you freak.'

Let me go, crazy one. Let me into the night. I don't belong here, locked up tight.

I lower the cloth and strap it tight around your mouth. I adore the look on your face, the fear; your eyes wild, pupils dancing; how your mouth widens and you squeal under your gag. I think it's a squeal. Maybe I'm wrong. Perhaps you *want* to be here.

I brought you food earlier. That was something. I thought you'd push it away, refuse, but you acted like a savage, leaning over the wooden floor, scavenging for every crumb you could get. It's only been a few hours, but I know how fear can drive the appetite.

I watched you eat, sitting there in your ripped dress, momentarily forgetting where you were.

Then the fear on your face.

You came back, into my world for a moment, then I quickly took you out.

10

I t's certainly an idea for our next documentary. And two people spoke of this person. Creeper, did you say?'

'That's what they call him.' Sean removed his T-shirt and threw it over the back of a chair next to the dressing table. He slipped out of his jeans and got into bed beside his wife. 'Some old guy at the garage, the owner – Bernie was his name. And a woman we picked up.'

'Whoa, woman? "Picked up"? You never mentioned this.' Jenny noticed he had started to blush.

'It's what they do in the countryside. The poor girl was getting soaked. Call it my good deed for the day.'

'Good deed schmeed. Was she wearing tight jean shorts and cowboy boots?' Jenny laughed as his face reddened.

'They both spoke of this guy who supposedly stalked the locals years ago. It's said that if you see him, it means he's picked you out. Get this: the people of Painswick believe he's responsible for those locals who went missing.' Sean kept quiet regarding the possibility that he'd hidden the bodies in their farmhouse.

'That's some scary shit. I'll give you that.'

'It all happened years ago. We should do some research, check it out. Speak with the people of Painswick, see what they think and if they still believe the story.'

Jenny reached to the bedside light and pressed the switch, plunging the room into darkness. 'What makes you think it's just a rumour?'

Sean paused. 'Because the reality is way too terrifying.'

Jenny lay in bed, thinking about the truck driver, the attack. She hoped they'd been in the wrong place at the wrong time, but the doubts were creeping in. It was all a little too coincidental.

Wednesday.

Sean woke early on Wednesday morning. With the decorators having made a sharp exit from the farmhouse, like a bank robbery gone wrong, he now had lots to do. He had called Mario numerous times, always reaching his voicemail with a message he struggled to understand. Mario had recorded it with a drill going in the background. Very professional.

After tapping out a text message that started with the letters WTF, he pressed send and moved upstairs to his daughter's room.

'You ready, Beth?'

He watched her straightening her long, brown hair, her head tilted to the side. Her makeup was scattered all over the dressing table.

'Two minutes, Dad. Be patient.'

'We're only going to decorate, not for a night out.'

Beth looked at him and tutted through her painted red lips.

'Oh, you have a bit of, you know, a smudge.' He pointed to her face.

Beth laughed, kicking the door shut.

Sean walked into the bedroom. 'OK, Jenny. We're off. I'll see you this evening. I've got everything we need, I think.'

'See you, babe. Oh, and don't go picking up any strange women. Beth will tell me.'

'Only if I knock one down.' Sean kissed the top of her head. 'I'll have a strange woman accompanying me to Painswick. She won't talk and insists on having music blasting through those strange shaped ear-plugs.

'Oh, Sean. It's good of her to help.'

'You should see the way she's dressed. Christ, you'd think she works for

Laboratory Garnier.'

'It's Laboratoire, you moron.'

* * *

Fifty-five minutes later, Sean and Beth pulled up to the farmhouse. Beth had provided little to no company, listening instead to music on AirPods tucked underneath her hair. Sean had to ask her how she was listening without wires and tried to grasp her explanation of Bluetooth, with little success.

'No wires? That's impossible. Try telling that to an electrician.'

'Oh, Dad. Get with the times. Surely you're winding me up.'

They stepped out of the car, and Beth looked at the farmhouse with a disparaging look.

'Yes, the place is a little rundown, but it's been shut for years. You've seen it from the outside but try and hold back on the sarcasm. Picture the potential, if you can. It's in need of work, but we'll get there.' Sean peered over the grounds. 'Eventually.'

'In need of a miracle, I'd say.'

Beth placed the AirPods into a small white box, which she placed into her handbag. Sean pointed at it. 'You are going to talk to me, aren't you?'

'Yes, Dad. I am going to talk.'

They laughed as he moved to where she stood and gave her a tight hug. 'Thanks, Beth. I mean it. I'm glad you came. I say we get the kettle on and make a start in the hall.'

She gave a 'Yes Sir' salute and followed him through the front door.

Inside, Sean watched Beth's face as she gasped. Words weren't needed, and for the first time, he felt embarrassed as he began to realise the mammoth task.

Beth looked along the long, dank hallway that led to the kitchen, glancing at the high ceilings and the mouldy walls, both of which were riddled with damp patches and deep black stains. The wood that once resembled a stair rail was rotten with woodworm.

As she walked along the hallway, she could smell the wet, soggy air. Her balance seemed unstable, as if the floors were about to collapse. The dust from where the builders had begun sanding collected under her feet. She brushed her hand along the walls, which were only partially coated in paint, feeling their rough texture.

What have my parents done?

Beth grabbed the kettle and turned on the tap, seeing yellow-stained water coming from the spout. She watched as it ran in spurts before eventually becoming clear.

'An airlock. It will rid itself,' Sean stated.

They drank tea from old, stained mugs retrieved from a cupboard on the kitchen wall loaded with cobwebs.

Wow. It must be years since this place has been cleaned, Sean had thought, but kept the assumption to himself. When he'd finished his tea, he moved towards the front door. It felt like the floorboards were bowing under his feet. He eyed his daughter from where he was unloading a couple of boxes, embarrassed. They both smiled.

'Right, where shall we start?'

He pointed at the wall to his left. 'Here's as good a place as any.'

While her father placed the containers on the floor and spread out the dust mat, Beth moved to the rooms.

'Wow. The space is incredible. I can see the potential.'

Sean searched his daughter's face, looking for a hint of criticism, but found none.

She moved towards a small box room to the left of the front door. Inside, she kicked the carpet back, revealing a large wooden hatch cut into the floor. 'Dad, come look.'

Sean could hear the excitement in her voice.

The wood was a brighter colour than the rest of the floor. There were two brass hinges on the left side, and on the top and bottom; a silver lock was on the right.

'Damn. It's locked.'

He watched as she struggled to push her fingers into the latch.

'Please tell me you have a key?'

'I do. But it's at home.'

'I wonder what's down there.' She stood up and made her way out of the room, back into the hall.

Sean stood over the hatch, remembering the rumours he'd heard. He felt a chill sweep through his body and kicked the carpet back over.

* * *

Sean clutched onto the last piece of sandpaper, which now resembled a moth-eaten rag. They'd smoothed out a good part of the wall in the hallway and he was pleased with their progress.

The clouds, thick in the sky, provided minimal light. The low energy bulbs the builders had fitted into the sockets were insufficient. 'We should have brought candles. What a heap of shit – another thing to add to the list.

Shall we call it a day?' He glanced at his watch: it had gone 2pm.

'Let's give it another couple of hours, Dad. I've got sod all else to do, and to be fair, it's quite therapeutic.'

'Therapeutic. I like it. Well then, we need to find a hardware store.' He held up the flattened piece of sandpaper.

'You go. I'll carry on. I have a bit of sandpaper left, but not enough for the two of us. Just be quick.'

Sean hesitated. 'Are you sure?'

'Yeah, I hate stopping once I get started.'

Ten minutes later, Beth had worn the sandpaper down to within an inch of its life. Her hands were covered in dust, and her hair was wet from perspiration.

She stepped back, admiring her work, then reached into her handbag to phone her father. The screen displayed the 'No signal' sign. 'For Christ's sake.'

She dropped the phone back in her bag and walked into the kitchen. She looked at the space, imagining what it would look like in a couple of months: a breakfast bar along the middle of the room, a small, widescreen telly; neighbours clinking glasses and sipping wine, toasting her mum and dad, welcoming them to the quiet life. It wasn't for her; Beth needed action, excitement. She wondered why anyone would want to live in the country, away from civilisation. The nights seemed to get darker much quicker, the solitude unbearable, and even the thought of people in the village knowing your life story made her feel like a headache was coming on.

Beth had plans. She'd study fashion at college, then move abroad – New York, Paris or Tokyo.

Her thoughts were interrupted by a sudden thump that seemed to come from the box room. It sounded as if someone had fallen.

Beth froze, holding her breath for a brief second. She turned, facing the front door and looked over. The box room door was closed. Beth slowly pushed it open. The room was empty. She backed out and stood in the hallway.

Hello? Is someone there?' She listened hard, then tiptoed along the wooden floor. Now, standing at the bottom of the steps, she felt her heart racing.

She grappled with her confidence, trying to reassure herself. *Get it together, Beth. It's an old house. You're bound to hear noises.*

'Come on. Where are you, Dad?'

She waited for a second. A vein began to throb in her neck. She was beginning to question whether the sound had even happened.

On tiptoes, she moved slowly along the hallway, watching the section of the old, dust-ridden carpet just above the hatch. She darted a look to the front door, then moved slowly back into the box room. Holding her breath for a moment, she lifted a corner of the carpet and pulled it away.

She knelt, placing her ear to the hatch, listening hard. 'Hello?'

She pushed her finger through the brass ring, tugging at it. It was solid. There was no way it would open without the key.

Beth stood, still troubled by the noise she'd heard. Then suddenly, the hatch jumped slightly, as if someone was in the basement below forcing themselves against it.

Beth screamed.

'What the hell?'

Petrified and her body shaking, she backed away, her hand over her mouth. She moved into the hall and towards the kitchen, her eyes remaining fixed on the box room. She clutched at the wall behind her to aid her path.

As she stood in the kitchen, Beth listened intently, her body still trembling. The house was silent again. She listened to her sharp breaths, her chest moving fast, in and out, in quick movements. She was struggling to breathe; panic temporarily paralysed her body. It felt as if her heart had stopped; the blood was struggling to circulate.

She slowly pulled herself together, knowing that she needed to get out of the farmhouse. As she moved back along the hall, she heard a pounding on the front door. Again, she screamed, holding her hands up to her face.

'Leave me alone!'

'It's me.'

She raced to the front door and pulled it hard.

'You OK, Beth? What's wrong?'

'I'm OK. I'm fine. Jesus, what took you?'

'The hardware shop had no sandpaper. Can you believe that? Drinks and food, but no bloody sandpaper. What's wrong with some people? Hardware shop? Hardluck shop, more like.'

Beth pushed out a sharp breath. 'It's just as well. Come on, let's go home.'

* * *

As the rain came down heavily, Sean cursed. He struggled to see and had to keep slowing to avoid the deep pools of water that had formed in the road, dotting the concrete like an attack of chickenpox. The windscreen wipers were working overtime, flicking back and forth like an erratic pendulum on an old grandfather clock. Water sprayed over the window. He wiped the glass with the back of his hand to see more clearly.

Beth was unusually quiet, and Sean was certain that she wasn't listening to the wireless headphones. He glanced at her in the passenger seat, her knees pulled up close to her face, staring out of the window, motionless.

'What are you thinking about? You seem a million miles away.'

Beth was troubled. 'Nothing. Just chilling. You worked me to the bone. I'm bloody exhausted.'

They approached a small cafe on the side of the road, its car park almost empty.

'Come on, I'll treat you to a bite to eat.'

He was pleased to see the sudden change in Beth's expression and slowly steered the car into a space.

They raced through the doors hand in hand, laughing at how soaked their clothes had become.

The cafe was brightly lit, decorated with pictures of famous golden oldie Hollywood actors and actresses: Marilyn Monroe in the famous dress standing over a subway grate; John Wayne and Maureen O'Hara in a clinch from *The Quiet Man*; Elvis in a cowboy hat and blue denim shirt – rows of pictures that Sean could happily study for hours if he had the time.

A waitress came over, offering a broad grin, and placed cutlery in front of them both.

'It looks like you just managed to beat the rain.'

'Yeah, it doesn't seem to be stopping lately. I love the pics by the way. Who's the fan?'

'Who doesn't like old movies? They don't make 'em like that anymore. We had someone famous here a couple of years back. God, who was it? Tall, skinny, British actress. What was her name again? It will come to me.'

The waitress took their orders and ripped off a piece of paper from a small pad. She returned a minute later with a pot of coffee.

'Kate Winslet! That was it. Unfortunately, I was on holiday. She signed autographs and had pictures with the staff.'

'Wow, she's amazing.' Sean searched the walls to see where the photos were. 'My wife and I are in the film business, you know.'

Beth tutted sarcastically at this.

'Oh, anything I'd have seen?' The waitress beamed enthusiastically.

'Possibly. We make documentaries: urban legends, unsolved mysteries, that kind of stuff. Mainly short, low budget films but we make a living.'

The waitress leant forward. 'You need to investigate Cree—'

'Rose!' A voice came from the kitchen. 'Get in here. We don't pay you to talk all day.'

Sean and Beth watched as the waitress left the table, disappearing out the back.

Beth looked at her father. 'Who was she talking about? What was she going to say?'

'I'm not sure.' Sean lied. He didn't want to frighten her with the stories.

When they'd finished eating and Sean had settled the bill, they got up from the table and thanked Rose for her hospitality. Sean placed a twenty-pound note onto the silver plate with the receipt, then they walked out to the car.

'What was she going to say? Before the other woman stopped her?'

Not wanting to worry his daughter unnecessarily, Sean had to distract her. 'Who knows? How was the food? Good?'

'It filled a hole, I guess.' Beth smiled.

The rain had eased, although the sky had become a deep grey colour, threatening another downpour.

Sean pulled his seatbelt around his waist and struggled to put it in the clip. 'Bloody hell, I need to stop eating so much.'

Beth laughed, glancing at her father. 'Salad, Dad. That's the way forward. Too many burgers are no good for anyone.'

'I had salad in my burger?'

'That's cheating.'

It had been ten minutes since they'd left the restaurant. The sky had now turned black, and as they drove along the empty country lanes, a light drizzle started.

'What did you think of the farmhouse then?'

Beth froze. The question had triggered her fright once more. 'I like it. Just a little too isolated for me,' she said. 'Won't you miss people though? The comforting sound of a hoover next door? A conversation over the fence?'

Sean laughed. 'Not in the slightest.'

He watched as heavy specks of water splashed onto the windscreen, hailstones bouncing like golf balls.

'Wow, it's ruthless. I suppose we've been lucky. It's been dry for so long.' He flicked the lights from standard to full and whenever they reached sharp bends in the road, jabbed on the brakes, water spraying the ground like a cascade. He twisted the knob on the dashboard, allowing more heat to penetrate through the grills.

'What about you? How long do you intend on staying with us, missy?'

Beth hesitated. 'A couple of years? I'm starting my new college soon, but in the meantime, I'm all yours.'

She needs a job. If she doesn't go to college, she'll have to find a trade in Painswick.

'Dad, look out.'

Sean's thoughts were sharply interrupted. Someone was standing in the middle of the road.

He slammed on the brakes. At the last second, the person dived into the bushes on the side of the lane.

'Who was that?'

Beth watched the bushes to her left side rustle, then pressed the button that turned on the central locking. The clicking sound eased her tension and made her feel a little safer. She eyed her father.

There was something on the road. Beth could make out an object through the brightness of their headlights.

'What's that?'

Sean guided the car forward. 'I don't know. Whoever was standing there dropped something.'

He leant forward until his head was nearly against the glass of the windscreen.

'I can't see. I need to get out. Wait here.'

'Dad, just keep going. Someone jumped into the bushes.'

'I have to check. What if it's something alive? It looks like it might be wrapped in a bundle. It's in the middle of the road anyway. I can't move around it.'

He stopped the car and stepped out onto the road. The hailstones had eased but the rain was now intense. The only sound was of the rain and the car engine as it idled.

He brushed the water from his jacket and suddenly, in his peripheral vision, noticed a shadow to his left. Although he couldn't see into the fields, he was sure someone was watching him.

He backed away, certain the figure had moved.

'Who's there? Hello?'

He waited a few moments, then looked towards the object in the road. He could feel his chest tightening, his body freezing as the rain whipped against his skin. He crouched down and touched the material. It was a red coat. Possibly the same one the hitchhiker had been wearing the previous night. He realised they were close to where he'd picked her up.

Surely it couldn't be her? Why would she hide? He glanced at the wet material. He felt uneasy.

Again, a rustling in the bushes distracted him. He turned and peered into the black hole.

'Marie? Is it you? It's me, Sean, from last night. I can give you a lift.'

No answer.

Something was wrong. Sean kicked the coat into the bushes and slowly backed away, his eyes never leaving the dark fields. Once he reached the car, he fumbled for the door handle and climbed into the driver's seat, locking the doors.

'What was it?'

'Last night, your brother and I drove along this way. We picked up a woman. She was hitchhiking.'

'What?' Beth looked back at him with a bewildered expression.

'She was getting soaked. Anyway, she had a red coat. She was holding it over her head to shield the rain.'

'And?'

'The object on the road. I think it's the same coat.'

Beth was silent for a moment, digesting what her father had just said. 'Dad, drive. Let's get the hell away from here.'

As he hit the accelerator, he took one last look at the red coat lying in the ditch.

He couldn't help worrying about Marie.

* * *

'Oh, Sean. You're being a little dramatic, don't you think?'

Jenny was in the living room, curled up on the sofa with her laptop. Their Greyshott Hall docufilm already had over 200,000 views.

Sean was standing beside her, eyeing the boxes that were tightly secured with Sellotape. Instructions were written on each one in black felt pen, describing the contents and where they should go once they arrived at the farmhouse.

'I'm not being dramatic. First, we had that loony in the truck attack us; then multiple people going on about some guy who kidnaps the residents of Painswick; the builders disappearing... Then, on the way home, another mysterious figure standing in the road. They dropped a coat that I'm sure belongs to the woman we picked up.'

'What did you do with the coat?'

'I kicked it into a ditch. I panicked. I thought it might have been a trap. You know, before they jumped us or tried to get into the car. There was someone standing in the rain. They saw us and hid in the bushes.'

Jenny stood and faced her husband, lifting her hands to his face and running her fingers through his hair. 'Sean, you're getting worked up. The attack was awful, but we were just in the wrong place at the wrong time. It's got nothing to do with your uncle's farmhouse. Builders, well, they do that – too many jobs going on; snagging is a trivial task to a lot of them. And you know how people like to talk. We need to grasp this opportunity. If there is a myth, if there is someone called Creeper who used to watch the people of Painswick, let's embrace it. Imagine the footage we could get, the interviews. The documentary could go viral, off the scale.'

Sean wrapped his arms around her. 'It's just weird, you know? I think the people of Painswick believe in this story. I'm worried about opening old wounds from the past.'

'What? The story of Creeper? Come on, Sean. Listen to yourself. It's not real. It's just a story fabricated to scare the locals, like The Bogeyman – an urban legend. Surely you can see that? If there was any truth to the rumours, it would be documented. People would know about it – outside of Painswick.'

She paused. Sean hoped that she was processing the possible danger of moving to the farmhouse, but somehow she didn't seem as fearful as him.

Maybe he needed rest. Once they moved, things would settle down. They'd be able to unwind and adapt to the stillness of the countryside.

'So, are we ready for the next chapter?'

Jenny moved across the living room, looking at the many boxes. 'As we'll ever be.'

11

Thursday.

Billy Huxton was sitting by the living room window, looking out. The clouds that had clogged the sky for the last few days had finally dissolved, disappearing to wherever the hell they would go to. The sun was warm as it pushed through the glass, and Billy was slightly less agitated than usual.

The living room was quiet; most of the residents were asleep.

Billy sipped at a mug of weak coffee. He winced, reaching for the remote control, and turned on the local news. He wasn't usually a fan of the television, preferring to sit in his room and read an autobiography, tackle the occasional crossword or look through pictures of him and his family. He also kept a scrapbook under the bed which he liked to flick through every so often.

The digital display in the bottom corner of the screen

stated the time as 8.53am, and as the main news bulletins were winding up, he watched the newsreader as she lifted a pile of papers, tapping them on her desk to stack them in order. He watched her turn to her colleague and wondered whether they were actually speaking or just mimicking conversation for the sake of the camera.

Oh, how was it for you? That was great, wasn't it? You read so clearly with your dulcet tones and your overzealous expression. Well done you. I can't wait until the local headlines are over and we're back on. Only a couple of minutes and we go again.

He turned the volume up, despite the possibility that the sleeping residents may wake up and complain about the noise. He had to listen to their shit all day though, so didn't feel too bad about it.

The newsreader started the local news with the report of a knife attack in Oxford town centre – two lads were critically ill in hospital – but it was the second story that caught Billy's attention. A picture of a young woman flashed up with the headline written above. He stood, watching the words appear. A missing woman from Painswick.

The newsreader started speaking, reading from her autocue.

'There are growing concerns this morning for a vulnerable woman missing in the Painswick area. Marie Nelson was last seen while out drinking with friends on Tuesday night. Her work colleagues are concerned for her safety, stating that it's "totally out of character". Reports suggest she was in good spirits when she left The Crown and Anchor pub at around 7.30pm. Marie is on medication and it's vital she is found as quickly as possible. Marie was last seen wearing a green dress with a bright red jacket. If anyone has information on her whereabouts, Gloucester Constabulary has asked that they call them directly. Onto sport now, and the annual boat race between Oxford and Cambridge—'

Billy hit the mute button and moved across the living room, stepping aside as Betty Gilroy edged through the door.

'Morning, Billy.' She patted her newly purple rinsed hair as she slowly twisted from left to right. 'What do you think then?'

'Of what?'

'My hair. I've had it done.'

'For me?'

'Of course not for you.'

'Well, don't ask then.' He left the room and moved along the corridor, heading back to his room at the far end.

The news report concerned him. He was struggling to deal with the explosion of thoughts and emotions that were racing through his mind.

He sat on the bed and reached underneath, feeling for the box he'd tucked away. Once he'd dragged it out, he placed it onto the bed, wiping the light coating of dust from the top of it, leaving a finger trail down the middle.

He undid the straps, then levered the lid away, letting it fall on the bedspread. The box contained a pile of paperwork, pictures, reports and private files.

He walked to the bedroom door to ensure it was properly closed, then returned to the bed. He lifted out half of the paperwork.

Billy could feel his heart racing, a knot of anxiety now rising from his stomach. He placed the papers beside the box and picked up the top few pages. He held his breath for a moment, composing himself, then began to look through the newspaper clippings. All of them were reports of missing women, all occurring in the Painswick area, all of them still missing. The accounts dated back almost twenty years.

Billy looked at the pictures, staring at the faces – all of them were young, late teens and early twenties, all still with their lives yet to live out.

He wiped the tears that were forming in his eyes as his memory took him back to the time it happened, his recollection still so vivid. He held the most recent clipping with shaking hands. The top corners were curled, stained a light brown colour with age. Thumbprints dirtied the paper. It was dated just over ten years ago, one year before the death of his wife. The headline was printed in six harrowing words.

'Another woman reported missing from Painswick.'

The picture was of a girl in her late teens – short, brown, shoulder-length hair, thin black glasses and a smile for the camera. She was sitting on a stool in her kitchen. Paintings hung on the wall behind her: a ballerina balancing her left foot in the air with her hands gracefully held above her head; a man and woman drinking coffee outside a cafe somewhere in Europe. Other pictures were also displayed in the background: a scribbled drawing that looked like it had been attacked by a toddler with crayons; a simple sketch of a house with smoke coming from the chimney, the front door larger than the windows on either side. This one made Billy smile the most.

He remembered this girl so vividly.

He remembered because the picture was of his daughter.

12

Sean woke early, needing to get to the farmhouse. It was just over twenty-four hours until they moved, and he intended on a quick visit to a hardware shop to purchase more sandpaper and some boarding to place over the holes on the stairs. He'd contemplated bringing Ethan or Beth but felt that they'd slow him down. Waiting for them to get ready was tedious.

He glanced at the clock in the kitchen just as two pieces of bread popped up from the toaster. Pleased he'd had the foresight to leave this as one of the remaining things to pack, he buttered the toast and headed out the door, determined that today he would make their new home a little more tolerable.

* * *

Jenny woke an hour later. She glanced at her mobile phone. 9.53am.

She sat up, eying the empty space in her bed. A sudden feeling of sadness washed over her as she realised this was their last day in this house. She loved this place. It was close to Oxford town centre, had great schools and the bus routes were convenient. Although the neighbours on both sides were not the type to pop over for a glass of wine or join them for a barbecue, Jenny knew they were there if they needed them – for a pint of milk, a bag of sugar, or if they needed someone to keep a watch on the house while they were away.

Once she had showered and dressed, she moved downstairs to the kitchen. The smell of Sean's toast still clung to the air. Ethan and Beth were still asleep; they'd had a late night eating pizza and watching Netflix.

She made herself a coffee, welcoming the sudden caffeine hit, then started up her laptop. Struggling to shake the nervous feeling that hung over her like a dark cloud, she Googled Painswick, recalling what Sean had said last night, his concerns about where they were moving.

The screen loaded with pictures of a winding road, an old church and a map of the village showing things like places to eat. The Rococo gardens were high on the results, but the rest were less picturesque. As she scrolled down the page, her heart raced as she saw the reports of eight missing women. Looking at the time stamps, they seemed to be over a twenty-year period.

She read a few of the reports, which stated that the locals and police were baffled as to the women's whereabouts. Some of the articles mentioned a cult; others talked about a pact or a belief the women had turned against the town and just left, practically walking away without any of their belongings.

Jenny tried to recall everything Sean had mentioned, the rumours he'd heard from the mechanic, the hitchhiker and the waitress. She struggled to remember what they'd called the man. She searched the words 'crawler' and 'croucher'. Nothing of significance showed. She leant back, struggling to remember the name, then it hit her.

'Creeper. That's it.'

She typed it into the search bar, but only found references to a roller coaster somewhere in America – a ride that boasted ten loops and a two hundred foot vertical drop – something to do with Minecraft and a band from Southampton. She added 'Painswick' to her search and a news article with the headline 'The Painswick Beacon' appeared, dated August 2012, but on closer inspection it was a small report about a magpie, with a picture of a cottage with the caption, 'Dormer creeper plant roof window'.

She scrolled through images of properties and more wildlife photos. The results below were mainly announcements about the Painswick fair. She found nothing remotely like the story that had bothered Sean so much. The only articles she'd seen relating to what Sean had told her were of the missing women, but there was nothing that mentioned Creeper, the mythical figure he had spoken so much about. None of the reports mentioned anything about people being watched from their homes nor anyone prowling around late at night, and there were no references to locals reporting of someone hiding in their homes.

Jenny sipped her coffee, then typed, 'Missing persons. Painswick'. She leant closer to the screen, reading more articles. She found more reports and pictures of the missing women, which made the hairs on her neck rise. The first one showed a woman in her early twenties with black hair tied in a bun. The headline read, 'Search continues for Chloe Madden.'

Jenny scanned over the article.

. . .

There are growing concerns for a woman missing in the Painswick area.

Chloe Madden was last seen exiting a taxi three nights ago after a night out with friends. Despite numerous efforts from the local police, family and friends, no evidence has been found to suggest where she might be. Her clothes and belongings are still untouched. The driver of the taxi has been questioned and is helping the police with their enquiry.

'The controller radioed my job over at around 11pm,' the driver, who wishes to remain anonymous, stated. 'I pulled over on Painswick High Street, and Chloe was standing with friends on the side of the road. I watched her hug them all as she said good-bye. Everyone was smiling. We spoke briefly on the way home – I know her well. I'm a friend of her parents. She's a great kid. And she seemed in good spirits. Then I dropped her off outside her house. I can't believe I was the last person to see her.'

Chloe had been twenty-one at the time, and the article described her as being five foot two with blue eyes and long black hair. The report included a description of the clothes she had last been seen wearing and a phone number to call with information.

Jenny read the article a second time. She wondered where Chloe was now. Had she simply walked away? Started a new life, leaving her family with so many unanswered questions? It was possible, but Jenny doubted it.

As she continued her search and moved down the page, she found more reports of missing Painswick women – all in mysterious circumstances; all had vanished into thin air. She counted eight in total.

Chloe Madden. Twenty-One.

Amelia Shaw. Eighteen.

Charlotte Ryan. Nineteen.
Emma Shawcroft. Twenty.
Ellie Simmonds. Nineteen.
Lily Painter. Eighteen.
Michelle Casey. Twenty-Two.
Katie Huxton. Eighteen.

Jenny read the report on Katie Huxton, the last woman to vanish, ten years ago. The article began with, 'Local investigator Billy Huxton is no closer to finding out what happened to his daughter.'

The picture showed a girl sitting on a stool with paintings in the background.

It's been over a month since Katie Huxton vanished from the Painswick area. The daughter of private investigator Billy Huxton, she was last seen at a family barbecue.

Billy said, 'We had a gathering of approximately twelve people, close friends. We were running out of wine so Katie left for the local shops at around 8.30pm. I offered to take her to the shop – it's only a few minutes' walk – but she refused, telling me to stop worrying. We haven't heard from her since. It's not like her; she would never leave like this. Katie's a happy kid with no mental problems, not that we know of. We need her to come home.'

Katie was last seen wearing blue jeans and a white blouse. Her credit cards, mobile phone and passport remain untouched.

Jenny scrolled down to the bottom of the page, finishing the article, but a door opened upstairs, causing her to close the laptop.

* * *

In a hardware store en route, Sean bought more sandpaper, paint, wooden boards and a couple of small blow heaters. He was determined to make an early start and get as much done as he could. He could just imagine Jenny stepping into the hallway of their new house and the first thing she saw being the bare walls and the gaping holes in the stairs. He couldn't have that happen.

He pulled into the drive at around 10am, still pissed off that the decorators had vanished. He'd continued to call Mario but each time he got his answer message.

It was a cold October morning. Frost still graced the tips of the grass, and as Sean stepped out of the car, his breath formed a smoke-like mist that pushed from his mouth. His body was warm from the heat of the car but his skin soon began to bite from the icy breeze. Thankfully, the rain had stopped.

He gazed around, noting the tranquil surroundings. The open fields opposite the farmhouse were bare, uninhabited. The grass was long, a dark green colour, which added to the natural beauty of the landscape. In the distance, he could hear cows and the faint sound of a cockerel screeching.

The driveway was substantial with enough room to park three or more vehicles. The farmhouse was painted a bright, white colour, but dirt marks and grubby stains had festered, spoiling its charm. The roof was high and timber-framed, with brown slate tiles that came into a sharp point at the top where the sides of the triangular structure met together. The outside windows were large and robust, single glazed and stylish – rectangular in shape with rustic barn wood frames. Wisteria hung from the front of the farmhouse, resembling claws from above, giving the impression of something trying to pull you into a vacuum.

To Sean's right was a stretch of winding road that

seemed to reach for miles. Jenny had wanted to live somewhere quiet, safe, secluded. He'd have to get used to being so
isolated.

He opened the front door, listening to the groan as he
slowly pushed. The smell of damp was evident. The house
was dark, and almost instantly, he felt alone. With Ethan
accompanying him a couple of days ago and Beth helping
him yesterday, he had never been alone here.

He stood in the hallway, taking in the old farmhouse,
peering along the hall to the kitchen, over to the broken
stairs and the box room to his right, which provided entry
into the basement. He shivered, a sinking feeling taking over
his body. He felt overwhelmed and lonely, verging on
depressed. He had to shake it off, fight the fear.

He set up the small blow heaters he'd purchased at the
hardware store. As the fans whirred into motion, causing a
low humming noise, he could smell a burning substance, oil
or lubricant.

A half-hour later, Sean had the radio on full blast, the
dust sheets spread out on the hallway floor and the sandpaper in action. He needed to keep busy, but was now
feeling a little more optimistic. He imagined the parties they
would have: neighbours sat at the breakfast bar with coffee
and biscuits, talking about the upcoming fair, telling stories
of the locals. They would have barbecues and invite friends
to stay over for the weekend. They could make as much
noise as they liked, blare the radio as loud as they wanted.
No more screaming at the kids to turn their music down, or
hearing the thumps when the next-door neighbour was
trying to sleep.

Sean continued to work over the walls, pushing the
sandpaper, feeling the ache settle into his shoulder. He
moved slowly along the hallway, pressing hard. He stopped

for a moment, wiping the thin coat of dust that had formed on his face. When he moved on to the next section of wall, he realised there was something there – scratch marks, five fingernail indents ingrained in the paint.

What the hell? He moved closer, his face almost pushed to the wall now, his eyes wide. The scratch marks were around eight inches long, deep in the fresh paint. Below, smudged into the wall, were bloodstains.

He slowly extended his arm and touched the blood. It was dry. He spun around, glancing at the front door, then walked over and locked it from the inside. He hoped it might be Beth's blood somehow, but he knew she would have told him if she'd cut herself.

A shiver raced through his body, causing him to jerk. He quickly grabbed the paint roller he had already prepared nearby, dipped it into the paint tray and spread it heavily on the wall. He stood back, checking the marks were gone, then went over the section of wall a second time, just to be sure.

He recalled the mugs of tea he and Ethan had found a couple of days ago. He thought about Mario and the other guys working here and wondered whether something had freaked them out – grown men, leaving the house in a hurry, unable to keep working, fearful of staying.

He moved into the kitchen and leant against the unit, the stories he'd heard from the locals playing in his mind. He worried that he and Jenny had made a mistake. This place was so isolated. How would they deal with the long winter months? The bitter cold? The remoteness? He fought the anxiety that was working its way up from the pit of his stomach.

Once he'd regained his composure, he returned to the hallway and continued to tackle the walls. He was determined to get everything finished before they moved in

Friday morning. He had to push through the fear of being here alone.

* * *

Jenny was in the kitchen, cooking eggs and bacon. Beth had been awake for an hour or so, hypnotised by the smell of food. She was still in her dressing gown, yawning as if she'd just emerged from hibernation.

'What are your plans today, love? Have you packed everything?'

The oil from the pan spat as she turned the eggs.

'Almost. Just a couple of things left to do. How are you feeling, Mum? Excited?'

'Overwhelmed is the word I'd use. It's daunting, you know?'

'Yeah. It'll be great though – all that space. It's amazing. I didn't realise how big the farmhouse is.'

Beth tried to push the dark images from her mind: the basement door, the slight jump as she'd knelt on the wood, the noises she'd heard from under the farmhouse, the figure standing on the isolated road. She had to stay positive.

Jenny also donned a brave face, masking the feeling of trepidation in her stomach. The missing women were playing on her mind. 'Yeah. It's what we want. Right, are you hungry?'

Beth turned from her chair with a wry smile; she didn't need to answer.

'Stupid question, I guess.'

Ethan joined them a short while after. He'd been lying in bed, listening to a grime album.

Jenny watched as he walked along the hallway and into the kitchen. His cropped blond hair was gelled forward and he wore bright blue pyjama bottoms with a white T-shirt. His excitement at the smell of food was evident.

Jenny cracked another couple of eggs into a saucepan and listened as the usual brother- sister niggles started.

'Beth, why do you do it? I was listening to a track. You know that.'

'Ethan, grow up. I was listening first. Deal with it.'

Jenny called this 'Spotifight', an argument resulting from when the siblings knocked each other off the playlist.

'Guys, not today. Try and get along, will you? Huh?' She walked towards them with two plates of bacon and eggs on toast.

Ethan and Beth were a year apart in age. They were close but often argued. It was usually music that caused the disputes, or who unloaded and restacked the dishwasher. All trivial. That, and Beth's boyfriends – no matter how Ethan tried, he couldn't get used to the idea of his younger sister getting attention from the opposite sex. He was extremely protective and didn't't like to see her get hurt.

The three of them ate together, then spent most of the day packing, shifting boxes downstairs and getting everything ready.

Later, as Ethan and Beth were in their rooms, Jenny was sitting at the laptop, sifting through the messages they'd received after she'd posted the Greyshott Hall documentary. She enjoyed responding to the comments, both the well-wishers and haters. She always tried to interact with as many people as possible.

As she scrolled down the Facebook page she'd originally posted the video on, she looked over the latest comments.

Blue Sue: 'Great film and background story of Greyshott Hall. Loved it. Keep up the amazing work.'

Kate311: 'Wow, I could feel the anxiety seeping through the screen. Your best yet. Much love to you both.'

RussandRubes: 'Loved, loved, loved this. Sean and Jenny, you are heroes. Always look forward to your films. Keep up the amazing work.'

Sech11: 'Mark Wheelan is one evil dude. Imagine if he's still out there? Love the new movie.'

Jenny typed out responses, thanking people for the messages. She wrote a post on the main wall too, thanking them all again. She kept scrolling: more likes, love hearts and questions about their future films and ideas. A couple of regular contributors recommended places to visit with additional back stories. Jenny made a mental note of these and would search their suggestions later.

Returning to the top of the page, she stopped abruptly. The last reply came in a couple of seconds ago.

Painswick Eight: 'I want to show you something?'

She moved her head closer to the screen, squinting her eyes. *Painswick Eight*. She ran the name over in her mind. It was possibly a fake account, a post from the many trolls who drowned her social media. There was something about the name that caused her body to shudder. She debated whether to interact, eventually deciding to reply.

'Show me what?' she typed.

Now perturbed that she'd responded, she clenched her hands on the edge of the table. She waited a few seconds, hovering over the post, then began to scroll down the page. Then another notification came in.

Painswick Eight: 'Do you want to see?'

Jenny felt numb, her body freezing as she tried to figure out what they meant. She braced herself, waiting to see how it played out.

Another message came through.

Painswick Eight: 'I have a picture you may like?'

Jenny sat still, waiting to see what they'd say next, wondering whether they might send the picture over. She hesitated. A wash of irritation crawled over her body.

Painswick Eight: 'Here it is.'

She leant forward and a picture appeared under the last comment. A red coat, lying on the road. She tapped the picture and zoomed in. It had been taken at night, the surroundings dark with a single light shining on the garment. Jenny remembered Sean talking about a red coat, lying on the ground.

This person was taunting her. But why?

Her fingers hovered over the keys. She wanted to reply, but to say what exactly? Then more words appeared.

Painswick Eight: 'The farmhouse is so isolated. Here's what's going to happen. Enjoy your stay.'

Jenny shrieked as another picture appeared. A farmhouse. The farmhouse they were moving into tomorrow. *Their* farmhouse.

Jenny wanted to close the laptop, slam the lid hard and run, but she had to inspect the picture. She clicked on it. Someone was standing at the front door. A lone figure. She zoomed in. The person was holding a key in the lock, ready to open it.

Jenny's body trembled with terror. The man in the photo was Sean. Someone had been watching him.

Someone may be watching him now.

13

J enny spent the rest of the day packing. She'd tried to call Sean, but each time it went through to his voice-mail due to there being no reception at the farm-house. She had to keep busy. The pictures that had been sent upset her. Trolls were a par for the course, but this was something sinister, personal.

She had debated calling the police, but could only imagine the person on the other end of the line asking stupid questions and not taking her seriously. How long has your husband been missing? When did you notice he was gone? When was the last time you saw him?

Sean had only left that morning and she feared looking stupid. She'd give it some more time, then if he still didn't answer his phone, she would have to do something.

She'd stayed away from the post as long as she could. She sat, her head in her hands and her body shaking. She gave herself a few moments to compose herself then slowly opened the lid of the laptop, as if she were waiting for a jack in the box to spring into life.

But she didn't manage to check the page again as she

was distracted by the front door opening. She could smell the paint as Sean walked into the kitchen.

'Oh, thank God!' She rushed towards him, gripping him tightly. Relief ebbed from her stomach.

Sean could feel how tense her body was. He kissed her on the head and, trying to ease the tension, ran his fingers through her hair. 'How about white highlights?' He lifted his paint-stained hands and Jenny gave him a playful slap on the arm.

'I missed you.'

'Hey. I was only gone a few hours.' He checked the clock on the kitchen wall. It was just gone 6pm. He felt something was wrong. Jenny seemed upset. 'Are you OK? Where are the kids?'

'Upstairs, packing, making sure they have everything. I think they're doing the final bits and pieces.'

Sean smiled and pulled her closer. 'I got lots done. The hallway is finished. I think you'll like it. I've just put boarding over the rotten steps until we can get them replaced. I'm just sorry the essential work isn't finished. And, oh shit, do I hate sanding.'

He kept the other details to himself, the scratch marks and the bloodstains.

Jenny noticed Sean was wearing the same clothes he'd been wearing in the picture. A black jacket and blue jeans. She reached for his hand and steered him towards the laptop.

The screen was open where she'd read the last comment. She pressed the refresh button and searched for the post.

'What are you looking for?'

'I wanted to show you something. Where the hell has it gone?' She searched through the comments and responses, but couldn't find it. 'Where the hell is it? It was horrible.'

The comments had disappeared. The pictures were gone.

'Jenny, keyboard warriors. Forget it; it's meaningless. Ignore the hate. You can't stop the weirdos and lowlifes of this world trying to freak you out.'

Jenny stood, facing her husband. 'It wasn't hatred.' She looked around the kitchen, knowing she had to tell him. 'Someone posted a picture of a red coat.'

Sean stared at her for a brief second, digesting what she had said. 'OK. That's weird.'

'It gets weirder. The same person posted another one of you, stood at the door of the farmhouse – in your black jacket and jeans. I could clearly see it was you, Sean. Someone was watching you.' She could feel her husband's demeanour change; his body began to visibly tremble. 'That's not the worst part. The person called themselves Painswick Eight.'

'It's a reference to the missing women.'

Jenny and Sean stared at the screen, both too frightened to say anything.

Later that evening, after calling his mum, Sean joined Jenny, Ethan and Beth in the living room. His mother had wanted to come over to spend the last night with them in Oxford but she was tired. Her hip was causing pain and she promised when she felt better she'd spend a weekend at the farmhouse.

They sat on boxes, eating Chinese takeaway from tin containers. They rarely ordered in, preferring home-cooked food, but this was a special occasion – and anyway, they'd packed away all the kitchenware.

Beth had her AirPods in, and Ethan was focused on his mobile, which he balanced in one hand while he scooped spoonfuls of egg fried rice into his mouth with the other.

Sean was deep in thought. He'd checked Beth's hands earlier for signs of blood, a cut – anything that could explain the scratch marks on the wall at the farmhouse. Nothing.

Once they'd finished eating, Jenny called for the family's attention. 'Right, you lot, I'm going to go around the room and you each need to say something – anything – you'll miss about this place.'

She turned to Beth who was oblivious to the comment. Ethan nudged her, and she removed the AirPods from her ears. He explained the game.

'Oh, OK. Well, I guess I'll miss my room. Whenever Ethan pisses me off, it's my hideout. My getaway. I liked my posters on the wall – arts, music, culture, different stages of my life. It's a small thing, but I'll miss it. Even if I put them up in the new house, it won't be the sa—'

'That's so lame. Your bedroom,' Ethan interjected.

Beth chose to ignore the sarcasm.

Jenny turned to Ethan. 'What about you, sunshine?'

'Well, I guess the garden.'

Beth laughed louder than she meant to. She turned to her brother. 'What about the garden?'

Ethan braced himself. 'OK, when I was younger—'

Beth burst into song. 'So much younger than today, oh, oh, oh.'

'Beth, let him talk. Go on, love.'

'Well, I know it seems weird, but I loved the connection, you know? Before school, I'd wake early, slide the kitchen door back, stand out on the patio and say a prayer. I'd hear the dog in Mrs Lovelock's garden, her coming out and calling him; Mr and Mrs Peters on the other side, pegging clothes to the line, the smell of washing powder in the air, or the sound of snipping as they pruned the bushes, shaping the hedges. Mr Peters would lean over the fence and ask how I was. He'd always say, "Have a pleasant day, son." It was comforting, knowing people were close.'

As the room fell silent, there was one word on Sean and Jenny's minds.

Creeper.

14

You nearly gave it away, didn't you? You couldn't keep calm as I carried you through the house. You should have listened to my simple instructions. We were almost caught. Stupid, stupid girl.

I watched over you this morning. You slept, only a little, but you did drift, I'm sure. When I came into the basement, you were quiet. I was surprised. I thought you'd screech. Maybe it's the gag around your mouth. I did tie it firmly. Your fingers were stained with paint – on the tips from where you'd dragged your arms as I carried you.

Above, I could hear the sound of scraping, the smell of paint strong in the air. He was so close.

The sun was shining this morning, the air filled with birdsong, the sound of a tractor in the distance. You should see it.

Tick tock, tick tock. Need to quickly grab my rock.

You sit up, pushing your body against the cold, damp wall. Ah, there it is at last. The fear has returned. I wondered where it went, having dissolved temporarily. Now it's back.

I remove the gag, watching as saliva drips from your

mouth, your lips, chapped and wet. Your screaming echoes through the room, a piercing noise. I scream too, louder than you. No one can hear. No one is coming to help.

Stop with the pathetic pleading. Your voice is husky now, raw, raspy from the shouting. You look beaten.

I get on my knees, push my scarred, disfigured face to yours and smell your hair. You struggle to focus. Being held against your will has broken you. Your nose is dripping, long strands of mucus dropping onto the floor, lips soaking, eyes streaming.

I imagine you want to run. You don't know where you'd go, but you want to race, fast now, your heart pumping, beads of sweat forming on your skin, the cold air stinging, filling your lungs. Your thoughts would only be on escape. Keep motivated. Get to someone. Keep going. You'd turn around. Is he behind me? Did I lose him? You'd keep push-ing, feeling the lactose as it quickly builds in your legs, rising now, taking over your body like an infection, smoth-ering your skin with bacteria.

Wait, you've ejected yourself from your stupor; your eyes are savage, feral. You're back, confused to see me crouching beside you. You push your hands on the ground, forcing your body further against the wall.

I touch the soft skin of your face. You're looking deep into my eyes. I like that.

'Who the hell are you? Let me go, you fucking freak.' Your voice is pleading, so boisterous now. 'Let me go.'

The woman was shackled. Thick, brass cuffs attached to a long pole were now tearing into her wrists.

'People are looking for me. You know that, right? You won't fucking get away with it.' She kicked out, wriggling like a fish on the end of a line. She spat blood, pushing air from her mouth, struggling to force her fringe from her eyes.

'I told you to keep quiet. You disobeyed me. Now, I have no alternative. We have to go; there's no choice.'

She screamed. 'Go where? What the hell is wrong with you? I can pay, anything you want. I beg you, don't do this.'

'They're coming. It's not safe here. But I'll be back; you can count on it.'

'Who's coming? What are you talking about? Let me go.'

He paused, now standing over the woman. The ground was covered in sheets. When he finished, he would dump them and the rock down the well at the side of the house. He'd dropped so much down there over the years. Always careful to clean up.

See-saw, Margery Daw. No need for this girl anymore.

He lifted the large rock that was placed beside him. He'd carried it into the basement earlier. Everything was set. He crouched on both knees, back straight, arms wide, his hands gripping the rough edges, the tips of his fingers tearing away.

See-saw, Margery Daw. No need for this girl anymore.

'No. Don't do it. No. No—'

He stood on the road by the front garden, his body turned slightly, looking to his left. He recalled the car pulling into the drive that morning, the smell of the exhaust as it filled the air, pumping that putrid smoke into the atmosphere. The stench was overbearing. The guy had got out, a proud smile on his face as he looked up at the farmhouse. He was on his own this time, gripping a carrier bag in his right hand. It swung a little as he walked.

He remembered the writing on the bag. Snap. He'd been to the same hardware shop. How weird was that? For different reasons, of course. But they were both making things better. *You drift in, a splash of paint, pictures adorning the walls, furniture. But I'm making things better too.*

He glanced down at the shovel he was holding, the body slumped over his left shoulder. He crossed over the road, stamped through the bushes along the field opposite the house and then strolled through the long grass casually, as if he were taking a picnic.

When the house was out of sight, he stopped, dropping the woman next to him. She bounced a little, then lay still.

You're proud of me, aren't you? I can hear it in your voice. Please say you are. I can't explain how I'm feeling. You are evidently jubilant at what I'm doing, what I'm achieving. I can hear your soft tone – distant, but it's there. You hold me now, patting my shoulder, pushing my hair to the side. You tell me it's better this way; it makes me look younger. I'll be a man before too long. You say I should enjoy the first stage; you only experience this part of life for a short time.

It's like you've called me into your room all over again. You haven't been pleased with my behaviour. I try. Honest. But now you've changed. The forlorn expression has gone, but I wonder for how long. You're proud of what I'm doing now, aren't you? Aren't you? Please say you are. You must.

He worked the shovel, pushing it into the earth, then lifted the sod and tipped it over his right shoulder. The woman was lying by his feet. He could see her in his peripheral vision, still, lifeless.

Once the hole was wide enough, deep enough, he rolled her over, watching her body drop slightly. Slump. That satisfying noise as she fell. He wiped his face with his shirt sleeve and began to fill the hole. Then he patted the mound with the flat end of the shovel.

His cry echoed through the fields.

See-saw, Margery Daw. You will never be seen anymore.

See-saw, See-saw. I'll watch them move in as they walk through the door.

15

I t was Friday morning, and Billy Huxton was watching the TV from his single bed. There were more reports on the missing girl, now a picture revealed, taken while out with friends. The last one before her disappearance.

It had been almost three days since she'd vanished and a search party was under way. A handful of locals had begun to explore the woodland. Billy watched the screen, seeing them traipse the grounds together, the community as one in time of tragedy, the sullen faces, arms around each other. His mind raced with memories of his daughter, the night of the barbecue ten years ago. He recalled how she'd opened the front door, assuring him she'd be fine.

'Stop worrying, Dad. It's not far to walk.'

Billy had followed her, stood in the hallway. He remembered that embarrassed smile that had adorned her beautiful face as she'd turned, as if to say, 'Stop it, Dad. You need to let me live my life.'

Then the door had closed and Billy waited alone, listening to the voices in the garden, the music loud, the sounds of dancing and laughter. Little did he know he'd never hear his daughter doing those things again.

Billy reached for the remote that lay on the bedside unit and turned off the TV, the blank screen now staring back at him. He reached under the bed and pulled out the box containing the picture of his daughter. His mind kept returning to that night, playing it over and over in his mind. He remembered the last words Katie had said. 'I'll be back in a few minutes. Go to Mum. Enjoy yourself. I love you, Dad.'

He had waited in the hall for a minute or so, and then he heard the sound of high-heeled shoes stepping over the wooden floor, Cheryl coming to him, cracking open a beer and handing it over. The liquid pushed over the top and dripped onto the floor as they smiled. His wife had told him to get it together, then led him into the garden, laughing at him in front of their guests, playfully grabbing his cheek and pinching the skin gently.

'We can't keep them children forever,' she'd said.

Even at the time, Billy had reason to be concerned. Seven women had gone missing from the Painswick area over the previous ten years. The story was on everyone's lips but it hadn't achieved the coverage it warranted. No bodies were found. If any had, even one, the police would have had more to go on – DNA, fingerprints, an autopsy to confirm foul play. But the police had nothing.

Many believed the women simply left Painswick. Some say they lived together, a pact, and they were hiding in a retreat or a commune. Others believed their lives were so boring they just left and went abroad to travel the world. This pissed Billy off more than anything. The conspiracists. It was a slap in the face to each of the families whose daughters were still missing. They wanted answers.

Billy Huxton still wanted answers.

He lay back in the bed, holding the picture of his daughter, tears now filling his eyes. He stroked her face with the tip of his forefinger, then glanced over at the picture of his wife on the night stand, in her green blouse and brown cardigan, her smile beaming and not a single hair out of place. He missed them both so much. At that moment, he had never felt so alone.

Suddenly, he burst, the emotion too raw, the pain too difficult to bear. He sobbed, pulling his daughter's picture close to his chest and staring at his wife.

A tap at the door forced him out of his overly emotional state.

'I've come to say goodbye.' Declan could hear Billy sniffing. 'Billy baby, what are you at in there? Watching re-runs of Little House On The Prairie? Get it together, Captain.'

Billy watched the door slowly open. Declan was standing in the hall.

'What's up, mate? Billy, are you OK?' Suddenly realising Billy was upset, he moved into the room and sat on the bed. 'Talk to me, Billy. What's going on, pal?'

Billy manoeuvred his body further up the bed, then held out the picture. 'This is my daughter.'

Declan took it in his hand. His face dropped as he suspected a sad story would follow.

'She was eighteen. She went missing – a trip to the local shops almost ten years ago. I've never seen her since.'

'Oh, Billy. I never knew. I'm so sorry.'

'How the hell would you know? I never mentioned it.'

Declan glanced at the picture. 'She was beautiful.'

'She *is* beautiful.'

Declan realised the mistake. 'Is. Sorry.'

Billy continued. 'It started twenty years ago. A woman went missing from Painswick. Then seven more. None of them have been seen since. My Katie was number eight.' He took the picture from Declan and placed it on the bedside table. 'I searched day after day. I couldn't give up. It became an obsession. I couldn't function or concentrate, not until she was home. I'd say I spoke to nearly everyone in Painswick, some twice, three times. I waited outside houses. I followed them. I searched woodland, fields, farms. I wasn't eating. I couldn't sleep. My wife grew more concerned for me. She told me I had to look after myself; she couldn't face losing two members of the family. But I didn't care. I wanted to rip the bastard's head off, kick it down the road and bounce it off the pavement. I wanted to rip his throat out, pull the rotten heart from his chest. I was consumed with rage and all I wanted was to hurt the fucker that took my daughter. When I did sleep, the dreams were of how I'd torture him, dismember his pathetic body, crush him until his insides squelched and came out, seeping from his skin.'

'Wow, remind me never to cross you.' Declan shifted slightly on the bed. 'So how did you deal with it?'

'Do I look like I'm bloody dealing with it? What's with the dumbass questions anyway? Time, Declan. Time has removed part of the pain – not all, but part of it. I still have the dreams. I still fantasise of being in a room with the evil bastard, the door locked – I'd only need a minute.'

'I think you need to talk to someone. Have you tried a bereavement therapist?'

'Talking isn't going to bring her back.'

Declan stood. 'Come on, I'll make you a coffee.'

'I'm leaving today, Declan. I think he's back. There's another girl gone missing. Her name is Marie Nelson. She's vulnerable. ' He looked into Declan's eyes. 'They call him Creeper. This time he's not going to escape.'

A shiver ran through Declan's body, causing him to jerk.

'You know, I'm off for a couple of weeks as well. I have some leave. Another person is taking over my duties, as if they could fill my boots. There'll be complaints, you know. I'll hear all about it when I come back.'

Billy smiled. 'Whoever fills in won't be able to lace your boots. What have you got planned?'

'Absolutely nothing. I was going to sit around the house and relax. Why?'

Billy took a deep breath and pushed even further up the bed. 'I want you to help me.'

Declan hesitated for a moment. He glanced at the picture of Katie, then over to Billy's wife. Billy was wiping the tears from his eyes. 'How long will we be away?'

Billy liked the way Declan said, 'we'.

'Until we catch the evil bastard.'

16

'OK. This is it. Our final goodbye.' Sean was standing on the pavement outside their semi-detached house, his arm around his wife. 'We'll miss it, that's for sure, but onwards and upwards. That's how we should think.'

Jenny wiped a tear from her eye, then blew a kiss towards their old home.

Feeling it was the right time, Ethan asked to say a prayer.

They stood on the street as he led the prayer, thanking God for the great times, the memories and hoping for even better ones in their new home.

Then they got into the car, and taking one last look at the house, they drove away.

* * *

They arrived fifty minutes later. The sky was unusually cloudless, and a light breeze blew across the drive from the fields opposite. Sean stepped out of the car, then taking a deep breath, he moved around to the passenger side where he opened the door for Jenny.

'Why, thank you, sir.'

'Anything for my lady. Welcome to your new home.'

Jenny smiled, eyeing the farmhouse.

A large truck was parked near the front door, 'Cotswolds Removals,' written in white along its side, and 'Everything from storage to a complete house move,' underneath. A picture of a man and woman carrying a small sofa was plastered on the driver's side. The same couple unloading the truck.

Sean and Jenny greeted them with a formal handshake.

The guy was mid-sixties, tall and strong-looking, while the woman was much shorter and appeared to be ten or so years his junior. They introduced themselves as husband and wife.

'Blow me down. Great place you've got here, Guv.' His accent was English, but oddly old-fashioned. 'Must have cost a bob or two, I'm thinking.'

'Thanks. There's work to do on the old place but we love it.'

'Bit quiet, though.' The woman noticed the odd look in Jenny's eyes – was that fear? – and smiled, hoping she hadn't perturbed her with her remark.

Sean let Jenny in first and held his breath, the expectation rife. This could go one of two ways. He braced himself, waiting for Jenny's reaction.

'Oh, Sean. It's amazing.'

'You like it?'

She turned to him, her body shaking with excitement. 'Of course! You've done so much since I came here. You should be proud. There's still work to do... We need a new floor in the hallway. The stairs can't stay like that. And I'm thinking a dark red colour for the walls.'

Sean laughed. 'But you like it?'

'I love it.'

They embraced where they stood by the front door, then Beth and Ethan interrupted them.

'Get a room already.'

Sean and Jenny laughed, then they all began to unload the boxes.

The builders had used an electrician to re-wire the house and yesterday, Sean had fitted some strong bulbs he'd picked up at the hardware store. He hoped they were still working, and as he flicked the switch in the kitchen, relief washed over him as the lights came on. He turned on the tap, again relieved to see the water still working.

Ethan and Beth were carrying boxes up the stairs, careful to step on the temporary boarding. Sean listened to the raised voices as they argued over who slept where.

As he carried a small table down the hall towards the kitchen, he glanced at the area of paint where he'd covered up the scratch marks yesterday. It still bothered him how they had got there. He hadn't mentioned anything to Jenny. She'd freak out. Her voice played in his mind, the things she'd told him were posted on Facebook – the red coat, the picture of him opening the front door to the farmhouse. He felt the hairs on his forearms stand up.

* * *

The truck now empty, Jenny was pushing boxes along the floor in the hallway.

'Jenny. Sit down. I have this. Rest, hun. I can bring every-thing in.'

'Thank you. It's just overwhelming.'

'Of course it is. But we'll get the place exactly how we want it. It's going to take time. But look around, look at the space.'

'It's incredible.' Jenny moved to the sink to fill the kettle. As the water ran a rusty yellow colour and began spitting, Sean pulled a face, waiting for her reaction. But after a minute, the water became clear.

He watched as she filled the kettle, and then listened to the comforting sound of it boiling. 'Well, we're here at last. Happy?'

'I will be once we sort this place out. I thought we'd start on the documentary straight away. I think people would love to see us moving into the farmhouse and maybe get some interviews with the locals on the Creeper legend.'

It was as though Sean's heart missed a beat. That name again. He had been uncertain on whether Jenny would want to make a documentary, but it was their work, their life, what they loved. And this was going to be an amazing experience – the chance to bring the story of a chilling urban legend to life.

'Sounds great. I'll settle up for the removal and then we're good to go.'

A few minutes later, when the truck was pulling out of the drive, Sean stood by the front door, listening as its engine faded until it disappeared around the corner.

The long grass in the fields opposite flickered like the light of a candle, reminding him of the post. The red coat. Someone watching him as he entered the farmhouse.

They could be hiding in the field opposite, watching.

He glanced across the road. For a moment, he thought he saw someone, crouching, like a sprinter ready to run the hundred metres. He wiped his eyes. The figure was gone. He forced himself to look away, up to the sky at the dark blue that had only patches of light cloud.

The air was much fresher than in Oxford, untainted and clear. He glanced at the tyre tracks cut deep into the pebbles and moved down the drive, smoothing them out with his shoes. He couldn't get the photo out of his mind. Someone had taken his picture while he stood by the front door, then taunted Jenny with it.

Jenny was at the far end of the kitchen, organising utensils. 'Ready?'

'No time like the present.'

A few minutes later, the camcorder was out of the box, and she was ready to go.

'Hello, I'm Jenny Freeman, and we're here filming a documentary in our new home in Painswick, a picturesque village in The Cotswolds, deep in the English countryside. I'm here with my partner and husband, Sean Freeman.'

Sean turned the camera around, and waved to introduce himself.

'We're putting a film together, a story from your very worst nightmares. Here in this sleepy village, it's rumoured that someone terrorised and tormented the local residents, watching them at night, entering their homes and moving around, undetected, for years.' She walked along the downstairs hallway slowly. 'We're going to get the story from the people who live here, residents who have heard the rumours over the years and witnesses who claim to have seen the person only known as Creeper.'

As he held the camera, Sean was captivated by his wife's presentation. She was glowing, always professional and informative, and as she spoke, it was clear she had done her research.

Whenever Sean had tried to speak in front of the camera

– mostly for short clips and trailers – he would freeze, often getting tongue-tied. He recalled numerous occasions when he'd broken into a sweat or used the wrong word completely out of context. Jenny always remained supportive behind the camera, reassuring and patient. The clip would usually finish with something like, 'Oh, sod this for a shit show,' or, 'Fuck it, Jenny. Roll again. You know what? Bollox to this crap.' He'd stare at his wife, who would be holding the camera on her shoulder, trying her utmost to keep a stern expression. Then the two of them would burst into laughter.

They'd met on a film-making course at college. Both had wanted to get into production. Sean had dreamed of a career in TV while Jenny wanted to produce adverts for local companies. The path they'd taken, making documentaries, was nothing like they'd anticipated; they'd never imagined they'd have such control over the work they did.'

'It's up to you whether you believe it's just a story – an urban legend – or whether you think Creeper is real. We'll bring you the interviews and the eyewitness accounts of locals who claim this person is very real.'

She moved to the front door – Sean stayed close behind as she opened it – and gazed out across the fields opposite. 'The story we brought you last week of Mark Wheelan, the psychiatric patient who escaped from Greyshott Hall, occurred only a stone's throw from here. Many residents say Creeper is still out there, watching, waiting, ready to make a move at any second. No one can forget the heartbreaking story of the missing women of Painswick. Eight young girls who disappeared without a trace, never seen again. It's a harrowing, tragic history that people would rather forget. But it makes for a terrifying story, one steeped in so much sadness, a story we'll try to resolve. We'll help you make up your own minds about this place.'

Jenny gave the nod, and Sean turned off the camera.

'Was I a little over the top?'

'No. It was superb. You did amazing. I'd say it was just enough. I love the way you finished, leaving people to judge for themselves. That's clever.' He returned the camcorder to the bag and zipped it up. 'I have an idea. I say we take a drive to town, see who we can speak to. What do you say?'

Now that they'd made a start, he was keen to keep going. His pet hate was filming something and then returning to it days later. It always felt like the momentum was gone.

'OK. Let me grab my handbag.' Jenny felt a rush of excitement as she moved out to the hallway. 'Ethan? Beth? Either of you fancy a trip to town? We're going to do a bit of filming.' The kids could do some shopping while she and Sean spoke to the locals, but the groans that came from upstairs were indicative of the way Ethan and Beth felt.

'That's a no, then?' Sean joined her in the hallway. 'Will they be OK?'

Jenny turned to him. 'Why wouldn't they? They're tired. Let them rest.'

* * *

Ten minutes later, Sean and Jenny arrived in the small village and parked on a side street beside a row of shops. As they'd driven the short journey along the main road from the farmhouse, a small, single path with sharp bends, potholes and wild bushes overhanging from the surrounding fields, Sean had wondered how the removal company had managed.

They stepped out of the car to see that the local fair was in full swing, with stalls covered by tarpaulin and market traders sipping from cardboard cups, wearing woollen hats, scarfs and thick coats to keep warm. The aroma of coffee was thick in the air.

They checked out the shops as they walked, large white buildings that were centuries-old, with an array of ornaments, gifts, cuddly toys and all manner of peculiar objects neatly displayed in their front windows.

They approached an elderly woman who was standing on her own at the end of the row. She stocked every confectionary imaginable. Her stall was packed with sweet jars that contained cough candy, cola cubes, army and navy sweets and chocolate mice.

'Hi, I'm Jenny. My husband and I have just moved here from Oxford. We make documentaries. Could I ask a few questions? We'd really appreciate a couple of minutes to talk with you.'

The lady smiled, though she appeared slightly embarrassed. She placed her cup of coffee on a shelf behind her, then stepped forward. 'Of course. Welcome to Painswick.' As she spoke, her breath formed like a plume of smoke in front of her.

Jenny held out her hand, and the lady shook it softly, her fingers peeping out through the end of her knitted gloves.

'OK, Sean. You ready?'

Sean removed the camcorder from the bag he held over his shoulder and started to film.

'We're here in the village of Painswick, a bustling place, full of life, full of market stalls, shops and thatched cottages. It's Friday afternoon, and we're going to be talking to a lady who runs a sweet stall.' She turned to the woman. 'If you could start with your name?'

The lady stared, motionless.

'If you could start with your name?' she asked again, nodding to the woman.

'Oh, sorry, dear. I thought you were talking to the camera. I'm not down with all these gadgets. My grand-daughter has a phone, one of those small ones – tiny it is. She can fit it in her pocket. In the old days, we used cups and string. Young ones don't even know they're born. Did I tell you about my Albert?'

Jenny smiled. 'Could I ask you how long you've lived in Painswick?'

'Well, let's see...'

The woman reached to the shelf at the back, grabbing a bag of mint humbugs and popping one into her mouth before offering them around. Sean and Jenny politely declined.

'Since before you were born, I'd say. They'll carry me out in a box.'

'And how is life in Painswick?'

The lady looked up to the sky, closing her hands together. 'Look around you. It's a community. We all help each other. You won't find a nicer, more friendly lot.'

'Thanks. And can you tell us about the rumours? We've heard the stories, but we'd love to hear about it from someone who lives here.'

'What rumours, dear?'

Jenny turned towards Sean, who was zooming in on the woman's face. Then she took a deep breath and turned back to the woman.

'Creeper.'

The woman's face dropped. Her body language instantly changed.

'Shut that bloody thing off. Now.'

Jenny froze, trying to grasp the sudden shift in the woman's demeanour.

'I'm sorry, I didn't mean to offend you.'

'Shut it off. Shut it off, I said. Do you hear me?' As she yelled, a couple of guys who worked on the stalls beside her walked over.

Sean instantly pressed the off button, then grabbed his wife by the arm and led her towards the car. They sat there for a couple of minutes, Sean in the driver's seat and Jenny beside him, stunned at how the woman had reacted.

'I guess she wasn't keen to speak.'

'Let's go home.' Jenny reached for the seatbelt and pushed it into the holder.

Sean started the car and turned on the heater. Luke-warm air pushed from the grills. 'I don't understand. Why do you think she acted like that? Is she frightened?'

He pulled out onto the main road and drove away from the village. Jenny remained silent for a few minutes, watching the fields on either side of the road. As they pulled into Gallows Lane, she broke the silence. 'What did you make of that?'

'Well, I'd say she was upset.'

'You don't say.' Jenny smacked him on the arm playfully. 'She seemed up for it. It was the mention of Creeper. I saw the fear; her expression changed immediately. She literally froze on the spot.'

Sean's mind jumped to the scratch marks, how the builders had left the farmhouse abruptly, but his train of thought was interrupted by his phone ringing. He pulled it from his pocket and answered, not recognising the number. 'Hello?'

'Sean, It's Bernie. Your vehicle is ready. I'm open until 5pm. Once that time shows on the clock, the doors are shut and locked until Monday morning.'

'OK, fine. I'll be over within the hour.' After he hung up, he looked at Jenny. 'That was Bernie. The car's ready. We'll go and interview him. He wouldn't stop talking about Creeper last time.'

En route, they stopped back at the farmhouse to check on Ethan and Beth. As they walked up the stairs, careful to avoid the holes, they heard Ethan struggling to put his bed together. He sounded breathless, and as he looked towards his parents, holding a flat blade screwdriver and trying to turn a circular screw, they noticed that the headboard was attached to the wrong end. Beth was standing at the bedroom door smirking.

'This side, Ethan. The headboard goes this side.'

'Beth, I know what I'm doing. You're stressing me out here.'

'Jeez, I'm just trying to help. You know what? Do it yourself.' She turned to her parents. 'What are your plans?'

'We're trying to make a start on the docufilm.' Jenny kept quiet about what had happened at the market. 'There's a guy at the garage. We're going to interview him.'

'About what?'

Sean and Jenny glanced at each other.

'Oh, just about life in Painswick. The place is steeped in history, you know?'

'I'll go with you guys. I could do with some fresh air.'

The three of them left the room just as Ethan threw the screwdriver onto the floor.

Not long later, they pulled into the yard. Bernie came rushing out, as if he'd been waiting at the window, watching for customers. He greeted them with a floppy handshake and proceeded to inspect the car like a sniffer dog, searching underneath, lying on the ground and prodding the metal. He finished by kicking the tyres.

'We didn't drive it across Europe,' Sean said sarcastically.

'Good baby to drive, isn't she?' He pointed towards their vehicle on the forecourt. Go take a look. As good as new.'

Sean walked over, tempted to give the car a thorough check in a mocking response to Bernie's actions, but he didn't want to piss him off.

Bernie had managed to take the dents out and had resprayed the paint and replaced the smashed windows.

'OK? Follow me inside, and we can put the payment through. How's Ed's place? You settled in yet?'

Sean turned towards Jenny, mouthing for her to get the camcorder off the back seat. He would keep Bernie talking.

He made his way into the office with Bernie, and Jenny returned a few seconds later. It seemed that Beth was going to wait outside, which he was thankful for. He didn't want her to hear any of this.

Sean watched Bernie fishing around in the cabinet behind the counter, while Jenny moved behind him, subtly passing him the bag. He bent down, unzipped the case and removed the camcorder. Then he moved back, pointing the camera at Bernie.

Jenny moved to the counter and began to narrate. 'We are at Bernie's autos—'

'The cheapest and best vehicles in the whole of the Cotswolds, I'll add.'

Jenny stalled. 'Thanks, Bernie. We're investigating rumours that for years have cast a dark shadow over the quaint, tranquil village of Painswick. The people in this quiet—'

'We just had a new batch last week, actually – vans, cars,

a couple of second-hand scooters. We fix most vehicles and hire 'em out as well.'

Sean pointed the camera at Bernie and zoomed in. 'Could you tell us a little about what you told me the other day?'

Bernie rubbed the stubble on his chin. 'Oh yeah, the Mercedes. It's a beaut—'

'No, the story you told me, about Ed's place.'

'What about Ed's place?'

'Creeper.'

Bernie leant forward. 'I haven't a clue what you're talking about, son. Now let's settle the bill, and you can be on your way.'

* * *

Sean had turned off the camcorder and placed it in the boot, aggravated by Bernie's lack of enthusiasm.

Jenny yanked at her seatbelt, the frustration evident as she forced the clip into the holder. 'Beth, the volume. I can't hear myself think.'

'Sorry.' Beth had been face-timing a friend, telling her about the farmhouse, but after her dad's words, she told her friend she'd call her later.

'Jesus, Sean,' Jenny said. 'I'm beginning to think you made this shit up.'

'I don't understand. Bernie told me about Painswick. The history. He warned me when I came here with Ethan. He sang like a friggin canary. It's like I've imagined the whole thing, for Christ's sake.'

Jenny felt discouraged. She was anxious to put the story together. She wanted to film, to start the documentary. It was a huge opportunity, and so far, they'd had nothing but false starts. This wasn't what she'd anticipated.

Sean looked out over the yard as he pulled the car away. He watched Bernie at the front desk, staring back at them. 'Let's call it a day.'

* * *

Ethan had assembled the bed. He'd finally worked out where to fit the headboard and now had the correct screw-driver. He dragged the large metal frame across the floor, scratching the wood, then pushed it against the back wall, placing it as centrally as possible. He stood back, making sure it looked correct and that the door wouldn't catch the frame when he opened it. Then he began to lift out his things from a cardboard box with 'Ethan's shit' written on the side and set them by his bed – aftershave, toiletries, rolled-up posters of the current Liverpool squad and a pair of Nike trainers. As he reached into the box for more items, he heard a key being placed in the front door and the loud, sluggish creak as it opened.

'Up here. I managed to sort the bed out. I'll be down as soon as I finish organising the room.' He listened as foot-steps came from down the hall. 'I wouldn't say no to a coffee.'

He removed a couple of picture frames that he'd care-fully encased in bubble wrap, lifting them out one by one. Proudly, he read the certificates enclosed in the glass, honours awarded for his behaviour at school: Ethan Freeman – Certificate of excellence; Ethan Freeman – Outstanding achievement.

He set them out on the floor, five in total, then looked around the room to see where was best to hang them. He grabbed one, offering it up to the wall by his bed, shifting it left and right.

'Dad, where's the drill?' He waited for an answer, then walked out of the bedroom and leant over the balcony. 'What are you guys doing? I'm on a roll here. Dad, the drill.'

He waited, listening, then moved along the upstairs hall to the large window that overlooked the drive. He looked out, searching for his family, but a small wooden balcony marred his view, allowing only half of the drive to be seen. He assumed they had been shopping and maybe were still unloading the car.

He stood on the top step and waited, looking down into the empty hallway below, listening for voices.

The front door was closed. He waited a moment longer, then moved back to his bedroom. One of the boxes contained a small telly, which he pulled out and set on top of a cabinet they'd brought from the old house. He pushed the plug into the socket, fished out the remote control and began to flick through the channels until he found a reception. He had to play with the ariel before he found a good signal.

Distracted from the footsteps and the lack of acknowledgement from his family, he watched the TV, appreciating the diversion from the stillness.

The newsreader began talking as a picture of a young woman appeared on the screen. The word 'Painswick' was displayed at the top.

Ethan turned up the volume and listened.

'Concerns are growing for a woman who has been missing since Tuesday evening. Marie Nelson was out drinking with friends at The Crown and Anchor on Tuesday evening and hasn't been seen since. Friends and work colleagues are concerned for her safety. Local police have asked that anyone who might know of her whereabouts dials 100, where all calls will be dealt with in the strictest confidence. Marie is nineteen years old and works at a local High Street bank. She's five foot two with green eyes and a fair complexion. Marie was last seen wearing a green dress and a red coat.'

Ethan dropped the remote control and stood in the bedroom, unable to move. He recognised the woman. Marie Nelson. It was the same woman they'd picked up, the hitch-hiker. His body felt numb.

He backed away out of the bedroom, then turned and moved along the hallway. 'Guys, where are you?'

He moved down the stairs, careful to avoid the holes his father had covered with wooden boards. The door to the box room was closed, Ethan was certain it was open when he was downstairs earlier and thinking they might have gone in there, he slowly pushed the handle down, easing the door back. The room was empty.

He closed the door hard, listening to the sound echo through the hallway. Then he stepped back and moved toward the kitchen, checking the rooms further down the hall – the living room to his left, empty, as was the bathroom next door. Ethan could feel his heart racing, his body shaking.

The back door was open, the room suddenly freezing. Ethan was sure he'd closed it earlier when he'd come down to get some tools. He'd gone out to take a look in the garden. He remembered twisting the key in the lock, then leaving it there. The key was still in position, but the door was now open.

He closed the door, locked it and backed away to the middle of the kitchen. His mouth open, breathing hard, he looked along the hall towards the front door.

Someone had been in the house.

He froze, his skin tingling with fear.

Ethan stood for a moment, then edged out of the kitchen and along the hall, watching the rooms on either side. At the front door, he awkwardly fumbled with the handle, checking behind him and glancing towards the kitchen, then up the stairs. He was sure he was alone. Whoever had been in the house had got out through the garden.

As he pulled the front door towards him, he jolted, staring at the figure in front of him.

'Ethan, are you OK?'

His breathing was erratic, his eyes wild. Relief swept over him as he saw his father. Behind him, his mother and Beth were stepping out of the car.

'Were— were you here a few minutes ago? Were you in the house?'

'We've just pulled into the drive. Are you all right?'

Ethan stood at the door while his family entered the house, then he glanced across at the fields.

A shiver ran down the back of his neck as he realised how secluded they were.

17

There are no cars on the drive, no work vans. I stand by the road, watching. I'm unsure for how long – ten minutes, maybe more; I can't tell. It's difficult to explain the feeling I get, the sensations my body goes through. My skin tingles with excitement, the first sense I taste. A warm glow works its way through me. It's as if I'm flying, floating in the air, or drifting on a wave. It's my happy place, where I belong. My tranquil mindset is unique, invaluable, something you could never purchase. It makes me calm, alleviates the tension. It takes me far away from the voices in my head. The air is still, the light, bright and warming – comfortable, yes; that's a word I'd use. Invigorating.

There are no vehicles on the road. No planes above me. Only the sound of a tractor in the distance and the smell of freshly-cut grass. I turn, unable to see it – only the empty, barren fields.

The grass moves; it sways with the cold breeze, but I feel only warmth. I glide up the path and turn the key in the front door, not expecting to find anyone inside. I could use the basement, but the hatch is locked – my first mistake.

From upstairs, I can hear the sound of furniture being dragged over the floor, and my body sinks. Suddenly, I'm clammy. My skin feels tight, itchy. It's as if I'm falling into a dank pit. I could go upstairs, but where is the fun in that? I must be patient. The hunt is the most fun part. It can't be over too quickly. I can't let that happen. Control and pace, that's the way forward.

From outside, the place looked void and lifeless. The lights in the hallway and living room were off. I walk through the downstairs hallway slowly. It feels tainted, like the farmhouse is contaminated.

I carry the shovel in my left hand, careful not to drop any soil on the floorboards. I'm inside now. It's too late. I hear a voice call from above. I need to be quick.

I move to the kitchen and find the key in the door. Carefully, I twist it and pull the handle towards me.

Outside, there's a tap. I watch the occasional drop of water spill from it and into the drain. Drip. Drip.

I count a ten-second gap. Maybe fifteen. Drip. It reminds me of blood, emptying from a body I just cut. The rustic smell would fill my lungs. And then there's the disposal. Sometimes I use the well. But it's more difficult with people here now. There's more chance of being caught.

I place the shovel underneath the tap and turn the brass handle anticlockwise – the water seeps out. Then I watch the mud as it disperses into the drain.

Once the shovel is clean and I can see the shiny metal again, I store it in the shed, hanging it on a hook with the other tools. I run my hands over them – an axe, a couple of brooms, a large hammer. It's almost as if I'm caressing them.

A display of immeasurable beauty. They seem to look back, teasing me.

I exit the shed and move back to the kitchen door. I can hear someone calling from the top of the stairs. As I stand there, I can hear steps coming towards me. It's time to go.

I head towards the garden and walk around the back of the house, through the black metal gate and out the front. I peer through the glass of the front door and see a shadow, a young man, tall, gangly looking. He's walking towards the kitchen, checking the doors along the hall.

The drive is still empty, but I hear the sound of a vehicle. Maybe a half-mile away. I make my way across the road and into the fields. The grass is damp and it works into my boots. I listen to the sludgy sound they make as I walk.

I crouch low behind a bush opposite the farmhouse and wait.

A car turns in from the road and parks near the front door. I see the man and woman, both sat in the front. She's pretty, petite. I imagine what it would be like to tie her up, starve her a little. Listen to her beg for her life. I feel elated and have to attempt to control my excitement. I imagine how it's going to feel, watching them.

I could make a move at any second. Tonight? Tomorrow? A week? I can't tell.

Oh, what's this? There is another woman. I watch as she opens the back door of the car. It's like all my birthdays have come at once. I can already imagine her face, how it will twist as she's tied in the basement. I can feel the energy bursting through my body. Control and restraint.

Curb the desire. Keep it in check. I make the rules. I'm the master of my own fortune. My time will come.

You'll be proud of me again. I see you, clasping your hands together, leaning over on your chair. You still look so young, fresh, your skin youthful, but there's disappointment. I can see it in your eyes. You looked out for me and I let you down. I know it. A smile adorns your face, as if you're watching me place the final piece into a jigsaw puzzle, the last brick in a Lego wall.

But if you're honest, you were never proud, were you? Never. Well, I'll soon change your way of thinking.

I can do anything.

You'll see.

See-saw, Margery Daw. The farmhouse was vacant and now there are four.

See-saw. See-saw.

18

'What do you mean someone came into the house?' Sean walked to the living room and tried to light the fire using large blocks of wood he'd purchased on the way back from the mechanic's yard. Jenny followed them in, listening as Ethan went through the afternoon's events.

Beth had gone upstairs to organise her bedroom, still peed off that her brother managed to get the larger room.

'First dibs, what does that even mean?' she'd said to herself as she reached the top step.

'Someone was in the house. I heard them. The front door opened, and I heard footsteps moving along the hall. When I came down, the kitchen door was open.'

'Ethan, come on. It's an old house. You're bound to hear noises. It happens.' He turned back to the fireplace, pleased that smoke was now starting to billow.

Ethan moved forward. 'Dad, I didn't imagine it. I know what I heard.'

Sean placed his hand on his son's shoulders. 'The farm-house has been unoccupied for a couple of years. No one has been in here since Ed left. I was working on my own here yesterday and even I heard multiple creaks and groans. It's going to happen. Your mind will play tricks. I assure you: no one came into the house.'

The fire became stronger, the flames now large and dancing in the centre of the living room, pushing out warmth.

'Dad, I have something to tell you.'

Sean removed his jacket and placed it on the sofa neatly. 'Go on?'

'A woman has gone missing.' He watched his father's demeanour change. His body became tense.

'Missing? From Painswick?'

'Yes. Marie Nelson.'

Sean hesitated for a moment. 'How do I know that name?'

'Dad, it's the hitchhiker, the woman we picked up the other night. She's missing.'

'How? How do you know this?'

'I saw a report on the news. She hasn't been seen since Tuesday evening. She's vanished, Dad.'

In a panic, Sean called the local police station and gave them an account of the other night, how he and Ethan had been driving and picked up a hitchhiker. He was certain it was Marie Nelson. He then described the red coat that he and Beth had found on the road.

The woman took a statement and then asked for further details on where the coat had been found. She took note of the location and said she'd get an officer to take a look.

* * *

For the next hour, they organised the downstairs rooms. Sean and Ethan moved the furniture in the hall and followed Jenny's instructions on where each piece should go. When Sean used a drill to fit a bracket to hold the flat-screen TV, he thought about how weird it was not having to worry about neighbours and the noise.

Marie Nelson played on his mind. His stomach was in knots and he was struggling to concentrate. He and Ethan may have been the last people to see her.

'Sean, people go missing. It happens all the time. How are you feeling?' She could see the shocked expression on his face.

'Sick, if I'm honest. I just hope she's all right.'

'She's probably gone away for a few days or just doesn't feel like answering the front door. It happens. She'll show up.'

'I hope so, but don't you think it's weird? The coat me and Beth found?'

Jenny paused for a moment. 'Just because she's missing it doesn't mean it's Creeper. Maybe she had too much to drink. She might be lying in a ditch somewhere, hurt, but still alive. The police will look into it. You did a brave thing, Sean, calling them.'

It might have seemed callous, but with the new disappearance, Jenny was itching to film more of the docufilm. Of course she was concerned about the missing woman, and she hoped she'd show up, but she had to justify it in her mind – it was probably a row with a lover or with her family. Maybe she was tired of the hassle and stress. There was usually another story in the background.

Ethan came down the stairs and into the living room.

He'd changed into a jumper and black jeans, and his after-shave was overbearing. 'I'm popping into town. I thought I might check out a local pub or two.'

'Why don't you ask your sister to join you?' Jenny stated.

'She's still in a huff.'

'Regardless, it will do you good. Go on, go and ask her. Ethan, soft drinks only for Beth, you hear?.

It goes without saying. She's too young anyway.

They watched him leave the living room, and after a couple of minutes, Beth came down the stairs wearing a coat, a thick scarf wrapped around her neck and a wide grin across her face.

'Here, I'll give you a lift.'

'Dad, it's fine. We'll walk.'

Ethan walked towards the front door, with Beth following.

Jenny could see the concern on her husband's face. 'They'll be fine. If we baby them, they'll hate this place.' She walked to the hallway and watched the kids leave. 'Have fun, you two.' She closed the door. 'Right. Get the camcorder. Let's get going.'

A couple of minutes later, Jenny was standing on the drive of the old farmhouse. Sean was behind her, the camcorder held on his right shoulder.

'Don't start filming until we go inside. I don't want anyone seeing the outside of the house. You know what some people are like.'

'OK, I understand.' He pressed the stop button and deleted the footage he had already started. He then waited until Jenny walked to the front door, then began recording again.

'We're finally here, our new home in the heart of The Cotswolds. We're making a documentary, a story it seems the residents of Painswick are often too afraid to talk about. Earlier today, we spoke to a couple of the locals who were adamant they didn't want to be filmed speaking about the rumours.

'Years ago, in this small village, the rumours were rife, circling like a fire out of control. It's said that Painswick has a secret, a story so chilling it would make your skin crawl – a terrifying urban legend that many locals believe to be true. I've done research myself. I've extensively searched the web, and there's not a shred of evidence that details what happened, what seems to have cast a dark cloud over this place. But local knowledge tells me it's the story of Creeper, an individual who's rumoured to have terrorised the locals many years ago. It's said that Creeper got into homes, often while the residents were inside, and watched them, preying on these people. If you're to believe the story of Creeper – and trust me, it seems many locals do – then whatever stalked the residents of Painswick over that ten-year period could also be responsible for a number of women who have vanished and remain missing today. Some of the locals are too frightened to talk about what supposedly happened, but we will find out the truth.'

She lifted her hand as a sign for Sean to end the recording.

He pressed the stop button. 'Brilliant.'

'Thanks, hun. I think people need to know how reluctant some of the locals are to talk. I wanted to get that in too. Right, let's go again. I think if you follow me, we can take a look in the rooms downstairs. Oh, do you have a key for the basement? That's always a good atmospheric place to record.'

Sean gave the camcorder to her and went to grab the set

of keys from the glove compartment of his car. He joined her a few seconds later.

'OK, great. Hit record. Let's go again.'

Sean took the camcorder and followed her as she went into each of the downstairs rooms, leaving the box room at the front until last.

'It's hard to think that whoever got into the locals' homes could have hidden somewhere just like here, where we're standing right now. If you believe the story of Creeper, this old farmhouse is as good a place as any.'

As she spoke, Sean felt the hairs stand on his arms. He still hadn't told Jenny about the links Bernie had made to their basement.

They moved to the box room and opened the door.

Jenny continued. 'Directly opposite where we are now, you'll see fields, as far as the eye can observe, a haven for someone like Creeper to watch, choosing their time to strike.'

At this, Jenny noticed that Sean's body seemed to jolt, like a shiver suddenly charging through his being. She knew how effective her delivery was. 'We're standing in a box room at the front of the farmhouse, which contains a basement. There's no need to explain why something like this is of importance. For years, basements or cellars have been considered places of terror, especially in our line of work, a place under a house where strange things can often occur, where children refuse to explore. I have to admit, the feeling I'm getting at the thought of unlocking this hatch is one of apprehension. We've yet to venture down these steps, so this is a first for all of us.'

She signed for Sean to pause the recording, then watched as he struggled with the lock, turning the key one way and then the other. She felt numb, unsure whether they should check the place out first before filming, but she knew the docufilm would be more atmospheric and raw if they played it out as it happened.

Sean finally unlocked the hatch. 'OK, Jenny. Ready?' He began to record again.

'Sean is lifting the hatch as we speak. Immediately, I can see cobwebs that are strong like rope. The smell is one of dampness – it's wet and cold, how you'd imagine the scent of a basement to be. As I walk down the wooden steps, which feel as if they could give way at any second, I have a strong feeling of remoteness – I think that's the right word. Unexplored territory, if you like.'

She reached the bottom step and searched for a light. As she pawed for the switch, Sean turned on the camcorder light.

'That's better. Wow. The ceiling is high, much taller than I expected. As you can see, the place is vacant, a large area with a wine shelf that's now empty. The walls have crumbled over the years, and there are watermarks on the concrete floor from the pipes overhead. As I move along the basement, I can see, whoa—'

'Jenny, what's happened? Jenny?' Sean pointed the camera onto the floor.

There were rats. He counted two, three of them, then saw more fleeing across the floor, climbing over each other to get away. The squealing noise penetrated through the basement and seemed to bounce off the walls. He spun in a circle then grabbed on to Jenny's arm to get her out to safety.

A few minutes later, they were back upstairs, the basement hatch closed, sitting on the living room floor in front of the fire.

Sean had made them both coffee, and they sipped the contents to warm themselves up.

'I'm sorry, I just freaked out. God, I hate rats. There must have been a dozen at least.'

'I know, it was disgusting.' Sean's body quivered. 'I feel dirty. It's like I can feel them running all over me. I'll have to call pest control so they can deal with it. Yuck.'

Jenny looked at him. 'Did you see they had something in their mouths? What the hell was that? It looked like skin. Maybe there's something rotting down there. The smell was rancid, Sean.'

They sat still, silent, composing themselves as they dealt with the shock. When they felt more comfortable, they opted to leave the docufilm for the day and focus on the farmhouse instead.

For the next couple of hours, they sat talking, planning the decor and discussing how they envisaged the final place would look. Sean fetched a bottle of whiskey from one of the boxes and poured a generous amount for Jenny. As they spoke, he saw the enthusiasm in his wife's face.

Realising the time, Sean jumped up. He'd organised to pick Beth and Ethan up at 10pm. 'I need to grab the kids. You coming?'

Jenny held her glass closer to her chest. 'No. I'll stay. I'll edit the recording, get it ready to continue next time. You won't be long, will you?'

'Half hour tops.' Sean wanted Jenny to go with him, but he knew if he insisted, she'd think he was babying her too. There'd be many times his family would be alone here; he had to get used to it. They all did.

He grabbed his keys from a small rack he'd screwed on the wall by the front door and made his way out.

Jenny sat in silence on the living room floor. Her heart had slowed to a more normal pace, her breathing more controlled. She thought about the rats in the basement. Out of all the things they could find in this old house, that was the worst. When it came to her fears, rats were top of the list. She listened to the fire, to the wood crackling, watching the bright yellow flames as they flickered. The heat warmed her skin and made her face a deep red colour.

She sipped at her whiskey, holding the glass with both hands as she glanced around the room. She envisioned how it would look when they'd settled. There was so much potential with the farmhouse. The place was huge, the rooms spacious. The garden was enormous, and the drive had so much space. She thought about her friends coming over for the weekend, the parties she and Sean could host.

She took a deep breath, immersing herself in the feeling of contentment.

Then she picked up the camera and started to play the recording. She started from the most recent recording, watching herself step into the rooms, narrating confidently as Sean recorded. She observed her impressive body language, her presentation skills. She watched as they entered the box room, then the recording cut to Sean lifting the hatch, and then her going down the stairs where she began to scream at the sight of the rats.

Jenny was adamant they wouldn't use any of this footage.

She froze the camera and zoomed in, watching the way the vermin scurried over each other, clawing to escape. She felt the fear all over again, as if she were there, among them. A shiver spiralled through her body. She scanned to where Sean began to panic, spinning the camera in a circle. From here, the recording was a blur.

She sat up, moving on to her knees. She rewound the recording and watched it a second time: her screaming, the rats scurrying over each other, Sean spinning. When the recording finished, she stopped the tape, an uneasy feeling in her gut. Something didn't look right. She rewound again. Her screaming. The rats. Sean spinning.

She pressed rewind and left the recording on pause, zooming in close and skipping through the footage frame by frame.

Her screaming. The rats. Sean spinning.

Someone was standing in the corner of the room.

Someone was down there with them.

* * *

Beth and Ethan had gone into the first pub they'd found in Painswick.

They'd ironed out their dispute over the bedrooms. Ethan's room contained a shower pump for the water, and he made the argument that the noise would drive her crazy. Still, he said she could have the room. With a curt smile on her face, Beth refused.

It was a typical country-style public house. The outside walls were decorated with small stones, which were painted bright white. The roof was embellished with dark brown straw, and a sign hanging above the door presented the name, The Harbour Inn.

The couple sat opposite them. The guy was around thirty with wavy brown hair and dark blue eyes. He was wearing a crisp white shirt and skinny jeans, his black coat placed on the back of his seat. His wife was a little older with long pinky-red hair, the colour looking like it had come from a bottle. She was plain looking, but had a kind face and was wearing a green jumper and blue jeans.

'It's good to meet you guys.' Beth sipped her sparkling water. A slice of lemon floated in it, while another piece clung to the edge of the glass. 'So, how long have you both lived here?'

'I was born here.' The guy wiped the cream of his Guinness from his top lip and placed the pint glass in front of him. He turned towards his wife. 'You've been here what, twelve, thirteen years now?'

'Don't remind me. No, there are worse places, that's for sure. I moved from London. It's tough at first. The winters are long and drawn out, but the quality of life is much better.'

The guy looked towards the bar, wondering if he had room in his stomach for another drink. 'So, where did you move to? Don't tell me, one of the new houses on Manor Road? Bloody hell, what I'd give to live there.'

'No, we've moved to the old farmhouse on Gallows Lane. Ed Berry's place.'

At Ethan's words, they both felt a sudden change in the atmosphere, the worried, almost pitiful, look on the couple's faces opposite. There was an embarrassing silence, which lasted longer than was comfortable. Beth and Ethan glanced at each other.

'Wow. What did we say?' Beth giggled, wondering how their demeanour could change so quickly.

The woman leant forward. 'You do know what happened there, don't you? The stories, I mean.'

'Stories? What are you talking about? What stories?' Ethan was growing more concerned by the minute.

Beth's eyes gave away her curiosity. She pulled her chair

closer to the table so she could hear better above the surrounding noise.

'Cath, what the hell? Leave it.' Her husband became uncomfortable.

'Fine. If you don't think they want to hear it, forget I mentioned anything.'

'Go on, Cath. You have to tell us now. You can't start something and not finish it. What about the farmhouse?' Beth felt nervous energy cultivating in her stomach, reminding her of those times someone wanted to show you something but insisted you shouldn't look. However hard you try to force yourself to turn away, part of you wants to see it for yourself.

Cath continued. 'Well, you know the guy who lived there, Ed Berry? Rumour has it that someone stalked his place. Ed reckoned he saw him outside, watching the farmhouse. Ed became paranoid and couldn't cope with living there, knowing that someone was stalking him. It was so isolated. He told people that someone was entering the farmhouse. Apparently, he could hear floorboards moving when he slept, and heavy breathing. It was proper freaky.

'Ed was sectioned. He couldn't cope. He spent the last few years in a psychiatric unit and died there. The locals don't talk about it. People have tried to keep it quiet for years. I think they're frightened. That, and the fact it might stop the tourists from visiting. Painswick makes a lot of money with visitors. But my father worked in mental health, so we know all about it. It's why we moved from London. Ed Berry ended up in a psychiatric unit where he spent the rest of his days. They say he went crazy and lost his mind. He spoke of this person watching him. He said he could see the figure from the farmhouse windows, standing on his drive, just staring. He was adamant the person got inside, moved around from room to room and watched him sleep.'

Beth glanced at Ethan. She suddenly felt numb, and the hairs rose on the back of her neck.

'That's not the worst part. Rumour has it, this man – if you see him, you die. They say he's responsible for the women who went missing all those years ago. He's never been caught, and people believe he's still out there, watching and waiting to strike again. Now, another woman has gone missing – Marie Nelson – so of course everyone is worried. I think he's back. He's called Creeper.'

'That's enough. Out. All of you, out now.' The pub owner was standing over the four of them, his large gut hanging over his trousers. His fists were tightly clenched.

* * *

Jenny's hands shook violently. Her heart raced as she fought to take deep breaths. She was still sitting on the floor of the living room, her body numb, struggling to make sense of the figure she'd seen in the recording. She began to doubt herself. She was tired; the move from Oxford had taken its toll on her body.

A minute passed. Jenny held her breath, too frightened to move. She felt queasy, petrified. Cautiously, she lifted the camcorder and pressed play. She had to check again. Her screaming, the rats, Sean spinning. Again, she jabbed the pause button and went through frame by frame. She watched the room turning in slow motion, the white walls with the crumbling paint, the damp marks, the empty wine rack. To the right, a figure appeared, standing motionless in the corner of the basement. Their basement. Watching them. It was blurry at first but after tapping through the frames, she could see the figure more clearly. Jenny gasped. A man, standing still, looking directly at them.

She turned to look at the living room door, and then glanced back to the camcorder. She zoomed in, but with her numb and trembling fingers, she hit delete by mistake.

'No, no, no. For God's sake, don't do this, please.'

She placed the camcorder on the floor by her side and edged her body slowly upwards, her full attention now on the hallway. Her legs were weak and her vision became blurry. She had to get out of the farmhouse. She grabbed her phone from the front pocket of her jeans. The reception bar was empty. She stepped to the side and waved the phone in the air, hoping for a change in status. She edged forward as she continued to try, placing one leg gently in front of the other, aware any noise would attract attention.

At the living room door, she leant forward and peered down the empty hallway. Cautiously, she stepped out of the room and glanced towards the front door, then back into the living room, where the comforting flames of the fire still burnt, then back along the hallway. She eased her legs forward, edging ahead, tiptoeing along the floor. The bare wooden boards creaked under her feet.

She was certain *he* was still down there – unless maybe there was another way out. Sean had locked the hatch. Or had he? She struggled to recall.

As she moved along the hall, she watched the box room door, which was closed. She eyed the handle, almost convincing herself that it was moving. She stopped, keeping as still as possible. Her heart throbbed through the skin of her neck.

She watched the handle. Did it move? Was her mind playing tricks? She sensed a presence on the other side of the door. A deep shadow under the gap.

Then her legs gave way, collapsing underneath her weight. She screamed, a high-pitched wail, and began to crawl along the cold wooden floorboards to the front door. Her hair was in her face, damp from sweat. Her hands moved meticulously slowly, supporting her body. Her back was arched and her breathing erratic.

She reached her arm upwards, her head swinging to the left, to the box room.

. She was stretching her arm out in front, feeling for the lock of the front door. She listened to the loud clicks of the lock that pounded through the hallway, and suddenly, the front door opened.

Using the weight of the heavy-duty lock, she hoisted herself upwards and stood. She ran, screaming, along the drive and out onto the dense country lane.

'What the hell was his problem?' Beth, Ethan and the couple they'd met earlier were standing on the corner of Painswick High Street.

'It's a touchy subject. People believe in the rumours. They believe in Creeper. It's still difficult for locals to talk about what happened. It's too raw.'

Ethan looked at his sister, then back to Cath. 'And you? What do you believe?' He could hear Beth shivering next to him, the cold air and adrenaline causing her body to tense as she struggled to get warm.

Cath glanced at her husband . 'Well, you can't deny there's something behind it, all those women who vanished without a trace. I believe something wicked happened in the village. Something evil lurked in the darkness. It doesn't bear thinking that someone could have taken them, but it was so long ago. You heard about the girl who went missing a few nights ago, right? It's just like the stories years ago. Like it's happening again.'

Ethan held his gaze on Cath as she spoke. She had genuine fear in her eyes.

Cath turned to her husband. 'Go on, Adam. You know the story better than me. You were here at the time.'

Adam wrapped his arms around himself, then cleared his throat. 'It happened when I was around twelve, maybe thirteen – the second year of high school. I can remember when the first girl went missing. Chloe Madden. I knew her younger brother. It was all over the news. The people in the village were shocked. Everyone searched for her. My mum, dad, me – we joined too – walking for miles to see if anything could be found, looking for any trace of her. We found nothing. The search went on for days. Everyone helped. I remember all the sullen faces as we walked side by side. I remember seeing the police, the sniffer dogs. Weeks went by, but everyone continued to talk about her. They always believed she'd come home, clinging on to her memory. I watched the news constantly. I was obsessed with the story, as were most of the local kids. It happened on our doorstep. Months passed, and the story was still in everyone's minds; Chloe's name was often mentioned – at church, in the supermarkets, everywhere.

'Then the next woman was reported missing, again in Painswick, again, in the same suspicious circumstances. I was home, chilling with Mum and Dad, watching the telly, when I found out. Over the next eight or nine years, six more women disappeared. Vanished without a trace. And now it's happened again. I'm worried Creeper is back.'

* * *

Jenny ran to the end of the drive, glancing over her shoulder. When she reached the narrow country lane, she paused briefly to look out over the vast fields, debating whether to jump the hedge and run for her life, or try to make it to the next house as quickly and directly as possible. She peered left, looking down the road that led towards the village. It went on for a half-mile or so, disappearing around a sharp bend.

She was unsure how far the next house was on either side, but she needed to get to someone, anyone.

She stood, her legs numb, a dull ache racing from her calves to the tops of her thighs.

Jenny looked back at the farmhouse, at the garage to the right. No one had come out, she was sure.

She took a deep breath, then began to jog along the country lane, the lights from the town slightly visible on the horizon. Then, she saw two lights in the distance, a vehicle making its way towards her. Jenny stood, hoping it was her family. She calculated how long Sean had been gone. Twenty, thirty minutes – it had to be them. They hadn't heard another vehicle since they'd arrived at the farmhouse that morning, or another person, for that matter.

She was frantically jumping, waving her arms, then watched as the lights suddenly stopped moving, though still shining in the direction of where she was standing.

Come on. What are you doing? Why aren't you moving?

She waited, watching to see if the lights would go out or move in another direction. They went off. *No, no. Why have the car lights gone off? Don't do that. Keep driving. You need to help me.* She waited for a second, then watched as the lights came back on, flashing towards her. Off. Then on again.

Shit, shit, shit.

This was just like Greyshott Hall – the truck driver, the

flashing lights. Her legs gave way and she fell to the floor. She edged to the side of the road, scuttling back on her hands, which she placed behind her cautiously. She pushed herself up onto the verge and pressed herself against the sharp bushes. She watched the vehicle head towards where she was hiding, building up speed as it moved. She pushed herself further into the bushes, desperately trying to keep herself concealed. She heard the engine, the crunch of the gearstick. The lights were getting brighter. The car was now beside her, revving. Then it stopped, conked out and the lights faded, casting the surroundings back into near darkness.

A guy got out of the driver's seat, followed by a younger man.

'What a piece of shit. I'd have more comfort if I'd ridden a camel. Hello, is anyone there?' He turned to his passenger. 'You sure you saw someone?'

'Yes. They were jumping around – frantically, like one of the ladies playing bingo. Either that, or she's a fan.'

Billy Huxton turned towards the car, watching steam coming from the bonnet. 'When was the last time you used oil, for Christ's sake?'

'Yesterday evening – to cook sausage and eggs.'

'Do you have a light?'

Declan responded. 'I don't smoke. Jesus is my light.'

'A torch? A phone light? Anything... I can't see for shit.'

Declan removed his phone from his jacket, concerned to see there was no reception, then he turned on the torch and handed it to Billy. He watched as his partner held the phone torch the wrong way round, directing the light into his eyes.

Billy walked along the road, shining the light along the path.

The smoke from the bonnet was now heavy in the air,

and there was a sharp hissing noise like water being thrown on a flame. Declan stood on a grass verge and looked towards a nearby farmhouse.

Suddenly, he saw a figure further along the road.

'There, Billy. On the road ahead.' He pointed along the path.

'Hello. Are you OK? I'm Billy Huxton. There's no need to be frightened. Come out so we can see you. We're here to help. Do you need a lift somewhere?'

Declan moved forward. 'Yeah, we'll take you wherever you need.' He looked over at the car, worried it would catch fire any second. '...as long as it's within walking distance. '

Billy watched as the figure moved. He shone the light ahead and saw a woman. She was dressed in blue jeans and a heavy jumper, and she looked frightened.

'Hey. What happened?'

Jenny moved towards the two guys.

'I'm Billy Huxton. This is my partner, Declan. We mean no harm. Are you all right? What happened?'

Jenny fell into Billy's arms. Declan hurried towards them, concerned she'd been attacked.

She looked at the men. 'There— there was someone in my house. My husband went to pick up the kids. I was filming.'

'Oh, kinky,' Declan joked.

'We make documentaries, my husband and I. I saw someone in our basement. When I watched it back, someone was standing in our fucking basement.'

Billy turned towards Declan, seeing the concerned look on his face. Then he turned back towards the woman, and pointed ahead. 'Is that where you live? The farmhouse?'

'Yeah, we moved this morning from Oxford.'

'Wait by the car. I'll take a look.' Billy walked along the

road while the woman waited with Declan. The two of them had now moved a safe distance from the car as smoke continued to push out from its engine.

'At least the heat will keep us warm,' Declan said.

Billy stood outside the farmhouse, looking over the grounds. The garage door to the right was closed, as was the front door. He moved to the living room window and cupped his hands against the glass. He could see the low flames of the fire and the cardboard boxes on the floor, but he couldn't see anyone.

As he backed away, his eyes fixed firmly on the building, he saw the road glow brightly from the lights of another vehicle. A car pulled up behind where Declan and Jenny stood, and a man ran out towards her, followed by two teenagers.

As Billy watched the family huddle together, he debated whether to tell them just how much he knew.

The problem was if he did, they might never step foot in their new home again.

19

'Hello. Is anyone down there? We have a gun, and we'll use it.' Sean was standing over the hatch, with Billy just behind him. He realised how ridiculous he sounded. He had neither a weapon nor any intention of shooting anyone.

He turned to Billy as he began to edge down the wooden steps.

'We came down earlier, Jenny and I. We were making a documentary.' He went on to explain how they filmed stories and shared them on the internet. 'She was freaked out. We saw rats. She panicked. I dropped the camera. That's when I got her out of here. Do you think someone is down there?'

Billy took a deep breath, suddenly feeling claustrophobic. 'We're never going to find out if you stand there babbling.'

They reached the bottom step. Again, the pungent smell was strong. 'This place has been closed for a few years.' Sean kept his voice low as he pointed, shining the torch around the basement. 'That's where they were. We'd walked a little further along.' He turned to Billy. 'Jenny said she saw some-one, standing in the corner.'

'Yes, she said.'

'Stay close to me, Willy.'

'It's Billy. And I've no choice if you don't bloody move.'

The two men walked slowly along the floor. Sean directed the torch ahead, the light jerking around because of his trembling hands. He scanned all four corners of the room and then cast the light along the back wall.

'They've gone.' He blew a hard breath from his mouth, a relief from the stress that had built. 'There's no one down here.'

'Well, if there was, they've made a sharp exit. Let's go back upstairs,' Billy suggested.

The two men climbed back up to the basement hatch. Sean watched as Billy struggled to pull himself up the wooden steps, and he stretched out his hand in case he fell backwards. As Billy gripped the handrail, it began to rattle. The screws had become rusted and weak over the years, and it vibrated as they pulled themselves upwards.

When they'd emerged back into the box room, they brushed their clothes down to rid themselves of the cobwebs.

'Well? Anything?' Jenny was still in the hallway, huddled into Declan, her face full of anticipation.

'Nothing. It's empty. I suggest you all get an early night,' Billy said. 'You've had a hectic day with the move and all. The mind can play cruel tricks when you're tired.'

Jenny moved forward and wrapped her arms around him. 'I can't thank you enough for stopping and, you know, helping me.'

Billy's face flushed. He struggled to cover the embarrass-ment and held his head down, turning away. 'I'm sure anyone would do the same. Just don't make a habit of running out on the road at night and talking to strange men.'

'Speak for yourself,' Declan fired back.

When their offer of coffee – or something stronger – was firmly declined, Jenny opened the front door.

Sean, Ethan and Declan moved to the men's car. The smoke had finally cleared from the bonnet, and they rolled it along the road and onto the drive. Sean said he would give them a lift. Billy called out to Jenny as he got into the front seat. 'Thanks for the parking spot. We'll be back as soon as possible with a mechanic to get the car started. Though on second thought, we might just leave the piece of shit here.'

'So, where are we heading?'

Billy gave sharp instructions as Sean began to drive.

'Turn left... the second right... around this bend – slow down, you drive like a bloody maniac.'

They reached a large, semi-detached house on the edge of the village.

'Stop. Here. We're here.'

As the two men stepped out of the car, Sean thanked them again for their help with Jenny, and as he drove away, Billy felt guilty that he hadn't mentioned anything about the history of their farmhouse.

Declan turned to Billy and gestured towards the house that stood before them.

'So, what's the deal with this place? Your son doesn't know you're coming, does he?'

Billy paused for a second. 'He's away. He leaves a spare key in the outhouse. It's a deal we made years ago. I used to live with him, but he got on my nerves – a groggy little shit, at the best of times.'

'Wow. I can't imagine. A miserable Huxton.' Declan's voice was tinged with sarcasm.

'Well, the key is his way of letting me know that I can come and go as I please. He struggles to deal with the idea of me living at Sheldon's, so I'm taking him up on the offer. I spoke to him a few days ago. He's gone skiing with friends.' He did an exaggerated shiver and turned to Declan. 'I don't get it. How can you go to a colder country in the winter? It doesn't make sense.'

'Have you never skied, Billy? It's so invigorating. Up on the mountains, the views, the thrill of gliding on the snow. It's like you're floating. You don't know what you're missing.'

'Traipsing up a mountain in the ice-cold, your fingers numb, icicles forming at your nostrils and unable to walk with the snow being so thick. Then, once you're down, if you bloody make it in one piece, you repeat the same torturous procedure, over and over. My idea of hell.'

'So maybe you'll think about it. I can book us tickets. We'd have such an adventure.' Declan turned and stared at the house, impressed with what would be his lodgings for the next few days.

'This is it. You can make yourself at home.' They walked side by side towards the front door. 'Just a few house rules. Shoes off, no loud music, don't raid the fridge and keep the windows closed. I suffer with the cold.'

'Wow, this will be one hell of a party.'

'Leave the biscuit tin, wash the shower out immediately after using it, don't leave your dirty clothes on the floor, don't pound up the stairs – or down, for that matter – turn the lights out when you leave a room – it wastes money – oh, and no guests overnight. This is my son's house. Please respect it.'

Declan pulled out his phone.

'What are you doing?'

'Letting a few women down gently.'

* * *

The Freeman family were standing in the kitchen. The kettle was almost boiled, and Jenny had laid out four cups on the worktop.

'Well, that was an eventful night.'

'Are you going to tell me what's going on?'

'Beth, there's nothing to worry about, really.'

'Nothing to worry about? Dad, come on. We find Mum out on the road with two strangers, scared to death; you and that old guy are crawling around in the basement like it's haunted; and Ethan and I find out that Painswick women keep going missing. So, if I then hear you and Mum discussing some oddball who used to watch houses late at night, I'd say there's something to worry about.'

Jenny placed her arm around her daughter, trying to smooth it over. 'Beth, what are you talking about?'

'Creeper... Who the hell is this Creeper that people keep talking about?'

Sean froze, shocked to hear his daughter spit out the word. 'Beth, it's gossip – an old wives' tale, a rumour made up by the people who live here. You don't need to worry. Creeper isn't real. It's just a story. Trust me. Do you think for one minute—'

Suddenly the security light came on. That wasn't a good sign. Sean had asked the builders to rig it up, a way of knowing if someone was on the drive.

'Shit.' He glanced at his watch. It was almost 11pm. 'Wait here, guys. I'll go check it out.'

'Sean, leave it. Maybe it's a fox or another wild animal.'

Jenny edged across the kitchen, looking towards the front door. She feared the person in the basement may still be outside.

'I have to go and see.' Sean moved along the hall. He turned back for a moment, seeing his family huddled together nervously.

As he reached the front door, he glanced towards the box room and shuddered. He wiped a trickle of sweat from the side of his face and slowly opened the front door. The cars were on the drive, and the lamp at the front of the garden glowed bright. He peered into the darkness.

'Hello? Who's there?' He moved from the step and walked towards the road. 'Hello? Is someone out here?'

He waited. No response.

He glanced back at his family, who were now standing in the hallway, looking out.

'Go back. Please, guys. It may not be safe. Please.'

He stopped when he reached the road and glanced in both directions, seeing only a sheet of darkness.

There was no sign of life, only specks of light in the distance. He walked across the road and stood on the grass verge. The barren fields seemed vacant. He tried to focus his eyes, wondering if someone had fled into the fields, but he didn't intend to find out.

Sean watched behind him for a moment and then made his way back to the house.

'There's no one there. Something small must have triggered the light. I'd say it's just sensitive.' He reached out and placed his arms around his wife. 'I don't know about you but I'm knackered. Shall we call it a night?'

Jenny nodded. 'I don't think I've ever looked forward to my bed more.'

Once Sean had checked the farmhouse was locked, he and Jenny went up to the bedroom.

Ethan and Beth stayed up for another half hour, and when they too retired to their rooms, Jenny listened as they climbed the stairs. She lay on the soft mattress, one of Sean's arms around her. He was already asleep.

The face in the basement plagued her mind. She lay still, her eyes fighting to see through the dimness, the blanket tight around her neck. She closed her eyes and turned one way, then the other. She sat up. The face was more clear in her mind now.

It felt as if he was in the room, a shadow in the darkness, watching her. She wanted to wake her husband, turn the light on and ask him to watch her until she slept. It was unfair; why was she the one that had to deal with it?

Her mind began to race – the truck that had chased them from Greyshott Hall, the terror she felt; she was now feeling the same anxiety, as if it was happening all over again. She pictured the red coat, the photo of Sean standing at the front door. She thought of Mark Wheelan and the atrocious acts he'd carried out while escaping Greyshott Hall.

It was like she was living in a horror movie. Only this was real – all too real.

She wiped her eyes and slumped back down.

She could hear breathing – not Sean, but someone else in the room.

She pulled the blanket over her face and the sound disappeared.

Eventually, she slept.

20

Sunday Morning.

The following morning, Sean woke early. He hadn't slept well. Jenny had tossed and turned all night and woke him numerous times. He wanted to let her sleep in and unwind, so he got dressed quietly and made his way downstairs.

He moved around the house, searching for reception on his iPhone, first going into the living room, the box room, the bathroom and then the toilet. He was elated to eventually find slight coverage in the corner of the kitchen. One bar would flicker on and off.

He switched on his hotspot and connected it to his laptop which rested on the kitchen counter. 'Yes. You beauty.'

He wanted to find out about his uncle. He had never met Ed and his parents rarely mentioned his name. As he made a pot of coffee, he searched his name and scrolled through the results, seeing reports of a football agent in Kentucky and a Twitter account with no pictures or posts. Sean's mother had said that Ed spent his last couple of years sectioned at a local psychiatric hospital, deemed unfit to live in the farmhouse on his own. His mother had gone to visit him a few months before he died, but she didn't say much with regards to his mental state. Sean needed to speak with her and find out how he had died, whether he had ever mentioned anything about the farmhouse.

Beth had said something last night about some couple they met in the village pub. They told Beth and Ethan that Ed had indeed been sectioned, unable to cope with the things he saw.

How did they know?

And was it true? Had someone been watching Ed while he lived here?

There were now a number of rumours mentioning the farmhouse directly, and Sean couldn't stop wondering what had happened that had caused his uncle to lose his mind.

* * *

'I could get used to this. A shower that actually throws out hot water and not finding false teeth in a glass on the toilet seat. I like.' Declan smiled at Billy who was standing over the breakfast bar, a jigsaw of pictures placed in front of him. 'What are you looking at?'

Billy had emptied his small brown satchel of newspaper clippings he'd brought from Sheldon's, and had laid them out in front of him. 'These, Declan, are the eight women who went missing over the last twenty years.' He called out the names as if he were a teacher taking the register, pausing out of respect after each one. The final woman was

Katie Huxton. He pushed the picture forward, out of the line. 'This one is my daughter.'

Declan placed an arm around him, watching him wipe the tears that had appeared in his eyes.

Once he'd composed himself, he continued. 'They are all still missing.'

Declan recognised a couple of the names. He'd only been a police officer for a couple of years, and the last woman to go missing had happened before he'd joined the force, but it was something many of the officers would sometimes speak about. 'Each case is still open; that's how it works. But they'd have run cold; no one will be assigned to look into them unless new information comes to light.'

'That's where we come in, Declan. Ten years ago, I spent every waking hour trying to find out what happened to my girl. I made myself sick. I couldn't eat or sleep. I even collapsed with exhaustion and was hospitalised. They put me on anti-depressants. Cheryl, God rest her soul, she saw me crumble as it ate away inside me. She begged me to take a break and let the police do their job. She died a year later. One of the last things she said to me –' Billy wiped his eyes '– was to enjoy the rest of my life and don't get ill again, to let it go. Well, I'm in a better place now, Declan. And it's happening again. I'm waiting for him.'

Declan remained silent for a moment before speaking. 'So, Captain. Where to first?'

Billy rubbed his grey moustache, contemplating the task ahead.

'I say we start at the beginning. Where the rumours started. Ed Berry's place. If you're to believe the rumours, he was plagued with visions of being watched. Let's start at the farmhouse on Gallows Lane.'

* * *

Billy grabbed his thick tweed jacket from the coat stand in the hallway, opened the front door and looked out at the drive. It was an icy morning, the sky was a clear blue and he could smell the damp grass and frost in the air.

'Oh shit, I forgot about your car, Declan.'

'Nothing a jump start and a drop of petrol won't sort out.'

Billy remembered the smoke coming from the bonnet last night. He feared it would take a miracle to get it going. 'Did you ever consider putting a drop of water in it from time to time?'

'Water, Billy, is for showering, drinking and brushing your teeth. I've never heard such nonsense.'

Billy watched as Declan closed the front door. He was wearing a bright yellow pair of jeans and a white, short-sleeved T-shirt. The temperature was below freezing, he didn't bother with a coat and Billy wondered how the man had managed to get himself through almost forty years of his life. He turned and eyed his son's flashy sports car. A Mazda MX-5. It was silver in colour, glistening and pristine. 'We'll take that. Henry won't be back for a while. Hopefully, he won't notice it left the drive.'

'Are you sure? Look what you did to mine.'

'What I did to yours? What the fu— Wait there. I'll go and find the keys.'

Billy went back into the house and returned a few minutes later, clicking the key mechanism, immobilising the car alarm. He listened to the clunk as the wing mirrors opened out and the locks popped up. 'Shit, I think I've broken it.'

They got into the car. It was spotless inside, and they

could smell that polished scent you only get with new vehicles.

'Right, let me see here.' Billy searched underneath the steering wheel.

'What are you doing?'

'The ignition. There's no place to put the key.'

'Press the button, Billy boy.'

'No. No radio on in the car. I need to be able to think.'

Declan pushed out an exasperated breath, then grabbed Billy's leg and nudged it onto the left-side pedal. He leant forward and pressed a small rubber button. 'That's how it's starts. We also have the steering wheel, accelerator and brake.' He gestured to each one as he spoke.

'I'll break you in a minute.' Billy pressed the accelerator and moved the gearstick. The car jolted backwards.

'Whoa! Shall I drive?'

'I'm more than capable, thank you. You didn't say it was automatic. I just need to learn how to go forward. It has to be here somewhere.'

Billy turned into Gallows Lane and when they reached the farmhouse, he parked at the front of the drive. They stood, peering across at the empty fields, the frost thick, the surroundings so still and composed.

'An exceptional hiding place,' Billy said, more to himself than to Declan. 'Right, let me do the talking. I need to chat with the family, tell them my business without freaking them out. We'll have to tread carefully.'

He knocked on the door, and around a minute later, Sean answered.

'Hey, how are you both?' Sean stepped to the side and beckoned them into the house.

Billy removed his jacket and placed it over the stair rail. He slowly turned full circle, taking in the size of the place. 'A beautiful home you have here.'

'Thank you. It was quite daunting, the idea of moving here. But we'll get used to it.'

Sean went on to explain how his uncle had died and how the old farmhouse had been left to him and Jenny. He spoke of the cost of refurbishments to get their home to a liveable standard.

Sean looked along the hall to the kitchen and up the stairs. 'It's hard to think that this place has been empty for so long. My Uncle Ed died in a psychiatric ward.' He kept his voice low. 'Bless him. I think he lost his mind.'

Billy already knew. He sharply changed the subject. 'I can imagine the renovation was costly. Building works aren't cheap.'

Declan pointed to the boarding on the stairs. The gaping holes could be seen from the sides. 'You keep elephants? Are they asleep upstairs?'

Billy fired Declan a disgruntled look.

'Huh? Oh, the builders left sharpish. They were supposed to be here until yesterday. I think another family were renting before we moved here. They carried out a lot of bodge jobs, so the builders said. They attempted to brick up parts of the house without the correct material, including a section of the basement. Damp has set in but I can't get hold of the boss, Mario. I think that's how the rats got in.'

Billy took a deep breath, steadying himself for what he was about to deliver. 'I need to have a chat with you.'

Sean looked concerned. 'By all means, let's move into the living room. My family are still asleep.' He offered tea or coffee, but Billy and Declan declined, choosing glasses of water instead.

They sat on a large sofa that ran along the back wall of the living room, careful to avoid the empty boxes.

Billy went on to explain his business.

Sean and Declan listened intently.

'I was born here in Painswick. I grew up here. It's where I met my wife, Cheryl, and where my daughter went to school. I love this place more than you could ever imagine.' Billy stared at the white wall opposite, then looked back to Sean. 'I was a private investigator. We both were – a husband and wife team, like yourselves.'

He spoke in depth about the cases they took on, the challenges they faced and how they'd busted everything from petty criminals and small drug gangs, to settling an array of family disputes and altercations.

'My daughter went missing ten years ago. One of the Painswick eight. She went out to the shops one evening and never returned.' Billy explained the extent of his search, how he'd become ill, struggling to function, and the anti-depressants, then finished by telling Sean of the death of his wife a year later. He held nothing back. 'We're going to re-open the case, investigate what happened here, and I'd like your help. I need to know what happened to these women. I have been sick for a very long time, but thankfully, I'm able to cope again. I'm stronger now. I need to know what happened to my Katie.'

'I'm so very sorry for your loss. It is unimaginable what you went through, and still are going through.' Sean glanced at both men. 'I'm here to help. Whatever our family can do.'

Billy smiled. 'You say your wife may have seen someone in the basement?'

'Yes.' Sean looked apologetic. 'Unfortunately, she deleted the footage.'

'Can you tell me what happened before you went into the basement?'

Sean stood in front of the two men, bringing his hand to the side of his face as he recalled their actions the previous day. 'Ethan and Beth left around 8.30pm – we arrived yesterday morning and they were anxious to see Painswick; you know how it is. Jenny wanted to continue with the docu-film. Once we start, we usually crack on, you know?'

'Are you sure the house was empty at this stage?'

'Yes. Apart from Jenny and I. We'd gone into town to conduct interviews, get the view of the locals in the area, but we returned shortly after. Oh, and we dropped by to pick up our car.' Sean told the men how their vehicle had been damaged at Greyshott Hall, how Bernie had been repairing it.

'Can I ask what you're filming?' Declan asked.

Sean turned a bright red colour. 'We're investigating Creeper.'

The atmosphere in the room dropped suddenly, as if they'd been transported to a wake. The silence lasted for almost a minute.

Sean's admission perturbed Billy. But as he sat, thinking, he realised it may help the investigation. It wasn't his place to tell Sean to stop. He had no control over their choices. He needed to keep the family onside. He would investigate the missing women while Sean and Jenny filmed the story – it may work in his favour. 'OK. So, you're certain it was just the two of you here? Your kids went out for a couple of hours and then what?'

'We began filming. I opened the hatch and we went into the basement. We saw the rats, Jenny freaked out and we came back up to the living room. Then, just before 10pm, I went to fetch Beth and Ethan. The rest, well, you know. Jenny ran onto the road and you guys turned up to help.'

Billy went to stand. He rocked back and forth like a broken Jack in the box, the spring pushing to try to release it.

Declan supported his arm and helped him up. 'Christ, do we need to call Cranes R Us? Here, tip the sofa, Sean. We'll spill him off.'

Billy slapped his arm away. 'Could we take a look in the basement? You say the house was empty? The builders had started dealing with the damp. If your wife did see someone down there, it's possible there's an entry point leading in from the outside.'

'By all means. Just keep quiet. I don't want to alarm my family.'

Billy stood and faced Sean. 'I'm going to be straight with you. You'll find there's no bullshit with me. I say what I think. I'm direct.'

'You tell him, Captain.'

Billy noted the apprehensive look on Sean's face, how vulnerable he and his family were. 'Make your film, I've no problem with that.' Billy glanced at Declan, then back to Sean. 'We're not here to stop you. It's what you do. But I will tell you something: what you're both doing is extremely dangerous. You're going back somewhere most are too frightened to.'

Sean hesitated a moment, taking in what Billy was saying. 'How so? With the documentary, you mean?'

'Investigating what happened here in Painswick. The women who disappeared. The person many say is responsible.'

'You mean Creeper? It's a story, surely? A fabricated myth to scare the locals.'

Declan moved towards the two men. 'If it's a myth, it's certainly working – someone watching the residents in their homes, the possibility he got inside, moved around.' Declan turned to Billy. 'Do you think this Creeper character really kidnapped those women?'

A tree branch slapped against the living room window, causing the three men to jolt. There was silence for a few seconds.

'Brace yourself, Sean. I won't hold back from telling you what I think or skim around the facts, cutting bits here and there to make you feel safer. A seamstress, I am not. There's a possibility the rumours are true. It's said that Ed Berry, while living here in the farmhouse, found bodies in the basement.'

Sean's calm expression dropped. The colour drained from his skin. 'How do you know this?' His voice was dry and weak.

'There's never been proof. It seemed there could have been a mass cover-up, but the rumour mill spilt over when Ed was moved into the psychiatric hospital. This place was abandoned for quite a while. I must say, it looks a heck of a lot better than I imagined.' He began to walk around the room. 'Ed was a recluse. He mostly kept himself to himself. But he had one very important friend – a man called Ronnie Hathaway. They were as thick as thieves. Ed, for whatever reason, had a certain hold over Ronnie.'

'Ronnie Hathaway. I've not heard of him.'

'Well, I have. He was an important man and didn't want his reputation tarnished. He was a Painswick MP. He stood up for the locals. He built houses, shops, the church. He brought prosperity here. The town folk will never forget what Ronnie Hathaway did for them, for their families.'

Sean listened, experiencing a sudden head rush. 'I'm not with you. How do you know bodies were found in the basement?'

'My daughter, Katie, was the last woman to disappear. I searched, tirelessly, for months and became psychically and mentally ill. But the more I researched and spoke with people, the more I believe it happened. Before Ed became ill, I called over here, numerous times. Oh, I knew he'd holed himself up here, how he was deteriorating.' He pointed towards the living room window and out to the drive. 'I stood there, knocking on the door, desperate to talk to him. I saw a shadow once, twice, while Ed came to a window above. He quickly moved out of view.

'A day or so later, Ronnie Hathaway phoned me. He told me not to call over to Ed's place again, to leave him alone. He told me he could have me arrested for harassment. Needless to say, I was fuming. This important person, this high and mighty so-called gent, warning me off. Something was going on, all right. Something happened here. But Ed never opened the door and I never found out.'

'So, what do you think happened?' Sean kept his voice low, at an almost whisper.

'I believe Ed found a body and that he was being watched. Why else hide? And why was I warned off?' Billy was standing by the window, looking out at the cold, crisp morning. The sun shone, reflecting off the glass, warming his body. He turned. 'Honestly, I think Ed was driven crazy – part fear, part guilt for what he'd seen. I strongly believe he was watched at night. When it first began, Ed told a couple of people, who inadvertently told me. They'd laughed, pointing out how Ed had lost his mind. And yes, he was losing his grip on reality. I spoke with many people here in Painswick. As the rumours spread, it drove Ed psychotic. I believe he became paranoid, delusional. There is no proof, but it's said that Ed Berry found a body in the basement.'

'You mean one of the missing women?' Declan asked.

'Yes, possibly more than one. I like to believe my Katie is still out there, but I'm not delusional. I have prepared for the worst. Ed was taken to the psychiatric hospital not long after I'd heard this story. The police managed to obtain a search warrant for this place but they found nothing to back up the allegations. They believed it was a hoax. Whether someone had managed a clean-up job after Ed was sectioned, covered up what he'd found, I don't know.'

Sean and Declan remained silent for a while, digesting the story. The more Sean heard, the more frightened he felt for he and his family.

'So, if Ed really saw someone outside, watching him, and there was the possibility that this person was responsible for what he may have found in his basement, why didn't he call the police?'

'He probably did. I don't think they took him seriously. Ed was a simple man and lived alone; he wasn't confident. He struggled to communicate.'

'So, you think bodies were found here in the farmhouse? And if the story of Creeper is true, then why has he waited so long to strike again?'

'How would I bloody know?' Billy felt hassled by all the questions. It was too much for him. Memories of his daughter were rushing into his mind. He wanted to run, as far away from here as possible. He wondered whether he was capable of facing the worst time of his life all over again. He could hear his wife's voice, urging him to rest, but he had to confront his fears. 'It's possible the person responsible felt they'd had enough. Maybe he got bored, dispassionate.'

Billy began to think aloud.

'A serial killer is usually defined as a person who murders three or more people, habitually, for abnormal psychological gratification. The murders take place over a period of more than one month, most often with a significant gap between them. The motives can include anger, thrill-seeking, financial gain, and often, attention-seeking. Many are active until they die, taking their secret to the grave. Some stop; others feel like they can go on forever, with massive gaps between their victims.' He paused and looked Sean in the eye, 'We may never know why my daughter's abductor has waited over ten years, but I know it's the same person. To answer your question about Ed, I think he covered it up, how he found the bodies. Maybe he'd lost touch with reality by then. It's possible he didn't even believe what he saw. Maybe he didn't want to think it was happening. As I said, Ed possibly suffered from delusions. He struggled to differentiate between reality and fantasy.'

Sean heard a floorboard creak above them. Fearing his family were going to come down, he needed Billy and Declan to move fast. 'Look, do what you have to do. You have a few minutes before Jenny and the kids are up. I'll tell them you've lost something, but make it quick. Please.'

He led the two men into the box room, and as he opened the hatch, a myriad of thoughts began to besiege his mind: the rats, the possibility of bodies previously being down there... He felt sick.

He watched as the two men disappeared down the steps.

Billy removed a flashlight from his pocket. 'OK, I was down here briefly with Sean last night. I don't know what we'll find. You heard what he said. The builders were dealing with damp. They've broken up part of the structure following temporary repair works made by the previous occupants. If Jenny saw someone down here, we need to find their route inside. Just keep your eyes open.'

'I won't see anything with them shut.'

They walked slowly along the ground. They could smell the sodden, saturated bricks, could hear the sound of water dripping in the distance and could feel the wetness in the air, like a blurry mist clinging to the atmosphere.

'There's more to it, isn't there, Billy? You seem certain bodies were found down here,' Declan whispered. 'There's never been any evidence. I searched the internet last night while I was lying in bed. Oh, it was comfy. Can I request an extra pillow and maybe a hot water bottle for tonight?'

Billy turned and shone the torch in his face. 'Anything else? Breakfast in bed? A newspaper? If you get too comfy, I'll never get rid of you.'

'Hey, if the invite is there...'

Billy turned back, facing the basement wall at the end of the room. 'I had a friend, a police officer who I went to school with. Glen Porter. He's retired now, but we kept in close contact most of our adult life. I spoke with him when Katie went missing. He wasn't supposed to tell me anything about the case – an investigator needs special permission – but Glen bent the rules. The police were desperate and probably embarrassed. Seven women had gone missing before my daughter, and they had no evidence, no leads. The spotlight was on them and people wanted answers.

'Phil was heavily involved with the case. We met for coffee, and he spoke of his suspicions, things he had heard. He couldn't reveal the source, but he assured me it was someone reliable. Phil held the source in good stead and he'd heard the stories, which backed it up. The source was the reason they were able to get a warrant and search the farmhouse.'

'A cover-up, then. So, it's possible Ed found something down here?' Declan looked to the ground. A chill ran through his body.

'The police never found a shred of evidence. I met with Phil a few days after. No fingerprints, no DNA, no blood or semen. No hair fibres, skin or bone fragments – nothing to suggest there was any truth to the story.' He turned to Declan. 'It's why I have to believe Katie will come home.'

'But you still think it could be true? It's possible?'

Billy pushed out a hard breath. His body was sore and his head ached from the questions. 'The rumours spread like wildfire. You know what small villages are like. It's a community. Everyone talks. Once people found out about Ed being watched and harassed, and then how he'd lost his mind and moved to a psychiatric ward, they had plenty of fuel for an already burning fire.'

'And so, the birth of Creeper. Like the Boogeyman.'

'Exactly. Parents would manage their unruly kids with the threat of him; teenagers would go to the abandoned farmhouse and dare each other to knock on the door. My son, Henry saw them many times as a teenager. Creeper became as real as you and me.'

Billy turned to Declan. He paused, wanting to make the delivery of his next sentence as effective as possible.

'Only the Boogeyman isn't real.'

21

The two men reached the wall at the end of the basement, and Billy shone the torch towards the area that had been knocked through, where Sean had told him the builders had widened the room to deal with the damp. The area immediately to the left looked like it had once housed an old boiler flue or toilet waste.

They stepped into this section, shining the torch across the floor and over the walls.

'I wonder what this room was used for?'

Declan moved further inside, running his hands along the walls, his fingers picking at the loose stones. The walls were formed with rock and breeze block – a false structure – and resembled a crumbling cave. It felt cold.

Billy stepped behind him, shadowing his movements.

'Pass the torch. There's gaps in the wall.'

Declan reached behind him and accepted the torch, which Billy slipped into his hand.

'No, the torch.'

'Can you be serious for one bloody minute?'

Declan shone the light through the minuscule gaps in

the rock. He pushed his face forward, closing one eye to see better, then moved along the room. 'There's something hidden in the wall.'

'What do you mean?'

'Well, from what I can see, there's an object, buried in the concrete. I think if we get a hammer we can dig at the loose stones.' He guided the torch further along the wall. The wall had become weak due to damp. 'It's a small, rectangular object – purposely buried in the wall, like someone has hidden it.'

'Pull at the wall. We have to see what it is.'

Suddenly the hatch opened and a voice echoed through the basement.

'Guys, please. You have to come out.' Sean's voice was urgent.

'For shit's sake,' Billy sniped. 'Fine.'

A minute later, the three men were standing back in the box room.

Sean locked the hatch and pulled the carpet over it.

Jenny came down the stairs. She was wearing a thick white jumper and jeans, and looked the picture of health. She saw Billy first, standing in the doorway.

He turned, a slightly guilty expression on his face, as if embarrassed they may have woken her.

'Morning, guys. How are you both? You're up early.' She offered them coffee, but they declined. 'Thanks again for last night. I don't know what I would have done if you hadn't come along.'

Billy's face flushed, his cheeks turning a bright scarlet colour. 'It's no problem.'

'They've come to try and sort the car.' Sean felt guilty for hiding the reason Billy and Declan had called. He couldn't have his family worrying.

'Are you sure you won't stay for a drink?'

Billy raised his voice, agitated for a moment. 'No. We're good. We need to get going. A tow truck is booked for Monday. I've given them the address. They'll get the car off your drive. You don't want that piece of shit cheapening the place.'

At this, Declan clutched at his chest, as if wounded by the comment.

Once Billy and Declan had left, Sean and Jenny moved into the kitchen. Jenny closed the door more harshly than she'd intended. 'What's going on?' She pointed to the two empty glasses. 'What time did they get here?'

Beth walked in, which saved him from having to explain what they'd wanted. He'd tell Jenny eventually – he'd have to – but he needed to choose his words carefully.

'Morning. How did you sleep?' Jenny asked.

Beth stretched, looking dishevelled. 'Not great. My room is freezing.'

'Well, we'll get some more blankets. There are loads in one of the boxes.'

Beth grabbed a cereal box from a cupboard and poured half the contents into a stained bowl.

'What do you say we chance filming, Jenny?

'We can certainly try.'

A half-hour later, after having eaten, Sean and Jenny were in the car.

They'd asked Beth and Ethan to join them, both Sean

and Jenny slightly desperate in their pleading, but Beth was planning on sorting her room and Ethan was having a lie-in – something that usually ended with him surfacing in the latter part of the afternoon.

They told Beth to call if there were any problems and not to answer the door under any circumstances. Their instructions were met with an eye roll and a sharp tut.

In the car, Sean reached forward and took his wife's hands in his. 'How are you feeling after last night?'

Jenny sat back in the passenger seat. 'Maybe I was wrong. I freaked out. The rats, the basement – Christ, it's a creepy old building. There are bound to be shadows, noises. I suppose it's something I'll get used to in time.' She looked at Sean. 'I'm not making it up. I'm certain I saw someone on the recording.'

'Baby, I know you're not making it up. But it's probably nothing – a local drunk who got in from the outside or kids messing around. You know how it is. We've boarded up the entrance. No one can get inside now.'

'I'm not happy with the kids staying behind.'

'Oh, Jenny. They're together. Ethan is eighteen, for Christ's sake. Look at the size of him. We can't lock them in a room every time we need to go out.'

'You're right. I need to get a grip.'

Sean started the engine and they were immediately met with cold air from the grills on the dashboard. The windows were lightly frosted, and as he pulled away from the drive, the tyres spun as they tried to get a grip on the road. He fought the feeling of anticipation, looking back at the farmhouse in the rear-view mirror. It had been a tough twenty-four hours.

Sean drove, holding the steering wheel tight in his right

hand, his left resting in Jenny's lap. His conscience had eased slightly, knowing Beth and Ethan were together.

He watched the narrow road, the window slightly cracked open, the cool breeze pushing against his skin. Out of the corner of his eye, he noticed Jenny fighting with her fringe. She demanded he shut the window.

'Where are we going?'

'Beth and I came here a few days ago. Remember when she offered to help with the decorating? We had a bite to eat at a local restaurant.'

'Yeah, you mentioned a waitress. She was going to talk to you and then she stopped.'

'That's right. She went to say something, something about Creeper.'

'Sean, we need to be careful. If the locals don't want to talk, we can't force them. We don't want to make enemies. Painswick is a small place.'

Sean smiled. 'Hey, we have each other. That's all we need.'

Jenny slapped his arm. 'You're so cringy.'

'I'm thinking we go have a coffee, see if she'll talk. There's no harm in that.'

'You wouldn't think so.'

* * *

Ten minutes later, they'd stopped beside the restaurant, parked and made their way inside.

Once seated, a waiter read them the specials from memory, dropped menus onto the table and said he'd be back in a couple of minutes to take their order.

'We're just having coffee. That's it.'

'That's all you want? We have an apple tart that goes lovely—'

Sean held up his hand. 'Just coffee, thanks.'

The waiter sauntered away. When he returned with the drinks a few minutes later, Sean took a deep breath, ready to ask again about Creeper.

'A couple of evenings ago, my daughter and I came here to eat. There was a girl. We spoke about the old Hollywood pictures. She's tall with blonde hair, striking features.'

Jenny darted a look at him that could have cut him in two.

'Oh yeah, Silvia. She doesn't work here anymore.'

The waiter went to leave, but Sean grabbed his arm. 'Doesn't work here? Why? What happened?'

The waiter leant forward. 'She was sacked.'

* * *

Beth was upstairs, unpacking from a large cardboard box.

She picked up a lamp, twisted the bulb to ensure it held in the connection, then placed it on the bedside table. She took out the posters of her favourite grime stars, Stormzy and Big Shack, which were neatly rolled and held with rubber bands, and ripped off small pieces of Blu Tack so she could pin them to the wall. Then she set up her dressing table, placing her makeup bag alongside some toiletries, her hairdryer, straighteners and hair curlers. Beth stood in the centre of the room, eyeing the posters, the dressing table and the bed that her father and Ethan had helped to put together. It was beginning to feel like home.

She walked to the window and looked out over the large garden and the fields further along. The frost was beginning to melt, grazing the tips of the grass, leaving a shiny green colour as it evaporated. She looked towards the shed to the right-hand side, the small rockery in the centre of the lawn and at a white marble flamingo water feature they hadn't yet managed to set up. She glanced at the washing line, which reached from one side of the garden to the other, a thin white wire that looked flimsy and weak.

She recalled how their garden in Oxford was so untidy – a trampoline with the net ripped, with wide holes you could put your arms through; swings that creaked as they moved, the seats lopsided and forever wet; a slide that usually tipped over on to its side as you came down – as a child, Beth had hated it because of the worms underneath the legs. Ethan would pick them up and hurl them towards her.

Beth's eyes were drawn to the end of the garden. There was a shadow in the fields, a figure, crouching low, partly concealed behind some bushes. She brought her face closer to the window, her panicked breaths forming condensation on the glass. She wiped it with the sleeve of her cardigan, then stepped back, glancing behind her at the open bedroom door and out to the empty hallway. For a second, she wondered where her brother was.

She edged to the middle of the bedroom, her eyes glued to the window. She waited. She tackled the thoughts in her mind. The figure had been low on the ground and resembled a person kneeling. They were facing towards her, watching her, like a creature in the night.

She wanted to wake Ethan, but she knew he'd be livid. She had to deal with this herself.

Was it was a shadow, her mind playing tricks? The farmhouse was isolated and barren. The fields that surrounded the land seemed like an empty void.

Beth waited, aware of her heavy breaths and the outer silence that encompassed her.

She backed out to the hallway, delicately stepping on the wooden floors, and then turned. She could see that the door to her brother's bedroom further along the hall was closed.

She listened to the calmness and took a large gulp of air, then moved back into her bedroom. She edged towards the window and pressed her hands against the cold glass. The figure was gone; only small trees and shrubs graced the space now.

I knew it. You're seeing things. Get a grip.

The view suddenly brought peace. Beth could see for miles – beautiful green pastures, a wild and mysterious landscape, which she suddenly devoured. She breathed out hard, absorbing the sight in front of her.

But the peace didn't last. Beth's vision seemed to move in slow motion back to the end of the garden, where a man was standing by the fence at the edge of the field. She could see him clearer this time. He was tall and was wearing a long jacket. His arms were extended, and in his hands, he held a red coat.

She dropped to the floor and screamed, a high-pitched wail that woke Ethan, bringing him racing into the bedroom.

'What's up?' He stood in his boxer shorts, his face swollen with sleep. He crouched and took her hands.

'There's someone in the garden, Ethan. He's watching me.'

Ethan stood, turned toward the window and stared.

The garden and fields were empty.

22

'Sacked? I don't understand.' Sean sipped at his latte, confused. 'I don't get it. She was so nice.' He leant into the table, moving closer to Jenny and kept his voice low. 'I think she was going to say something. I remember another woman stopping her mid-sentence.'

Jenny placed her espresso on the table. 'Oh, this is ridiculous. We're getting nowhere.'

In a moment of madness, she stood, picking up the camcorder and began recording. The counter was empty – the staff were all in the kitchen out the back. It was her time.

'Hello?' she shouted, circling the restaurant, zooming in on the patrons' astonished faces. 'Can I have your attention for a second, please? Hello, can I have your attention?'

The restaurant fell into complete silence, only the noise of cutlery rattling out as people paused their eating.

'My name is Jenny Freeman. This is my husband, Sean. We've just moved to Painswick and we make documentaries. I'm recording here this morning off the cuff.' She raised her voice, watching the piercing eyes on her. 'So far, we've hit a blank wall. But I'm sure someone wants to talk. We're investigating the story of Creeper.'

It was as if everyone in the room emitted a low gasp in unison. Jenny watched the faces, the prudent, subtle movements of those around her.

'Why will no one talk? What? If you say his name three times while looking in a mirror, he will come for you? This village has been quiet for too long and it's time to speak. I know there has been a lot of pain here, the history, and all those missing women, but nothing gets resolved if we don't talk about it. Another girl has gone missing; maybe we can help find her.' She moved towards a couple to her left, their empty plates on the table in front of them. 'You two, do you know the story of Creeper? Is it true?'

The lady leant forward on the table. 'Sorry, we're here for the weekend. Who's this Creeper? Sounds bloody terrifying.'

An elderly guy on his own spoke up. 'I know about him.'

Jenny suddenly felt excitement as she moved towards the guy. She handed the camcorder to Sean.

'It's all anyone spoke about round here for years. They say he's seven, eight-foot-tall, gets into folks' houses late at night. If he chooses you, well, you're in for it. He'll rip ya fucking heart out and shove it up your ass.'

Jenny moved beside him and crouched down. 'Have you seen him?'

'Don't want to see him. I mind my business, which is what you guys should be doing.'

Another person, two tables from where the old guy was seated, spoke next, an elderly lady with her husband. Not catching what she said, Jenny dashed over. Jumping from person to person like this, she felt like Oprah Winfrey.

The woman fixed her hair as Jenny sat in the seat opposite.

'You said something a moment ago. Could you repeat it?' Jenny asked.

'My cousin, Bob, saw him. He reckoned he had someone slumped over his shoulder, one of those girls that went missing. Of course, they're only rumours but he swore blind. He saw him while driving up Gallows Lane late one night. Bob would tell you about it himself if he were here. Said he had a face like the devil himself, all burned, melted. He said it was the scariest thing he'd ever seen.'

'Could we speak with Bob?'

'Doubt it. He died a few years back.'

'Oh, I'm sorry.'

'Don't be. He was an arsehole.'

'OK, turn it off this instant. The camera. Turn it off. We don't allow filming in here.'

Jenny and Sean turned to see a woman coming out of the kitchen, making her way towards them. She wore a stained white apron, and her hair was held in a net.

'They're not causing any trouble, Sue. They're only asking what happened to the people who went missing,' the lady who'd spoken about her cousin said, trying to reason with the owner.

'Not in my place, they don't. Come on, pay up and leave.' Sue walked to the bar, her voice raised so everyone could hear. 'It's tough enough trying to deal with the tragedy without the likes of you bringing it up again, you hear me?' She stood behind the counter and picked up a card machine. She tapped in some numbers and then placed the device on the counter.

Sean recognised the woman. The night he called here with Beth, she had been the one who'd stopped the waitress mid-sentence. She'd probably fired her for talking. *What was she hiding?*

Jenny tried to explain. 'We're not trying to cause any problems. We make documentaries. It's our line of work. We make a living from it. And we live here now; we've moved to the farmhouse on Gallows Lane. Honestly, we don't mean to upset anyone or cause complications.'

Sue's expression suddenly changed, now full of horror. 'The farmhouse on Gallows Lane, you say?'

'That's right. We've just moved there. Ed Berry was my husband's uncle.'

Sean stepped to the counter and placed his card over the machine. He watched as the lady took the card reader, her eyes never leaving Jenny's face. She looked stunned, briefly frozen in time. After a moment, she refocused, her gaze passing between the two of them.

'Well then, welcome to Painswick. But a word of advice.' She dropped her voice to a hush. 'Lock your doors at night, keep the blinds shut and pray you don't see him.'

* * *

Ethan and Beth were crouched under the bedroom window. Ethan had his hand placed on Beth's shoulder. 'I'll go and take a look. Wait here.'

'No, don't leave me.'

'Beth, there's no one there. You're seeing things. It's an old house. You know, I thought I heard someone downstairs yesterday. Remember when you all went out? Our minds play tricks. This place is creepy. We're going to hear shit all the time. I'll be back before you know it.'

Beth faced her brother. 'What about the stories? What people are saying about this place? The bodies?'

'Oh, Beth. People love a story. They're probably all having a good laugh at us.' He made his way out of the bedroom and leant over the balcony. 'Hello? Is anyone down there?' He turned to Beth. 'See? No one there.' He slammed the bedroom door shut.

'That's it? That's you checking if the house is empty?'

'What do you suggest?'

Beth took a deep breath. 'We can't stay up here all day. Go and check.'

'What? Why should I go?'

'Because you're the man. Now go.'

Ethan looked hassled. 'Beth, there's no one downstairs.'

'You won't know until you check. I'll wait here.'

Ethan moved slowly out to the hallway, closing the bedroom door behind him.

Beth heard his footsteps as he walked down the stairs, moving one slow step at a time. Eventually, the noise faded.

* * *

A couple of minutes had passed, and Beth remained crouched under the window.

Visions flashed in her mind – the man standing in the field, holding a red jacket. Her legs began to cramp. She slid them out, straightening them, turning her ankles to relieve the discomfort. She struggled to control the panic that was rising in her body so she forced herself to listen for sounds on the ground floor – anything to clarify Ethan was OK.

The farmhouse was silent. Beth didn't like it. She felt guilty for making Ethan go and check. They should have remained hidden, together, up here where it was safe.

She pushed her hands on the ground and rose, then peered out the window at the empty garden, the barren fields. There was no sign of Ethan. *Where are you?* Her mind conjured up scenarios: Ethan lying on the kitchen floor, in the back of a van or buried in the fields opposite. She had to do something.

A sound came from outside the bedroom. Beth was certain. She spun.

'Hello? Ethan? Is that you?' She moved forward, her eyes fixated on the door handle. Did it move? A slight turn? Beth was unsure. 'This isn't funny.'

She paused, aware of her heavy breaths, her body suddenly hot, a flush creeping over her skin. She reached forward, placing her fingers on the door handle and turned it gently. The door opened. She looked out to the empty hallway.

'Hello? Is someone there?' Delicately, she stepped over the floorboards, too frightened to peer over the balcony. When she reached the stairs, she eased her leg down the first step. She whispered. 'Please, Ethan. Are you there?'

No reply.

She moved further down the stairs, eyeing the boards that her father had fitted over the holes. The door to the box room was closed, and further down, she could see into the living room, the bathroom and the kitchen. The lights were off and the farmhouse was in near-darkness.

A shadow stood in the far corner of the kitchen. Tall, menacing-looking. Beth cried out. She turned, debating whether to run out the front door or race back upstairs and lock herself in her bedroom.

'Beth, it's me.'

'Christ, Ethan! What the hell is wrong with you? You scared the shit out of me.'

Beth stepped off the stairs and walked along the hall,

now able to see her brother more clearly. He was standing motionless, staring at something on the wall.

'Don't come in here. Stay back.'

Beth had now reached the kitchen door. 'What's wrong? Ethan? You're scaring me.' She turned on the lights, then moved beside him, looking in the direction he was staring.

On the chalkboard their father had nailed to the wall, four stick people had been drawn in black felt tip, standing side by side. The largest was on the left, around six inches in height. The three other drawings were identical, but shorter as you went down the line – only, the one at the end had a line drawn through it.

And a noose around its neck.

23

I t was almost midday, and Billy wanted to take a drive over to the psychiatric hospital where Ed Berry had lived out the remainder of his life. He needed to understand the man: his state of mind and how he spent his last few years; he needed to take a walk in his shoes, get into the mind of this elusive, ambiguous recluse.

He'd thought about calling ahead to announce the reason for his visit, but decided it was best to turn up unannounced; that way, he'd catch them on the hop. Hospital staff couldn't talk about residents, and Billy knew he'd get little – if any – information if they knew he was coming.

Declan's mind was preoccupied with the findings at the farmhouse. Something had been buried in the basement wall. The builders had told Sean that Ed Berry had works done, a false wall and other minor jobs, but the structure wasn't safe. Something had been placed there, purposefully. And whatever it was, it needed to be kept hidden.

He turned to Billy and watched him struggle with the seatbelt. 'I'm trying to understand why Ronnie Hathaway warned you off from talking with Ed Berry. How did you know Ronnie?'

'He was a complicated character. A right miserable bastard.'

'So, you had one thing in common then.'

Billy ignored him. 'He was an MP, a man who liked to be in control. He thought anything that happened in Painswick was his responsibility. And to a point, it was. But Ronnie made everything his business. He'd hear of a break-in, a child having a tough time at school, a car accident, a deceiving partner; then he'd play the role that was required of him: psychologist, doctor, priest. He poked his nose in everyone's business.' Billy clicked the belt into the holder and sighed. He shifted in the seat, trying to get comfortable. 'Ronnie indulged in self-importance. It was like he thought a spotlight glowed down on him wherever he went and he expected applause at the slightest thing he accomplished. He was proud, illustrious – a man who thought he was far above anyone else.'

'Classy.'

Billy pulled out onto the road. His hands were awkward on the steering wheel and he struggled to find the brake pedal, his legs stamping, as if he was putting out a fire.

Declan clung to the overhead grip. 'What was he like at school?'

'He was a year above me so I didn't have much to do with him. But I remember seeing him in the playground, swanning around like he owned the place. He was the type that thought he was a hit with the ladies, that kind of kid.'

'And was he?'

'What the hell does it matter?'

'Aw. I detect a hint of jealousy.' Declan reached out and rubbed Billy's head playfully.

'I ended up with the princess.'

Declan went quiet at that, feeling his friend's pain.

They left Painswick and drove the three miles along the A46 towards Stroud, a market town and civil parish that acted as a centre point for the surrounding villages. Billy eyed the sign for Stroud Hospital and followed the directions to the psychiatric ward.

'There's a space. Quick before someone takes it.' Declan pointed, watching as Billy struggled to move the gearstick.

Billy shifted it back and forth while pushing out a frustrated breath.

A couple of cars waited behind, and an irate driver began to pound his horn.

'I'll never get in there.' Billy adjusted the rear-view mirror while Declan waved his hand out of the window to apologise. The trail of vehicles was starting to grow.

'Look, let me get out and guide you.' Declan opened the passenger door and climbed out. 'Keep coming, that's it, further, you're doing great.' Drivers began to shout obscenities. 'Backwards, Captain. Press the accelerator and put the gear into reverse.'

After several attempts, Billy stopped, finally parking in the space. He tried to open the driver's door but it bumped against the car next to him. 'Oh, for shit's sake. Why do they park so close to each other?' He crawled into the passenger seat, and exited from the other side.

People continued to curse him as each car drove away.

'Did you ever think about getting a moped?' Declan asked.

'It's too cold; besides, cars are much easier.'

'What about the bus?'

'I'd never drive one of those.'

* * *

The hospital was a large, old-fashioned brick building that looked in need of refurbishment. The outside was painted a dull, brown colour, and the windows were large and stained with a greasy substance. Flowers that had once flourished with life were now hanging over, bowing forward and lifeless.

They followed a narrow path, heading for a sign that declared, 'Psychiatric Ward. Main Entrance.'

Declan pressed the buzzer on the wall to their right and waited.

A women's voice came out of the speaker. 'Can I help you?'

Declan stood back, making sure that he and Billy could be seen, and then spoke in a muffled voice. The lady had to ask him to repeat himself twice, then she sighed and pressed the buzzer.

Declan pulled the heavy glass door towards him.

'Right, you know the plan. Let's do this.'

He held on to Billy's arm, guiding him through the doors. 'That's it, Pops. Another step. Keep going. You're nearly there.'

'Don't overact,' Billy whispered. 'They may end up keeping you here.'

A lady dressed in a brightly-coloured nurses uniform greeted them at the reception.

'That's it, another step. And another. Come on, Pops. You can do it.'

The nurse stood. 'Can I help you both?' She watched as

the young, flamboyant man stepped slowly towards her, admiring how considerate and attentive he was with the man she presumed to be his father.

'Yes, I'd like to make some enquiries about Shergar here.'

'Shergar?' The nurse looked confused for a moment. 'Oh, I get it – the racehorse. Oh, that's funny. 'I'm afraid you can't make enquiries without an appointment.'

'Please. You need to help my father. We've driven for miles. The journey was tedious. Painswick seems a world away.'

'Painswick, you say?' The nurse asked.

'That's right. Have you heard of it?'

'Of course. It's a couple of miles down the road. Look, what's your father's surname?'

'Berry. He's a brother of Ed Berry. I believe Ed stayed here a few years back.'

'I'm sorry, I can't release information like that. I have to follow protocol.'

Declan turned to Billy. 'You're going to stay here now, Pops. I think you'll like it. I say: I think you'll like it.'

'I'm not bloody deaf, you imbecile.'

The nurse sat back in her seat. 'It's not as easy as that, I'm afraid. There are rules, referrals that must be made. I'm afraid you can't just come here and expect us to take your father. Let me take some details. I can refer him to a specialist. Has he been assessed?'

'Only by me.'

Please tell me some of your father's symptoms?'

'Oh, where do I start? Aggression, that's one. Rudeness. He's always rude – blunt, coarse, insulting, ignorant.' Declan heard a muffled growl coming from where Billy stood next to him.

'How long has he been like this?' the nurse asked.

'Oh, let's see.' Declan began counting on his fingers. 'One, two – about forty years. Ever since I can remember.'

The woman looked up and blew her fringe from her face in frustration. 'OK, look. Those are not reasons to place your father in a psychiatric ward. You say he's always been this way?'

'Pretty much. I've come to the end of my tether. I've told him over and over till I'm blue in the face. He's had umpteen chances. So, here we are. He's all yours. I can visit once a month, but you'll have to pay for the taxi. I'd love one of those eight-door air-conditioned ones.'

'I don't think it's him who needs the help,' she said under her breath.

Declan knew he was irritating the nurse. It was almost time to hatch their plan. 'I'll gladly stay if he goes home. Not a problem. Do you have Sky? I'll need a telly to myself and a large room with a view of the grounds. I'd like breakfast in bed but not before 10am.'

The nurse eyed Declan. 'I'm beginning to lose my patience.'

Declan glanced at the main entrance. 'Well, have you looked under the beds? No one has come out this way.'

He jolted as Billy kicked him hard in the shin.

'Let me see what I can do.'

Declan watched as she opened the laptop.

'I'll see who your nearest doctor is. If you're concerned about your father, I may be able to get him an appointment.'

Declan peered over at her screen. He could see that she'd been updating a programme called Care Notes. A list of patients' details showed.

'I need the loo.'

'Oh, Pops. You went this morning. You can't seriously need the toilet again.'

'Quick. I'll end up going here.'

'I can't bring you in, Pops. You know me and closed spaces. I'll panic. I can't do it. I'll get stuck in there and never get out.'

'Quickly. I'm about to go here. I mean it.'

The nurse stood. 'Look, I'll take him.'

'He needs help with his trousers. You'll have to wait while he sits on the toilet. I usually do it at home, but I freak out in strange places. He also likes the door to be locked. Don't leave him in there on his own.'

'I'm well able to cope,' the nurse sniped. 'Come on then, Mr Berry, let's get you sorted.'

Declan watched as Billy and the nurse made their way to the toilet, and when the door was closed behind them, he lifted the hatch and jumped into the chair by the laptop.

He needed to find something on Ed Berry. He clicked on the 'files' folder and typed Ed's name into the search bar. Immediately, a report came up. Opening it, he was relieved to see all of his details displayed: his age, date of birth, medication, a description of his condition, and his length at the psychiatric ward. According to the records, Ed Berry had had a breakdown. He'd been admitted under section 136 of the 1983 mental health act. Ed suffered from depression and hallucinations, and was diagnosed with paranoid schizophrenia.

Declan eyed the toilet door, watching for any movement, then turned back to the laptop. He scrolled further down the screen, then stopped abruptly. He moved closer, studying the last entry.

After significant progress, Ed Berry was discharged.

Towards the bottom of the page, on the left side of the screen, the word 'Visitors' was written, under which was a list of names.

One name came up time and again. Ronnie Hathaway. He'd called here the night before Ed left. *Did Ronnie have something to do with his release? Did he pull some strings to get Ed out?*

Declan heard the toilet door unlock and saw Billy step out a few seconds later.

Billy put his thumb up.

Declan responded with a nod.

* * *

'Ed Berry stayed there, all right. I saw the records. But get this: he left before he died.'

Billy yanked the seatbelt and again, struggled with the clip. 'What do you mean?'

'Ed was discharged. He must have returned to the farmhouse and I guess he died there.'

Billy turned to Declan. 'Why would they let him leave? I don't understand.'

'That's what the records say.'

Billy rubbed the stubble on his chin. 'So, he spent a few years at the psychiatric ward after suffering a breakdown, a breakdown possibly brought on from finding bodies in the basement of the farmhouse, only to return there. I don't get it.'

'I saw Ronnie Hathaway's name too. He visited Ed before he left. I can't help but think that whatever Ronnie said that night possibly caused Ed to leave, like Ronnie was in control.'

Billy paused, digesting the information. 'I'd say Ronnie Hathaway had a great deal to do with Ed's release. But why?'

As Billy pulled out of the car park, Declan turned to face him.

'So how did it go with the nurse? Number one or two?'

'Huh? Oh, sod off. I'm embarrassed enough. Have you ever gone with someone watching you?'

'Well, no but—'

'Well, then. You wouldn't understand how flustered I got in there.'

He drove away from the hospital grounds, the car jolting as if it had springs for wheels.

Sean and Jenny drove back to the farmhouse in silence, both trying to understand what had happened at the restaurant. The words Sue had said as they'd paid the bill resonated in Sean's mind. *Lock your doors at night, keep the blinds shut and pray you don't see him.* He was stunned, and for the first time, he was scared. The fact that people didn't want to talk and Sue's words of advice worried him.

He had to protect his family. Later, when everything had settled down, he'd talk to Jenny. Maybe it was time to call a halt on the documentary and start a new project.

As they pulled onto the drive, Jenny broke the silence. 'Sean, I need to know we're safe.'

He took a deep breath and stopped the car. The pebbles crunched under the tyres, and a cloud of dust formed around them. 'We're safe, Jenny. It's not true. Any of it. Ed was my uncle. I'd know if bodies were found in the basement.'

'How? You never met him. You told me he had nothing to do with your family. How would you know anything about him or his life?'

Jenny was right. Sean knew nothing of his uncle. His mother never spoke of him, whether out of embarrassment or because they'd lost contact, he didn't know. Sean had never quizzed her on such matters. Despite the fact they'd lived fifty minutes from each other, she, nor his father, never spoke about Ed.

His dad had died a few years ago after a stroke, his second. His death had hit Sean hard, and he'd struggled to come to terms with the loss. His mother now lived alone in Oxford and Sean kept in regular contact. She'd refused to move in with them, stating that she needed her independence. She wasn't someone who tolerated people fussing over or feeling sorry for her.

He could ask his mother about Ed but he knew he'd get no answers, at least, not the ones he needed.

As he opened the front door, taking in the enormity of the place, he fought the feeling of trepidation that rose within. He was determined to make a life for himself and his family.

He looked towards the kitchen, the stairs and the box room to his right. His mind began to develop images of what might have happened here, but he had to keep telling himself they were only rumours.

Beth and Ethan were upstairs. They'd wiped the picture of the stickmen from the chalkboard, deciding it would freak their mother out if she saw it. Part of Beth hoped that her brother had done it to wind her up – he often pranked her: worms in her bed, tapping at her window with a long pole, salt in her coffee – but somehow, she knew even Ethan wouldn't go this far.

The reality seemed altogether too frightening.

24

That evening, the family were in the living room together. They all had their own private concerns.

Beth was freaked out by the stickmen Ethan had shown her on the chalkboard. She hoped it had just been him fooling around, but with the tall figure she had seen goading her in the field at the back of the garden, holding a red coat, she wasn't so sure.

Ethan was thinking about the missing woman he and his father had picked up. It had been five days – he'd kept an eye on the story – and still no one knew where Marie Nelson was. He was also concerned about what the couple had told them, of bodies being found in the farmhouse. He glared around the room and into the hallway, his stomach turning over as he imagined what may have happened there.

Sean needed to speak with Jenny. He was contemplating putting a halt to their filming. It just seemed too dangerous. People were agitated; they didn't want the past brought up again.

Jenny had her own troubles. Though she'd deleted the

footage from the basement, she was still sure she'd seen someone hiding down there last night.

Despite their internal struggles, each member of the family put a brave face on. The telly was on low, and they were sitting on the floor playing cards. Sean had a fire going. Already, it was dark outside.

'Snap.' Jenny gathered the pile of cards from the floor. 'Oh, the WIFI company are calling over to do the installation tomorrow.'

'About time. It's crazy with no phone reception here,' Beth said.

'I've told you. There's a corner of the kitchen. It seems to work there.'

'I've tried but it's pointless. You have to be lucky.'

'How do you think your mother and I survived for years as kids? No mobiles, no WIFI, four channels on the telly. We had to record our favourite songs from the radio every Sunday evening.' Beth and Ethan mouthed his sentence back at him word for word. It was a common refrain of his. He turned to Jenny. 'Can you believe these two?'

Jenny tried to hold her laughter. 'I'm so sorry, but you do say the same thing all the time.'

'I have no chance, do I? The three of you. You're unreal. Mocking me.'

As he was placing a playing card on the floor, a loud thud came from the box room. They all looked towards the hallway.

'What the hell? Sean, go see what that was.'

'I'll come, Dad. It came from the box room.' Ethan stood.

'It sounded like the basement hatch.' Sean also rose to his feet. His eyes were wild, fearful. He glanced at Jenny as she placed her arm around their daughter. 'Stay here, the two of you. Don't move.' They both nodded. 'Ethan, stay behind me.'

He moved across the wooden floor to the hallway. Ethan followed.

'Who's there?' Sean waited, though he did not expect an answer. He raised his voice louder. 'If someone is in our house, you need to leave. Now.'

He turned towards his wife and daughter, who were staring back at him, their faces flush with shock.

'You need to leave the house,' he called out again.

'Sean, Ethan, be careful.'

The two men edged along the hallway. The door to the box room was closed.

As he moved to the side of the door, he held his hand out to stop his son. 'Ethan,' he whispered. 'You open the door so I can be ready. If anyone is there, I'll jump them. You understand?'

Ethan placed a shaky hand on the door handle. The brass was cold and heavy. 'I got it. Ready?'

'On three. One. Two. Go.'

Ethan turned the handle and pushed the door hard while Sean glared around the room. The light was on. It was how they'd left it. The basement hatch was closed. Sean stared. The window further along resembled a dank pit. He wondered if someone was outside, watching them.

He turned to Ethan. 'False alarm. There's no one in here.' He stepped forward and placed his hands into the groove of the wood, straightened his back, then slightly edged the hatch upwards. The basement door was open. He crouched as Ethan moved behind him. 'I locked this earlier.'

'Are you sure?'

'Yes. Absolutely.' He could picture that morning when Billy and Declan had gone into the basement. He'd heard

Jenny coming down the stairs and had told them to come back up. He'd definitely locked the hatch.

Then they heard footsteps, pounding along the ground below. Sean and Ethan stared at each other, remaining silent, mute with fear. They waited. The footsteps stopped. It sounded as if someone had run the length of the basement floor.

'I'm going down there. Wait here.'

Ethan placed a hand on his father's chest. 'No. You're not going down there.'

Suddenly another bang came. The two men jumped. It was definitely coming from below, towards the back.

After a moment, Sean spoke. 'Ethan, I have to. Someone is down there. Stay here. I'm sure everywhere is locked, so this would be the only entry to the farmhouse. If you see anything, shout for me. I'll come straight back out.'

'Dad, please listen to me. It's not safe.'

'Wait here. I'll be back in a minute.' Sean moved into the hatch and began the slow decline. The wood creaked like an old boat. For a moment, he lost his stepping and he had to grab the handle to his side to steady himself.

'Dad, hurry up.'

He watched Ethan's face become distant, and when it became too dark to see, he removed his phone from his pocket and fumbled with the light. 'Come on. Which way around are you?' He pressed buttons, struggling to summon the torch app.

He moved forward, glaring into the darkness, his left hand held out in front, swiping the air. He stopped, listening. 'Hello? Is someone down here?'

After another bout of pressing buttons, the light came on. Sean pointed the phone to the back wall. Suddenly, he heard a noise around five yards from where he stood.

'Another rat. It's a rodent, Ethan. There's one next to me. Yuck. I think this place is infested with them.'

'OK, well, come back up. We'll deal with it tomorrow.'

But then, Sean heard another crash coming from the back of the basement. He spun, pointing the torch towards the area. A fox was scurrying by the back wall. It turned, the bushy tail moving through a hole..

He watched as the animal disappeared. He waited – what for, he was uncertain. He stood, immobile, still, realising how easy it was to get into the farmhouse. Would the next intruder leave so easily?

Come on, Sean. Get a grip. He hesitated, thinking of his family. Jenny, Beth, Ethan. He had to make their home secure. Now he thought he could hear someone outside. His mind busy, paranoid they were coming through the hole. He crouched, facing the back wall, then charged forward and crawled through the gap. His knees hurt from the rough stones, he felt claustrophobic and he struggled to breathe.

The small, narrow tunnel that led to the outside had been part of the structure the builders had created and demolished. A long piece of boarding had been placed over the hole.

It now lay on the floor.

Sean clawed his way through the tunnel, gripping on to the sides, his fingers pressing against the rough stone.

Once outside, the cold air hit him hard. He stood for a moment, brushing down his clothes, looking across the road to the fields opposite. The security light at the front of the drive had come on.

Sean quickly moved around the cars and waited in the darkness. Once he was sure no one was outside, he made his way back into the basement, keeping low, edging back through the tunnel. He could hear Ethan calling his name.

He placed the board back over the hole. Then shouted for Ethan to grab his drill, a handful of raw plugs and some screws and was astonished when Ethan returned a few minutes later with everything he'd asked for.

He secured the board to the wall, satisfied

'It seems we have a visitor. A fox has been getting into the farmhouse. I found a hole where the builders broke through that leads outside.'

Jenny and Beth were still huddled on the living room floor. Sean could see the relief on their faces. He went on to explain how it crawled out of the tunnel when it saw him and how he'd secured the basement with strong wooden boarding. 'It won't get back inside.' Sean was fearful someone had got in through the hole. Someone may have a key to the basement hatch. He was certain he'd locked it this morning after Billy and Declan had left.

He kept his fears to himself. 'I'm going to check over the house.'

'Dad, I'll check upstairs; you look down here.'

Sean started with the living room while Ethan climbed the stairs. He checked the window handles, making sure they were closed and locked. Then he moved out to the hallway and to the front door – also closed and locked. The boarding he'd fitted over the basement hole was strong but it wouldn't take much effort to break it. They'd need to be on high alert tonight.

After checking the box room, kitchen and bathroom, and after Ethan confirmed all was secure above, Sean was satisfied there were no other intruders.

Before returning to Jenny and Beth, he had a quiet word with Ethan.

'We need to keep attentive. The fox has shown how easy it is to get in here. Next time we may not be as lucky.

Keep watch but I don't want you freaking out Mum and Beth.'

'Got it. I understand.'

Sean placed his hand on his son's shoulder. 'I love you, mate. Thanks.'

'Love you too, Dad.'

Back in the living room, the fire was smouldering, the coals emitting a bright orange glow. Playing cards were scattered on the wooden floor.

Jenny and Beth sat side by side; their expressions riddled with concern.

'Is the house empty, Dad? What if someone's hiding?'

Sean crouched. 'Beth, no one is here. Ethan and I have checked everywhere.'

Jenny stood and rubbed the knuckles of her right hand against her forehead to release the stress. 'Anyone fancy a sandwich? Beth, are you hungry? Ethan?'

They both nodded.

'I'll help. Beth, Ethan, stay here – oh, and don't open any windows.'

Sean followed Jenny into the kitchen, where she turned and threw her arms around him. It was all getting on top of her. She held him tight, her quivering body almost melting in his arms.

'Are you certain we're alone?' She kept her voice low and gazed past him, first eyeing the long, dark hallway, then the front door. She squeezed him harder, sensing his short, sharp breaths.

Sean gazed into her eyes. How he wanted to reassure her, protect her from all this. He needed to be confident, to bury any negativity. The unlocked basement still concerned him. 'I won't let anything happen to us. We'll make this place a wonderful home, somewhere to be proud of, you hear me? Tomorrow, I'll get the locks changed and enquire about a home security—'

'Dad!' Beth's shout came from the living room.

As he rushed back to them, he heard Ethan reassuring his sister.

'There's no one there, Beth.'

When he entered the room, Ethan was standing by the window, his hands cupped together, his face pressed against the glass.

'I heard something. I swear. There was a noise from outside.'

'What happened?' He moved to his daughter.

'I was talking with Ethan. Then I heard a thump, like a bin falling over.'

Sean moved back into the hallway. He inspected the front door.

'What's happened, Sean?' Jenny's voice, echoing from the kitchen, startled him.

'Oh, nothing. I think Beth is trying to spook her brother.' He grabbed the keys from the rack and slowly twisted the lock. He listened for the clunk, then eased the door towards him.

Outside, the road was empty. The security light was off. Sean moved towards it. He felt faint as he reached forward, realising the bulb had been removed.

Shit, Beth was right. Someone has been here.

He walked back to the front of the farmhouse and looked through the living room window. The lights were off ,and from where he stood, he couldn't see inside. Only the glow from the fire was visible.

'Dad, is everything OK?' Ethan called from the front door.

'I don't know. Go back inside to your mum and sister.'

Next, Sean moved around the side of the farmhouse and pushed down the latch on the door that led to the garden. Although it was dark, he could sense the vast space around him. The wind churned, groaning in his ears, the cold pressing against his face, his skin wet from the light drizzle.

Sean stood at the back of the farmhouse. He could see Jenny in the kitchen, a loaf of bread in her hand, a few slices already piled on a plate. She placed the bread on the counter and reached into the fridge for the butter. Then she opened the cutlery drawer. *How exposed we are.* He glanced to the first floor. The lights were also out. The farmhouse was just a silhouette, its contours hidden, shaded.

He stood for a moment, immersed in the cold. This was their home. A fresh start. The beginning of a new—

The rustle of bushes sounded to his left. A brief flicker, a slight stirring noise, as if someone was trying to stay hidden.

He spun around, expecting to see his son, but saw no one.

'Ethan, is that you?'

But he could see him in the kitchen, biting into a sandwich.

Sean was terrified. He edged to his left, taking tiny sideward steps, his heart racing, his legs awkward.

'Who's there? Leave us alone, you hear?'

A shadow moved towards him from the bleakness. Sean could sense it. He backed away, his eyes fixed on the area where he'd heard the noise. He hesitated, unsure which way to turn. He ran around the side of the house, the sound of grass being trampled ringing from behind him, moving faster. Someone was following him. He grabbed the garden gate, rushed through and closed it behind him. A darting shiver pulsed through his body.

When he reached the front of the house, he listened for the sounds of being followed, but there were none. He stopped, bent over, catching his breath. The lights were still off in the living room, the front door still open.

He was sure someone was outside, but he knew he couldn't say anything to his family. He needed to get into the farmhouse and keep it locked.

As he paused on the doorstep, he was certain he saw a shadow drift out onto the road. He was too frightened to follow.

As he went to step through the front door, he heard the sound of a vehicle door closing.

He had to take a look.

When he reached the edge of the drive, he saw the lights of a truck parked further along the road. The engine started, a sharp, fiery rasp that pierced through the stillness of the night.

He stood in disbelief as memories from the other night flooded his mind. Fear drenched his body as he saw the truck pull away, possibly the same truck they'd seen a few nights ago at Greyshott Hall.

* * *

It was late Sunday evening. Billy and Declan had returned to Billy's son's house after visiting the psychiatric ward. They'd had a bite to eat and decided to take a drive to the Freemans' place.

On arriving, they saw a black truck parked along the road, pulled tight into the ditch a hundred yards from the farmhouse. Billy hit the brakes, causing them both to jolt forward, then attempted to reverse behind the truck.

'Do I need to get out again?'

'I have it under control.'

'If you're sure, Captain. Anyway, your parking always gives me good exercise. I enjoy the walk to the kerb.'

Billy parked up and turned sharply, once again finding himself entangled in the seatbelt. 'For shit's sake. Keep your observations to yourself.' Billy eventually released the belt and opened the car door.

He walked towards the truck.

'The engine's warm. It hasn't been here for long. It seems the Freemans have a visitor.' Billy moved back to his son's car and stood by the driver's door. 'I don't have a good feeling about this. Sean mentioned something about being pursued by a man in a black truck. The Freemans may be in trouble.'

Declan watched ahead. He saw a figure move onto the road. 'Someone is coming out.'

The truck lights blinked and a man got into the front seat. A moment later the truck pulled away.

'Right, buckle up. We're going to follow him?' Billy got back into the car. He jabbed for the button to start it, poking the dashboard, flicking the light switch. The windscreen wipers creaked and then the radio came on. 'For shit's sake. What a piece of crap.'

Declan leant forward, grinning to himself, then reminded him he needed to place his foot on the brake. Billy followed the instructions and Declan jabbed the button to start the car. 'You have to learn to touch it in the right places.'

'I'll touch you in a minute with my fist. Are you strapped in?'

Declan plucked the seatbelt out from his waist, showing he was buckled up. 'Ladies and gentlemen, this is your captain speaking. We're clear for take-off. Buckle up, relax and have a pleasant journey. Your fears are warranted, but I can assure you all the captain here is—'

Declan jolted forward as Billy jammed his foot on the accelerator, then the brake.

'I'm surprised the airbags aren't inflated.'

Billy turned the radio on full blast to cut out the din.

* * *

The radio was off and their eyes were glued to the truck in front. They stayed a safe distance so as not to be seen. It was gone 9pm, the roads were deserted and it seemed that the truck driver was not suspicious. Even so, Billy knew that if he pulled away, they would lose him instantly.

As he drove, an air of apprehension smothering them, Billy summed up their thinking. 'If it's Ronnie driving, as we think, we need to figure out why he's calling to the farm-house. Something is going on with him.'

'Was he sussing the place out? There's a reason he's trying to get in there. Something must be hidden inside.'

Billy hesitated before answering. 'You have a point. So, what are you thinking?'

'I'm thinking it's the item we found in the wall.' He turned to Billy. 'The builders were smashing up the base-ment before the Freemans moved in. They exposed part of the underground section. What if – I'm thinking out loud here – what if whatever is hidden down there has something to do with Ronnie? Hence him going to see Ed at the hospital?'

'Are you sure Ronnie Hathaway visited Ed Berry?'

'One hundred per cent. I saw his name on the computer. It seems that whatever Ronnie wanted, it caused Ed Berry to leave the psychiatric ward and die alone in the farmhouse.'

'Then we need to find out why.'

They drove along the narrow country lanes for another ten minutes, watching the truck ease around bends, swerving to avoid the gaping potholes and accelerating on the long, open stretches of road.

Then, on the outskirts of Painswick, it swung a left. Billy's reflexes weren't quick enough and he passed the turning.

'We're going to lose him. Back up.'

He hit the brakes, pushed the gearstick into reverse and slowly moved the car backwards. The truck was gone.

'For shit's sake.'

'I think we've lost him.'

'I know where Ronnie lives,' Billy announced. 'It's not far from here. Let's check the place out.'

'The driver is on to us. It's not safe, Billy.'

That's why you're going to keep watch from the street. I'll get inside.'

* * *

Five minutes later, Billy pulled into a side road and parked, mounting the kerb. 'Piece of cake.' He gestured to a house at the end of the street. 'That's his place. The last one on the left. Call me if you see the truck.'

'Billy, I can go instead. It may not be safe.'

'You'll probably burn the house down. Just wait here. I'll be fine.'

Declan watched as Billy walked towards the house. He was feeling nervous. Ronnie may be dangerous. If it was him in the truck, he would have seen them following. He would know they were on to him.

The street was a dead end; there was nowhere for them to go.

Billy opened the small metal gate that stood in front of the large, semi-detached house. He walked along the path and peered through the glass of the front door. It didn't seem like anyone was inside. He moved down the narrow alleyway that led to the back of the house, until he reached a tall, wooden gate that secured the back garden. He twisted the handle but it was locked. He looked up to the dark windows. The curtains were open but no lights were on.

He moved back to the front and pressed his face against the glass again.

'Can I help you?'

Billy turned to the side and saw an elderly lady standing at her front door. She was wearing a white blouse and black skirt, with an apron tied around her waist.

'Yes, sorry. I'm Ronnie's brother. We haven't spoken for a while. Is he inside?'

'Oh no. He's gone away for a while. I think he went to Spain or Madrid. One of the two.'

Billy didn't bother correcting her. 'How long has he been gone?'

'I'd say a few months. Terrible thing what happened to his wife. Cancer. She was brave. Fought it all the way.'

'It's certainly a horrible disease. How do you know he's gone?'

'WhatsApp.'

He spoke louder. 'I said: how do you know he's gone?'

'Oh, you are daft.' The lady held her phone up to his face. 'He put it on WhatsApp. We have neighbourhood watch. Though I didn't think he'd be gone this long. But he's retired. He's stepped down from his duties, so why not? Maybe he's finding himself.'

'Finding himself indeed. He just needs a mirror. Do you have a key? I need the loo.'

'I do somewhere. I keep it just in case he gets locked out. Wait there a second.' The woman returned with two keys, a Chubb and a Yale. She instructed him on where they went.

'I do know how to open a door.' Billy used the Chubb first. The lock clunked loudly. Then he put the yale key in and twisted.

'That's it. Push it gently, dear.'

'Oh, for shit's sake. You can go now. I'll drop the key back when I've finished.'

The woman grabbed his arm. 'Have a look in there, would you? There's been a terrible smell. I've got it many times. Maybe it's the drains. I'd appreciate it if you check.'

Billy smiled – it was the excuse he needed in case the police got involved.

He moved quickly along the downstairs hall and opened the door on his left, which he discovered led to the living room. He needed to find something, anything on this guy.

There was a small telly in the corner, a black sofa to his left, pressed against the wall, and a small circular table, placed centrally, with magazines and paperwork neatly stacked atop it, pressed together in an orderly structure. A bookshelf spread out across the back wall, each book in alphabetical order by author, held tight against each other like a jigsaw puzzle. The house was immaculate; nothing seemed out of place.

Billy backed out of the living room and moved along the hall to the kitchen. Here, the decor was retro and vintage. Old-style pictures were hanging on the back walls, one of the Bisto gravy kids, another featuring the Ovaltine drink. Others displayed machinery and forms of transport from many years ago.

He opened the back door, and a security light blinked on, lighting the small garden. He glimpsed a shed towards the back, and something within him knew that's where he needed to check. He stood for a moment, turned around, watching the front door, then made his way towards it.

* * *

Sean and his family sat in the kitchen, eating the last of the sandwiches Jenny had made. Sean had kept silent regarding the figure he'd spotted racing across the lawn. He'd stood by the front door, watching in agitation as the truck passed the house, his eyes following the vehicle until the noise faded. He'd then moved into the hallway, about to close the front door, when he heard another vehicle approach. Bursting with anticipation, he'd watched as the window wound down and a familiar voice called to him.

Billy asked him about their visitor and when Sean informed them that no one had called over, Billy had decided to follow the truck. As Sean watched the sports car jump along the road, he thought about what Billy had said. He didn't have time to question him. They seemed in a hurry.

Now, he sat with his family. Ethan was holding his stomach, complaining he'd eaten too much and was struggling with the carb overload. Beth was moaning that they needed jam as she hated bread without it. And Jenny was washing the plates in the sink.

Sean joined her. She smiled and handed him a plate, running her finger along the middle to highlight the squeak, meaning that in her terms, it was washed correctly.

Once they were finished, he addressed the room.

'Shall we call it a night?' He needed his family upstairs, together, where it was safe.

'Yeah, but I'm bringing my mattress into your room. I'm not sleeping on my own,' Beth said.

Ethan peered down the hallway towards the box room. 'Sounds like a plan.'

Jenny woke with a jerk. The alarm clock showed it was 11.59pm. She scanned the bedroom, momentarily forgetting her surroundings. She pawed at the bedside table and grabbed her phone so she could light the room.

She looked at Sean, who was lying on his side, the blanket pulled up over his shoulders, then down at Beth and Ethan, who were lying top and tails on the mattress in the middle of the floor.

The house was silent, and her mind raced with thoughts about the events of the last twenty-four hours. Tomorrow would be the start of a new day, she told herself. Things would seem easier and less strenuous. They'd just had a lot to deal with and needed to get used to their surroundings.

She eased the blanket back and made her way out of the room, down the hall and to the toilet. When she was finished, she used the flush, though regretted it instantly for the noise it caused.

She washed her hands, flicking the water from her fingers and made a mental note to unpack the towels, then pulled back the lock and pushed the door away. The action suddenly sent her mind to the box room, the rats, the figure in the corner of the basement, standing, watching her. She felt her chest tighten as it fought to catch a breath.

She moved out to the hallway, and then, from nowhere, a voice whispered her name.

'Jenny.'

She spun to the side, now facing away from their bedroom, the heels of her feet burning on the wooden floor.

'Jenny.'

She let out a loud, gurgling scream. She had to reach her family, get away from the voice. She urged her body to move, but like a nightmare, it didn't budge. She struggled to place one leg in front of the other, and they both gave way, causing her to drop to her knees.

She sensed its presence, heavy breaths, advancing, slowly propelling itself along the upstairs hallway. The hairs on her neck stood as the voice surrounded her, was almost upon her, seeping into her skin.

'Jenny.'

A door opened and she saw Sean come running out of the bedroom.

'What happened? Jenny?' He leant forward and held her, feeling her quivering body, a limp wreck. 'You're having a nightmare or sleepwalking. It's OK. I'm here. You're safe.' Sean crouched, easing both hands under her arms and slowly lifted her to her feet.

He made his way to the bedroom, pleased to see Beth and Ethan still asleep.

He laid her on the bed and gently rubbed her face, then ran his fingers through her hair. He looked down at the cute mole on her left cheek that rose when she laughed, the soft lines under her eyes and her clear, pale skin.

He couldn't bear to think of life without her. Whatever was going on in this farmhouse, he knew he had to protect his family.

He held Jenny until she fell asleep in his arms.

* * *

Billy found the shed locked. He needed to be quick. Concern was setting in. The next door neighbour may message the other residents. He turned, and looked over at the garden. The kitchen light was off. He hoped it stayed that way.

The shed was dark and the overcast sky provided no aid. He stepped back, again glancing over his shoulder. He reached to the ground, scanned the darkness and found a heavy stone. He began to pound it against the lock. A moment later, the screws worked loose from the wood and the frame dropped.

He opened the shed door, stepped inside and felt the wall for a switch. He needed light. Once the inside was visible, he moved to the centre of the room. There were pictures everywhere – old black and white photos he presumed were Ronnie's parents; another with a young boy holding hands with the same people; others showed Ronnie, out with friends. The pictures went back thirty years – he could tell by the date imprinted on the bottom. The old photos were in bad condition and stained, but there were more recent photos, taken in colour, at award ceremonies and speeches. He moved closer, eying more pictures until he spotted a box on a shelf.

Keeping an eye on the kitchen, he grabbed the box, blew dust from the top, which caused him to sneeze, and removed the lid. Billy took out the contents and held them under the light. He flicked through newspaper articles, pictures of local buildings and information about new developments and projects happening in Painswick. After a few minutes of inspection, he placed them back in the box and put it on the shelf.

He moved towards a table in the corner. He pulled on the drawer, hoping it would open, but it was locked with a padlock. He grabbed the stone again and began to smash the lock. Due to its position, Billy hit the table a few times and he worried the crashing noise would draw attention, but a minute later, he'd got it open. The lock collapsed onto the floor as did the drawer handle. He pulled the drawer open and found more newspaper clippings.

Here, Ronnie was pictured with another man. The headline read, 'Fund for War Heroes.'

The article explained how Ronnie had started a charity to help victims of war. In this picture, Ronnie and the man held a large cheque for thousands of pounds, the man holding one side, with Ronnie on the other.

The person receiving the vast sum of money was Ed Berry.

Billy read on. Apparently Ronnie had taken Ed under his wing, making him his protege. He'd found him lost and destitute, and he wanted to show how Painswick and the larger area looked after their war veterans.

Yeah, win voters, more like.

With the story that Ronnie himself had found Ed Berry living on the street, the residents had even raised enough money to buy him the old farmhouse.

Ed Berry had many issues. He suffered delusions and paranoia, and claimed he had no memory of his previous life. When questioned, he stated he had no recollection of his past.

It seemed that Ed Berry had become a local hero, and the people of Painswick had pulled together to help him.

Billy tipped the contents onto the table.

He separated the paper clips and photos.

He held one photo in the air, his legs suddenly feeling weak. His heart began to pound.

The picture showed a girl lying on the floor, face down, her head turned to the side. Her hands and legs were strapped with rope.

Billy felt a thump on the side of his face and fell to the ground.

* * *

The man stood over Billy Huxton, holding the rock in one hand and a phone torch in the other. He looked to the corner table and saw the broken lock, the drawer open and the photo of the girl.

His body was trembling. He realised they were moving in on him. He couldn't let that happen. He refused to be caught. It couldn't end here, like this. He called the shots and said when it finished. He still had so much life in him. So much still to achieve. The feeling was too great for it to stop.

He gripped the stone, watching as the man began to regain consciousness.

Billy held his head in his hands, then looked up.

As the man held the stone high in the air, he heard a voice.

'Billy, where are you? Is everything OK?'

He dropped the stone on the floor. A man was walking through the house, and a light was shining from the hallway. He had to go. It was too dangerous being here. But he'd be back.

As the light disappeared into the living room, he squeezed through a broken railing in the fence and ran into the park behind the house.

* * *

'Billy! Christ, what happened?' Declan was pleased to see the man conscious. His head was cut and as he sat on the floor, he was unsteady.

'What do you think? I was jumped?' Billy turned around.

The photo was gone.

25

Monday.

The following morning, Billy and Declan rose early. A call from a mechanic came at 7.30am, informing Billy he'd grab Declan's car from the farmhouse within the next half-hour. For this, he'd suffered an ear-bashing from Billy.

The mechanic finished the call with, 'Whatever, mate,' and hung up.

Billy had a thumping headache from where he'd been bashed in the head. He swallowed a couple of painkillers when he got home last night and two more this morning with a glass of water. After leaving Ronnie's house, he was adamant that he'd drive but after stumbling up the street and falling against the Mazda, he let Declan take the wheel. He was shocked when they'd made it home in one piece.

Billy had not given Ronnie's keys back to the neighbour. With the attack and all, he'd completely forgotten. He'd wanted to call the police, but he did enter the house without permission, and with the photo that he'd found there, he was stumped.

They needed to speak with Sean and let him know their findings. It was obvious Ronnie Hathaway was extremely dangerous.

'So how do we approach this?' Declan asked as they pulled up outside the farmhouse. 'Sean wants his family kept out of it. It's understandable. You saw the way he reacted yesterday morning. He's nervous.'

'Wouldn't you be? But if the family is at risk, they need to know.'

They approached the front door and Billy tapped the knocker against the thick wood. A moment later, Sean answered.

'Hey, do you two ever sleep?' Sean glanced at his wrist-watch, a subtle reminder of how early it was. He was wearing a white bathrobe and proceeded to tighten the belt. 'Sorry, I've just got out of the shower.'

He saw the cut above Billy's eye but decided not to ask anything.

Billy and Declan saw Jenny coming down the stairs, awkwardly stepping over the boards. 'Come in! It's good to see you. I was about to make a pot of coffee.' After the episode last night, with someone calling her name, she was glad of the company. She saw the cut. 'Ouch. That looks nasty.'

'That's Billy Huxton for you. He's harmless. His bark is worse than his bite.'

Ignoring Declan, Billy spoke. 'I need to chat with you both. It's quite urgent.'

They followed Jenny into the kitchen.

Sean pulled out a chair and gestured for them to sit. 'What's happened?'

Jenny began to fill the kettle with water. She looked tense and her eyebrows were knotted into a scowl. 'Is everything OK?'

Sean interrupted. 'Look.' He turned to his wife. 'I didn't say anything as I didn't want to worry you.'

She moved to the table. 'What's happened?'

Sean proceeded to explain the full events of the previous night, the shadow he'd seen moving along the front lawn and the truck that resembled the one the pursuer had had at Greyshott Hall. Billy remained silent. He didn't want to say anything out of place.

When Sean had finished, Jenny sat open-mouthed, her eyes wide and fearsome.

'For Christ's sake, Sean. You need to tell me these things. I need to know. What is it with you?'

He took her hand, feeling her cold skin, and held it tight. 'I'm sorry. I didn't want to worry you.'

Billy picked up where Sean had left off. 'We followed the truck, but we lost it. I'm convinced it was Ronnie Hathaway so we went to his house. In the shed, I found something, a picture.'

Sean leant forward. 'Of what?'

'A woman tied up, lying on the floor. It looked like she was in your basement.'

The kettle boiled, and Jenny moved over to the side to prepare the drinks. Panic was rising through her body, and she was glad of the distraction. She began spooning coffee into the mugs, her hand trembling. She spilt the contents onto the sideboard. Regaining composure, she placed her hands beside the kettle and breathed deeply, struggling to control her emotions. Her face began to flush. Once the head rush had passed, she poured the hot water in and placed the mugs on the table. 'Are you sure it was our basement?' She directed the question at all three men. 'Why on earth would he have a picture of a woman tied up?'

'We've reason to believe Ronnie Hathaway is looking for something in your home, something that may have been hidden and needs to stay there.'

Jenny stirred her drink. 'I don't get it. Why the hell would he start looking now? The farmhouse has been vacant for months.'

Billy looked at Sean. 'Before Ed Berry died, he'd had minor building works done. I think you said a false wall had been built. And your builders knocked part of the basement wall out.'

'That's right. We wanted a bigger space for storage. They knocked part of the wall through before they scarpered.' Sean explained how the builders had left and were now uncontactable. 'I think we'll need to add a lintel down there too. The last thing Mario said was his concern about the strength of the basement ceiling.'

'Look, I think the builders exposed something that was supposed to remain buried. We know Ed and Ronnie were close. I saw them in pictures together last night. I believe that's why Ronnie Hathaway was calling over here, trying to gain access, to find whatever it is that's hidden. I strongly believe the building works have exposed a secret. And I think your uncle was involved. Is it possible to take another look down there?'

Jenny sipped her coffee. 'By all means. Be our guest.'

Sean was irritated. He stood and began to pace, listening for sounds of Beth and Ethan upstairs. He couldn't have them overhearing this conversation. He thought about what had happened at Greyshott Hall again, the attempt on their life, the way the truck driver had tried to ram them off the road. It was all beginning to slot together. Was this the reason for the attempt on their life? Had Ronnie Hathaway been that desperate to stop them moving into the farmhouse, worried about being exposed? Could Ronnie be responsible for the rumours?

'How is my uncle involved?'

Billy took a deep breath. Now wasn't the time to hold back. 'I knew Ronnie. He was a vindictive, untrustworthy, deceitful old bastard.' He looked around as everyone stared at him with open mouths.

'Why don't you say what you really mean, Billy? Don't hold back.' Declan quipped.

Billy went on to explain how important Ronnie was, how he became an MP, his exceptional ego and how he interfered in everyone's business. He told them of the time his daughter went missing, how Ronnie had told him to back off and how when he called around to the farmhouse for help, he got nothing but curtain twitching and Ed hiding.

He finished with the accusations and the police searching the basement.

Billy sat back. He removed a handkerchief from his jacket pocket and wiped the tears from his eyes. 'You won't like what I have to say, but I'll say it anyway. Ronnie turned his back on me when I needed him most. He knew what I was going through, what my beautiful wife had to suffer and endure, the pain, the heartache. He advised me to stop searching for my Katie, to give it up. To back off.' Looking around, he could see the pity in everyone's faces. The atmosphere was tense. 'Ed spoke of a person watching him. He believed it to the point he was sectioned, locked away in a mental institution. It drove him crazy. Ronnie Hath-away visited him there, and whatever was said, it was enough to bring Ed back here to live out the remainder of his days.'

Sean and Jenny sat in silence, watching as Billy spoke.

'So Ed returned here? I don't understand. Why come back to the farmhouse? I believed he died in a mental insti-tution.' Sean was stunned. He saw the frustration on Billy's face. Sorry, I'm trying to comprehend what you're saying. Please, continue.'

Can you imagine how terrified he must have been? A tortured soul, petrified, returning to his hell on earth. His worst nightmare. Ed Berry came back for a reason, and I believe Ronnie Hathaway had a significant part to play in this. For many years, people believed Ed Berry found bodies in the basement of this place.'

At this, Jenny gasped.

'I think Ronnie Hathaway was involved. Maybe Ed called on his friend to help. Maybe they hid the bodies, kept quiet about it. As I said, he was an MP. Something like that couldn't get out. It would have destroyed his reputation. Can you imagine? Families wanting to know where their missing loved ones had gone, wanting answers about the fate of their daughters, the possibility of finally being able to lay them to rest, to bury them with dignity and respect? Ed and Ronnie could have given closure to the families and the atrocities that happened in Painswick. But they chose to cover it up to save face. That's what I believe.'

Everyone was shocked by Billy's allegations. Sean, Jenny and Declan sat still, absorbing what they'd heard.

Sean broke the silence. 'Look, we need answers, and so do you. Anything you need to do, please feel free. We'll help any way we can.'

Jenny nodded. She reached forward and held Billy's trembling hands.

A couple of minutes later, they'd opened the hatch once more, and armed with a hammer, chisel and a torch that Sean had grabbed from the shed, Billy was making his way down the wooden steps. Declan followed close behind.

When they reached the basement floor, Billy turned on the torch and tapped one end to make it brighter. 'OK, it may be nothing, in which case, we're back at square one. Do you think you can reach whatever is hidden in the wall?'

'I think so. The cement is loose. Have faith, Captain.'

They moved towards the back of the room, observing the wood Sean had placed over the hole that led outside.

'OK, do your best. I'm counting on you.'

'I'm not an abacus. Hold the torch still.' Declan began to knock the wall with the hammer and chisel. The cement dropped like dust. He chiselled for over half an hour.

'Good lad, Declan. That's it. It's coming. It's coming.'

'Christ, I feel like a mother in labour. Let me concentrate.' Declan pressed his body against the wall, pushing his left hand into the crack. The stones tore at his skin. His clothes were wet and his face was dirty. 'Almost there. Keep the light shining this way. I've nearly got it.'

His hands touched the object. He gripped it with the thumb and forefinger of his right hand and edged it out.

'Well done. Now, keep a hold of it, Declan. Easy does it.'

Declan slowly moved his hand out. He was bleeding. Scratch marks now decorated his forearm. 'Bloody hell. The things I do. I want sick pay if this goes septic.'

In his hand, he held a memory stick.

Sean and Jenny both grabbed Billy when he emerged,

helping him out. When Declan followed, they did the same with him.

'How did it go? Any luck? Was there something there?'

Declan held the memory stick in the air as if it was The Holy Grail, just at the same time they heard a door opening above them.

'Shit. It's one of the kids.' Sean was evidently disappointed that they couldn't go and see what was on the stick immediately. 'Sorry guys, we need to call a wrap on this.' He turned around, facing the stairs. 'Beth. Good morning, lovely. How did you sleep?'

Beth scanned their faces: her mother, Declan, Billy and then back to her father. 'Fine, thank you. What's going on?'

Billy had already grabbed the memory stick and put it in his jacket pocket.

'Nothing. The guys are just sorting out the details of the car, is all. There's a mechanic calling over—'

The knocker thumping against the front door caused them all to jump.

Saved by the bell.

Jenny opened the door and Billy and Sean followed the mechanic out. Sean pulled the belt tighter around his bathrobe, worried it may open while he stood on the drive.

'Where's your brother?' Jenny questioned.

'Need you ask?'

A few minutes later, the broken-down car was loaded onto a truck.

Billy turned, thanking Sean and Jenny for the parking space. He tapped his jacket pocket. 'We'll be in touch.'

. . .

Not long later, Billy and Declan were back at his son's house. The tension was rife, both men anxious as to what they would find.

'What do you think it will show?'

'There's only one way to find out.' Billy opened the door and moved into the living room. He crouched down by the telly and proceeded to press buttons. The lights came on, and again, Billy pressed more buttons.

'What are you doing?'

'Waiting for this contraption to open.'

'It's not an envelope. Place the stick into the side.'

Billy did as Declan instructed, fishing for the slot.

Once it was in place, Declan pressed a few buttons with the remote control. A picture formed on the screen.

'I've been away from this modern technology for a while, you know.' Billy sat beside him.

Declan grabbed the remote control from the coffee table and pressed the play button.

A man appeared in a darkened room, and it looked like he was holding a camcorder, pointing it towards his face.

26

Billy and Declan sat in the living room, watching the video on the memory stick – a guy perched alone on a small wooden stool, the camcorder pointing at his face.

'I don't have long. I need to explain why I'm here, talking into a camcorder. I need to clarify what's happened recently.'

Sweat was dripping down his forehead, and his eyes were wild and startled. His demeanour was nervous, his voice raspy, as if he was struggling to talk. He darted a look behind him, as if someone was going to walk in at any moment. He leant forward, and you could hear the terror in his voice. He fought to hold the camcorder still as it shook in both hands.

'I'm going to make a confession. Something I'm ashamed of. Really ashamed. Don't judge me. Don't think any less of me and don't ridicule me. I'm Ed Berry, and I'm in the basement of my farmhouse on Gallows Lane on the outskirts of Painswick. OK, here goes.

'You'll have heard the rumours of the missing women,

the pain and anguish brought to the people here, the broken families who are grieving and in need of answers.

'I left the farmhouse a few years ago. The reason for my actions, I'm ashamed to say, is that I found a body, here – where I'm sitting now in my basement, in fact. A woman, mutilated, her body ripped apart and left like a rag doll. I've never seen anything like it – it's something from your worst nightmare. I recognised her face. Chloe Madden.

'I freaked out. I'm not proud to say it, but I panicked. I locked the basement and refused to ever come down here again. I left the body to rot. Over the next few days and weeks, the smell became unbearable. It seeped through the floorboards, the stench getting worse every day.

'It became unable to function. See, I'm a sick man. I've had therapy most of my life. I take medication, but some-times I forget. That's when I'm at my worst. I became para-noid, smelling the rotten copse everywhere: on my clothes, my hair, in the hallway and in my bedroom. But I left her there. I panicked. You know, in my condition I shouldn't have had to deal with that. It wasn't my responsibility. I'm a war veteran – local hero, if you will. The people of Painswick have done so much for me. My name would be tarnished. Imagine what would happen if people found out. They'd say I did it. I'm guilty. A judge would throw the book at me. I'd rot in the cell for the rest of my days. "Ed Berry? Yes, he's responsible for the women who are missing. That's him. Hang the fucker." Mr Bury Man, that's the nickname they would have used. That's what people would have called me. So, I left her there, decaying, wasting away under the farmhouse.

'I'm unsure of the next piece of the story. I'm struggling with the facts. I need to get it straight, place the puzzle together properly. My name is in jeopardy here, so bear with me.

'Not long after I found the body, I began hearing things, only slight at first. Footsteps walking along the hall as I sat watching TV. Shadows sweeping the walls. The sound of breathing in the distance. It happened as I slept too. I'd flick the light off, get under the blanket and I'd hear noises. I began to get paranoid. I saw a face at the window – many times. I'd be cooking in the kitchen and I'd see the door handle move downwards.

'First, I thought the place was haunted, from the soul drifting up from the woman buried deep below. But it couldn't be. Because the face I kept seeing was of a man, watching me, peering in, staring.

'I had a breakdown. I became delusional. Not only was I seeing this person more but I believed the ghost of the woman in the basement was trying to kill me.

'I ran to the village. I think I screamed as I fled down the dark country road. When I reached Painswick, someone called an ambulance. I was out of my mind, unable to talk, function or think for myself. They sectioned me, sedated me. I was lost, alone.

'As the days passed, I watched the door, fearful the body had been found at the farmhouse.

'But no one came.

'No one knew she was there.

'The few years I stayed there, I never stopped thinking about her. What if someone noticed the smell? What if someone found out?

'I discovered her and did nothing about it. It's as bad as killing her myself. When it became too much, I rang the only person I trusted. Ronnie Hathaway. My oldest friend. I hadn't seen him for a while. His wife was ill and he was caring for her. Anyway – fuck it, I thought – I waited until I was being released from the ward and I called him. I told him to meet me at the farmhouse.

'I remember when I walked through the front door – that rancid, dank stickiness in the air. There were flies, everywhere, dead on the floor, the windowsills. My boots crunched as I walked through the hallway.

'I rang Ronnie Hathaway again. He came over a couple of hours later, and I explained what I'd found in the basement, how I'd panicked and left the body there to rot. He looked at me in disbelief, as if he never knew me at all. His face was full of horror at what I'd done. The first thing he did was take a look in the basement. When he returned, he vomited all over the floor. He was anxious, concerned about what was down there and he kept questioning me – asking why I hadn't done something about it. He compared me to a hit and run driver – I was cowardly. I knew he was right. What I'd done was unforgivable. But I had my name to preserve.

'Ronnie ran out of the house without saying another word. I thought he'd gone, legged it, but he returned half an hour later with some large industrial bags. We wrapped them around the girl's skeleton and carried her out. Then we buried her in woodland nearby.

Afterwards, Ronnie grabbed hold of me. He shook me and told me never to mention it to anyone, to never, ever, discuss it as long as I lived.

'I understood. Of course I did. What Ronnie and I had done was criminal, the lowest of the low, but I was selfish. All I cared about was the reputation I'd built and what the people of Painswick thought of me.

'A couple of days passed. I didn't hear from Ronnie. Then, a few days after, he called me, asking for money to help his wife. She was dying and cash was tight – private care was excruciatingly expensive. He'd raised thousands for me and he wanted a favour. I helped him out, but he kept coming back, asking for more until I had to refuse. He told me that if I didn't give him everything I had, he'd go to the police and tell them what we'd done, how we'd found a woman and buried her. I couldn't let that happen. It would destroy me. The people of Painswick loved me, respected me. I was like an adopted son to them.

'So, the next time he called, I refused outright. I told him I couldn't give him any more money. I told him I'd blame everything on him. I'd use my contacts and they would make it seem like Ronnie had found the body. He didn't like it. He said he'd come after me. He'd end me. That's the long and short of it. Ronnie Hathaway was blackmailing me.

'I've just heard his truck pull up to the farmhouse. I don't have much time. If you're watching this, you'll now understand what's happened. You know the outcome. I hope this recording is found while Ronnie is still alive. He must get the justice he deserves.

'The person responsible for murdering these women is still out there. They call him Creeper. The body I found in the basement is testimony to what he will do. I only hope the others are found and given the burials they deserve. Their families deserve closure.

'I'm going to finish this now. I just heard the front door being slammed open, which means Ronnie is inside my house. I can hear him above, traipsing along the floorboards. I could escape through the basement, through the small hole, but he'd shoot me like a dog on the street. I'd rather die with dignity, here in the farmhouse – my home. So, while there's time, I'm putting this recording onto an SD card and leaving it in the wall. I hope you find it. I'll drop the camcorder in the pit; there's a gaping hole that runs deep right where I'm sat. That way he won't know I've made this recording.

'If you're watching this, I'm Ed Berry, and I found a dead woman in my basement. Ronnie Hathaway helped me to get rid of her. Now, he's going to kill me.

'This is my confession and my account of what happened.

'Ronnie needs to pay for the crime he's about to commit.

'Do me a favour, if you're watching this, show someone.

'I'm going now. I need to hide this recording.

'But please. Ronnie Hathaway is going to kill me.

'He needs to pay.'

Declan turned to Billy. 'Well, that was unsettling. It said light-hearted romance on the cover.'

Billy stood. 'Chloe Madden was the first girl to go missing. I know her family well. Maybe it was her. Or it could be.' Billy stopped for a moment. 'This is devastating.' Tears began to form in his eyes. He dabbed at them with a handkerchief.

'Billy, it doesn't mean Katie is—'

'We need to go to the farmhouse. Sean and Jenny need to see this before a decision is made. Are you ready?'

Declan placed a hand on his shoulder. 'Let's go.'

* * *

It was almost 11am, and Billy and Declan were standing in the hallway of the farmhouse. As usual, Billy was dressed impeccably in a white shirt, a smart jacket and trousers. His grey hair was combed back and held like glue. His grey goatee beard glistened. By contrast, Declan was wearing jeans and a casual jumper. His hair was ruffled, resembling the top of a pineapple. Billy wondered if he'd ever seen a comb.

Sean had greeted them at the door. His eyes immediately jumped to the memory stick Billy held in his hand.

He called for Jenny to join them in the living room. Ethan and Beth were in their rooms –Billy thought it best they didn't see the recording.

'I need you to both sit down.' Billy's voice was authoritative. The atmosphere was tense.

'What's on it?' Sean asked, noting the concern on Jenny's face.

Billy straightened his jacket, pulling it slightly off his shoulders. 'What you're about to see will come as a shock. To say it's difficult viewing is an understatement. But you need to see it. I'm sorry, but it involves the death of your uncle and his final moments.'

Declan held his head down in respect.

Sean and Jenny sat open-mouthed, their faces still and expressionless.

Billy continued. 'It's a harrowing watch. I am warning you now in order to save you distress later.'

'I'd like to see it.' Jenny was resolute.

'Me too.'

A drilling sound echoed through the house, which made Billy jump.

'Sorry, we're having WIFI installed. It's been two whole days.' Jenny tried to lift the sombre mood, but her smile didn't reach her eyes.

. . .

Sean held Jenny's hand as they watched the recording. When it was finished, they were both too shocked to speak.

'I'm sorry you had to see that. We'll give you time to digest the situation. I'm going to call the police, have them pick it up. I'll keep the memory stick safe. I'm sure there'll be a warrant for Ronnie Hathaway's arrest. In the meantime, I'd suggest you all stay put. Don't open the front door under any circumstances.'

Billy stood, nodding to Declan – a silent request to retrieve the memory stick from the laptop.

They made their own way out.

27

Monday afternoon.

'We have WIFI!' Beth tapped in the password, and a signal appeared in the right-hand corner of her phone. The elation was evident in her face. 'You don't know what this means. Oh, my goodness.'

'Yes, I do. Minimal conversation, message alerts every few seconds and a constant tapping noise. Oh, what did we do without it?' Sean stood, listening to the incessant beeping noise as Beth's texts and alerts began to filter through. 'Happy now?' He stepped forward and hugged his daughter.

'Yeah, you don't understand how difficult it's been, like you're cut off from the rest of the world.'

Sean glanced at Jenny, and the two of them smirked privately.

'Cut off indeed. What are you like? It's been a couple of days.'

Beth's face was glued to the screen as she made her way out of the living room, her shoulder bumping into the door frame as she left.

Jenny moved to the door, watching Beth slowly make her way up the stairs, the phone still pinging.

'Be careful. Watch where you're going. The stairs are weak.'

Her daughter muttered back a response.

Jenny turned to Sean. 'What do you make of the recording? Tell me how you feel.' Her voice was anxious and weak.

'I feel sick, Jenny, to tell you the truth. To think what happened here, under the floor where we're standing. Ed and Ronnie. What the fuck? My mother didn't know any of this – she hasn't seen Ed for years – but it's still her brother. How do I tell her what happened? How he died?'

Jenny stepped towards him and placed her arms around his waist.

'When Mum handed us the keys to this place, she'd said her brother had died. As far as she knew Ed, had passed away at the psychiatric ward. She didn't attend the funeral. She told them to cremate his body. She didn't come to Painswick. Maybe it was too painful for her, dredging up the past. They hadn't spoken for so long. She has to know how he died, back here in such a cruel way.'

'I'm scared, Sean. Have we made a mistake moving here?'

Sean kissed her cheek, running his fingers through her hair. 'Billy is dealing with it. He's going to give the recording to the police. Ronnie cold-heartedly murdered my uncle. We have the footage. He's going to go away for the rest of his life. It's what he deserves.'

'What if he comes back? He's obviously aware of the

recording and he knows it's hidden here. Somehow he found out.' Jenny's face was filled with dread. 'What if he tries to get in?'

'I'm not going to let anything happen to my family. I'm going to get the locks replaced tomorrow. I called earlier and organised someone to come over.'

Jenny pulled him closer. He could feel her body shaking with anticipation.

'What about Ronnie? Do you think he's—' She struggled to say the word Creeper. 'He murdered Ed. Maybe he killed all those women too.'

Sean thought for a second. 'I doubt it. The recording shows a feud between two friends. It even explains the attack at Greyshott Hall: Ronnie knew we were moving in; he knew that building works were being carried out. Obviously, he knew the hard drive could be exposed and he was frightened of the footage being discovered. He was here last night. I saw his truck again, and Billy and Declan followed it to his house. They know where he lives. It's only a matter of time before he's caught.'

'And Creeper?'

'I don't believe there was ever a Creeper. It's possible someone may know what happened here. Maybe people had their suspicions about Ronnie and Ed – their dispute, feud, whatever you want to call it. I believe Ed found a body, and they both buried her. Christ knows what happened. Perhaps he did it – Ed locked her up, fathomed a story of a man who watched him at night, someone to blame. It drove him crazy, delusional. Creeper may have been a figment of his imagination, or something to help stem the guilt. There could be endless possibilities. Or maybe Ronnie killed her. Who knows? This is between them.'

'What about the other missing women? The red coat you found on the side of the road?'

Sean didn't have an answer for that. He hoped it was a hoax. But, somehow, he doubted it.

* * *

After showing the recording to the Freemans, Billy returned to his son's house and sat in the kitchen. He was still shocked at what they'd seen. He thought about Katie. Was it possible Ronnie had something to do with her murder? Was the video unravelling the secret, getting closer to the truth? Maybe that's why Ronnie killed Ed.

The more Billy thought about the footage, the clearer it became. Ed Berry had found a body in the basement, which Ronnie had placed there, knowing that Ed was confused. It would explain why he'd called over to the farmhouse.

The face Jenny had seen in the basement. The truck parked outside. It was all coming together.

Billy opened his laptop and searched the names of the eight missing women. Chloe Madden was the first girl to go missing. He did an advanced person search, which provided deeper information: aliases, relatives' names, phone numbers. Her parents had died in a car crash on the M25 a couple of years after she vanished. He bowed his head for a moment in respect. She had no siblings, and no one else was listed for her next of kin.

He then Googled Amelia Shaw, the second woman to go missing. Her parents had divorced a few years after she had gone missing. Her father had died of a heart attack five years ago, but Greta, her mother, was still alive. After an address report, Billy found she still lived in Painswick. He managed to get a phone number, then grabbed his mobile from the breakfast bar and dialled it.

The phone rang four times before a withered, tired voice answered.

'Hello?'

'Greta Shaw?'

'Speaking.'

'I hope you don't mind me calling.' When the woman didn't interrupt, Billy continued. 'I'm Billy Huxton. I'm the father of Katie Huxton, one of the missing girls. I'm a private investigator and I've re-opened the case. I'd like to talk to you if possible. I've found something that's relevant and need to ask a couple of questions. I promise it won't take long. I know this is extremely tough. I've gone through the same as you.'

There was silence. Billy thought Greta had hung up.

'Do you have my address?'

Billy answered no even though it was a lie. That way, Greta would hopefully feel more relaxed. He didn't want her thinking he was too pushy.

Once Greta told him where she lived, he made arrangements to call over. 'As I said, I won't take up too much of your time.'

'None of this will bring Amelia back.'

'I know. But hopefully we can catch the bastard and put him behind bars where he belongs.'

* * *

Twenty minutes later, Billy pulled up outside a small terraced house a few miles outside Painswick.

Declan was in the passenger seat, his hands gripping the holder above his head so tightly that veins started to show.

They got out of the car and glanced over the house. It was dull looking, the exterior painted a dark grey colour. The windows were large, with grubby marks staining the glass. The front garden had pockets of flower beds, though the soil was unkempt with thick, gloopy mud besieged with light green weeds. The glass in the front door was cracked and the letterbox was accompanied with a sign proclaiming, 'No junk mail.' On the doormat were the words, 'Not you again.'

'This is going to be fun,' Declan said.

Billy banged on the door with his fist. They watched a shadow move along the hallway, and then the front door opened with a struggle, revealing a woman in a blue dress and crocs, her hair high in a beehive style. Her face was heavily wrinkled, with a smoker's crease around her mouth. There was a faint stink of cigarettes in the air under the smell of damp and mildew, which was overbearing.

'Greta, it's me. Billy Huxton.'

She offered no handshake nor greeting. Instead, she turned and glided along the hallway towards the kitchen. 'Follow me.' She spoke with a raspy tone.

Declan pulled a face, expressing that he was frightened. He shut the front door with a struggle, and then they walked along the hallway. The carpet was thick with dust, and mites clung to the air. He glanced behind and saw prints left by his shoes.

'Nice place you have here.'

'I think so.' Greta beckoned for them to take a stool each and the two men sat.

'Thank you for allowing us to speak with you,' Billy started. 'I'm sorry for your loss.'

Greta smiled and waved a veiny hand in the air. Her fingers were long, the nails painted a light purple colour. 'No need to be, really. It was so long ago. I've done my grieving. I'm an old woman. I doubt I have much time left. I'll be dammed if I spend it being bitter. It's no good for the soul. What's done is done. No amount of sorrow will bring her back.' She paused and then added, 'I'm also sorry for your loss.'

Billy went on to explain the events of the night Katie went missing, how he had spent months searching for her, tirelessly struggling to find answers, how he became sick and his wife had to put a halt to it before it killed him.

Greta eyed both men. 'Sometimes you have to deal with the cards you're dealt. I miss Amelia. Every day I pray for her safe return. But I know she's not coming back. I've told myself it was her time. God wanted her for whatever reason. I have come to terms with that.'

'You're a very brave woman, Greta.'

'Who are you?'

'Oh, sorry.' Declan placed out his hand but Greta just stared at it. 'I'm Declan Ryan. I'm helping Billy with the investigation.'

'Do you think you'll catch the man responsible?'

'We hope so.'

'Another girl has gone missing. Did you hear about it? I heard them talking on the radio. Here in Painswick. It's like it's all starting over again.' She looked up to the grubby ceiling and clasped her hands together. 'They couldn't catch him then. They won't catch him now.'

Billy leant closer to her. 'Did the police interview you? At the time, I mean.'

'Fat lot of good it did. They came here, asking questions, with their promises and words of encouragement. It was meaningless. I miss her voice the most. I hear her some-times, in my dreams, calling out. "Help me" is what she shouts. But how can I help her when I don't know where she is?'

'Sorry to have to ask.' Billy began his line of questioning. 'Did you have a row? Or had she spoken about going anywhere?'

'A row? Goodness, no. Amelia was the most calm, placid person you could meet. I can't remember us ever raising our voices at one other.'

'And your husband? Are you certain he never had anything to do with it?'

Declan gripped the side of the table, waiting for a barrage of abuse.

'Absolutely certain. He was a drinker. He'd rather prop up a bar than deal with Amelia going missing. That's the way he handled it. It tore us apart. He spent all our savings on booze. He left, unable to cope. We sold the house and I downsized. We spoke, we were civil, but we dealt with Amelia's disappearance in different ways. But if you saw the drunk he became, you'd know he had nothing to do with it.'

'Thank you, Greta. I appreciate it greatly.' Billy stood and Declan followed.

'You can see yourselves out.'

They were walking along the hallway towards the front door, when Greta called out from the kitchen.

'There is one thing – the night Amelia disappeared.'

The men turned, staring along the hallway. 'Yes?'

'I remember the phone ringing. When I answered, no one was there. It was like a warning. Ring after ring. It was most odd. Eventually, I had to take it off the hook. I spoke to another mother at the time. Michelle Madden. Her daughter was the first. Chloe. She said it happened to her too. She answered, and no one was there. But it kept ringing. Later that evening, Chloe disappeared.'

Billy grabbed the door, forcing it open. 'Thank you for your time, Greta.'

* * *

'I'm Jenny Freeman, and we're recording live at the farmhouse in Painswick. So much has happened in a short space of time. We're pleased to say we now have WIFI, much to my children's delight. Tomorrow, we'll post a teaser for the docufilm we've been putting together. We're exploring a story that's infamous in this part of the world – someone called Creeper. Myth or fact, we'll let you decide.

'Yesterday, Sean and I spoke to the people of Painswick. The footage is raw, profound and very much a reality of how people feel about this individual. We spoke to locals who claim they have seen him. One person gave an account of their cousin who saw a man late at night with a body slumped over his shoulder; others claim to have heard stories, how he stalks the lonely country lanes, waiting for his next victim. Eight women have been allegedly abducted from the streets late at night, and most residents believe that Creeper is responsible.

'Closer to home, we've also witnessed some strange events. The first night after we moved here, I saw a face in our basement, and last night, I heard voices in the upstairs hallway. We're setting up a camera to catch any further happenings. I'm Jenny Freeman, it's 10.50pm here in the UK, and if anything happens, we'll upload the footage tomorrow. Sleep well.'

'Right, I'm placing the camera by the stairs, camouflaged under a blanket. It will record anything that moves. You ready for bed?' Sean asked.

'Yeah. You go upstairs. I'll be there in a second. Have you locked up?'

Sean walked to the front door to make sure the chain was in place, then he grabbed the key from the rack and turned it. The lock was secure. 'All good. See you up there.'

Jenny watched the red light of the camera illuminate as he walked up the stairs.

She moved to the kitchen, glancing outside. The half-moon, set far back in the clear sky, allowed light to shine on one corner of the garden. She stood alone, her family upstairs. A shiver ran up her body as she thought about the tape they'd seen earlier, the brutal murder of Ed Berry.

Jenny wanted to leave the house, pack their belongings and go, never to come back. She didn't feel safe here. She knew Sean would protect her, and Ethan – he was fit and strong; he'd guard both her and Beth – but still, she didn't want to be here anymore.

She struggled to stem the fear that was now taking over her body, panic spreading, pumping through her veins.

She slowly edged out of the kitchen and screamed. She felt someone behind her at the door. Her body jolted. Her legs were suddenly weak.

'Christ, Ethan. You frightened the shit out of me.'

'Sorry, I thought you guys went to bed. I came down for a glass of water. Are you OK?'

Jenny placed her hand on the door frame. Her face was pale and it seemed as if the blood had momentarily drained from her body.

'I'm good. You just made me jump. Are you staying up for a while?'

'No, I'm so tired. I've been revising all afternoon and need sleep.'

'Revising, my arse. You've been asleep all day.' Jenny

laughed. She ruffled her son's hair then leant forward and kissed him on the cheek. 'Don't stay up too late. See you in the morning.'

'Night, Mum.'

* * *

After their visit to Greta, Billy decided to return to Ronnie's house. He'd called the local police and arranged for the footage to be picked up the following morning.

He found a space close to the house, and after a tenacious battle with the steering wheel, he parked up. For once, Declan didn't comment on his driving abilities.

Declan had tried to dissuade him from coming but Billy was hellbent on it. He had the key and nothing would stop him.

'I need to delve further into Ronnie's life. There has to be something else. If we're building a case against him, I need more evidence.'

'I'm coming with you then. We're a team. If you go, I go too.'

Billy and Declan glanced down the street. There was no sign of the black truck. They crossed the road and headed for the semi-detached house.

The gate made a screeching sound as Billy pushed it, and they stopped for a moment.

Declan looked through the window. The curtains were open, and the living room was dark. He turned around to make sure no one could see him. They were both anxious. Nerves began to overwhelm their bodies.

The door opened next door, and the old lady from the previous night stepped out on the steps.

'Oh, there's two of you now? You didn't return my key, young man.'

Billy was agitated. 'I need to go back inside. I'll drop it through the letterbox when we're done.'

'Did you check the source of the smell? It was terrible today. It's like it's seeping through the walls.'

'I'll take a look. You can go back inside.' Billy moved to Ronnie's front door, peering through the glass.

Declan stood beside him. 'I think she wants you. Look how she's staring.'

Ignoring him, Billy stood back and stared up towards the first-floor windows, all of which were dark. The house seemed vacant. He placed the key in the lock and gently turned it.

The stench was now unbearable. Last night had been bad – the smell of drains or something rotting – but this was horrendous. It felt like their lungs were clogging up, the putrid, vile odour working its way into their skin, as if about to possess them.

Billy covered his hand with his jacket sleeve and pushed the door wider. The rotten, fleshy smell filled the hallway. They stood there, wondering if Ronnie Hathaway was hiding, waiting for them.

Declan was struggling to breathe. Billy grabbed a handkerchief and covered his mouth.

The two men began to heave, struggling to stem the odour entering their noses and mouths.

It was pitch black. They listened hard, then moved further into the house, pushing their hands in front to guide their way. Something was in front of them. A large, heavy object. Billy felt it first. He removed his phone and turned on the torch. As the figure became clear, both men backed away.

Billy's legs were weak, and he fell against the wall. He dropped the phone and the hallway was plunged back into darkness. 'No. Please.' He scrabbled around on the floor, searching for the phone. What he'd seen moments ago was the scariest thing he'd ever witnessed.

Declan grabbed him, helping to steady his body. He grabbed his own phone, turned on the torch and used the light to find Billy's.

'Billy, who is it?' He pointed the torch to the body, feeling like he'd vomit at any second.

A person was strung up on the wall, naked. Ropes were strapped around their arms, which were attached to strong clamps that had been drilled and screwed into the brick. The body was completely skinless, like a morbid piece of artwork from the sickest mind. Their eyes, nose and fingers had been removed. The person looked alien-like.

Billy darted his eyes towards the stairs, then further up into the bleakness. His body had frozen, his mind turned off, attempting to block his brain from processing the terror he'd just seen. He placed his hands underneath him and tried to manoeuvre his body backwards. His legs felt incompetent, his body a dead weight. Declan guided him, helping him back.

As they reached the front door, someone was standing there already.

Declan spun his head to the side.

The person moved further into the house.

'What on earth is going on?'

Billy recognised the voice. The old lady next door.

'Don't come in here,' he shouted. 'Please. Go back outside. You can't see this. Go outside.'

'Is it Ronnie?'

Billy and Declan were too stunned to answer.

* * *

As Jenny walked along the upstairs hallway, she heard Beth talking to someone. She stood outside her room for a second, then tapped the door. 'Can I come in?'

'Yes, you don't need to ask.'

Who are you talking to?' Jenny saw the laptop open and a girl's face on the screen.

'Lauren.'

'Hi, Mrs Freeman. Good to see you. How's the new house?'

'Getting there, Lauren. Still so much to organise. Say hello to your mum for me. Night, girls.'

She moved to the hallway and listened to Ethan shuffling around in the kitchen, hearing the familiar sounds of bread popping up from the toaster and the kettle beginning to hiss. Hearing Beth's voice and Ethan downstairs was a comforting release. She moved to the bedroom, took off her clothes and got into bed.

Sean was asleep, turned towards the window. She placed her mobile phone on the bedside unit and settled into bed, pulling the soft duvet over her shoulders and sinking her head into the cold pillow. She closed her eyes.

A beeping sound came from her side. A message had come through on WhatsApp.

Jenny pulled herself up and reached for the phone.

It was a message from Ethan. *Where are the crisps?*

Jenny smiled. She tapped a message back. *In a cardboard box on the floor near the door. Don't eat too many. Night, Ethan. Love you.*

Love you too.

She glanced at her screensaver, a picture of the four of them on a beach in Tenerife. They were so happy. She leant forward, stroking the screen with her finger. The light went out, her phone becoming a black rectangle, and she placed it on her bedside table.

* * *

Billy and Declan stood by the front door, shining their phone lights over the body.

'Who is it?' Declan's hands shook. The smell was unbearable. The body was in a shocking state of decomposition.

'I can't tell. Wait, let me see if there is ID on it,' Billy sniped. 'Someone is fucking with us. This wasn't here last night. Someone knew. They knew we'd return. From the looks of the condition, this body has been dead for months. Whoever is responsible went to great lengths so we'd find it.'

'Why, though?'

'Because they're sick, Declan. Look at the state of the corpse. What person in their right mind could do such a thing? It's evil. Barbaric.'

'It has to be Ronnie. He knows we're onto him. He's done this as a warning. Maybe to scare us off.'

'Well, it's not going to work. It's only a matter of time before we catch up with him. And I assure you I've thought about it, what I'll do to the person responsible for my Katie.'

Declan dialled 999 and explained what had happened, who he and Billy were, then waited for the emergency services to arrive.

Billy took pictures of the corpse in the hopes of identifying the body. But due to the appalling state it had been left in, he knew that it would probably only be dental records that could show who it was now.

Once they'd given a statement, they were free to go, but they remained for a moment, sat in the car, watching the chaos unfold. They watched as the blue lights illuminated the night sky and as the body bag was taken into the ambulance.

'I've never seen anything so disgusting.'

Declan reached forward and tilted the rear-view mirror. 'There you go. You can't see it now.'

'Sod off. How are we going to find Ronnie?' Billy glanced to the street. 'He's out there now. He could be watching us as we speak.'

'Or watching the farmhouse.'

Billy started the car and manoeuvred along the road.

'We're closing in on him, Billy. He won't get away with it for much longer.'

'I hope you're right. Something is telling me he's coming for us.'

* * *

Beth was lying on her bed, the lights on, keeping her voice low as she spoke to Lauren. She stuffed a fistful of crisps into her mouth and then washed it down with a glass of coke.

'It's an amazing place. The farmhouse is huge. I can't wait for you to come over for a weekend. I can have the music as loud as I want when my parents are out, though the seclusion takes a bit of getting used to. When you stand on the doorstep, you can't see any other houses at all. It's mad.'

'Wow, doesn't that freak you out?'

Beth wanted to tell her the strange things that were happening, but one, she was worried Lauren would tell people and two, she didn't want to frighten her friend and sabotage any chance of her visiting. 'It's all right. I don't know if I'll stay for long. God, I need to sort my life out.' She pushed a frustrated hand through her hair.

'And how's your hot brother?'

Lauren laughed as Beth pulled an awkward face.

'Ethan is, well... Ethan. He's got the bigger room, of course. And we fight over the smallest things. We did have a good night though in town. You should see the road leading into Painswick. It's proper scary.'

'How's Ethan getting on at college?'

'Studying and pissing around, I'd say. He starts at Stroud soon. Failure is lurking.'

The girls laughed.

'I heard that.' Ethan poked his head around the bedroom door.

'You were meant to.'

'Hi, Ethan. You all right?'

'Good thanks, Lauren. When are you coming over for a visit? It's been a while since we've seen you.'

Beth watched Lauren's face on the screen turn bright red. She was stuck for words.

'Night, ladies.'

'Why does he have to be your brother?' Lauren asked with a hint of disappointment after he'd walked off down the hall.

'What are you like?' Beth laughed.

'Hi, Mr Freeman.'

Lauren's face froze for a second, then came back into view. The screen was losing signal.

'Are you still there?'

'Yeah, sorry. I'm not sure what's going on. How are you, Mr Freeman? Enjoying the new house? Beth's going to give me a virtual tour tomorrow.'

Beth's face dropped. 'Who are you talking to?'

'Your father. He's gone now, but he was standing behind you in the doorway.'

Beth turned her head. Her heart seemed to stop and her chest became tight. She looked towards the door and out to the empty hallway, then she stood, moving out of the room. She crept along the wooden floorboards and opened Ethan's door without knocking, finding her brother under the covers, listening to music. A lamp placed on the bedside table illuminated the room, and his eyes were closed. She watched him for a brief moment, then made her way back out.

She turned, holding her breath momentarily, then walked further along the hallway, peering over the railing to look downstairs.

The ground floor seemed empty.

Beth moved quickly to her mum and dad's room and pushed the handle down, opening the door.

Her mum sat up. Her father was lying on his side asleep, his arm hanging out of the bed.

'Beth, what's wrong?'

'Did either of you come out a minute ago? To use the toilet or something?'

'No, love. Why?'

'It doesn't matter. Goodnight.'

Beth closed the door and stood, listening. A creak, a floorboard bowing on the stairs. She fought to stem the fabricated noises in her mind, her imagination running wild. *Get a grip, Beth. No one is in the house.*

An image flashed in front of her eyes, the figure standing at the end of the garden, holding the red coat. But she saw him here, at the end of the hallway, standing, like a matador, waving the garment each side of his body. She pressed her hands against the stair rail, closed her eyes and brought her hands to her face, rubbing her eyelids with the knuckles of bent forefingers. She opened her eyes again.

The figure was gone.

Just a figment brought on by her fear.

But Lauren had seen someone at her bedroom door, had been convinced a man was standing there. She had spoken to him. She believed he was real.

But her father and Ethan were in bed.

Still outside her parents' room, she tried to compose herself. *Deep breaths – inhale, exhale – bring your mind to your happy place. A garden filled with flowers, the smell of cut grass. A bar selling margaritas. The sun, penetrating heat from a clear sky.*

She straightened her back and edged along the hall, coming to stand under the doorframe of her bedroom. She heard Lauren calling out to see what was happening. She tiptoed along the floor with heavy, deep breaths, carefully placing her legs in front of one another. She grabbed the laptop. 'Lauren, I need to go. It's late. I'll call you tomorrow.'

'Is everything OK? What's happened?'

Beth moved her finger over the trackpad. 'Nothing. I'm tired. See you soon.' She glided the cursor across the screen and ended the call. Then she closed the laptop and placed it on her dressing table.

Beth stood for a moment, listening hard, wondering if someone was in the house. Only moments ago, Lauren had seen a figure at her bedroom door.

Was it possible someone had got in? She had to check.

Slowly she backed out of the room, peeling her eyes away from the wall, the comfortable bed, the dressing table, the closed laptop.

I need to wake Ethan; he'll come down with me. She moved along the hallway, watching the stairs, the dark shadows looming over the space. She tapped on Ethan's door, pushed the handle down, then walked towards his bed. 'Ethan. Hey. Wake up. Ethan.'

Something caught her eye in her peripheral vision. She turned, sure the door had just moved behind her – a sudden rasp, the flicker of a figure, bulky, wide, standing and waiting for her to come out.

But nothing.

She turned back to Ethan. The light was still on beside the bed, and he was lying still, motionless, on his side, his face towards hers.

She tugged on his shoulders, watching him turn over and face away from her.

'You arsehole. I know you're awake.'

Frustrated, she moved out of the room, her eyes fixed on the door. She glanced up the hallway towards her parents' room, where the door was closed tight.

Beth debated what to do, tackling her inner voice that wanted to go to bed, place a chair under the door handle and hide under the covers. But she knew she had to go down, check the rooms. She had to take charge and make sure the farmhouse was empty.

Downstairs, she opened the door to the box room. Empty. She moved to the window and

looked out at the darkness.

The front door was locked. Beth pulled the handle and made sure it couldn't open. The chain was secure, though flimsy and weak. The living room was next. She lifted her phone, turned on the torch and pointed it inside. The fireplace was stacked with charred coal, and the telly sat on its robust stand with the standby light blinking a bright red. She felt for the switch, running her hands along the cold plastic and turned it off.

The small bathroom with a toilet and washbasin was vacant; so too was the store cupboard opposite.

In the kitchen, the cold tiles stunned her feet and pushed a chill through her body. She pressed on the handle of the back door. Closed and locked. She leant against the frame, pushing out a sigh of relief. She felt proud. She was able to look after herself. She'd taken the matter into her own hands and dealt with it.

But as she turned, she pointed the torch to the corner of the room, across the wall and onto the chalkboard. She tensed. Her mind became cloudy and confused. Fear shot through her body. She reached for the chair in front of her, leaning against its back to steady herself.

The chalk drawings were back – four stick people in a row.

The one at the end had another line drawn through it, this time, accompanied by the word, 'Tomorrow.'

* * *

Beth stood over her brother. She watched him sleeping, facing towards where she stood. The cold glass numbed her fingers, a feeling of frostbite working to the tips.

She steadied herself, lifting her arms high in the air with both hands. She was going to do it. Ethan was driving her mad. He'd forced her to do this.

She hesitated for a second, took a deep breath and lifted the glass higher, holding it like a trophy.

Then, she tipped it, spilling the water over his face.

'What the hell?' He opened his eyes, wild, ferocious. 'Are you bloody crazy? Why would you do that?'

Beth grabbed his arm and tried to drag his body down to the floor. 'Get up. If you don't, I swear I'll scream.'

Ethan rolled over, revealing that he was wearing only boxer shorts. His pale, skinny body shook with the cold. He stood, wiping himself down. 'What the hell has gotten into you?'

'I know it's you. I know.'

Ethan stood. 'What? What's me?'

'You were the last to leave the kitchen. I fucking hate you sometimes.'

'Beth, I haven't got a clue what you're talking about.'

'No? Well, follow me then.'

She led the way into the kitchen. She pointed at the chalkboard.

The stick people had gone.

The board was clear.

They suddenly felt a chill, a breeze sweeping towards them.

As they made their way to the middle of the kitchen, they looked past the cupboard on the wall.

The back door was open.

Someone had been in the farmhouse.

28

'What a night. I'm going to have a whisky – a bloody large one.' Billy turned towards Declan, and from the kitchen, watched as he removed his shoes by the front door.

'Sounds good to me. We need it after the night we've had.'

'It was horrible, wasn't it? Are you going to join me or what?' He reached into a cupboard above his head and grabbed two tumblers. 'Now, let's see what my son has in his stash. I know he likes his drink. It's just finding where he's hidden it.'

Declan pulled out a chair and sat at the table. 'Try the shelves underneath. Watch you don't put your back out.'

'I'll have you know I'm extremely robust. I used to be a gymnast in my early years. I can still touch my toes.'

'Yeah, maybe with a broom.'

'I can think of a place I'd ram with a broom if you carry on.' Billy's face lit up as he found a half bottle of whisky. 'Yes, beauty.' He opened the fridge. 'There must be ice somewhere.'

'The fridge door – it's an ice maker. Place the glass into the compartment, and it will drop.'

Declan watched as Billy held the first glass, carefully placing it into the gap in the fridge door.

'Blasted thing isn't working. Come on, what's wrong with modern technology? Why does everything have to be so damn complicated?'

Declan moved towards the fridge door and had a look. 'You don't *pull* the bloody lever. It's not a beer tap. Push. Push the glass against it, and the ice will drop.' He sat back at the table and watched Billy play with his new toy.

Billy turned and looked him in the eye. Struggling to hold in his laughter, Declan had turned red in the face and his cheeks puffed with mirth.

Billy was ready to snap. Then he burst into hysterics himself. It was a much-needed release, a welcome tonic. Tears were rolling down his face as the laughter took hold of him. He couldn't recall the last time that had happened.

As he took the first sip of his drink, Declan witnessed the Jekyll and Hyde moment – Billy instantly relaxed

Billy placed both glasses on the table, each half-filled with ice, then removed the cap on the bottle and poured out equal measures.

Billy had his drink on the rocks, while Declan found a can of coke, which he added.

'Cheers.' Billy raised his glass.

Declan lifted his, listening to the fizzing noise as the coke settled, and clunked his drink with Billy's. 'Back at ya. Well, this is cosy.'

Billy smiled, though the strain of the last few hours was evident in his rounded shoulders, his tight lips and deep eyebrows..

Declan watched as he began to unwind, suddenly realising who he reminded him of. 'Have you ever been told you look like Dick Van Dyke? I've been trying to work it out. That's it.'

'You mean that chimney sweep from Mary Poppins with the stupid accent? That's a bloody insult.'

'Not really. In his later years, he was quite the stud. He played a detective and acted with his son. A real lady killer.'

'The son?'

'No, Dick.'

'Who's a dick?'

'Oh, for frig sake. Not you. His name is—'

Billy smiled. 'See, I can be funny too. Dick.'

'Oh, very good. I asked for that.'

Declan swirled the ice in his glass. The whisky was starting to take effect, and he suddenly felt tired. 'What was that tonight? I can't believe what we witnessed. The body, I mean. It was like it had been dug up from a grave. I'll never forget the way it looked. The smell. Christ, Billy. The corpse had disintegrated. How?'

'Someone put it there. They wanted us to find it.'

'How are we going to tell Sean and Jenny?'

Billy hesitated. 'It will take some time to identify the body. It may not be Ed.'

'I wouldn't bet against it.'

'Christ. After seeing the state of the body, maybe it's possible Ronnie is responsible for the missing—' Declan stopped. He didn't want to upset Billy.

'Ronnie knew we'd return. He attacked me at the house last night. Were it not for you, he probably would have killed me. The body hanging in the hallway was his way of telling us he's one step ahead. He knew we'd find it.' Billy drained the glass, then refilled it. He thought about his daughter and the seven other missing women. 'A person so wicked, so twisted – he's capable of anything.'

Declan sat forward in the chair, revolution oozing from his body as he tried to piece the puzzle together.

Billy froze, though his mind continued to tick while his body remained stiff. 'Let's take another look at the recording.'

Declan and Billy moved to the sofa in the living room. They sat side by side as the tape played.

Ed Berry sat on the stool, facing the camera, his eyes wild, ferocious.

Billy asked Declan to fast forward to near the end. When Declan had skipped forward enough, Billy pushed forward on the edge of the sofa, instructing him to turn up the volume.

'The person responsible for murdering these women is still out there. They call him Creeper. I have proof that he exists. The body I found in the basement is testimony to what he will do. I only hope the others are found and given the burials they deserve. Their families deserve closure.

'I'm going to finish this now. I just heard the front door being slammed open, which means Ronnie is inside my house. I can hear him above, traipsing along the floor-boards. I could escape through the basement, through the small hole, but he'd shoot me like a dog on the street. I'd rather die with dignity, here in the farmhouse – my home. So, while there's time, I'm putting this recording onto a memory stick and leaving it in the wall. I hope you find it. I'll drop the camcorder in the pit; there's a gaping hole that runs deep right where I'm sat. That way he won't know I've made this recording.

'If you're watching this, I'm Ed Berry, and I found a dead

woman in my basement. Ronnie Hathaway helped me to get rid of her. Now, he's going to kill me.

'This is my confession and my account of what happened.

'Ronnie needs to pay for the crime he's about to commit.

'Do me a favour, if you're watching this, show someone.

'I'm going now. I need to hide this recording.

'But please. Ronnie Hathaway is going to kill me.

'He needs to pay.'

White noise took over the screen, and Declan turned the volume down.

'Why did you want to see it again?' He dropped the remote control on the sofa.

'How did Ronnie know the recording had been exposed?'

'I'm not with you?'

Billy leant back in the sofa, which caused Declan to give him a mock stern look.

'Are you sure that's a good idea? Look at the trouble we had last time getting you off that thing.'

'We have footage of Ronnie entering the farmhouse. But how did Ronnie know Ed made a recording? It doesn't make sense.'

'Oh, I see what you mean. In other words, he's looking for something he doesn't know exists.'

They sat in silence for what felt like minutes.

Billy broke the ice. 'What are we missing?'

'Look, let's hit the sack. Things may seem clearer in the morning.'

Declan picked up the remote control and pointed it towards the telly, ready to turn it off, but the white noise shifted back to a clear picture: a wall, still and unmoving. It was as if the camera had been dropped. There were voices.

Billy turned to Declan. 'Turn it up.'

A loud, clunking sound could be heard, then a shuffle, then a panting noise. Something was being dragged along the floor.

Billy and Declan hadn't seen this. It seemed to be several minutes later, after the footage of Ed Berry sitting and announcing that Ronnie Hathaway had a gun and was entering the farmhouse.

The two men in the recording were unaware the camera was still filming.

Billy and Declan struggled to make out what was being said.

More shuffling, someone panting. Then a picture came into view. A man, his face bloody, being placed on the chair. Another man tied rope around his body, strapping him securely to the frame.

'I know it's you. You'll never get away with it. The body I helped bury, it's only the beginning, isn't it? There are more. You sick bastard. How could you do it?'

The man continued to tie the rope, the veins in his forearms protruding, the breaths he was taking hard, firm.

'I knew you'd betray me. That money you raised wasn't yours. You had to keep asking for more. I've made a recording. I'm going to hide it in the walls. If they catch me, if my time is up, they'll blame you, Ronnie. I have the footage of you entering the house. No one will know.'

The man struggled as the rope circled his body, the blood weakening in his limbs. His lips had become a deep purple colour and his eyes became blurry. 'How could you? Those innocent girls. You killed each of them, didn't you? It's true, Ed. What people say. There is a creeper. You're Cree—'

Ed Berry lifted a hammer and began to smash it over Ronnie's head, unaware the camera was still rolling.

His screams for help were chilling.

When Ronnie ceased moving, Ed moved out of the frame and returned a few minutes later.

He carefully began cutting, delicately removing the skin from Ronnie Hathaway's face.

He placed it over his own and began to scream like a madman.

'See-saw, Margery Daw. Ronnie can tell his story no more.

'See-saw.

'See-saw.'

* * *

Ethan twisted the key in the kitchen door, then yanked the handle downwards to ensure it was locked. He glanced back at the chalkboard. A few minutes ago, his sister had seen the drawing of the chalk people. Now they were gone.

Beth stood close to him, too frightened to speak.

Ethan looked at her intently. 'Are you OK?'

'What a stupid question. How do you think I feel? What the hell is going on?'

'I think we should stay in Mum and Dad's bedroom. We're safer together.' He cradled her in an embrace, feeling her body shake from fear.

'I want to go home, Ethan. I hate it here. What do the drawings mean?'

'I won't let anything happen to you.'

'You promise?'

'Yes. Someone was here, but they're gone now. You're safe.'

'How do you know?'

Ethan had no answer. 'Let's go.'

They edged out of the kitchen, walking backwards towards the stairs, their eyes glued to the kitchen door. When they were sure there was no one following them, they turned and charged up the steps.

At the bedroom door, Ethan grabbed Beth's arm. 'Wait. Go in quietly. It's not fair to wake them. Whoever was here won't come back tonight.'

Beth opened the bedroom door. Ethan followed her.

Their father was asleep, on his side as he had been before.

Jenny sat up. 'Guys, what time is it?' She reached for her phone on the bedside table, and jabbed her finger on the screen. She held the phone in front of her face briefly, then screamed, a chilling wail bellowing from deep in her lungs.

The screensaver of her and her family had been replaced with another picture.

A photo of Jenny, lying asleep in her bed.

29

Beth and Ethan stood in the bedroom, both with their hands cupped over their mouths.

Jenny was staring at her phone. A picture, taken that evening, was on her screensaver, a photo of her, lying in bed. She could see the shape of Sean lying next to her. 'How the hell could this happen? How did someone do this? Sean, wake up. Sean!'

He stirred, then turned over. 'What's up?'

Jenny told him what had happened. Beth and Ethan were stunned into silence.

He took the phone and looked at the picture, his body flush with anxiety.

He sat up. 'Christ, someone was in our house. Ethan, come with me. Jenny, Beth, lean against the bedroom door; use your bodies as a shield. We'll be back in a minute. We have to make sure he's gone. How the hell did he get in here and take a picture?'

'Mum's iPhone is locked with her fingerprint.'

Sean paused, taking in what Ethan had said. 'So, he must have lifted her hand.'

Sean and Ethan left to check over the house. Jenny put on her dressing gown, then her and Beth leant against the bedroom door. They heard doors slamming, footsteps racing over the old wooden boards and loud commands from both men, telling the person to leave them alone.

'Mum, I'm so scared.' Suddenly the house went silent. 'Are they OK? I can't hear them.'

Jenny grabbed her daughter's hand and squeezed it hard. 'If someone is in the house, Sean and Ethan will find them.'

'I can't hear them, Mum.' Beth looked over the bedroom. The walls were still bare but freshly painted. A white set of drawers, which her father and Ethan had carried up together, leant against the far wall. The old bed, with its deep-brown-coloured wooden frame, sat in the middle of the room and the duvet was draped over the side. Beth stared at it, sure it had just moved. She focused her eyes, staring hard. A shadow that she hadn't seen before caught her attention. Now she saw a hand resting by the corner of the mattress. Did it move? She was uncertain. She swallowed hard, staring at it. It seemed to push out from under the bed.

No, no, no.

She listened for the voices of her father, brother, but the farmhouse was still, only the noise of her mother's breaths, light, sharp.

Beth whispered, 'Mum, I think someone is under the bed.' She pressed her back against the door.

'Where?'

She pointed. 'The mattress. I saw it move. I think someone is under the bed.'

Jenny felt sick with fear. She focused on the area and

was now sure she could see it herself too. 'Where's Sean and Ethan? They've been gone a long time.'

'Should we run?' Beth's voice was weak, frail. Her body was tense. 'I have to check.'

Jenny grabbed her leg. 'Don't, Beth.'

She moved towards the bed, her eyes staring at the mattress. It seemed to sway. She checked the pockets of her tracksuit, but realised her phone was in her bedroom. Her mother's rested on the bedside cabinet.

'Hello? If someone is under the bed, you need to get out.'

Jenny stood, silent, raw, as if she'd been anaesthetised. She watched Beth move closer to the bed. 'We need to run. Beth, don't.'

Beth crouched, panic rising through her body. An ache seemed to twist in her stomach, like a fist, turning, rotating in her gut. 'Hello? Please leave us alone.' She reached forward, gripped a corner of the mattress. Her heart pounded, her fingers ached. She turned back towards her mother, who was moving towards her. As she ripped the mattress back, she stared at the figure – a long, cardboard box was tucked under the bed.

Jenny sighed, the relief spilling out of her.

Beth turned and began to laugh.

Suddenly, the bedroom door opened.

Beth and Jenny screamed.

'No one is in the house,' Sean announced.

Ethan stood behind his father. 'What's happened?'

They stepped inside, and listened to Jenny and Beth as they explained, the tension pouring out with each word, draining from their bodies. Beth told them about the shadow, her voice drifting off with tiredness.

'We're all in here tonight. Tomorrow, the locksmith is coming. No one will get in after that.'

'Should we call the police?'

Sean climbed into bed. 'It's useless. What are they going to do? Check over the place and leave? Whoever was here has gone. And I doubt they'll return. Ethan and I have looked. There's no one here. It's pointless calling the police.'

'Dad's right. If we stay together, we're safe. We'll get the locks replaced tomorrow and stop this lunatic getting into the house.'

The four of them settled into bed, Sean and Jenny in the double, Ethan and Beth on the mattress in the middle of the floor.

Sean turned out the bedside light, drenching the room in darkness.

The alarm clock showed 2.59am. Jenny opened her eyes and peered through the dimness that surrounded her. She sat up, pressed her back against the headboard and into the soft, velvet cushion. She needed the toilet but couldn't move from the spot. Her mind was racing, visions exploding in her head: the truck at Greyshott Hall, the red coat Beth and Sean found on the side of the road, Marie Nelson, the figure in the cellar. Jenny felt like she'd burst with pressure. It was becoming too much. She didn't want to be here anymore.

As she sunk back down into the bed, she heard a rattling noise, like a see-saw, moving up and down. She reached for her phone, pressed the screen and was faced with the picture of her sleeping. Someone had been in the room, had held her finger against her phone and taken a photograph. She struggled to think, and a panic attack began to develop deep in her stomach. It rose rapidly, working its way up her body, controlling her. Her chest tightened; her skin became hot.

She turned on the phone's light and shone it around the room.

Beth and Ethan were asleep, as was Sean next to her. The light hovered over the bedroom door. Jenny swore she could see the handle move. She stared hard, listening for footsteps, wanting to wake her husband.

'Sean. Are you up?' She guided the torch towards his face.

The squeaking sound by the bedroom door returned. She was too frightened to move the light back. Instead, she turned the phone off, placed it on the bedside table and lay back with the blanket pulled over her face.

Finally, the door handle ceased moving.

A minute later, she was asleep.

30

Tuesday.

.

At just gone 7.30am, someone knocked at the front door.

Jenny bolted awake, briefly confused as to where she was. As she glanced around the room, her heart sank, realising they were still at the farmhouse.

Another rap on the door.

'Sean.'

'Huh?'

'Sean, someone's at the door.'

He sat up. His hair was dishevelled and his eyes bloodshot from the tiredness. He looked at the alarm clock. 'Shit. The locksmith.' He pushed the blanket back and pulled a T-shirt from a folded pile of clean clothes.

On the way down the stairs, he heard another loud knock. The tradesperson was obviously agitated. Sean didn't want to start the day off with an argument.

He opened the door to find a young lad with his back turned, as if he was about to walk away. He was clutching a metal box, which looked awkward and heavy. In his other hand, he gripped a mobile phone.

'Mr Freeman?'

'Yes, welcome. You must be the locksmith?'

Sean glared at the man for a moment. He looked confident but his attitude gave him a cocky, arrogant image. He chewed on a piece of gum, his mouth open, revealing stained, yellow teeth. His dark blue hoodie was oversized, the sleeves covering his hands. He smiled, but not in a friendly way, more sarcastic.

Sean stood aside. 'Please, come in.'

The young man walked into the farmhouse without removing his shoes and instantly asked for tea. He took in the house, moving his head as if in slow motion. 'How many locks are we replacing?'

'I think this door, the kitchen, oh, and the basement has a hatch. I'd like that replaced too.'

'Lovely, Guv. We'll have the place secure in no time. This place needs it.'

Sean thought it was an odd thing to say but just nodded.

The man started to inspect the lock, then pulled hard on the catch. Sean passed him the keys and he began to twist the first hard in the mechanism.

'Christ, these are older than my nan.'

'Hence the reason to get them replaced.' Sean tried to answer politely but he was hindered by the man's cockiness. 'Can I leave you to it?'

'Er, tea?'

Sean turned and walked into the kitchen. He returned a few minutes later with a tray carrying a teapot filled with hot water, two teabags and a mug. 'I'll be upstairs.'

'Oh, yeah?'

Sean moved up the steps, struggling to stem the desire to lash out.

He grabbed the camcorder from the stairs, watching the smirk on the locksmith widen.

'Oh, making a private film, are we?'

Sean ignored his lewd remark.

Jenny was sitting on the edge of the bed, bent forward, resting her head on her hands. As the bedroom door opened, she jumped.

'What a rude little shit.'

'Who?'

'The locksmith. No manners. Christ knows how he has any customers. I think he's been dragged up.'

'Oh, Sean. You were young once.'

'Indeed. A very long time ago, it seems. Right, let's see what we have here.' He placed the camcorder on the bed. 'If someone got into the house, we'll see it. We can take any incriminating footage to the police.' Sean pressed play. He saw the stairs, the camera pointing downward to the hallway.

He and Jenny watched in anticipation. A few minutes in, they could see Ethan moving up the steps, quickly followed by a crash. It sounded like clothes being dropped onto the floor. The screen became dark.

'I don't believe it. He must have knocked something and covered the camera. What is he like?'

Jenny placed a hand on his leg. 'He didn't know.'

Sean jolted as a drill started downstairs.

At least they didn't have to worry about noise.

* * *

Jenny stood by the window. The sky was a deep, grey colour, laden with clouds. It had started to drizzle and the rainwater seeped down the glass. The grass in the fields opposite swayed violently, pushing from side to side.

She thought about their home, the farmhouse in Painswick. At that moment, she'd swap this place for anywhere else in England. She hated it. The townsfolk were withdrawn, disengaged and had no intention of speaking about Creeper. Now she knew why. The story itself was terrifying. Was this how the eight women went missing? Marie Nelson, just the other day. Who'd be next?

Jenny leapt as she felt a hand grab her arm. 'Jesus, Sean. Don't creep up on me.'

'Sorry.' He glanced at Ethan and Beth, who were still sleeping at either end of the mattress on the floor. 'I'm so sorry.' He reached out and held his wife, cradling her as she burst into tears. 'We can leave. Tonight. Pack up our things and say goodbye to this place.'

'How can we?'

'Easy. We'll get an Airbnb – the four of us. Until we can sell this place. Just say the word, Jenny, and we're gone.'

Jenny hesitated, thinking about the offer. She was stronger than this. They'd looked forward to this for so long, moving to the Cotswolds, the space, tranquillity. She couldn't give up. It wasn't her. They were paying to have the locks changed. After today, no one would get into the house. They were secure, guarded from the outside, from Cree—

She couldn't even muster the strength to think his name.

She turned towards the window, then back to her husband, suddenly mustering the courage.

'Let's carry on.'

'Living here?'

'Here, together, the four of us. I'm also talking about the documentary.'

Sean stood back, appraising his wife. Her face had changed: her eyes were alive, her cheeks a sudden pink colour. She smiled.

'Are you sure?'

'It's what we do. We have an opportunity to bring this story to the world, the secret Painswick strives to keep – a story so chilling that the locals refuse to even speak about it. I'm not saying we should go out and try to lure him here, but we have the chance to make something great, as long as we don't put ourselves in danger. Just think about it. We're living it now, here in the farmhouse, where it all happened. Let's film some more, speak to a few people and then close up, move on to something else. It's our life – that's why people love our films. Come on, let's do this.'

Sean looked out over the fields, fearful of what they might uncover next. He had to be strong, to continue what they'd started. 'OK, but one whiff of trouble and we cut loose.'

Jenny nodded. 'We cut loose.'

* * *

'We're filming live at our farmhouse in the Cotswolds. I'm keeping my voice as quiet as possible. I'll explain why in a minute. So much has happened in the short time we've moved to Painswick, and we want to share our story with our thousands of subscribers across the world. For those of you who are watching this later, we're currently live on YouTube – for the first time since we moved as we've only just had WIFI installed. I'm with my husband, Sean Free-man, my daughter, Beth, and my son, Ethan.

'Moving here has been a brave decision for our family and one we hope will work out for us. But Painswick has a secret, a terrifying story that only the brave will dare to mention. We've tried: we've spoken to the locals and asked people to tell us their beliefs, but it seems no one wants to talk about it. The more Sean and myself delve into the case, the more real the story becomes.

'Creeper.'

Sean watched the screen as Jenny spoke. Hundreds of people were watching, with many commenting and posting an array of emojis.

'My husband came here a couple of days before we moved in. The decorators who promised to finish the refurbishment had vanished and have been unreachable since. We don't know what caused them to leave so abruptly.

'We believe someone or something got into our home last night. Expecting something like this to happen, we'd set up a camera, but due to technical issues, it didn't record. I won't go into the reason behind our beliefs but be assured we have strong logic to why we think this happened.

'Saturday night, while filming in our basement, I saw a figure standing in the corner of the room. Unfortunately, that footage got deleted.'

Sean watched as loads of sad face emojis appeared. A sign he perceived as the viewers feeling their pain. He leant back, his eyes scanning down the screen.

Jenny continued. 'We'll post snippets to our usual social media channels where you can view the footage we've taken so far. We'll also add a link to the description for anyone unfamiliar with our work.

'Our job is dangerous. We often find ourselves in demanding and terrifying situations, but we do it because we enjoy it. We want to share stories, feed your appetite for what you want to see. I'll finish off by saying my family and I have felt under threat, here in this farmhouse. This is a story we seem to have been dropped into the middle of and we're vulnerable. If it becomes too much, Sean and I have decided to call a halt to the documentary. For now, we'll keep going. As always, thanks for the support and speak later.'

As Jenny finished, Sean watched an explosion of hearts appear on the screen.

* * *

Sean and Jenny moved back into the bedroom, glancing at Beth and Ethan who were still asleep.

The hundreds of people who had watched their YouTube live inspired them to keep going with the documentary.

They sat on the end of the bed, listening to the drilling noise start again, this time from the box room underneath.

'I'm starving. Do you want to eat?'

'Are you cooking?'

'It can be arranged.' Sean leant forward and kissed her on the lips.

* * *

Twenty minutes later, as Jenny was checking her phone and Sean was downstairs frying bacon, she heard Ethan wake, as if on cue. 'Morning, sunshine.'

Ethan stretched, blinking a few times to adjust to the dim light coming from the window. 'What time is it?'

'Time you got up and studied, young man. You're starting a new Uni soon. Those high grades won't appear themselves.'

Ethan threw his head back on the pillow. He turned away. 'Is Dad cooking?'

'Yes. Come on, up you get.'

Ethan stood, pulled on a pair of jeans and a T-shirt, and left the room. As he moved to the stairs, he met his father on his way up, holding four plates on a tray.

'Wow. You're a legend, Dad.'

'No, I'm a bloody slave.'

Ethan let him pass and followed him into the bedroom.

Sean turned on the light and was greeted with the pleasure on his family's faces. 'Don't get used to it. I've only brought this up as I'd rather keep away from Mr Personality downstairs.'

Sean went on to complain that the guy would never win tradesperson of the year.

After they'd eaten, Beth asked if Ethan would like to go for a walk. She felt cooped up and needed some fresh air.

Sean stared at Jenny. His anxiety was rife. He couldn't carry on like this.

They'd be fine. They were together.

As Beth opened the bedroom door, the locksmith shouted up from the stairs.

'Just the kitchen to do now. Not long. I need to go to the van. Tea was great, but I'd love biscuits with the next one.'

Sean went to say something but Jenny covered his mouth, laughing.

'Where should we go?'

'Wherever you like. Shall we walk up the road to the right? I haven't been there yet.'

Beth nodded. She'd only suggested the walk because she wanted to speak with him about her concerns. The chalk people on the board distressed her. She needed to understand what was going on.

Ethan grabbed the key from the rack and twisted it in the kitchen door.

'You OK, Beth?'

She smiled weakly.

'Damn.' Ethan paused, looking forlorn. 'I don't believe it.'

'What's happened?'

'The key. It's broken in the door.'

'Come on, we'll go out the front.' Beth moved down the drive. As she walked past, the locksmith stuck his head out from the side of the van. 'All right, beautiful?'

She continued walking, without turning back to look at him. 'Sod off.'

As Ethan followed her, the tradesman slid back inside the van, worried that he may be her partner.

* * *

They walked a half-mile or so along the country road. They hadn't seen any vehicles or pedestrians, and the only sound was birdsong coming from the trees.

They passed a large, detached house. The lawn was neat and the grass trimmed short. The driveway was empty, and it looked as if paving had recently been laid. A shed to the right-hand side of the house contained a pile of coal.

'That's a good sign.'

'What is?' asked Beth.

'The house. The new driveway. It means they're staying. See? It can't be that bad.'

Beth stopped. 'What does it mean?'

Ethan knew Beth was talking about the chalk people. 'Look. It's probably some local tosser trying to scare us.'

'You really think that?'

Ethan was careful with his answer. 'Beth, we're together. I won't let anything happen. There's quite obviously a local weirdo who gets their kicks out of scaring people. Try not to think about it.'

'Oh, OK then. Thanks for making it so easy for me.'

'Beth, come on. Nothing is going to happen, you hear?'

She turned, staring across at the fields. 'It's so secluded.'

'Come on, let's go back.'

Beth gasped as they turned around. A figure was standing to the side of the road – a huge guy in a long, black coat, possibly the same person she'd seen in the garden. He was staring in their direction.

She pulled at her brother's sleeve. 'Someone is there, Ethan.'

'Where?'

She moved out onto the road.

The figure was gone.

'I swear, he was there a second ago. He was watching us.'

Ethan joined her where she stood. 'I can't see anything. Maybe you saw a shadow?'

'He's waiting, Ethan. I think he's moved into the ditch.'

They continued along the narrow pavement, both firmly staring ahead, watching for the watcher.

Beth was struggling to move. She felt dizzy.

Her surroundings began to turn, spinning around her like a carousel. 'Wait, I don't feel good.' She sat on the kerb. Ethan sat down next to her. 'It's too much. I hate this place.'

He waited until she calmed down, offering reassuring plati-tudes. After a couple of minutes, she assured him she felt better.

He helped her up and they continued walking.

'He was there.' Beth pointed to a bush approximately twenty yards to her left.

Ethan walked in front, upping the pace. He stared at the bush. Was it moving? He couldn't be sure. A bramble sway-ing, the snap of a twig under someone's foot.

'Hello? I have a knife. I'll use it, I swear.' Ethan waited, not expecting an answer. He moved forward and paused, adjusting his stance, then he reached for the bushes and pulled them apart.

The space was empty.

Ethan blew out a sigh of relief.

He needed to get them back to the farmhouse.

Now.

It was all becoming too much.

They walked down the drive, past the van and around to the side door, which was closed. Beth didn't like that the lock-smith was still here working. She didn't want strangers in the house. She just wanted to go to her bedroom and chill out. Her nerves were playing up and she needed time out.

Ethan knocked on the front door. Beth stood beside him.

'How was the walk?' Sean asked, standing aside to let them in.

A loud, drilling noise echoed from the kitchen.

'How much longer do we have to put up with this?' Beth moaned.

'I don't know. Your mum and I have been upstairs.'

'I have a few things to do. I'm going to my room.' Beth pushed past them.

'And you?' Sean looked at Ethan.

'Same.'

They both disappeared up the stairs.

'All OK in there?' Sean screamed.

In the kitchen, a thumb was held up through the roar.

Sean blocked his ears, noting the cloud of dust that hung in the air, then made his way up the stairs too.

* * *

Beth opened her laptop. She needed to find a job. She was too old to rely on her parents. Although they never mentioned it, she felt like she should be contributing and able to pay for the odd meal or takeaway, or offer to share in the bills.

She searched for local recruitment agencies, and a list of jobs showed for which she had no credentials or experience. She moved to pages two and three, then closed the laptop, feeling uninspired.

She stood and moved to the window. The rain had ceased, but the clouds were still blanketing the sky. She looked to where she had seen the figure at the end of the garden a couple of days ago and thought about the walk earlier. Was there someone watching her? Her body began to spasm, like an electrical charge pulsing through her bones. She needed to take her mind off things.

She went downstairs and into the kitchen. The lock-smith had finished and the noise had ceased.

The kitchen door opened, and the man moved past her into the hallway.

'All done. Tell your father I'll send the invoice. I have another emergency to get to.'

'Fine. Bye.'

She grabbed a loaf of bread from the fridge, popped a couple of slices in the toaster, then turned on the radio to keep herself distracted.

When she finished her food, she washed the plate in the sink and moved out of the kitchen. The smell of paint was still notable in the air.

Beth thought back to when she and her father first came here. She remembered being so excited, so hopeful. Now, she wanted to run and keep running, as far away as possible. She climbed the stairs, her eyes focused on the steps in front of her, determined that nothing would enter her mind – no visions, no lurking shadows; only pleasant thoughts. She opened the door to her parents' bedroom. Her mother and father were sitting on the edge of the bed, chatting and laughing together. She instantly felt at ease.

'He's finally done.'

Jenny smiled, feeling a little safer.

'Oh, he said he'd send the invoice.'

'Did he leave spare keys?' her father asked.

'I'm not sure. He rushed off. He had another emergency, he said.'

'Fine. Well, I'll wait for his invoice. I hope he was polite to you?'

'He was fine. I feel sorry for him, having to work.'

'Everyone has to work, Beth. How else do bills get paid?'

'Yeah, but at his age?'

'He's not that young. I'd say eighteen, nineteen. He's making a living. You have to admire him for that.'

Beth paused, taking in what her father had just said. 'Eighteen or nineteen? More like seventy.'

'What are you talking about?' Sean looked at his daughter, his eyebrows furrowed and his lips tight.

'The locksmith. Who do you think?'

'Yes, but he's not seventy. I think your eyes are playing up.'

Beth turned towards the front door. 'The guy that was downstairs. He's an old man.'

Sean stood. 'What did he look like?'

'I don't know. Like an old man.'

'Cut the sarcasm. What did he look like, Beth?'

'He was wearing a hoodie, with the hood pulled down over his face, dark greyish trousers, and dark glasses. His skin looked an odd yellow colour, like he'd suffered burns. And it looked like he was wearing canoes instead of boots. The guy was enormous.'

Sean stood. He looked at Jenny. Her face had dropped as if she'd had a stroke. His mind raced, a mass of hysteria bombarding his thoughts. His skin became red hot, like he'd break into blisters at any second. 'Stay here. Whatever happens, wait. Barricade yourselves inside.'

'Sean. Don't go downstairs.'

He closed the door, then turned, speaking through the crack in the wood. 'Place something against the door. Do it.'

He charged along the hallway and thumped on Ethan's door. 'Ethan, are you in there?'

'Yeah. What's up?'

'I don't have time to explain. Sit against the door and stay there.'

As he raced down the stairs, his mobile rang. He looked at the screen, not recognising the number. 'Hello?'

'Sean, It's Billy. Billy Huxton.'

When he reached the ground floor, he ran along the hallway and opened the door to the living room. He rushed towards the sofa, kicking boxes over as he moved, and checked under the table.

'Billy. What can I do for you?'

'Sean, we need to talk. Is it a good time?'

Sean moved out of the living room and opened the door to the toilet room, pushing it hard against the wall. He stared at the toilet and sink.

'Not really. A little pre-occupied here, Billy.'

He turned and opened the store cupboard.

'It's a matter of urgency. I do need to talk to you. It's about your uncle.'

Sean went to the kitchen. First, he checked behind the door, then behind the breakfast bar, and lastly, he moved to the kitchen door. 'What about him?' He tried the key that sat in the lock. It wouldn't turn.

He backed out, his eyes focused on the kitchen door. He called up the stairs. 'Did anyone break a key in the lock?'

'Me. I did it earlier, when Beth and I went for a walk. We used the front door instead. I thought the locksmith would replace it.'

'What did you do with the other half?'

'I left it in the barrel.'

Sean turned, looking back down the hallway and seeing the shiny new lock on the front door. He pushed the box room open and pulled back the carpet. Another new barrel, glistening like a mirror.

He moved back to the kitchen. He reached forward, removing the key from the lock. He shone his phone torch. Again, the lock looked new, shiny, polished, but Sean had a suspicion. He felt paranoid, his brain was aching and his body pumped with adrenaline.

Sean had to prove it to himself.

He removed the key, again shining the torch into the barrel. There it was. The piece Ethan had broken earlier.

The lock had been polished to look new.

But the old key remained broken and stuck in the mechanism. The locksmith replaced the other two, but not this one.

He listened to Billy's voice.

'Sean, we need to come over now. Your uncle, Ed Berry. I think he's Creeper.'

Sean dropped his phone on the floor.

The only thing that registered was that someone had been in the farmhouse.

Someone may get in again tonight.

31

S ean placed the memory stick in the slot and they watched the unseen footage, proof that Ed Berry had murdered Ronnie Hathaway – evidence that he'd likely killed all eight women. When the recording finished, he sat, stunned.

Jenny squeezed his leg supportively.

'It's my uncle. How could he do it? Why?' Tears rolled down his cheeks. He felt ashamed, embarrassed – the same blood ran through their veins. 'What now?'

Billy had stayed standing to avoid the trouble he'd had last time getting off the sofa. 'We'll give the footage to the police. Someone is coming by later to collect it. I called them again last night to update them.'

'Billy, Declan, thank you both. It's certainly a shock.' He watched as both men dropped their heads in respect. 'I'm going to see my mother.'

Jenny moved closer to Sean. 'What are you going to say?'

'I need answers.' He moved out to the hallway and called up the stairs. 'Beth, Ethan, come on. We're going to see your grandmother.'

* * *

On the drive to Oxford, Sean was silent. His mind raced with questions, things he needed to know. He needed to find out more about Ed Berry.

'Sean, look out.' Jenny watched as a fox sprung out onto the road.

He spun the wheel and hit the brakes, then sat for a moment. He straightened his back.

'Do you want me to drive?'

'I'm good.'

Beth leant forward. 'What's going on, Dad?'

Jenny turned. She couldn't hide it from her kids. They'd find out eventually. 'We think Ed Berry may still be alive.'

'What?' Ethan removed an AirPod from his ear. 'Alive, you said?'

'Not only that. He may have returned to the farmhouse,' Sean added.

'Oh my God. What is going on?' Beth looked between her parents. 'Did he murder those women? Has he taken Marie Nelson?'

'Beth, we don't know. It's possible. We're going to your grandmother. We need to talk with her.'

'When did you speak to her last?' Jenny asked.

'The other day.'

'How did she seem?'

'Oh, the usual. Tired and missing us. She'd have me move home tomorrow if she could.'

* * *

They drove through Oxford High Street. The road was busy, and the cafes and restaurants were bustling with students from the local university. The streets were filled with families, couples and tourists, all taking in the beautiful city.

The Satnav instructed them to take a left. Sean eased the steering wheel and drove to the end of the street. He hadn't been to see his mother for a few weeks, and as he got nearer to the house, he felt a tad guilty. He pondered the upcoming conversation. What would he say to her?

Hey, Mum. I know I haven't been here for a while – there's no excuse, but I do Facetime, just so you remember what I look like. I need to chat. Over in Painswick, there's a shady character called Creeper. Oh, he lurks in the darkness and loves to watch the locals. You know what? Sometimes he even gets into their houses, crawls around in the basement and enters their bedrooms while they sleep. Why, only the other day, we think he got into our bedroom. He photographed Jenny

while she slept. There are also eight missing women, and people believe Creeper has taken them. Mad, isn't it? Oh, by the way, we think it may be your brother. How crazy is that? Good old uncle Ed. Dead Ed is back. He's going to kill us while we sleep.

'Your destination is on the left.'

He sighed, stretched his back, then undid his seatbelt.

They all stood together on the street, peering up at the house.

It looked like something from the Hansel and Gretel story, a place you'd stumble upon if you were lost in the woods. The only comfort were the adjoining houses on each side. The house was dark; Sean had never realised how sinister it looked. The large, black brickwork was chipped and crumbling. Wisteria swept around the walls as if grasping the building in its claws. The gate was hanging to its side, held only by one rusted hinge. The path was camouflaged with tall weeds, and the front garden dotted with dead flowers, bent and distorted.

Sean approached first. He pressed the doorbell and waited. A minute later, a woman answered.

'Sean. Jenny.' She looked past them, seeing her grand-kids. 'What a pleasant surprise.'

Mary Freeman was almost seventy but looked much older. She was small, frail-looking, and due to her back problems, her posture was slightly arched. Her hair was full but had long turned grey and her fingers were bony and distorted from arthritis.

Beth moved forward and hugged her grandmother. Then Ethan did the same.

'Well, this is wonderful. Come in.' Mary pushed the door back and they stepped inside.

The house was dark, and a faint, damp smell hung in the hallway. The floor was tiled with the grout missing, and the walls were decorated with pictures – most hanging lopsided – held with rusted nails. Patches of the paint had crusted and large bubbles were notable across the walls.

The kitchen was old-fashioned. Mary had a gas stove but no kettle, toaster or modern commodities.

She beckoned them over to an old, wooden table, the legs unsteady and rotten with woodworm, where six chairs were stationed, some pushed close to the table while others clumsily leant back against the wall.

'Tea?'

'Yes, please, Mum.'

'Beth, Ethan, can you occupy yourselves? Maybe go into the garden?'

Ethan looked miffed. 'Dad...'

Jenny darted a look at her son as if to say, go.

Once the kids were outside, Sean took a deep breath. He felt sick, his stomach was in knots and an ache was working up the back of his neck.

'Mum, we need to talk.'

'Isn't that what we're doing?'

'I need to know about Ed Berry.'

She dropped the teapot, spilling water over the floor.

'I've got it. Sit down, Mary. I'll make the tea.' Jenny grabbed a mop and soaked up the water.

His mother sat opposite him and placed her hands on the table. He watched as they began to tremble.

'Why do you want to know about Ed?'

He explained what was happening at the farmhouse, and Mary listened, her mouth open, her hollow cheeks almost pinching together. When he'd finished explaining what had happened the last couple of days, he prepared to tell her about the footage they'd found. Mary stared at the wall behind where he sat. Tears formed in her eyes.

'I don't know anything about him.'

Sean tried to be as delicate as possible. 'Mum, please. We've seen a recording. It was buried deep in the walls of the basement.' He briefly told his mother what was on it.

Again, Mary denied knowing anything about his adult life.

Jenny brought the teapot and three cups to the table, then sat, placing her hands over Mary's. Her skin was icy cold and her fingers felt like broken twigs. 'Mary, we may be in danger. We're begging you, if you know anything about Ed Berry, please tell us. Please.'

Mary closed her eyes as if in a trance. She stayed that way for over a minute.

Jenny locked eyes with Sean, desperately.

They both jumped as Mary suddenly pounded her fists on the table.

'It was all so long ago. It's like a distant memory now, a past that no one wants to hear or discuss.' She looked at her son and then at Jenny. 'Ed was my younger brother – you already know that. My father, Cecil Berry, was a good man. He worked long hours, often leaving before I got up and was home after I went to bed. My mother was always there for us. She was a housewife and took care of the run of the house, cooking, cleaning. You have to understand times were different back then. There weren't the opportunities women have now.

'I'd look forward to the weekends. Mum, Dad, Ed and myself would go to the park and walk for hours in the sunshine. Later Ed and I would sip iced lemonade at a local pub, while Dad had a pint of beer and Mum, a Bacardi and coke. Funny, the things you remember. We had little money, but we didn't care – as long as we had a roof over our head and hot food.

'I think I was about ten. Ed would have been eight. It was the first time I noticed anything was wrong. I loved having a brother, someone to share my childhood with, to cherish memories together. A unique bond – that's what I thought we had. I recall the first time, one Saturday morning: I went into Ed's room. He had posters of cars on the wall and a stack of comics that he'd collected. *Star Wars* toys filled the bedside cabinet and sat in frames. As I entered the room, I heard him talking to someone. He was on his knees, but not praying. The things he said I wouldn't repeat to this day. I backed out, pretending I wasn't there.

'Later, when Mum and Dad went out, I heard an almighty crash. I went running up the stairs and peered at Ed through the gap in the bedroom door. He was smashing the room like a bull had run loose. He was swearing, frothing at the mouth, throwing himself against the wall. I didn't know what was happening to him, but I was too frightened to go inside. I sunk to the floor, crying. As I sat, watching him, he seemed to come out of whatever trance he'd been in. He looked around, shocked, trying to figure out what he'd done.

'When Mum and Dad returned, I told them what had happened. They told me to wait downstairs. I heard them shouting at Ed, trying to control him. Mum began sobbing, Dad was screaming at the top of his voice. Ed was swearing at them, yelling all manner of profanities.

'Life became unbearable. The more we tried to help Ed, the worse it got.

'Remember, like Ed, I was just a child. We didn't have mobile phones or the internet or any other way of finding out what was happening to him. The day it happened, I can recall the incident so vividly. It's locked in my mind, like a birthmark. It never goes.

'A doctor called over – he was a friend of my father's and he wanted to help. My mum thought we should call a priest. It was a good day. We'd been playing in the garden. Ed loved the slide while I preferred the swings. Anyway, Doctor Conway was his name. He spoke to Ed. I listened from the top step. Doctor Conway was talking to my brother in his bedroom. He asked Ed what happens in his mind. Ed said he heard voices. The doctor asked him if he could control them. Ed said no; they came into his mind and they told him things, wicked acts he should carry out – cruelty, disruption, anguish, as much wickedness as possible.

'They continued speaking, and the doctor eventually recommended a course of tablets – Chlorpromazine. I don't know why I still remember that. The doctor told Ed he'd help. He said not to worry, that everything would iron itself out and he'd be well again.

'But as the doctor went to leave the room, Ed pushed

him down the stairs. He broke his neck. He was—' Mary paused, in grief. 'He was killed instantly.'

Sean and Jenny gasped, speechless.

Mary coughed. The story was taking its toll on her. She looked to the ceiling, her cheeks rosy, her lips dry.

'Let me get you a glass of water.' Jenny filled a glass from the cupboard and placed it in front of Mary on the table.

'Mum, I know this is difficult. Look, take a break. You don't have to—'

'And what? Live with the guilt?' she fired back. 'I need to get it out. You need to know what happened.'

Sean took a sip of his tea. 'So, what happened after Ed—' He couldn't finish the sentence.

'—murdered Doctor Conway?' Mary finished for him. 'They put him away. Locked him up like an animal.'

'Oh, my goodness. That's awful,' Jenny uttered. 'I'm so sorry. You must have been devastated.'

Mary stared at the wall. She began to rock slightly, as if she was under hypnosis. Tears rolled down her cheeks. She tilted her head forward.

'He was given electric shock treatment. My family believe it drove him over the edge. Doctor Conway was an accident, but the seven inmates and the nurse was an act of wickedness. That wasn't Ed, not the Ed I knew. He wouldn't do such an evil thing. They drove him mad in there.'

'What are you talking about?' Sean asked. 'Seven inmates? A nurse?' The words were familiar, but distant, characters from a different story, completely unrelated to this, to his family.

Mary paused. 'The slaughter at Greyshott Hall Psychiatric Hospital.'

32

'Hang on – the slaughter at Greyshott Hall, the seven inmates, Nurse Eastwood.' Sean turned to Jenny. 'A hideous, despicable atrocity, yes. But you're wrong. That was Mark Wheelan. He escaped and fled into the night.'

Mary clasped her hands together to help ease the next part of the story. 'Ed was a minor. When he was taken in, they changed his name. My father insisted on it. That way, if a news story leaked, his real name would be kept from the papers. It would shame the family. So, he became Mark Wheelan. It's well documented: minors who commit crimes and have their identities kept a secret.'

'How do you know this?'

Mary began to sob.

'What is it?'

'My parents didn't die in a road accident.'

'I thought they died on the M1; that's what I've believed all my life. You told me, Mum. My grandfather fell asleep at the wheel and he drove into the back of a lorry. He and Nan were killed instantly. That's what you said.'

'I lied!' Mary screamed.

Sean stood, brushing a hand through his hair. He looked into the garden, where Beth and Ethan were sitting on the sidewall, deep in conversation. He turned back. 'You lied? Why?' He placed a hand on the side unit to steady himself.

His skin felt tight and he wanted to run, far away from here. The more he heard, the more macabre the story became. He sat, not wanting to pose a threat by standing over his mother. 'Why did you lie?'

'Because the truth is so wicked and depraved, you wouldn't have dealt with it.'

'Try me now.'

Mary sat back, her fingers clasped together on top of her stomach. 'I remember my father, standing out there in the hallway, calling Greyshott Hall and asking to speak with Ed. They'd say they had no one of that name institutionalised. He'd forget. I told you the authorities changed his name, due to Ed being a minor. And even when they found Mark, he was always unavailable to talk. They were carrying out tests on him. Shock treatment.

'When Ed pushed Doctor Conway down the stairs, my father believed that he was just delusional, that tablets would stop any more episodes from happening. But the staff at Greyshott Hall continued with their experiments, tormenting Ed, driving him over the edge.

'We went to go see him – well, my parents did. I was never allowed in. I remember waiting by the front door. I heard the screams, women and children. I was terrified. I turned and ran into the woods. I still hear those screams to this day.'

'So, what happened? With your brother, I mean?'

'They came out – five, ten minutes later. My father was shouting. His fists were clenched, his eyes rabid, his face damp from sweat. Mum tried to calm him. They'd managed to see my brother. They'd got into the building, evading the security. They saw Ed – or Mark, as they'd named him – strapped to a bed in a cell and lying unconscious with machines, drips, this whole array of equipment. Dad was crying, biting the knuckles of his hand; Mum was holding him, saying that Ed would be fine. He was in the best care. They were the professionals.

'As we drove home, I sat in silence, weeping for my brother. My parents argued for days. My father wanted to file a case against Greyshott Hall, to bring them down. He spoke with a solicitor about it. He blamed them for Ed's deterioration.

'Then one evening, while we were sitting in the living room, we heard about what he'd done. A news bulletin interrupted the radio programme we had on. There had been a massacre. An inmate at Greyshott Hall had murdered eight people, then escaped. They warned people not to approach Mark Wheelan, to lock their doors and windows and call 999 if anyone saw him.'

Sean and Jenny sat, open-mouthed, as Mary relayed the truth.

'I don't understand, Mum. You say, Mark – sorry, Uncle Ed – escaped. We know the story. We covered it last week.' He thought back to the truck, the lunatic who'd chased them along the dark country road. It was all falling into place. 'How the hell did he get away with it?'

Mary took a deep breath. She appeared flustered, her body trembling slightly. 'I told you my parents didn't die in a car crash. Mark – sorry, I'm going to call him Ed – returned here a week after he escaped. Mum and Dad were down-stairs listening to the radio. I could hear them fighting from my room. Mum was shouting, saying they had to find him. I heard someone outside. I saw my brother crouched behind a tree in the garden. I was so scared. I waved at him, but he just stared at me, his face blank, empty.

'He moved to the shed. I saw the lights go on, and he began pulling out all these things – pots of paint, cloths, tools from the drawers. He found a container. I watched him lift it. It looked heavy. I opened the window and called out, asking him what he was doing. He looked up, but didn't say anything. Again, I questioned him, but he never responded.

'When he was younger, he'd try to please me, always worried about my opinion of him. I had a signal, a way to subliminally message that I wasn't angry at him, that I loved him – I'd often do it at parties or gatherings. I'd sing that old nursery rhyme, See-saw, Margery Daw. That way, Ed knew I wasn't cross. I'd sing it to him for hours, comforting him, showing him I loved him and wasn't annoyed.

'That night, as he stood by the shed door, he only said one thing. He asked me to sing it again. But I couldn't. He looked broken, distraught. I watched as he grabbed the container and opened the back door. I leant out of the window, trying to see what he was doing. I could hear liquid spilling onto the floor. I thought it was water. Ed came out, without looking up, and moved around to the front of the house.

'I walked to the top of the stairs. The radio was loud and Mum and Dad didn't hear him enter. He emptied most of the container, the rest he poured over a rag from his pocket, he lit a match and dropped the rag on the liquid. The flames spread instantly.

'I screamed, shouting for Mum and Dad to get out. Ed went round to the back door and must have dropped another cloth doused with petrol in the kitchen.

'I watched him digging in the garden with a shovel. He

went back into the house, through the flames, carrying something. I didn't realise what it was until later.

'I was terrified. I raced along the upstairs hallway. Ed had gone back into the garden. I could see him from the window. He was engulfed in flames. The screams still haunt me. He was a fireball, a bright, yellow mass. He rolled over on the lawn, but he'd been badly burned.

'I went to go downstairs. Mum and Dad tried to get to me but the fire was too ferocious.

It swept from the front and back of the house, meeting in the middle. They couldn't get out.

'I climbed out of my bedroom window and slid down the drainpipe. I'd done it before. Then I stood in the garden, just watching as the house began to collapse, caving in on itself. Ed had gone.

'When the fire brigade arrived, I lied. I said that my brother, mum and dad were all inside.'

'But Ed wasn't. He wasn't inside?'

'I covered for him. I don't know why. I was terrified. Ed had planned it all along. I saw him drag a body into the house, through the flames. I don't know who it was, how Ed had killed him. I don't want to know. When the police arrived, I lay on the grass, crying my eyes out. They asked me who was inside, and I lied again. I told them my brother was inside. His name was Ed Berry.

'The fire destroyed everything. No one realised the guy inside was not my brother. The body, lying charred and consumed by the flames, was far beyond recognition. And anyway, the police were looking for Mark Wheelan.

'I was taken into care for a year and when I was old enough, I began working. The house was left to me in the will. The insurance paid for the renovation work. I wanted to live here. After everything that had happened, it was the only way I could feel close to Mum and Dad.

'I saw Ed a couple of times after that night. He was unrecognisable. He would come and stand in the garden. He'd watch me. Although his face was completely disfigured, melted and unrecognisable, I knew. I knew it was him.

'I still have regrets. I'm petrified of the past. That's why I've held onto the secret for so long.

'If only I'd sang the nursery rhyme, maybe it all would have turned out differently. He may not have burned the house down. My brother needed me. He needed to hear it.

'See-saw, Margery Daw.'

33

B illy was sitting at the table in his son's kitchen. He was going through the list of names of the eight missing women. His finger smudged the paper as he moved it down the page.

He'd made notes under each name.

Chloe Madden. Twenty-One.

The first girl to go missing twenty years ago.

Parents died in a car crash on the M25. No next of kin.

Amelia Shaw. Eighteen.

Went to see Greta, Amelia's mother. Confirmed she and Amelia hadn't rowed before vanishing. She disappeared with no reasoning. Greta and her husband, divorced. He was an alcoholic. Greta downsized to a smaller house.

Police interviewed her at the time. She did mention that the day Amelia disappeared, the phone kept ringing. Greta had to disconnect it.

Anything to do with Amelia vanishing? Greta said she spoke to another mother at the time. Michelle Madden, Chloe's mother. She said the same thing happened the day Chloe went missing.

Charlotte Ryan. Eighteen.

Parents moved abroad. Untraceable at present. Voice messages left on both phones.

Her brother is in the army and we have left a message. Phone went straight to voicemail.

Emma Shawcroft. Twenty.

Father has dementia and currently in a care home. Mother died six years after Emma vanished. No siblings.

Ellie Simmonds. Nineteen.

Father hung himself two years after Ellie vanished. Have phone number for mother. No answer. One brother who moved to America. Possibly in Arizona. Phone has a weird dialling tone. Someone answered but said it was a wrong number.

Lily Painter. Eighteen.

Billy stopped, his finger pointed at the name.

'Declan, did you call the Painters?'

'No. Are they coming today? I think you should run it past your son first before you start decorating.'

Declan moved beside Billy at the table.

'Can you take anything seriously? Did you call them or not?'

'Yes, Captain. An elderly woman answered. I presume it was Lily's mother. I told her we were looking into the case, that there was new evidence. She told me she wasn't prepared to help. The police did little to nothing to find her daughter and she'd rather be left alone.'

Billy wrote a brief summary under Lily's name.

Michelle Casey. Twenty-Two.

Billy grabbed his mobile phone from the table and dialled the numbers he had for the Casey's. The first one was dead. The second rang out. It was a local number. He waited. On the fifth ring, someone answered.

'Hello?'

'Mrs Casey?' There was no response so he continued. 'I'm Billy Huxton. I'm a private investigator looking into the disappearance of the eight Painswick women. We have new information that we think may be relevant to the case. Would it be possible to call over?'

'I'm afraid not.'

'Is it possible to talk to you for a few minutes? It really is important.'

'I have nothing to say.'

'Please, Mrs Casey. It could help us catch the person responsible.'

There was a pause. Billy thought she'd hung up. 'Responsible! So why did nothing happen at the time? You think you'll catch him now? After all these years? Don't make me laugh! Do you know what it's like? Having a child go missing? Watching the front door, day after day, clinging to the hope that they'll return? To wake in the morning and go to bed at night with nothing but your child's image ingrained in your mind? Not being able to say goodbye or know what happened? To hang in limbo for eternity, always guessing, trying to piece together what happened, hoping she's out there, that she loves you and it wasn't your fault. Going over each day, trying to figure out why they left. Did I say something wrong? Did I listen enough? Was I an attentive mother, teacher, provider? These are questions I will never have answered. So, no. I don't want to talk. Because I'm better off dead. I know she's not alive. Because Michelle would never put me through this. I've been to hell and back many times. Sometimes I wish I'd found her with her throat slit. At least I could grieve. But you pick up the phone with your questions, theories and all measure of bullshit. You'll never know what it's like for a child to go missing. You'll never understand.'

The phone went dead.

Billy looked at the last name on the list.

Katie Huxton. Eighteen.

* * *

The four of them got into the car.

Mary stood at the gate, waving. 'Don't leave it so long next time.'

Beth opened the window. 'I can come for a few days during the Christmas Break.'

Ethan leant over his sister. 'Me too.'

'Forget it,' Beth said.

Mary dabbed her tears with a tissue and smiled. 'I'll call

you at the weekend.' She watched as the car disappeared along the road, then stood for a few minutes, her body drained.

She closed the door and walked back into the kitchen. She sat, exhausted from the strain of telling Sean and Jenny what had happened, the truth about her brother. Bringing it all back had made her an emotional wreck.

She thought about Ed, the secret she'd carried for so long. What was he doing now? And were the rumours true? Was her brother still living in Painswick and responsible for the women who had gone missing? As a child, Mary had witnessed the worst atrocity. She'd heard her mother and father as they burned alive, hearing the bellows of her parents as the flames tore them apart.

The things her brother was capable of didn't bear thinking about. He was wicked, demonic, evil beyond any comprehension.

As she sat at the table, the nursery rhyme played in her head. If only she'd sang it, maybe her parents' lives could have been spared.

She sat with her back straight, her hands placed on the table. She began to sing, softly at first, a slight smile on her face.

See-saw, Margery Daw.
    Johnny shall have a new master.
    He shall earn but a penny a day,
    Because he can't work any faster.

Suddenly a voice joined her.
    'See-saw, Margery Daw.'

Mary looked up.

Ed was standing in the hallway.

'Keep going,' he said. 'It means you approve, that you're not mad at me. You're not, are you? Please keep singing the song.'

She jumped up. She moved towards the kitchen door. She stared at her brother's face.

In all her life, she had never seen anything so hideous. His skin was distorted, like a melted rubber mask. Only it was real. His eyes were hollow, pushed back in his head, his nose seemed like one large nostril and his eyebrows were missing.

He looked more ghastly than she could ever have imagined, an evil, chilling face to match his wicked soul.

'Get out. I don't want you here.' She moved around the table.

Ed Berry ran at her.

'Please. Leave me alone. Get out of my house. All those terrible things you've done. I will never approve.'

'Sing the song, Mary. Make the voices better. Make them stop.'

'Get out. Do you hear me?'

She picked up a vase and hurled it towards him, watching it bounce off the wall near where he stood.

'Sing the song, Mary. Just one more time.'

'I'll never sing it.'

'Come on, Mary. See-saw, Margery Daw.'

'Get out.' She grabbed a frying pan from the side unit. She threw it, and it crashed against Ed's face. He fell back, losing his footing, giving Mary time to rush past him. She ran along the hallway, screaming at the top of her voice. She heard him push himself off the wall, his footsteps close behind her.

She grabbed the front door handle but it was locked. She turned around.

Ed was holding a key. 'You left it in the door. You're getting forgetful, Mary.'

He was almost on top of her.

She clambered for the stairs, falling on her knees, and crawled upwards, pulling herself towards the first floor with trembling hands. 'Why are you doing this? Leave me alone.'

Ed was behind her. She could feel his breath against her skin.

'You told them, didn't you?'

When she reached the top step, Ed grabbed on to her left leg and held it.

'Let me go. Please. I told them nothing, you hear?'

Mary broke loose and kicked out, catching him above his eye.

'You told them, Mary.' Ed stood, watching as the bedroom door closed. His face was sore, his eye was cut and he was struggling to breathe.

In her bedroom, Mary dropped to the floor. She listened. It was silent. Had Ed gone? Left her alone? She doubted it.

She hoisted her legs up, clambering against the door, using all her strength to press against it. She waited. She could feel her heart throbbing in the side of her neck. Her body was pained. Her legs were weak.

Seconds turned to minutes. Mary was unsure how much time had passed. Her mobile phone was downstairs, otherwise she'd have no hesitation in calling the police. She'd tell them everything, that Ed Berry, her brother, was responsible for the murder of their parents, a number of inmates and a string of missing women.

The house remained still. Nothing had changed in minutes – no sounds, no stirrings.

Mary stood. She was going to get her phone. She stretched her tired body, pushing her neck upwards, her back cracking. She turned and opened the bedroom door.

'Hello?' No answer.

She moved out to the hallway and peered over the rail towards the ground floor. Once she was sure it was safe, she crept towards the stairs.

Ed Berry was standing in the corner of the hallway, partly hidden behind a wall that led to another part of the house.

'No, Ed. I beg you.'

He grabbed her, threw her over his shoulders and marched into the bedroom.

Mary was shouting, kicking her feet against his back. But it was no use. It was as if he couldn't even feel it.

'Put me down. I'll sing the song, Ed. I'll sing it for you. See-saw, Margery Daw.'

Ed dropped his sister on the floor. Then he grabbed her cardigan and threw her headfirst out of the bedroom window.

He stood, looking down on her mangled body as it lay lifeless on the grass.

34

I watch your mangled, twisted body for what feels like days. I didn't expect the noise as the glass shattered, the shards breaking all over the bedroom floor, the mess on the carpet – hundreds of crystal-like specks lying under my feet.

I look out over the garden. The frost from this morning has long evaporated, the chill having disintegrated as the sun broke through the blanket of clouds.

You are so still now as you lie, slumped, on the damp grass. It's long, pushing up to your elbows. You've neglected it. It's not what I'd have expected of you.

I don't have long. I need to act fast. My time is quickly drawing to a close and I know I'll need to move on soon, take shelter elsewhere. I'm good at that. I'm able to adapt to my situations, adjust to my surroundings and melt into the background.

Please don't be mad at me, Mary. I had to take such dramatic action. I know that, eventually, you'll forgive my behaviour. You always do.

I hope you can hear my thoughts. As you lie there, I hope that the worries of this world are far behind you, dissolving as you move on to a better place – well, that's the plan. It's what we all hope. But if you can hear, if you're already watching me, listening, curious as to how I work, then understand why, why I had to do the things I've done. Mary, you've never judged, never incriminated me or scalded me for my wrongdoings. You were the one person who saw past the wickedness that infested my mind.

I was fourteen. I know I did a wicked thing – the doctor. I remember Mum and Dad, how infuriated they were. It was the last straw, I know.

Dad had a friend, someone in the medical profession – he knew lots of people: doctors, surgeons. Well, one of them assured him it was the correct thing to do. Greyshott Hall Psychiatric Hospital.

Ed just needed help, he said, a push in the right direction, a finger pointing to the right path.

This man was also able to convince the people who ran the place to keep my identity a secret. To make me someone else. Mark Wheelan.

I was a minor, fourteen years old, a child. Locked in a dark, dingy cell around the clock. As I lay there, I became more sick; the voices in my head were louder, amplified. I heard screams from my peers long into the night.

I remember the rooms with bright lights and people standing over me, holding all manner of implements. The staff told me it needed to be done, that I'd be better soon and the voices would cease. But they only increased in frequency; they came for me regularly.

Greyshott Hall was hell. That's how I look back at my time there.

When I left, the main thing I remember was the air, that first inhale of freedom; it was indescribable.

I felt like I could fly. I remember walking for hours, catching lifts from strangers, not knowing where I was going, just keeping moving, getting far away from Greyshott Hall and the intimidating shadow it cast.

I was invisible. My father had made it so; my slate was clean, my identity deleted, erased.

As I said, Mary, he knew people in high places. He must have paid vast amounts of money for this to happen.

The police had nothing to go on: no address, no phone number, no details of Mark Wheelan. Not even any photographs. I had a fresh start.

Mary, I hope you can hear me. I never forgave Mum and Dad for leaving me there to rot, another psychiatric patient adrift, misplaced in the system. It eats me up inside, what they put me through, having me sectioned – the experiments. I feel it only added to the burden I carry – my development. The way I think, function – the lack of help and support.

At my worst, the voices are constant, the cycles repetitive, monotonous.

I made my way to Oxford. If you want to know whether I meant to kill them, burn the house to the ground and watch them engulfed in flames, then yes. I did. I planned it all. Every second.

I knew there'd be details, records of my family and who we were. I was Ed Berry. I had a life before moving to Painswick. So, I befriended a homeless person, I brought him food, offered my company. Then I beat him to death. I removed his teeth so he couldn't be identified, I doused him in petrol and I placed him in the house with my parents.

When the police investigated the fire, they found three

bodies: my mother, my father and an unidentified body they presumed to be me, Ed. You also confirmed this, Mary. Thank you for covering it up.

When I moved to Painswick, no one realised that I was the Ed Berry who died that night. The authorities presumed Mark Wheelan was still at large, and still do to this day. Quite the scam I pulled, thanks to you and my parents. But I will never forgive them.

I'm sorry, Mary. You were the one who I salvaged. The only person exempt from our vile bloodline. But you couldn't keep your mouth shut. I feared it for so long.

And now they know.

I hid the recording in the farmhouse. It had to stay there – my way out, my alibi. I would frame Ronnie Hathaway and make it look like he was involved, that he committed the murders.

Ronnie's problem was greed. He made me a lot of money, raised enough funds for the farmhouse, but he couldn't control his selfishness, threatening to tell everyone what I'd done. I had to kill him. But I also had to make it look like he'd come for me.

Now, you've gone and spoiled everything. You couldn't keep it to yourself.

I've been watching your son and his family. The Free-mans. The last in the bloodline. For so long I've planned the things I will do to them.

Now they have moved to Gallows Lane, my home. It's time.

Ed Berry looked down at his sister, lying on her side. He was sure he saw her mouth moving.

'See-saw, Margery Daw. I give you my blessing while slumped on the floor.

'See-saw.

'See-saw.'

35

S ean pulled into the farmhouse and stared at the enormity of the building in front of him. They'd pinned so much on this place. A feeling of sadness washed over him.

After speaking with his mother and learning of the terrible things she'd gone through, it was all falling into place. Ed Berry, his uncle, was the person everyone in Painswick was so frightened to discuss. The dark cloud that had lurked over this village for so long was finally becoming lighter with the truth.

'Sean.'

'Sorry, I was miles away.'

Jenny turned to him. 'You didn't hear a thing I said, did you? I suggested we get a takeaway tonight. Christ knows we need to have family time, a release.'

'Good shout.'

As they entered through the front door, a dull cloud hanging over their heads, Beth asked what she'd been holding back for the whole car ride.

'What were you and Mum talking about with Nan?'

'Oh, nothing in particular.' Sean couldn't tell them the details of their conversation. He had to let it sink in, mull it over for a while. In time, he'd tell his kids who their grand-uncle was, but not now.

Sean stood and watched as his family walked into the kitchen, his eyes sweeping along the hallway and up the stairs. He didn't feel safe here anymore. But how would it look? Packing their stuff and fleeing? Running into the night, giving in to the monster that provoked fear in the village for so long? They had nowhere to go.

Sean wanted to call the police. He wanted surveillance put in place, someone to watch the farmhouse as they slept. But how could he prove they were in grave danger? How could he get it through to them that this was a matter of life and death? His victims have all been a particular type: young women on the cusp of adulthood. Until Creeper was caught, surely everyone in Painswick was at risk?. He could pick any of the homes here. What made the Freemans so special?

'Dad,' Beth called from the kitchen.

Sean broke himself away from his thoughts. 'Yes? What is it?'

'I have to tell you something.'

Sean joined his family. 'What's up?'

Beth began to cry. Her brother, who was standing beside her, moved closer. Jenny and Sean joined him.

'Beth, what's wrong?'

She was shaking, acting in a nervous manner. 'I think someone got into the house.'

'When? Talk to me, Beth.'

She described the chalk people, the first time they

appeared and then again last night. She spoke of how she'd called Ethan, the chalkboard being wiped clean. As she spoke, she had to keep stopping to gasp for breath, and her body was bent forward, as if she would throw up any second. She finished by telling them about the man she'd seen at the end of the garden, holding a red coat.

Ethan chose to remain silent. He was peeved that Beth had brought this up. He didn't want his parents worrying. They had enough to deal with.

'Bloody hell, Beth. How could you keep this from us?' Jenny pulled her daughter into her arms and kissed her head.

'Because I'm scared. I don't want to be here anymore. I hate this place.'

'Mum and I won't let anything happen to you. I mean it. We'll protect you, you hear?'

Beth nodded.

'The locks have been replaced. Well, not the kitchen but we'll deal with that matter. The hole in the basement is sealed. No one is getting into the house, OK?'

Again, Beth nodded.

Sean glanced at his watch. 'Right, what do you say we grab a takeaway, watch a film and have some us time?'

'Dad, I have to—'

Sean cut Ethan short. 'You have to do nothing. It's an order. Come on.'

'Fine. Just don't put on a tear-jerker. I hate those films.'

Sean opened the laptop and looked up the local curry house. The top half of the page was splashed with photographs: dishes they served, the staff with local celebrities and awards they had won for their cuisine.

Once everyone had chosen their meals, he gave their

order to a chirpy man on the phone who told them they could have a twenty-five percent discount if they collected.

Sean was adamant he wouldn't leave his family alone.

* * *

An hour later, there was a knock at the door.

The four of them were in the living room, halfway through the new Quentin Tarantino film.

'I got it.' Sean heaved himself off the sofa and walked to the living room window. It was beginning to get dark. He pushed his face to the glass and saw a man wearing biker clothes and a helmet, carrying a large paper bag.

'Everything OK?' Jenny asked.

'Yes, just checking. Be back in a minute.' On the way to the front door, he dipped into his pocket and removed two twenty pound notes.

'That's forty-one pounds in total.' The man kept his helmet on, only opening his visor.

Sean handed the notes over and another five pound note from his pocket.

The man placed it in a bumbag and turned to walk away.

'Er, my change?'

'Oh, hang on.'

Nice try.

The guy dipped into a box on the back of his scooter and returned a minute later.

With that attitude, Sean was adamant he wasn't going to give him a tip.

As the delivery guy moved down the drive, revving the bike profusely, Sean went to shut the front door. But he paused when he saw a car pull up on the road. There was a woman in the driver's seat. She wound the window down and waved frantically.

Sean dropped the food on the hallway floor and moved towards her. 'Can I help you?'

'I'm Angela Burrows. I'm your neighbour.'

'Oh wow. Sorry if I seemed a little rude. It's so good to meet you.'

The woman was in her early thirties and had short black hair with streaks of purple running through the middle. She wore glasses that were perched way down on her nose. She smiled eagerly.

Sean leant in the window and shook her hand. He could feel the warm air as it pushed from the vents. He told her about his family, how they were settling in, and how they were just about to try some food from the local curry house.

'Ooh, which one?'

'Bombay Dreams, I think.'

'Well, you and your family are welcome over to ours anytime. I cook a mean curry. We'll let you settle in first, though. Won't we, Abigail?'

Sean hadn't noticed the small girl sitting in the back seat.

'Hello. How old are you?'

'I'm five. It's nice to meet you.'

'Wow. And so polite.'

The girl was looking at the farmhouse. She breathed hard on the window and began to draw in the condensation. First, she drew a square, then added the windows, front door and finished with the chimney, adding smoke for effect.

'You're very talented,' he said.

Then she drew a stick man. 'That's you.'

'Wow, I wish I was that skinny.'

Sean and Angela laughed.

She then drew another one.

'Is that my wife?'

Abigail leant forward, and in a calm voice, she whispered, 'No. It's the man who has just gone into your house.'

36

Billy stared at his daughter's name at the bottom of the list. Katie Huxton. Eighteen. He fought the lump in his throat.

'We're gaining on him, Billy. The net is closing in. We're going to catch the bastard. We're going to catch Ed Berry.' Declan placed his hand on Billy's shoulder. 'You hear me?'

Billy parted his lips. For a moment, Declan thought he was going to smile.

'I hear you. Look, I haven't had a chance to thank you. You gave up a week's holiday. You came down here, to the middle of nowhere, out of the goodness of your heart. You gave up your time, your generosity. You've kept me going during this awful time. Thank you, Declan.'

'You mean I'm not getting paid?'

'Seriously, let me acknowledge what you're doing for me. You won't often hear a compliment out of my mouth so take it while it's offered.'

'Billy, I wouldn't be doing anything interesting instead. I would wake, probably about 7am. I would take a shower, go downstairs, watch a bit of daytime telly. Mope around, order a takeaway, feel guilty for the pleasure, then wallow in self-pity that I have no company, sink a beer or two and go to bed. Then repeat. So no, you don't have to thank me. If anything, you're doing me a favour.'

'It sounds like the perfect day to me.' Billy did smile at that moment. He glanced down at the sheet of paper, the names. Katie. 'Look, I'm not deluded. I've had my time to mourn. I know deep down she's not coming home. Christ, I've had years to deal with it. But I need to catch the man responsible. I'm not under any illusions.' His eyes began to fill with tears. 'I know Katie isn't coming home. Let's just put a stop to anyone else going missing.'

'So, what now?'

The doorbell rang. Billy tensed. He walked into the living room and saw a police car on the drive. 'At last.'

At the front door, a man in a police uniform introduced himself. PC Stratford from Stroud Police station.

'Billy Huxton?'

'That's me. Come in, Officer.'

'Thank you. I got a message to call over. I understand you have footage of a possible confession.'

The two men walked through to the kitchen where Declan was waiting.

Billy handed over the memory stick. 'Not a possible confession – that's what we first thought. But further into the footage, you'll hear Ed Berry, a local who resided at a farmhouse in Painswick, take a hostage. I have no reason to doubt he murdered Ronnie Hathaway.'

'Any cause to think this?'

'Yes. Watch the tape. Make up your own bloody mind—'

Declan interrupted. 'We found this recording in the

walls of a farmhouse in Gallows Lane. You'll see for yourself. Billy is a private investigator and I used to work for the force myself.'

'Oh, right. Which station?'

'The Met, East London. Many moons ago. I have since moved on to better things: a job with solid prospects and a nice pension.'

'Sounds like you've landed on your feet. Doing what, may I ask?'

'A bingo caller at an old people's home. Lines and full houses, that's where it's at nowadays, PC Stratford. I firmly hold the balls, if you get my drift.'

'Yes, quite.' The officer turned to Billy, his face flushed with embarrassment. 'Can I ask? You said you believe a Mr Ed Berry could be responsible for the death of Ronnie Hathaway. Any reason you may think this?'

'If you listen to the recording, you'll know.' Billy was losing his patience. 'The other night, we called at Mr Hathaway's residence. I know it was wrong – I hold my hands up – but I strongly felt I had reason to enter the house.'

He went on to explain the events that had led to them following the black truck, the person who was entering the farmhouse and them finding the tape. He finished by describing how they'd seen a body, hanging from a wall at his home.

'So it was you who called it in?'

'Yes, I have an incident serial number. I suggest you listen to the footage.'

The officer finished writing his notes. He told them he'd get the footage looked at and would be in touch. He left his card in case anything else came up.

'Future bingo caller in the making there,' Declan said

once Billy had returned from walking PC Stratford to the door.

'You think?' He laughed for the second time in as many days. He could get used to working with Declan Ryan.

37

Not waiting to watch the car pull away from the drive, Sean spun and ran back to the farmhouse, the conversation with the little girl fresh in his mind.

'Is that my wife?' he'd said.

'No. It's the man who has just gone into your house.'

He couldn't get the images of the stickman she'd drawn on the window out of his head.

When he reached the front door, he passed the food in the hallway and moved to the living room.

'Ah, at last. What took you? The food must be freezing.'

Beth and Ethan looked at their father. On the TV, the film was paused.

'Did you see someone?' Sean directed the question at the three of them.

'What do you mean?' Jenny sat forward on the sofa.

'Did someone come into the house?'

'No, we've been sat here. I thought you were at the front door?'

Sean explained how their neighbour had pulled over

and introduced herself, and what the girl in the back seat had said.

The three of them stood up, worried expressions on their faces.

'I need to look over the house. This is fucking ridiculous.' He backed out of the room. 'Ethan, check down here. I'll check the basement and upstairs. Jenny, Beth, close this door. Sit against it.'

Sean darted up the stairs, avoiding the broken steps. Downstairs, Jenny and Beth could hear him pounding across the landing.

Ethan checked the box room, then moved along the hallway, peering into the storeroom, bathroom and the kitchen. 'Anything, Dad?'

'No. You?'

'Nothing. Seems clear.' Sean had opened Ethan's bedroom, the en-suite and the airing cupboard. He paced along the hallway and entered Beth's room, checking under the bed as he'd done with Ethan's room, looking to each corner and then out of the window. The garden seemed empty.

He checked his and Jenny's bedroom and the spare room and finished by pulling down the loft hatch to investigate the space at the top of the house.

He rushed down the stairs and opened the hatch in the box room. He shone his phone over the basement. Empty.

He climbed out, locked the hatch and closed the box room door.

Ethan was standing in the kitchen. 'No one is here, Dad. Come on, let's eat our food.'

Sean tapped his knuckles against the living room door. Beth and Jenny stood to the side to let he and Ethan in.

'No one got in, Sean. We'd hear them, surely.' Jenny moved to the sofa.

Beth got the plates and cutlery from the kitchen. She glanced down at the three mobile phones on the sideboard. 'Er, Dad. Your phone. Come on. There are the rules. If we watch a film, they're barred. Too much distraction.'

Reluctantly, Sean handed his phone to Ethan, who delivered it to Beth.

When am I going to feel normal? To not live in fear in my own home?

The evening got darker, the view now minimal outside the living room window.

As they ate, the family talked and reminisced, remembering the last time they'd had a takeaway, when they'd spent the last night in their old house. It all seemed so long ago. These days, the only thing the four of them could think about was survival.

Once they'd finished eating, Sean took the cartons, cutlery and plates into the kitchen. He washed the dishes in the sink and put the cartons in the recycling container.

Their landline phone in the hallway began to ring. Sean let it ring out, knowing it had to be a wrong number. Their friends would call their mobiles. Or it could be someone associated with the previous owner. He didn't want to get into a conversation.

It stopped, and Sean returned to drying the plates and placing them in the cupboard by his feet.

The phone rang again. Sean spun, looking towards the sound. 'Oh, for crying out loud.' He moved past the living room.

'Come on, Dad. We want to continue the film.'

'One second.' Sean stood over the phone. It had been here when they moved in, already connected. He watched it. The ringing seemed to get more aggressive as it continued, like an alarm pounding at 6am. Get up, out of bed and face the world.

He picked up the receiver. 'Hello?' He didn't want to announce his name. He listened. 'Hello?'

After a moment of silence, he placed the receiver back.

The phone rang again instantly.

'Oh, for God's sake.' He picked it up again. 'Hello? Who is this?' He waited, but nothing again. When he returned the receiver a second time, he watched it, his body cold. Warming the farmhouse was a mammoth task. He wondered if they'd ever be able to deal with the list of problems.

He moved away from the phone, hearing his family's voices coming from the living room. Beth was talking, telling Jenny about how she had to find a job.

The phone rang again. Sean almost expected it now and debated whether to leave it. The noise seemed to vibrate off the walls, crawling along the ceiling, pushing towards him. But he could not leave it alone. He walked forward and swiped the receiver. 'Hello? Who is this? Is someone there?'

He waited, a minute, two – no voice, no communication. He hammered the receiver back. When he turned and moved to the living room, the ringing came again.

'Who is it?' Jenny asked.

'I don't know. It has to be a wrong number, but when I answer it, no one is there.'

'Just leave it. They'll get bored.'

Sean sat on the one-seater they'd moved from the old house. He began thinking of all the great times they'd had together while living in Oxford. He hoped they could emulate the same here. He pulled the seat forward, now sitting next to Ethan who was perched on the sofa. 'Come on then, put it on.'

As Beth pressed play, Sean could still hear the phone ringing. He couldn't ignore it.

'Oh, for goodness sake.' He got off the seat, charged to the phone and answered. 'What the hell do you want? Hello? Stop ringing. Do you hear?' He waited. No one spoke. 'Stop ringing the bloody phone. Do you understand?'

He slammed the phone back. It rang again.

'Oh, this is ridiculous.' Sean ducked under the small table and removed the cord. 'Try now, arsehole.'

A loud clunking sound echoed around him. The lights went out. The farmhouse was drenched in darkness. 'Are you for real?'

'Sean, what's happened?'

'A power cut. This is all we need.' He couldn't see anything in front of him. He held his hands up, pushing through the darkness and moving slowly towards the living room. 'Guys, sit tight. I just need to get my phone and find the junction box.'

He continued along the hallway and into the kitchen, reaching out to find the sideboard. He patted along the wood, then swiped his hands, making circles as he searched.

The phones were gone.

* * *

'What's he doing? Come on, Dad.' Beth was on the sofa, the remote control perched next to her lap.

'Are you OK, Sean?'

His voice at the living room door startled them. 'The phones are gone.'

'Did you move them, Beth?'

'What? Gone? They're in the kitchen where I left them.'

'Someone has moved them,' Sean said. 'I need to find the junction box. I don't even know where it is.'

Beth stood and made her way to the kitchen to check, while her dad moved into the living room. 'They were here. I remember placing them together. How can they have moved?'

'Where's the torch?' Sean asked. 'I have to find the junction box.'

'I'm not sure. Maybe it's in one of the boxes we haven't unpacked yet, but we'll struggle to find it in the darkness,' Jenny answered.

'Are you OK, Beth?' Sean called out.

Her voice came from the hallway. 'I'm fine.'

'What are we going to do, Sean? We have no light, no power. We can't sit like this all night.' Jenny moved to the edge of the sofa. 'Shall we go somewhere? A hotel, maybe?'

'Good shout, Mum,' Ethan said.

'It may be best, at least until we can sort this nightmare out. Maybe the whole village has a power cut. I'll go out onto the road, see if I can see any lights in the distance. Beth, are you OK?'

They waited. Seconds passed. Then Beth answered. 'I'm fine.'

Sean laughed. 'What are you doing? Come here.'

'I'm fine.'

'What the hell?' Sean moved towards the living room door.

'I'm fine.'

'Beth, you're acting weird. What's going on?'

'I'm fine. I'm fine. I'm fine.'

Sean crouched in the hallway where the voice was coming from. He reached to the floor and found a small dictaphone by his foot.

'I'm fine.'

Sean realised that someone had taped Beth's voice earlier and it was a recording that played over and over.

He screamed and smashed the dictaphone on the floor.

Beth was gone.

38

'I say we call over to the farmhouse. Maybe chat some more with the Freemans. It's no use sat here waiting for someone from the list to call.'

'I don't want to bother them. They have enough on their plate, dealing with the footage of Ed Berry.'

'All the more reason to go and check in on them. Come on, we need to keep moving.' Declan watched Billy, taking in his contrary expression, the knotted eyebrows. 'Come on, Billy. Mr Grouch. Come on.'

'I'm not a grouch.'

'You so are. The grouchiest person I've ever met. Mr Grouch from Grouchville. You were born there. It's your town.'

'Grow up.'

'Grouch. Grouchy wowchy. Big grouch.'

'What the heck is wro—'

'Grouch.'

'Fine. We'll go to the bloody farmhouse. Anything to stop you babbling on.'

'Mr Grouch has finally given in, boys and girls. Look at his mean, angry face, ready to snap at anyone who upsets him. Mr Grouch is not a happy grouch today. He's an angry grouch.'

Billy walked out of the front door.

A minute later, Declan followed.

* * *

As they drove towards the farmhouse, they could see lights in the road in the distance, heading towards them. Billy slowed as they approached, but the vehicle headed straight for them. Billy swore loudly and grabbed the steering wheel, trying to move out of the way. He swerved into a ditch, narrowly avoiding the vehicle.

'For shit's sake. What is it with people?'

'I think that was the truck. The one we followed last night.'

'Are you sure?'

'I think so.'

'Well, it's gone now. We'll never know. There's nowhere to turn around anyway.'

'Yeah, it would be in London by the time that happened.' Declan turned on the radio, which was playing 'Sweet Home Alabama'.

'Do we have to? I detest music, any kind of noise – anything that distracts me while I'm driving.'

'Only one of the greatest songs ever. Lynyrd Skynyrd.'

'Aren't they a shoe shop?'

'No. That's Lilly and Skinner.'

'Oh.'

Declan pointed. 'We're here.'

Billy turned into the drive of the farmhouse. Concern

addled him as he pulled up; the lights were off despite the car being on the drive.

They got out and walked towards the front door. Billy knocked.

They heard a tap at the window.

Billy turned and saw a figure, unsure who it was. 'It's Billy and Declan. Is everything OK?'

They heard someone shouting. Then the front door opened.

Jenny stood, frantic. She was talking so fast they struggled to understand her.

'Calm down. Take deep breaths. What's happened?'

'Beth. Beth is gone.'

Billy removed his phone from his pocket, turned on the torch and shone it in the direction of the hallway.

'How? What happened?'

Sean joined them at the door and – only slightly less frantically – explained how Beth had gone missing from the kitchen and how he'd found the dictaphone.

'When did this happen?'

'Just moments ago. I've searched the house. We need to call the police.'

Declan handed his phone over, and Sean made the call.

Billy stood inside the farmhouse. He searched the walls, looking for the junction box. 'It has to be here somewhere. Are there any cupboards in the hallway?'

'Yes, a storeroom further down.' Jenny pointed, then dropped to her knees, crying hysterically. 'He's taken her, hasn't he? He's taken my baby. No, no. Please don't let this happen.'

Sean was shouting into the phone. He had to move around the drive to keep the reception. 'Yes, I can hear you.

It's Gallows Lane, the old farmhouse... Yes, we've looked everywhere. I just need someone to come out... Huh? About ten minutes ago. I know she's been taken. I need to find her... Yes, she's tall, has blonde hair and is sixteen... I don't know.'

Declan moved to Jenny, who was now thumping her fists on the floor. The torch from Billy's phone allowed him to see her face clearly. 'We're going to find her. Please, Jenny. We need to focus. Did anyone come into the house?'

'He's taken my baby.' She screamed, a deathly wail spilling from her mouth.

Declan lifted her gently and held her close as she sobbed into his jumper.

'The police will get here as quickly as possible.' Sean handed Declan his phone back.

It was only then that Declan noticed that Ethan was there, stood by the living room door, stunned into silence.

When he'd got the lights on, Billy turned off his phone touch and moved away from the cupboard. 'Declan, the truck we passed. It's possible Ed Berry was driving it.'

'Maybe so, but the road out forks off to different towns. He could be anywhere by now.'

Billy watched as Sean moved inside and held his wife tight, Ethan hovering above them helplessly. He prayed they didn't have to go through the same torment he and Cheryl had suffered.

'Wait here for the police. They'll look around, probably ask for a recent picture. Beth may show up, so it's best you stay here. Declan, let's see if we can find the truck. We know what direction it went in. We might get lucky.'

'Sounds like a plan.' Declan turned to Sean, Jenny and Ethan, who were still huddled together, gripping each other tightly. 'We'll do our best to find her.'

The Freemans watched as the car left the drive and raced along the dark road.

* * *

'You're coming around. I thought you would. It was so easy. Your father was talking to the lady in the car, heedless of the front door being wide open, an opportunity I couldn't give up.'

Beth was lying in the backseat, duct tape over her mouth and rope secured to her hands and tied behind her back.

Back in the kitchen, all within a matter of seconds, Ed Berry had grabbed her and placed a chloroform-soaked cloth over her face. He'd dragged her body along the garden, one hand holding the cloth over her nose and mouth, the other clinging to her blouse as he waited for the effects to kick in. Five minutes later, she was out.

From the front of the truck, he could hear her stirring. She hadn't been out for long. Ed was pleased. It meant she'd suffer longer.

Beth was lying face down, her head turned to the side. Suddenly, she began to panic. Muffled screeching came from her taped mouth. She tried to free her hands. Her head felt as if it could explode at any moment.

'That's it. Welcome back. You're the first. I'll deal with you now. I couldn't take you all together. It would be too difficult. But I'll return to the farmhouse. I have wonderful things lined up for you. But first, I need to savour my catch. It's no good taking a ball at a football match and throwing it straight back. Not me. I like to appreciate it.'

Beth squealed. Her eyes were wild. She began to rock from where she lay.

Ed steered the truck up an old dirt track and soon

arrived at a deserted container the size of a small warehouse. 'This will do. In the early days, I used the farmhouse. It was easy to dispose of the bodies down the well. Can you imagine what it looks like down there now? All bones and skulls. I must take a look someday. The most recent one is in the fields.' Ed pointed. 'Over there somewhere. Maybe you'll join her. Or perhaps the well, for old times' sake. I'll think about it later – so many options.' Ed turned. 'Excuse my manners. I'll give you the choice. Where would you like to be buried?'

Beth was hysterical. She began to hyperventilate, pushing air out through her nostrils forcefully. Mucus dripped out too. She arched her back and moaned through the tape.

'Easy there. Easy.' He got out of the truck and opened the side door. He dragged her out, watching her legs smash onto the ground, and moved her over to the container.

A small torch clamped in his mouth, he pulled the metal door back and entered, dragging her body across the rough ground. Stones were cutting her clothes, tearing the skin on her back. He reached the steps in the far corner, then eased her down into the basement.

Ed went to grab more rope from the truck, which he tied around Beth, then strapped the other end to the bars of a small window above her.

Then he walked out.

39

The lights of Billy's sports car pushed through the dark road. He pressed the accelerator, while Declan leant forward to squint through the darkness, his hands flat on the dashboard.

The fields on either side were a mass of obscurity.

Declan watched the shadows flow past, as if they were on a conveyor belt, a blank continuation of bleakness. 'He could be anywhere. It may not have even been the truck. I couldn't see it clearly.'

'Watch for any lights on the road,' Billy insisted. 'It came past here only minutes ago. We need to find it.'

'It's dark. There's nothing. Where the hell are we going to start? He could have pulled off and be heading to Oxford or London or somewhere else entirely.'

'We're so close, Declan. I can feel it. I won't rest until we catch him.'

A few minutes later, Billy and Declan drove past the dirt track.

They couldn't see it from the road.

* * *

Beth lay on the ground, the smell of her own urine filling her lungs. She tried to scream but the tape prevented any effective noise from coming through.

Her head was pulsating, and an ache worked its way down the side of her face. She could feel her jeans sodden from where she couldn't hold it in anymore. Her back felt like she'd been whipped and her hands were cut.

She tried to work the tape, pushing out her tongue to loosen it, but it was too tight. It was dark; she was in a container, held secure and unable to move. She didn't want to die, but she knew her time was almost up.

Her mind raced with memories of her life, events from her school days, family vacations, her job at the cafe, days out to the park and weekends away.

Desperately, she tried to think of happy thoughts to lift her from the terror surrounding her. She thought of a field, the sun shining bright, adorned with buttercups and daisies, the feeling of standing there in a bright-coloured dress, her skin warm, her mood upbeat and jubilant.

She sees her mother and father, Ethan – all calling her. She runs, the light, warm breeze pushing against her face, the sound of birdsong in the trees close by. A peacock opens its feathers and she's lost in the array of colours – her happy place.

Beth was quickly pulled from her thoughts when she heard footsteps moving above her head. Her body tensed. She clenched her fists, pulling hard against the ropes, trying to break them so she could free herself. She began to cry, tears spilling from her eyes, making her face itchy.

Again, she moaned, hearing the muffled screams trying

to escape her mouth. She tried hard to listen. Were the steps moving away or towards her? She couldn't tell.

Until it was too late.

They were moving down the stairs.

* * *

Billy stopped the car at a junction. He looked left and right. Both roads were empty. He mused aloud to himself. 'Where now?'

'My father had a saying...' Declan began.

'OK. I hope it's wise.'

'He'd say, "right is right, left should be left."'

'What kind of a stupid saying is that?'

'He lived his life by it. He made it to seventy-two years, so it can't have been that stupid.'

'Well, how many times was he stuck at a junction, chasing a kidnapped woman, with a serial killer on the loose, huh?'

'Go left then.'

Billy pushed his hands through his hair. 'Didn't you say left should be left?'

'He did also say "anti-clockwise is wise."'

'Oh, for shit's sake. We'll go right.' Billy pulled out onto the road.

They emerged on a dual carriageway, heading to Oxford. Declan had a sinking feeling in his stomach. 'I don't think he's on this road.'

'Why do you say that?'

'He'd jeopardise his plan. He'd stay close to the farmhouse. It's too risky, taking a woman, driving with her in the truck. He knows he's vulnerable. The eight women all disappeared from Painswick, and the stories were of people seeing Creeper lurking outside their houses in the village. It was all in Painswick. It's where he feels safe. We need to go back.'

Billy turned off at the next junction and headed back towards the farmhouse.

* * *

Beth could hear him breathing. He stood beside her, a tall silhouette – still, motionless.

Her wrists ached; the skin was raw and sensitive. She lay on her front, straining her neck; her head felt heavy, a dead weight, unnatural. She turned on her side, pushing her boots into the ground to try to turn towards him. She tried to speak, to ask him what he wanted, why he'd brought her here – and how she was going to die. Beth wanted it to be quick, painless. This was it; her time was almost over.

She listened as he moved closer, the breaths louder in her ears. He sounded like a monster, wheezing, short but loudly, as if he was doing it for effect. But he was a monster, a lowlife piece of scum who preyed on the vulnerable, the person who'd terrorised the village for so long. She knew she'd be just another casualty, another name on the long list of murdered people. She wanted to tell him what she thought of him, her last words being the truth: what kind of creature this man really was.

As she listened to his wheezing breaths, his head pushing closer to where she lay, she knew it was over. She thought about the missing women, wondered whether their ends had been the same as this.

A light appeared beside her, then a face – something horrific from the worst kind of nightmare. That face – she'd never get it out of her head. It was staring at her, mere inches away. The flesh had melted, and blood wept from the scars. His eyes were sunk into his face, two slits, empty and hollow, as if he had no soul. He was completely bald, and his lips were distorted, his mouth a huge vacant pit, resembling a cauldron. He smiled. His breath was rank, stale, like rotten flesh.

Beth turned, unable to look anymore. She didn't want her last memory to be of this troll, this horror from another world.

But it would be; this was going to be the last person she saw.

And there was nothing she could do about it.

The light went off. Beth heard the footsteps moving away into the distance.

He was gone.

But he'd be back.

* * *

Billy pulled over and parked in a ditch, five hundred yards from the container where Beth was being held. He held his head in his hands. 'What are we missing, Declan? Where has he taken her?'

'Assuming it was even the same truck... Should we go and check out Ronnie's house?'

'I think we'd be wasting our time. He knows the police are all over it from the other night. He's already taunted us there, hanging a body on the wall. No, he'd have to be stupid to go back. He's here somewhere. I can feel it.'

Both men sat in the car, staring along the deserted road.

'I have an ache in my back. I need to stand for a moment.' Declan opened the car door and got out. Billy followed him.

'It's so peaceful. Do you miss it out here?'

'Sometimes. I liked it here when I lived with my son, but we didn't get on. I love him to bits, but he got on my nerves. Moody little bugger.'

'I bet he'd say the same about you. Wow, I'd love to meet him. The three of us could have a bitch-about-Billy party and swap stories. Imagine the fun!'

'Parties were never my thing.'

'I gathered that. It doesn't take a scientist to know from watching you at Sheldon's. Not a great mixer, are you?'

'People dancing, the sweat, the smell; boozed up people telling you how much they love you and then forgetting a minute later. A load of bullshit.'

'So, what do you do for fun? You don't like music, singing, noise; I never see you reading; you don't participate in any games. Do you watch boxsets?'

'I tried watching that Screwfix. A waste of my time. Too much swearing.'

Declan laughed. 'You mean Netflix?'

'Netflix, Screwfix, Tisylix – whatever it's called. It's not for me. I have no interest. A programme should finish within the hour. I don't see the relevance of dragging it out. My time is precious.'

'I can see that. Come on, let's take a drive around. We can call in to the farmhouse, see if they've heard anything.'

Billy got into the driver's seat and waited for Declan to join him. 'You know, I could get used to this toy. I'm understanding how it works. You have to treat it with respect. Let it know who's in control. I can see myself in one of these babies.' He jabbed the accelerator, feeling the thrill as the engine powered to life.

'Yeah, do you know how much it costs? Not just an arm and a leg; try your fingers, toes and add your winky in there for good measure. I'm telling you, your son will hit the roof if he knows you've taken it out.'

'How's he going to know?' He had to hit the brakes as a fox ran across the road, causing them to jolt forward. 'Bloody thing.'

A truck came out of the turning, its lights off, the wheels skidding along the stones. It was too dark for Ed Berry to see the road. He smashed straight into the side of the car and then reversed, almost bringing the driver's door with him.

'For shit's sake. My son is going to bloody kill me. I'm finished.' Billy pushed glass from the broken window and screamed all manner of profanities. His face was beetroot red and his fists were clenched so tight his nails were ripping into his skin. He got out, stamping on the ground like Rumpelstiltskin. 'You stupid, stupid, stupid bastard of a bastard. I'll kick you all over the bloody road.'

The lights came on. Billy shielded his eyes with his hands, and the truck sped around the car, fleeing down the dark country lane.

* * *

Billy stood with his head pushed into his hands. Feeling stressed, he pulled down on the skin of his face.

Declan stood beside him, having grabbed a torch from the back seat. The car door looked like a couple of bulls had rammed into it. The glass was shattered and huge gaps had appeared. 'Well, this isn't good.'

'Not one word, you hear me? Nothing. Don't say anything at all. I'm a dead man. My son is going to hit the bloody roof. What the heck do I tell him?'

Declan pulled the driver's door open, the sound grating and making flakes of paint drop to the ground. 'He may not notice. Why don't you park it the other way around? Keep it tight to the house?'

'I'm finished. I can't believe this.'

'At least we're keeping the local garage in business. They must be rubbing their hands together. They'll miss us when we're gone.'

Billy grabbed the torch and pointed it towards Declan. He watched his face as he struggled to hold the laughter. His eyes circled around, looking anywhere but at Billy.

'Did you get a look at the truck?'

'No, it was too dark. But it was him, all right. Ed Berry. Why is he out here? There has to be a reason. He had the lights off, obviously trying to keep concealed. Beth must be close. Come on, let's take a drive along the dirt track.'

Declan climbed into the passenger seat while Billy grappled with the driver's door. He leant across, trying to force it open with his legs.

Finally, Billy managed to squeeze through.

He tapped the accelerator and rolled the car along the path, the lights revealing the area in front.

Billy pushed his face closer to the windscreen. 'There's something there. Look.'

Declan leant forward. 'It's a small building.'

'That has to be where he's taken Beth.' Billy pulled the car around the back.

The construction was brick-built with a timber roof. The felt was cut in large rectangular patches but had gaps, as if it had been repaired many times.

Billy moved towards the front door, keeping the torch low. Declan followed behind him.

They pulled the wooden door, the paint on which had begun to peel from the cold weather, and the bottom dragged along the gravel path. One of the hinges were missing which made it awkward to manoeuvre. A strong smell of manure hit them hard and got into their throats. Billy suddenly felt ill.

Inside, he called out in a low voice. 'Beth, are you here?' He waited, looking and listening for any indication she was there. 'Beth, are you here?'

No answer.

They moved around inside, traipsing in mud. Billy shone the torch to the walls and over the ceilings. It was an empty space, possibly used at one time to house cattle, but now just a shell, standing solemn, derelict.

To the left, there were a couple of empty, plastic barrels. There was something behind them. Billy lit the area with his torch and the men moved closer. They heaved the barrels, rolling them out of the way, to reveal steps that led to an area downstairs.

They moved to the top and looked down.

'She has to be down there.'

* * *

Billy held the torch in front of him. His hands were trembling. Declan was holding on to his shoulder, both men fearful as to what they'd find. Had he killed her? If so, how would they tell Sean, Jenny and Ethan?

Billy had to fight to rid himself of the negativity.

They reached the bottom step, anticipating the worst, their bodies tense and cold. Billy moved the torch along the ground.

Suddenly, they heard a chilling groan. Beth was slumped in the corner, lying on her side, her hands tied behind her back and another rope secured around her waist. They raced towards her.

She was writhing on the floor, like she was lying on hot coals. Her eyes were wild and she looked petrified.

'It's me, Beth. Billy. I'm with Declan. You're safe.' He crouched and gently removed the tape from her mouth.

When she was free, Beth screamed. Relief drenched her body and she broke down, crying hysterically.

When she'd calmed enough, they untied her. The rope had cut into her skin, her legs were unstable and her clothes ripped. But she was alive.

They helped her to stand, then she threw her arms around them and sobbed.

Above them, they could hear a faint whistling noise. It seemed to bounce off the stairs and reverberate through the walls. It got closer.

Billy recognised it. An old nursery rhyme. See-saw, Margery Daw.

He looked at Declan. Then he called out. 'Who's there?'

The whistling continued. See-saw, see-saw.

'It's him.' Beth screamed and gripped on to Billy's jacket. 'He's never going to let me go. You have to help me. I'm begging you.'

Again, Billy shouted. 'Ed. It's over. We know what you've done. You'll never get away with it.'

More whistling. It seemed to come from the top of the stairs.

'Is there another way out?' Declan asked.

The three moved towards the back of the building. Beth was still weak and struggled to move, so they had to support her as she walked. The only window was the one that had bars, which Ed had used to tie Beth up. There was no other way out.

'We need to tackle him. I've dreamt about this moment.

I've thought about it for years. Let me go. Declan, you stay with Beth.'

'No, Billy.' Beth sobbed. 'He'll be armed – there's no doubt. He'll be ready for you. Leave it to the police.'

'Beth's right. Tackling him is suicide. We'll also be putting her at risk.' Declan looked at his phone. Still no reception. 'But how do we get out of here?'

The whistling suddenly seemed distant, as if Ed had moved back towards the door. It was much fainter now, drifting into the night. Then it stopped.

'I think he's gone. Please tell me he's gone,' Beth cried.

Declan reached for the torch and moved to the stairs. He began to climb the steps, shining the torch towards the walls and door. 'I think we should go. He's not here. Now's the chance. Come on. Quickly.' He reached forward, helping Beth, then assisted Billy.

'I'm well able to walk on my own, damn it.'

They crept along the ground, Declan swirling the torch, checking in all directions, the light darting off the brickwork.

'Wait. We need to be sure. Stop a second,' Billy ordered.

They listened but all they could hear was Beth and the strange whimpering noises coming from her mouth.

'Please, we need to make sure it's safe.'

The three of them stood in silence, monitoring the surroundings. They listened for footsteps, the noise of a twig breaking or the parting of bushes. Billy was sure he could still hear the song, a low whistle being pushed from the perpetrator's mouth. Could he still hear it? Or was it his imagination?

See-saw. See-saw.

The song would always haunt him.

Declan broke his concentration. 'Let's get to the car. Beth, are you OK? Can you manage?'

'Yes, I just want to get out of here. Is he gone?'

'I think so.' He placed his arm through hers and helped her walk. Billy followed behind.

They pulled at the container's front door, all three helping to ease it backwards. As it scraped, they held their breath.

'Quick. Get the car, Billy, and pull it round. I'll wait here with Beth.'

Billy took the torch and approached the car. His heart sank as he saw the driver's door, momentarily forgetting what had happened. He pulled it, then squeezed his body through the gap, first checking the car was empty. He struggled to start the engine, forgetting how to work the car in his panic. He pushed at the array of buttons. 'For shit's sake.'

'Place your foot on the brake, Captain,' Declan insisted.

Billy managed to start the car, then drove over to where Declan and Beth waited at the container. They both climbed into the back seat.

Billy adjusted the rear-view mirror. 'Let's get you home.'

Ed Berry watched as the car pulled away.

He continued whistling, drowning out the voices in his head.

Then he walked along the fields and got into the truck.

Billy hit the brakes just before reaching the farmhouse. He saw a shadow walking towards him. The person was frantic, screaming Beth's name.

Billy shoved the car door and got out. 'Jenny.'

She raced towards him. 'Oh, Billy. Where's my daughter? Where has he taken her?'

The back door opened. Declan got out first, then he turned back and took Beth by the hands, leading her out.

Jenny dropped to her knees for a moment, crying hysterically. Then she stood and walked to her daughter slowly, her body trembling with excitement. She pulled her in close and kissed her forehead. 'Did he hurt you, Beth?'

'No, I'm fine. A little bruised, but I'm OK.'

They heard Sean and Ethan calling her name from the garden.

'Guys, she's here! Beth is here!'

They came running, sprinting across the grass.

Billy and Declan stood back as the four of them gripped each other in a circle.

'How can we ever thank you both?' Sean asked.

Declan's eyes lit up. 'A cup of tea would be good. Oh, and a few Jaffa Cakes. I do love those.'

Jenny looked up. She smiled at Declan. 'It's the least we can do.'

Declan pointed to the damaged car door. 'Oh, and a big shovel for Billy here so he can dig himself a hole.'

40

————————

The six of them sat in the kitchen. Sean, Jenny and Ethan couldn't take their eyes off Beth. She'd only been gone an hour but it had seemed like days.

Declan was stuffing Jaffa Cakes into his mouth two at a time. He wiped the chocolate from his mouth with a satisfied smile.

Billy was still focused on what he was going to say to his son. He'd been so careful with the car. He wanted a pit to appear, which he could fall deep inside. Henry would be livid.

Jenny turned to the two of them. 'So, what happens now?'

'Well, the police are looking for Ed Berry. We can't prove anything yet, but the net is closing in. So far, they have no bodies and until Beth gives a statement, no way of knowing that it was him that took her. We'll do all we can to bring him down.'

He turned to Declan. 'Come on. Let's give these people their privacy.'

'What? And leave half a packet of Jaffas? You must be mad.'

'We'll get some on the way home if you're that desperate.'

The two men stood, and the family thanked them for their help.

'We'll talk tomorrow. Get some rest and make sure to lock up. He's still out there.'

As Billy and Declan moved from the kitchen, they could smell petrol.

Billy turned back. 'Hey, check over the farmhouse. Something isn't right.'

'What's happening, Mum?'

'I don't know.'

Sean moved to the hallway. 'Guys, go out the front door. Quickly. I'll check over the place.'

The three of them moved along the hall and tried to open the front door.

'It's locked,' Jenny said. 'Something is stopping it from opening.'

'It's him. Out the back way. Quick. Everyone go.' Declan waited until they'd moved to the kitchen, then walked behind them.

Sean stood next to Billy. 'Go on. You go. I'll be fine.'

'I'm staying with you.'

The smell of smoke began to fill the air, rising from the basement. Sean started to cough. 'Billy, I'm ordering you: go.'

Billy growled and joined the others.

'The back door is locked too.' Ethan began to pull on the handle. He placed his foot on the wall for a better grip. 'It's no use. He's been here. He's locked us inside. Where are the keys?'

Jenny could see the smoke beginning to rise through the floorboards.

By the front door, Sean was bent over and struggling to breathe. The fire had spread quickly and was now ferocious. He could feel the heat from the floorboards under his feet.

Flames were pushing through the gaps, forcing their way through.

He tried smashing the glass of the front door, but he didn't have the strength. The hallway was a mass of smoke, the heat unbearable. The flames were making him nauseous. He fell against the wall and dropped headfirst onto the ground.

Ethan was hurling objects at the window to no avail. He jumped up onto the sideboard and began to kick the glass. His foot went through, creating an intense noise as it smashed. He climbed through the gap, then moved to the back door. A heavy piece of wood had been placed across it and secured with nails. Ed Berry must have done it while they'd been out on the road with Beth.

Ethan took a step back then barged into the kitchen door. It took him four attempts to open it.

'Where's Sean?' Declan shouted.

Billy turned. 'I thought he was with us.'

Declan took Billy's coat, placed it over his head, and went back in, fighting through the thick fog. 'Sean, where are you?'

The sound of flames reverberated around him. He could hear parts of the building beginning to collapse.

'Sean, you've got to get out.' He dropped to the ground and began crawling. Declan swept his hands along the floor, using the jacket as a shield against the heat. 'Sean, please, where are you?'

Declan began to cough. His lungs felt raw, his skin hot.

All of a sudden, he could feel a body. It was Sean. He was lying by the front door.

'You aren't going anywhere yet, Mister. It's not your time.' Declan placed his hands under his shoulders, then carefully stood and heaved backwards, pulling Sean with him, dragging him along the hallway. As he made through to the kitchen and outside, Sean started to cough, then turned on his side and puked.

Declan sat beside him, proud that they'd all made it out.

They stood back, watching the farmhouse. The fire had now intensified. They heard loud explosions from the heat. The flames were working their way through the farmhouse, eating everything in its path.

Billy called the emergency services and explained what had happened. When he hung up, he thought about Ed Berry. He'd wreaked havoc on so many people's lives.

He had to put a stop to it.

* * *

By the time the fire brigade arrived, most of the farmhouse had gone up in flames. The heat was intense, the flames roaring, eating everything in its path, rising like a serpent and gaining in strength.

Some of the locals arrived, having seen the smoke from the village. They checked on the family to make sure everyone had got out and to offer help.

The ambulance crew checked on Sean. He'd inhaled a lot of smoke but was now fully conscious. They said he'd probably have an intense headache and would need rest.

They'd praised Declan's bravery for going back inside for him.

As the firefighters entered the building, strapped with water hoses, Sean stood with his family. He stared at the fire, his body in shock. He was sure he could see Ed Berry's smiling face in the flames.

When the police arrived, he gave a statement. The police also wanted statements from Jenny and Ethan. When it was Beth's turn, she relayed the full incident. As she gave a description of the perpetrator, she broke down.

'We'll catch him. I'm sorry your first week in Painswick has been so trying. It's a great place to live. Please don't let this put you off. I want you all to stay in a safe house tonight. It's for the best – at least until we search the local fields. He may still be here. It's not safe.'

Sean nodded. He wasn't going to put his family in jeopardy.

More police arrived and began to search the fields with bright flashlights. They found a well in the back garden.

One of the officers pointed a flashlight deep into it. 'Over here.'

More officers joined him.

They needed to go down.

* * *

Once the fire had been extinguished and after they'd given their statements, Billy and Declan went to leave.

Jenny, Sean, Beth and Ethan thanked them for everything.

'I just hope the bastard is put behind bars tonight.' Billy turned, watching the bright lights illuminate the fields. His body ached and his stomach was in knots, knowing that the person responsible for the death of his daughter was so close. 'You're welcome to stay with us, at my son's house.'

'No. You've done enough for us. We're going to a safe house. The police said they'll organise it.'

'It's for the best. At least until he's caught.' Billy watched the farmhouse, looking at the wisps of smoke that smouldered inside. He turned to Declan. 'If you say anything about a bonfire, you're walking home. Do you hear me?'

'Billy, as if.'

'I wouldn't put it past you.'

'I didn't need the jacket in the end. How good is the heating in their house?'

'Right. That's it. Off you go. You're walking home.'

* * *

'I'm so sorry this has happened.' Sean addressed the rest of his family.

'Dad, we were all up for moving to Painswick. You weren't to know this would happen.'

'She's right, Dad. Don't blame yourself. You and Mum spoke about it for months. You did everything you could. It was your dream – a new beginning, more space. I'm just sorry for you both.'

Jenny moved to stand next to Sean. 'You're my hero, you know that?'

'Oh, Jenny. Stop.'

'I mean it. I love you so much. Sod the farmhouse and everything that was inside. All we need is each other. It could have been so much worse.' They both looked at Beth. Her smile was beginning to return but she looked so tired and washed out.

'So, what happens now?'

'I guess we stay someplace safe. For how long is anyone's guess.' Sean looked out over the fields. The police were combing the area in full force, the lights from their torches dancing through the tall grass.

It looked like they were going to look inside the well. There appeared to be enough evidence to assume they might find something.

Suddenly, one of the officers shouted from the field opposite.

'I've found something. The soil has been disturbed.'

The Freemans felt numb.

They recalled the red coat.

Somehow, they knew it was Marie Nelson.

* * *

Billy had told Declan to walk. As they walked from the farmhouse, Billy pulled the driver's door back and watched as his partner made his way along the dark road. He suddenly felt guilty. 'Get in then. It's freezing.' Billy drove the car slowly beside where Declan walked.

Declan peered through the broken window of the car, the door hanging almost on the ground. 'I think it's colder in there.' He strolled with his hands in his pockets. The air was fresh and it stung his cheeks.

'Last chance. There's still a couple of miles to go. We could be sat in the kitchen, warming ourselves with a glass of whisky. Your choice.'

Declan reached for the door and climbed into the passenger seat. 'Have you got diet coke?'

'I'm sure there'll be something to deaden the taste, lightweight.'

Billy hit the accelerator, and Declan fell back in his seat.

'Christ, go easy.'

'What the hell am I going to tell my son?'

Suddenly, lights came on behind the car. Billy adjusted the rear-view mirror. 'Back off, you arse wipe. Look how close this idiot is.' He turned, moving his hand in the air, motioning for the driver to slow down. 'I can't go anyway. You'll have to be patient.'

The lights were getting closer. Then *bang*, the vehicle rammed into the back of them, knocking Billy and Declan forward.

'What the hell? Is it him?'

'I don't know. But he's going to ram us off the bloody road.' Billy pressed the accelerator, pushing the Mazda faster to thirty miles an hour.

Declan crossed one leg over the other and gripped the overhead handle. He regretted getting into the car. 'Can we turn off?'

'How would I bloody know? What am I? A Satnav?'

The truck hit them from behind again. They charged forward, Billy almost hitting his head on the windscreen. The vehicle had dropped back then rammed into the car.

'I don't believe this. For shit's sake. It's going to be crushed to the size of a tub of butter by the time I get it back. Henry is going to kill me.'

'Billy, you have to turn off. It's too dangerous.'

'Where? It's one long road. I can't stop or turn around.'

'Well, drive faster then.'

'Quick. Dial 999. Tell them what's happening. There are police at the farmhouse.'

Declan dialled and told the call handler what was happening. 'I think it's Ed Berry.'

'Who else would it be?'

Declan turned away, holding the phone close to his ear. 'Sorry, I'm with Billy Huxton – a private investigator. We're in danger and we need assistance now.'

The call handler asked Declan to stay on the line. A

minute later, she assured him that police were on their way. 'And you say you can't pull over?'

'We could, but we'd risk a truck being rammed up our arse.' Declan hung up. 'Is there anything I can throw out of the car? Maybe distract him?'

'How about yourself?' Billy pushed forward, wiping the screen with his right hand. He was struggling to see. The road seemed more narrow now, though thankfully the lights behind had dropped away.

He thought about Katie. He'd always envisioned beating her murderer to a pulp, only needing one moment in a room with him to rip him apart. This wasn't how he expected events to pan out.

As he drove, he felt fearful. Ed Berry was a madman. He wouldn't stop until he and Declan were dead in a ditch. He thought about his beautiful wife, what they'd gone through during those days and weeks after Katie had gone missing, not to mention her illness and final breath. Then his thoughts shifted to his new friend and comrade, Declan, how he'd given up his leave to help him catch the person responsible for Katie's death.

Ed Berry. Creeper. The person so many were terrified to mention, or to even think about. The terror he'd brought to Painswick. Their own Bogeyman.

Billy couldn't let it end here. He wouldn't. If he was going to die, he had to bring down Ed as well.

He stamped on the accelerator, the speedometer almost hitting forty miles an hour, the long, narrow road rolling out ahead.

The lights appeared, gaining, moving closer.

* * *

Ed Berry was laughing hysterically. As he watched the Mazda swerving along the road, he bounced in his seat with excitement. The person in front was driving for his life, but it was all of his own making.

The recording had been put to bed, buried deep in the walls of the basement. By finding it again, this man had started a new chain of events.

Ed had sprung on Jenny and Sean Freeman as soon as he'd found out about the move to the farmhouse. This had always been his fear, and he needed the recording to stay hidden.

He knew that one day the net may close in; people would find out what he'd done. The eight women in Painswick. Marie Nelson and maybe more in the near future.

He had a recording. Ronnie Hathaway entering the farmhouse. His get out clause, his ticket to freedom. He'd killed Ronnie and hid the body. If the police made their move, Ed would steer them to the footage. A tip-off from a burner phone. An anonymous call. Ronnie Hathaway entering the farmhouse. Ed, talking to the camera. The cold-blooded murder. Who would know any different? Ed would be far away from here when it happened. Just like before.

Missing.

Presumed dead.

And Ronnie would take the blame.

Ed had made a mistake. He'd panicked. The men in the sports car had called over to Ronnie's house. His wife had died recently, and he was supposed to be away for much-needed rest and relaxation. Ed had Ronnie's phone; he'd posted on the street WhatsApp group that he intended to go away, unsure when he'd return.

He'd buried Ronnie's body in a field close to the farmhouse. The night he'd found Billy snooping in Ronnie's shed, he thought it was over. He had to act fast; he had to plant something to scare them off, something to put the fear of God into the both of them.

Ed had intended to dig up the skeletal remains of one of his victims. Any of the women he'd murdered would do.

He grabbed a shovel from the back of the truck and began digging the earth, finding Ronnie Hathaway's body. He panicked; his head became cloudy with the pressure he was under, the voices so loud in his head. He saw lights in the distance, and his cover was about to be blown.

Ed needed Ronnie hidden. How else could he blame him? But he was digging at the wrong grave. Ronnie's grave.

Ed was running out of time. He couldn't recall at this moment where the other bodies were.

So he took Ronnie, loading his dead body into the back of the truck.

He returned the next day and strung him up like a piece of art, his masterpiece for all to see.

It seemed the only way to scare Billy and Declan off the trail.

But Ed knew.

He knew once Ronnie Hathaway was identified; his cover would be blown.

A mistake he'd made in the heat of the moment.

The only way he thought he could frighten them into backing off.

The fire had gone so wrong. In his moment of enthusiasm, after nailing the door shut and locking the front, the Mazda had pulled onto the drive. He hadn't had time to deal with the windows to secure them too.

But it was OK. He'd return and deal with the family once the police left.

He thought about his sister, lying in her garden. He pictured her, her body distorted, crushed and broken. It had to happen. Who else would she tell? Or were there others she'd confided in already? It was supposed to be a family secret between the two of them. Mary would always make it better. She had his back.

But not this time.

Ed had followed the Freemans' car and had waited outside his sister's house. He was going to break in, maybe as she slept, but he got lucky much sooner. As she said goodbye to her family, waving at the front door, she'd moved out onto the road. As she'd watched the car, Ed had managed to get inside and hide in the living room.

He'd heard everything.

Now, he watched the car ahead, maybe thirty or forty yards in front. As he slammed his foot on the accelerator, he listened for the nursery rhyme, but all he heard was the crunching sound as he battered into the back of the Mazda.

Sing it, God damn you. Sing the song. I'll start, Mary. See-saw— Come on, I mean it. Sing it for me. But Ed no longer heard the voice in his head. Not a murmur. His sister had died and so too had her blessing.

He watched the car in front, the man in the driver's seat turning, pushing his hand in the air to ward him off. The guy in the passenger seat was moving his body around, watching the truck behind.

Ed saw the brake lights come on just as the car swerved to the left. Then, bright beams were upon him, an oncoming van with scaffolding tied to the roof. He could see the driver's mouth open in shock as he forced the van to an abrupt halt.

Ed didn't have time to move. Four huge metal poles

worked loose from the van and hurled through the windscreen of his pickup truck.

One of them went straight through his head and ended up smashing the window behind him.

* * *

'I'm so sorry. I didn't see you. The bend was so sharp. Are you both OK? Oh my God. I'm sorry.' The driver was tall, in his mid-thirties and had a London accent. He explained how he was coming back from a refurbishment job – they'd finished for the weekend – and he was collecting some of the scaffolding. A surge in adrenaline was causing him to ramble. He forced the Mazda's driver's door open and helped Billy out onto the road. Then he went around to assist Declan.

'We're fine. Just stop going on.' Billy turned around and looked at his son's car in the ditch. 'Well, it's a bloody write-off now.'

'I'll go and check on the guy in the truck.' The man looked up, seeing the scaffolding planted through the glass. 'Oh no. No, no! Please, no.'

Declan placed his hand on the guy's shoulder. 'Go and wait in your van. It looks messy.'

Police sirens rang out over the village, and Billy watched the blue lights illuminate the sky as they approached. He turned to Declan. 'This is the moment I've been waiting for. Give me a minute, will you?'

'Take all the time you need.'

Billy walked towards the truck. The poles were sticking out over the bonnet. The windscreen was shattered and the airbag had engaged.

He shone the torch inside, staring at Ed Berry. 'Well, this

is karma. I've dreamt of this moment for years. It's also kept me awake all that time too. I feared you'd be locked up when they eventually caught you, given your own cell, a comfortable bed – a telly or a radio. My Katie had none of those privileges. So why should you? Let me tell you about my daughter, Ed.' Billy wiped the tears from his eyes. 'She was the most kind-hearted, generous, wonderful person you could meet. Most fathers will say that about their little girl, but you can't explain the joy that such a little person can bring to you. You'd do anything for her. When she was bullied at school and I saw the fear in her eyes, the tears she choked back, it broke me. I would have swapped places with her in a flash.

'When her first boyfriend mistreated her, I told her I'd rip him limb from limb. The night she disappeared, I'd never wish that pain upon anyone. It swallowed me up, took my spirit, my soul. I was never the same again. I searched for her until I became sick, too ill to keep going. It ate me up inside.

'I still remember one time when she was sitting on my knee. She was about five or six at the time. She was pulling on my moustache, asking why I had it. She said it was silly. It looked daft. She stared at me – I mean, she really looked into my eyes – and asked me if I was going to die. I told her not for many years. Then she said she loved me so much. Little did I think she'd go first.

'Ed Berry, I'm not going to curse. I'm not going to stand here and tell you what I hope will happen to you or where I hope you'll go. It's not down to me. I just wanted to try and get it through to you. What you have taken from us.

'I'll say a prayer tonight. I'll thank God for letting me have this moment. But I will never, *ever* forgive you, Ed Berry. You got what you deserved.'

Billy inspected his body closely. The scaffolding poles made it look like his head had exploded.

He hoped that Ed Berry saw them coming towards him. He hoped that as he saw his life flash before his eyes, knowing he was about to die, that he was sorry.

Somehow, he didn't think so.

41

As two police officers took the family to the safe house, one of them answered her radio and confirmed that they were all safe and in protective care.

The Freemans were sitting in the back of the unmarked car.

In the passenger seat, the officer held the radio up to her ear as she was told what had happened to Mary Freeman. Thankfully, Sean was speaking with Jenny in the back and didn't hear the story – how a neighbour had heard a disturbance, a window being smashed and saw a body lying in the garden. They'd dialled 999 in a panic.

The officer asked the driver to pull the car over, then turned to Sean. 'I'm so sorry to have to tell you this.'

'Go on.'

'Could I ask you to confirm your mother's address in Oxford?' She spoke as gently and politely as she could.

Sean recited the address.

'A colleague has just informed me that your mother was found dead in the garden of her home.'

'What? How? In the garden? You must be mistaken. We were with her this morning.' Sean felt dizzy, fearing he'd vomit . 'Let me out. I need air, please. Let me out of the car.' He stood on the road, weeping as panic washed over his body. The officers stood with him, showing him compassion. This wasn't the first time they had had to deliver news such as this.

Jenny, Beth and Ethan joined him outside the car, huddling together, numb and silent as they digested what the officer had said.

Ed Berry had easily burned the farmhouse to the ground, so Sean was sure he was guilty of murdering his mother too.

Sean was insistent that he was going to go to Oxford, but Jenny told him he needed rest. They all did. They would stay in the safe house tonight. Tomorrow they could deal with it. They'd had the week from hell and needed time to recover.

Sean was bent over, sobbing. His family held him as he spilled out all his anger.

They'd be there for each other.

Wednesday.

The Freemans left early the following morning. The four of them were in shock and they hadn't slept well. Jenny had had nightmares. She dreamt that Ed Berry was standing over her bed. He'd killed Beth and was wrapping her body in a red coat.

On the drive to Oxford, they listened to the local radio

station, where news was beginning to filter in about a body being recovered in Painswick. They didn't announce who it was but said she was female. They were currently breaking up the well at the side of the house so officers could take a look.

The newsreader also spoke of Ed Berry, how he'd burned a farmhouse to the ground and he was suspected of murder. He had been found dead in his truck.

The residents of Painswick will sleep better tonight, Sean thought.

An hour later, they arrived in Oxford. Two police officers stood outside his mother's house, guarding it.

The driveway was taped across and when Sean approached, one of the officers told him it was a crime scene and that no one could enter.

Although he showed her his identification, the officer didn't relent, explaining she'd just started her shift and knew little about what had happened. They'd have to book into a hotel until the police were finished with the investigation.

Sean stood, staring at his family home. He had been here just yesterday. Tears began to spill from his eyes as he recalled his childhood. There were so many happy memories in this house. Sean wondered if he and his family would ever be able to create a real home after what had happened.

They checked into a hotel in Oxford, a sanctuary for the time being, but after that, they had nowhere to go. Their world had been turned upside down and arse ways.

They were worried for the future but at least they had each other. That's what counted.

* * *

As Sean and Jenny entered their room, Jenny reached out and held him. 'I'm so sorry, Sean. This is terrible. Talk to me?'

He took a deep breath. His body was filled with anxiety, and he began to tremble. 'I'm struggling to deal with it. We only saw her yesterday. I'm still digesting what she told us.'

'I know. It's devastating.' Jenny ran her hands through his hair. 'You're so strong. You know you can deal with this. We'll gain the strength from each other.'

'I need to keep occupied.' Sean opened his laptop, typed in the WIFI password and began to look at all the breaking news in Painswick. Jenny grabbed a chair and sat beside him. They checked what was being said on social media, the comments, the trolls, the well-wishers and the opinions of what had happened.

One post caught Sean's eye, a woman on Twitter commenting on the body found in Oxford. Mary's name had been leaked.

'I'm distraught. I worked at Greyshott Hall and knew the family well. RIP Mary.'

Sean clicked on her profile and then followed a link that led to her website.

She was a mental health psychologist. Now retired.

Sean needed to talk to her. He had to have closure, and maybe she could give more of an insight into Ed Berry. He needed to know what happened at Greyshott Hall and the true story behind Creeper.

He found a contact number for her and dialled. She answered almost instantly.

'Fiona Beeston speaking.'

'Fiona, I'm Sean Freeman. Mary Freeman was my mother.' He listened to her as she gasped, then continued. 'I saw your post on Twitter and wondered if it was possible to talk to you?'

'I'm sorry for your loss.' The woman began to cry.

Sean eyed Jenny. 'I understand you worked at Greyshott Hall?'

'Yes. A long time ago. Look, I don't have anything to say.'

'Please, Fiona. I have unanswered questions. I'd be grateful if we could talk. I'm pleading with you.'

The woman sighed.

'Please, Fiona. Please help me.'

She gave her address and hung up.

Sean closed the laptop. Then he and Jenny grabbed Ethan and Beth, and got into the car.

Not long after, they pulled into a side street. Beth and Ethan were told to wait in the car, while Sean and Jenny stepped out.

The semi-detached house was bright and looked welcoming. The walls were clean, painted white and the windows were double glazed. The garden was decorated with flowers and plants, and the front door was a deep red colour with a Ring doorbell hung on the wall to the side.

Sean knocked on the door.

A tall, elderly woman answered. She was elegant. Her hair was blonde and she wore a thick woollen jumper and jeans. Her smile was warm and her dark brown eyes looked watery, as if she'd just been crying.

She stood to the side and let them in. She led them into the living room and pointed to a dark blue sofa, while she settled on an armchair opposite. She didn't offer any drinks – a sign that Sean and Jenny didn't have long.

'Thank you so much for seeing us. It really means a lot.'

'I don't have much to say. I was a friend of the family. I knew your mother.'

Suddenly, the woman seemed to collapse. She folded like a deck of cards. Her emotions poured out, as if she was feeling guilty over something.

'Talk to me. What happened?'

The woman was crying heavily. Her shoulders were shaking, her face damp with both sweat and tears. 'I'm so sorry.'

Sean leant forward as the lady began to rock in her chair.

'I've tried so hard. It has eaten me up inside.'

'What? What has eaten you up?'

Whether from guilt, frustration or a mixture of the two, the woman began to confess.

'Your grandmother was a very dear friend. I'd known her since our childhood. They were having problems with their youngest, Ed.'

'Yes, he was my uncle.' Sean was embarrassed by his own connection to him.

'She came to me. I've studied psychology all my life. At the time, I ran Greyshott Hall. I was the hospital director. It was a private institution, so we had our own rules, more or less. Ed was a sociopath with antisocial personality disorder, also known as ASPD. His brain hadn't developed correctly. Your grandmother confided in me. She believed her husband was abusing Ed. Physically. He struck him on many occasions. Many times, she'd found him beaten to within an inch of his life. She watched how he regressed, closed up and began hearing voices. He hallucinated and spoke to people who weren't there. She struggled to deal with him, his violent behaviour and wanted so much for Ed to get better. Given the beatings Ed received at the hands of his father and how he was deteriorating, she didn't want him to stay in their home anymore.

'So, I suggested Greyshott Hall. I convinced her we could take care of Ed. She didn't want to entertain it, saying she'd lose him if he was institutionalised, but I promised her I'd take care of him, that I'd let nothing happen to him. He'd be in the best care. I was used to children with mental problems coming in; I could look after Ed.

'Then, one evening, her husband brought a doctor to the house. He believed this person could cure Ed, make him better. He left them alone in the house. Ed had felt awkward with all the questions, the doctor asking about everything from his personal life to his thoughts and emotions. Ed threw him down the stairs.

'Your grandmother was distraught. She blamed her husband for not doing anything about it, for the beatings which exacerbated it and for sweeping his condition under the carpet. She believed he caused Ed's condition. In a way, he did.'

As Sean listened, his emotions began to take over, hearing this side to his grandparents that he'd never known. He watched as Fiona struggled to tell the story.

'Ed was brought to Greyshott Hall by a section 12 specialist doctor as an emergency. I gave him a new start, wiped the slate clean. I ran the place, so I could do anything. He became Mark Wheelan. I protected him and kept him under my wing. I separated him from the other patients, gave him his medication and had full confidence that we could help him to recover. Yes, he was held in a cell, but it was for his own good.

'Ed became worse. His condition deteriorated. He was fifteen and unable to function. I'd tried everything. He screamed continuously and used to slam his head against the wall of his cell. I couldn't get him to eat and he became weak. I thought he was going to die. I couldn't let that happen, not after the promise I'd made to your grandmother. So, I called over to the house and explained his condition. We had to get him out of there.

'Mary, your mother, said she would take his position. She would swap places with him. She said she owed it to him. She was strong. She could cope.

'So, after some persuasion from Mary, I organised for Ed to leave and for your mother to take his place. Your grandparents were terrified, of course. At first, they didn't want to entertain the idea, but with Ed's condition getting more serious, they agreed. Mary would step in and take Ed's place. He had two years to serve for the murder of Doctor Conway.'

Sean leant forward on the sofa. 'What the hell are you saying? That you sneaked my mother into Greyshott? That she pretended to be Ed Berry?'

'That's what I'm saying. She already looked like him. Once she cut her hair, coloured it and put on the uniform, there was little difference. The patients were kept in their cells. They never spoke to each other, and I was the one who dished out the medication. No one knew a thing. I could do anything I liked. It was easy time for Mary to serve.'

'So, what happened then?' Jenny asked.

'I had a complaint made against me. One of the nurses said that she saw me with a patient, that I'd sexually assaulted him while he was in my care. He was eighteen and brought in suffering with psychosis. Although there was no proof, I had to leave the hospital immediately. The allegations were enough for me to lose my job. I was finished at

Greyshott Hall. I was distraught. Later, I was found innocent of all charges but it was too late.

'A new doctor took my place, a young, suave egotistic bastard who thought he had all the answers. He wanted to make a name for himself. He began ECT – electroconvulsive therapy – which triggered the patients to fit and forget about their depression. He was all for it. He strongly believed the treatment was the way forward in mental health.

'While doing the rounds, he saw Mary, but of course her chart said Mark Wheelan. He eventually put two and two together. He forced her to tell him what had happened, how she'd swapped places with her brother. The doctor kept quiet, but he had his own plans; she was going to be his toy. He raped her over and over. She was only seventeen. I let her down.

'Mary developed a form of psychosis that was brought on by the severe trauma. The man continually injected her with LSD, and at night, after one of the two nurses would inject her with 10mg of Lorazepam to help her sleep, he'd get into her cell and abuse her.

'One night while the nurses were on their rounds, Mary played dead. Nurse Eastwood had sedated the other patients, and the second nurse had gone back upstairs.

'Mary lay on the floor.

'The rest is history.'

* * *

Sean felt sick. The room began to spin and he thought he was going to faint. He had listened to the woman in front of him, unable to comprehend what she had said. 'So, my mother, Mary Freeman, was—' He couldn't say the words. 'How do you know all this?'

'I had a friend, one of the nurses who was there the night it happened. She told me the dosage and what the new doctor had ordered them to do. Mary escaped that night. She went home. Of course, the police were looking for Mark Wheelan but couldn't find him.'

Sean struggled to comprehend the story. He tried to get it straight in his head. 'Yes, my Uncle Ed returned to the family home and burned it to the ground. My mother told me. Ed faked his death by dragging a body into the kitchen. The police believed he had died that night along with his mother and father. No one was any the wiser with regards to Mark Wheelan. Why would they be? As far as they knew, Mark Wheelan had nothing to do with my family. And only Mary survived. She kept the secret that Ed faked his death.' Sean glanced at Jenny, who was stunned into silence, and then back at the woman. 'Why the hell didn't you say anything?'

The woman began to cry again. 'Because I owed it to your grandmother. I let Mary down. I promised I'd look after her and I didn't. It was the least I could do. I owed them that much.'

'And Mary?' Jenny asked.

'Mary made a full recovery. She didn't remember what happened that night in Greyshott Hall, and no one ever told her. She still believed it was her brother who had gone on the murderous rampage.'

'What about the doctor? What happened to him?'

'He knew the authorities were coming for him. The staff at Greyshott Hall were going to testify. A case was being made against him. When the police broke into his house, they found him hanging from a beam in the garage.'

'So, no one knew the truth about what happened, that

my mother took Ed's place, was driven into a condition of psychosis and murdered eight people.'

Sean stood. He turned and walked out of the house without saying goodbye.

* * *

Sean stood on the road, watching his kids in the back of the car, AirPods in their ears. He loved them so much. He turned to Jenny. 'I didn't know my family at all.'

'Sean, we're your family. We have each other. We'll deal with this. It's a shock, but we're a strong unit. Nothing will ever break us.'

'I'm embarrassed.' He looked back up at the house. The woman watched them from a first-floor window. 'The things she revealed – how are we supposed to deal with it?'

Jenny held her husband tight. 'We will. Because nothing will ever come between us.'

'Where do we go from here?'

'We go back to the hotel, relax and have some us time. The police will be at your mother's house for a few days, but we'll move there temporarily afterwards. Then, I know of a rundown farmhouse in Stroud that's going cheap.'

'Forget it. No way. Not on your life.'

They got into the car and drove away from the house.

42

Five Days Later.

Monday.

I think it's on. The red light was flashing before; now it's still. That means it's recording, right? OK, I'm sure it's recording – oh God, where to start. You know, it's weird, looking into the lens of a camcorder, talking to myself, alone in the house. At least I think I am. I have a few minutes – that's it, no more. That's all I have. So, bear with me. Watch this recording and make up your own mind, but promise me you'll do something.

'I look dirty. Bloody hell, I've aged ten years overnight. My long brown hair is dishevelled and has grey wisps starting to show – large swathes of them are pushing their way through. I can see laughter lines cut deep into the skin of my face, only there's nothing to smile about. Not now, not anymore.

'You may wonder why I'm whispering, why I'm keeping my voice low, faint. The truth is, I'm fucking terrified. I'm guessing if you're watching this, you've found the recording. Perhaps you've just moved in and you're settling down, making a new life for yourself, a better life that's peaceful, quiet. You have a family, a partner, children. Well, get out. Get the fuck out before it's too late.

'Listen to me. Please.

'You'll hear the stories, the rumours, that's for sure. If you've found this, whoever you are, I beg you, don't just watch this. Promise me you'll do something. Take this recording to the police, put it on YouTube, Facebook, Instagram... All of your social media platforms. Make people aware. Tell them our story. You will, won't you?

'It can't all have been for nothing. I won't let that happen.

'Fucking Creeper. God, what were we thinking? Why didn't we listen? We were so keen to make the documentary. Now look where it's ended up.

'I don't have long, but you need to understand my story, how I came to be here, hiding in the upstairs bedroom, sitting in front of a camcorder, waiting.

'Wait...

'Hello? Who's there? Hello?

'Sorry, I know my voice is low. It may be hard to hear me. I get it. But I thought I heard the front door open.

'Hello?

'Shit. I think someone's in the house. I knew this would happen. I knew it.

'But what was I saying? All I ask is that you tell people about us. About Creeper.

'This is weird, right? You're watching this, maybe months after I made the recording, perhaps even years. I might look strange. My clothes may look peculiar, out of fashion, like an odd picture from a century ago. You may snigger, mock my appearance, laugh. Go on then. It doesn't matter. I don't care.

'I need to stand. I have cramp; my legs have gone to sleep. My body is aching and sore.

'Wait, stay with me. There's the bedroom door. I'm going to be quiet so I can listen. If you can't hear me, it doesn't mean I've gone or the battery has run out. I'm going to keep quiet because I want to draw it out, being found. I want to last as long as possible. That's all.

'Is the camera steady? Can you still see me? I can see my reflection, my worried expression, in the glass of the lens, but only just. I have visions of the video coming out blurry, the lens filthy, so you won't be able to make anything out.

'Wow, that would be a waste of time. Can you imagine? How stupid would that make me look? I guess I'll never know. I'll never find out.

'If that was the case, I could be saying anything, couldn't I? I'll exaggerate my lip movements. I'll speak louder. You need to hear what I'm saying.

'Here goes.

'CALL. THE. POLICE. PUT. THIS. ON. YOUTUBE.

'There. I've made it clear. If the sound's gone, you'll still have no excuse.

'You may think I'm delusional, drugged, pissed up. Well, I'm none of those. I wish I was.

'What I'd do for a drink though – an ice-cold beer. Just the one, mind, to take the pain away, place it far enough away for a short while.

'If you can't see where I am, I'm stood by the bedroom

door, listening. I'm sure I heard the front door open a few minutes ago.

'Yes, there's someone at the top of the stairs, getting closer. I'm backing away to the middle of the bedroom. I'm going to place the camcorder in a bolt hole; there's a cupboard behind me with a section cut out. Can you see it? I'll place it in there. One of you will find it, I'm certain.

'The handle of the bedroom door is moving downwards slowly. This is it. I think my time is up. Please do something. When you find this, do som—'

Sean sat beside Jenny in their hotel room, both of them staring at the laptop.

Beth and Ethan were out shopping in Oxford.

In another day or two, they were going to move into Sean's parents' house. They'd get their heads clear first, then decide where to go next.

He wasn't going to let the ghosts of the past spoil their future.

Jenny placed her hand in Sean's lap, leant forward and kissed his cheek. 'So, you definitely want to delete this part?'

'Yes, it's too much. Now we know what happened in Painswick – the suffering, the anguish – it's not right. I want to take it out. Let's just go with the docufilm, the story of Creeper. That's enough.'

Jenny leant back in the chair. 'I must say, it's great acting on your part.'

'Thanks. It only seems like yesterday when we recorded it. Things were so innocent then – our dreams of the farm-house, the story – but now we know it's real, I don't feel comfortable leaving this intro in. It's a little morbid, don't you think?'

'I'll go with you, Sean. I will accept any decision you make.'

Sean moved the mouse to the start of the footage, then highlighted it until the end. He listened to the last part again.

'The handle of the bedroom door is moving downwards slowly. This is it. I think my time is up. Please do something. When you find this, do som—'

He looked at Jenny, then pressed delete.

* * *

'Testing. One, two. Testing. Hello, darlings. Have you missed me?' Declan stood at the front of the living room in Sheldon's Residential Retirement Home. The room was packed with wild, elated eyes.

'Right then, let's get to it – a game of Bingo to start the day. Get set now, loves. Pens at the ready. Six and three, I need a wee. Anyone? Two and four, I've shit on the floor. Gladys? Betty? Are you marking your cards, treacles?'

Billy walked into the living room and sat in his chair towards the back.

'Here he is, the life and soul: Sheldon's own Michael Douglas! Do you all remember that film? Fatal Extraction?'

'Attraction,' a voice shouted from the room.

'I think you will find it's Extraction,' Declan pushed. 'Where they had to remove a rabbit from his arse.'

Betty sat up. 'Oh, Declan, you are funny.'

Billy sat, watching the joker at the front. He owed everything to him, the person who'd kept him going the last couple of weeks, the reason why he was able to put a stop to his daughter's murderer and have that moment he'd dreamed about for so long.

The police had found more bodies in the woodland. They'd also dug up the well and found skeletal remains. Nine bodies in total had been discovered: Marie Nelson and the Painswick eight.

Although some hadn't been identified yet, Billy knew his daughter was one of them. He was pleased that he could finally say goodbye to her and have a place to go whenever he needed to talk. The families in Painswick were going to have a proper burial with a memorial.

'Right then, mini disco. Let's see you all on the floor. Come on, everyone up. That includes you, Billy.'

'I have a wooden leg?'

'No excuses. Up you get.'

A nursery rhyme came on the speaker system.

See-saw, Margery Daw.

Declan froze, then turned to Billy. Both knew what the other was thinking.

'OK, not that one. Let's do another. Here's a great one. The Wheels on the Bus. Off you go, now. Let's see those hips moving, you lot.'

When the pensioners were up and dancing, Declan moved down towards Billy. 'Hey, how are you?'

'Oh, I'm all right. It's great to finally have closure, you know? And it's great to see you back here. This lot have missed you.'

Declan smiled. 'Yeah. Apparently, the stand-in was useless. He played the crap songs, called the wrong Bingo numbers and complained about Gladys and Betty being too touchy-feely. Can you imagine?'

'You'd never have complained.' Billy laughed.

'What? You don't know the half of it. They treat me like a piece of meat.' Declan turned, watching everyone dance.

'You're a special person, Declan. Thanks again for your help.'

'Oh, it's nothing. Hey, you want to do it again? I'm sure you'll be bombarded with phone calls now you're a mini-celebrity. I'm sure there's a cat that needs bringing down from a tree or an old dear locked in her bathroom.'

'Not a hope. And with you? Never. You do my bloody head in.'

A nurse made her way over to them. 'Mr Huxton, the telephone.'

'See? You're in demand now. Off you go, Grouch.'

'Oh, for shit's sake. Who is it?'

The nurse shrugged. 'I don't know.'

Billy followed her out of the room, while Declan stood at the door listening.

'Down here, Mr Huxton. This way.'

'I know where the bloody thing is. I've been here long enough.' Billy picked up the phone. 'Hello? Who? Oh, hey, son. How was your holiday? The car? What do you mean? No, I didn't touch it. I don't know what you're talking about.'

Declan placed his hand over his mouth, sniggered to himself and walked back into the living room.

The End

ABOUT THE AUTHOR

Stuart James is an award-winning psychological thriller and horror author and his books are constantly top of the Amazon charts.

His thriller, The House On Rectory Lane, recently won The International Book Award in horror fiction.

Books by Stuart James.

The House On Rectory Lane.
Turn The Other Way.
Apartment Six.
Stranded.
Selfie.
Creeper.

ACKNOWLEDGMENTS

Thank you so much for choosing Creeper and I hope you enjoyed it.
You can sign up to my mailing list and keep up to date with other projects I have planned.
I'll also send you a short story for free.
Just go to:
https://www.stuartjamesthrillers.com

I'd like to say a huge thank you to my family for your extreme patience and listening to my ideas constantly ha ha. I feel you know my thrillers as well as I do.
Sara Maria, you have helped so much with this thriller and I can't thank you enough for your expert knowledge in mental health.
The same goes to PC Ali Hickman-Jameson who is also such an amazing lady and your help will never be forgotten.
Thank you both so very much.

Special thanks to the Facebook groups who continually promote my works and support me so much.
The Fiction Cafe.
Tracy Fenton and her wonderful book club, TBC.
The Reading Corner Book Lounge.
UK Crime Book Club.
Donna's Interviews, Reviews and Giveaways.
Mark Fearn. Book Mark.

Also to the incredible book bloggers who have supported my journey so much and to all you wonderful readers and authors.

Also massive thanks to Adam Croft, Alan Gorevan and Lindsay Detwiler.

And lastly, special thanks to Zoe O'Farrell, Chloe Jordan, Kate Eveleigh, Donna Morfett, Emma Louise Bunting, Michaela Balfour, Kiltie Jackson, Mark Fearn and all the readers who requested an arc of Creeper.

Your support is forever grateful.

You really are amazing and I can't thank you enough.

Thanks to my wonderful family for all your patience and support. I love you all so very much.

Make sure to keep up to date with projects I'm working on and sign up to my mailing list at:
https://www.stuartjamesthrillers.com
I'll also send you a free short story.

Also, you can follow me on social media.
I love to hear from readers and will always respond.
Twitter: StuartJames73
Instagram: Stuart James Author
Facebook: Stuart James Author.
TikToc: Stuart James Author

I'm hoping Billy Huxton and Declan Ryan return for another chilling tale in 2022.